Crosshairs of the Devil

A Novel

By

Yancey Williams

ISBN: ISBN: 978-0-9860316-5-6 (Paperback)
ISBN: ISBN: 978-0-9860316-6-3 (eBook)

The Library of Congress has catalogued the YPress edition as follows:

Names: Williams, Yancey, author.
Title: Crosshairs of the Devil: a novel/ Yancey Williams
Fiction/Satire | Fiction/ Suspense.

Published in the United States by YPress.

To
Pops aka P. Bailey Williams
Provider, World War ll Army Air Corps Captain,
Football All American & United States Olympic Team

To
Jean Balle Denman

To
VMP Sammie KRE Goddess

To
Anndel Kininmonth Williams Powers
&
Kendall Drew Williams Hoak

Cruelty is the law pervading all nature and society; and we can't get out of it if we would.

Jude the Obscure by Thomas Hardy

He is deformed, crooked, old and sere,
Ill-faced, worse bodied, shapeless everywhere;
Vicious, ungentle, foolish, blunt, unkind;
Stigmatical in making, worse in mind.

A Comedy of Errors by William Shakespeare

The resolution to avoid an evil is seldom framed till the evil is so far advanced as to make avoidance impossible.

Far from the Madding Crowd by Thomas Hardy

Contents

Pray, do not mock me:
I am a very foolish fond old man,
Fourscore and upward, not an hour more or less;
And, to deal plainly,
I fear I am not in my perfect mind.
King Lear (2.7.70-4) by William Shakespeare

CHAPTER 1

The Making of a Hit Man

Location: Room 315. The Garden of Eden, Retirement Village & Nursing Facility. Senior Living and Memory Care at its Finest.

Edek Jablonski, or Eddie, the resident, sits comfortably with Jenkins, his attendant-orderly. Jenkins has been Employee of the Month four straight months in a row. Jenkins doesn't play favorites ... against company policy. But Eddie is his favorite.

On this day, the morning had almost passed before the two men realized that it was a shade and sliver before high noon. Their A.M. time on the clock had disappeared, vanished into thin air like flower petals into fall. Poof. Just that quickly. Their routine, patient-pensioner to caregiver-confidant, attendant-orderly to his geriatric convalescent-sidekick, it was intuitive, respectful, discerning, just the other side of cordial, and even at times beneficent and heartfelt one man to the other.

Jenkins looked away. He put down the bed pan and the tray. He paused then stopped to listen. It was clear to him that Eddie was on deck, next at bat, Eddie being Eddie. Without a hitch or further ado, Eddie began.

"I was a small boy. Not much bigger than this." (Lifts his hand just so high from where he sits.) "If that," he continued. "The old man, my father came back into the room a third time. I was already bleeding and dazed from the other times he'd been into the room with me. Beatings each time. Ranting. Railing. Obscenities. I was a *little motherfucker* he said. *You little bastard,* he shouted out. Me? No bigger than this. (Raises his hand again to the same small height.) Then, he clubbed me twice more, then backhanded me again across the cheek so that the blood splattered once more against the far wall where the other blood stains drooled down the whitewashed plaster. Stained in blood red and teardrops, Jenkins. Blood red and teardrops, mind you. And me, a little boy. Beaten senseless. Submitted. God's child? That's what the priest called me in church ... God's child. More the devil's whipping boy in the crosshairs of the devil, J. It's what I grew up in ... the crosshairs of the devil, mind you. The devil was my old man. Wasn't any fun. I can attest to that. Me. A spindly legged colt, a young lad barely out of the womb. No more than a tyke.

No bigger than this, mind you. (Once again, for a third time, Eddie sizes himself off the floor, not much taller than the chair's armrest, for disturbing emphasis and horrifying clarity.) A little boy. A child. Harmless. Frail. Innocent. Unknowing. And this man ... this *father* so called, this monster is tossing me about like garden confetti or candy at a Christmas parade all for the sake of his own demonic pleasure and whim.

(In remembrance, the perspiration beads gathered at the top of Eddie's old weathered forehead. It was a personal, holocaustic memory. Trauma, even its recollection, wears a hole in any man's soul no matter his age, no matter the tough luck he's known, or his down and out, makeshift experience. Eddie shook it off and continued.)

Me. Imagine this if you can? That same small boy ... me, J ... could have been a different man I'm sure, but it's what happens to you that makes you who and what you are. So, you play the hand you're dealt and all that. Didn't do anything to that so-called father of mine, Jenkins. Didn't do one blasted thing. And what do I get? Beatings. Beatings day in and day out. All over my body. Up one side and down the other. For the entire first half of my boyhood. He started and then he continued even until his final day, that day, and I sat there, lay there, curled up like a tiny homeless kitten, like any small child, whimpering and crying and sniffling and pleading with him to stop because it hurt, because it was painful and his beatings left bruises and marks up and down my face and body even to my toes and not once did I ever question the drunken man's insanity because I didn't know how and wasn't old enough to know that I could.

That came later."

(Eddie smiled. Revenge, simple and plain and homespun, homeschooled revenge, it makes any man smile. It's sweeter than honey, more satisfying than the love of a beautiful woman, more delightful than the adulation of all mankind in a skyscraper ticker tape tribute and city-wide procession.)

"The man holding the clinched fist by his side was my father. Each time, he salivated. Spittle like white sea foam surfaced at the periphery and corners of his mouth and around his lips. It was the usual ... disgusting and vile and the signal, the green light, of what was coming. Each time, I could smell his breath from where I lay in a heap, a clump of cowardice, a child's repose of fear, of self-preservation and muted, muffled hysteria, my own kind of paranormal paralysis. Rarely do these go together, but all of these emotions and reactions and defenses paired themselves within me as I was being beaten and knocked about without protection or recourse.

I remember the cut below my eye, my shattered nose bleeding, the new cleft (as wound) also bloody in my lower lip, the cuticle from my thumbnail torn away from gripping my father's shirtsleeve (self-defense) which left him angrier and more determined to teach me the same demented and unhinged lesson that I was always being taught … of being a human in this, *his* household … me, a child, a small boy in the wrong place at the wrong time in the wrong, so-called home occupied by a madman, a tyrant, a diabolical dipsomaniac, a filthy, intemperate louse, the worthless and depraved lunatic that he was.

Each time, he stared back across at me, I shriveled into a careless, disheveled clump, irrespective of any life or breath or thought of either of our futures together or apart. Human-to-human was never on the table for consideration. It was only about the here and now … his drunken *here and now* … and my *here and now*, his target surviving or outlasting the moment and the pain it bore.

I could and would never laugh the same. That side of life … the gaiety, the boyish tease of chuckles and giggles and laughter, the frivolity, the juvenile insouciance … had been stripped from me forever.

He came at me again with his belt strap and then crossed himself and my face with one, two, three, four, five, six lashes that left me whimpering, holding my arms in such a way as to try and deflect the blows, then crying, then wailing as he told me to, "*Shut up! Quit your crying, you little sniveling dog, you dreadful piece of manure, you … you,*" … until he became lost in his own, loose-knit, jaded and preposterous liquored language which finally left him speechless, confused, energy-less, and tired inside his own, tormented, tortured-torturing shell.

I hated him more than all things ill and evil and miserable and bad made one as well as that same, dark, next nightfall that I associated with these beatings that left me alone and desolate and crying and destitute of any feeling, good or bad, in fear that he would come for me again and repeat what he had just done to me in the previous hours and the days prior. A horror for any man to experience let alone a small boy. A predestined hell for an unknowing, unsuspecting child, it's what I grew accustomed to, what I came to know as my own distilled if not fractured subsistence at such a tender age.

The good eye, the one not swollen shut, I can still see him toppled over, only to rise again, then topple over again while I lay there thinking, '*Stay down, devil man, stay down.*' What a way to grow up, to live?

If there was a god (thoughts of a tiny, young boy, mind you, J), I knew that he would come and save me and place me in an empty corner, a safe corner of another house or another building somewhere far away, and I could sleep, in the cold if need be, in the comfort of knowing I would not be beaten anymore, again and again and again like now and before this so many times. But god, he never showed up. Not once. And god, the other one, as the newfangled, contemporary, tonier version, *she* never showed up either. Not once.

That is how you become a hit man, J. First, your childhood is tortured. Then it is stripped away and murdered. Stripped away, stabbed, and murdered as you watch, you the luckless and forgotten child, you get to witness all of it firsthand. Up close. In full, living color, in the bright, red color of your own blood. In your next life, the grownup, adult side, your victims, the insulting slobs and deadbeat bums and gutless rogues and rakish villains that come later, they mean nothing … deserving in the final analysis … even less than the devil-personified that had whipped you over and over and over again until you cannot feel anything inside any longer. Compassion is erased. Love, too. Fear is forgotten. Reality banished. What's more, don't kid yourself, it is everlasting and forever. For the right price, anyone or everyone, they all have a name tag with a dollar amount on their collar fixed and marked as undeserving to live.

Later, J, that was in my eighth year, not even nine, that was when I shot that miserable bastard. Shot him in the face with his own revolver what's more. It took me several seconds (a lifetime for me, the small boy) to pull the hammer back on the pistol. Mimicked the good guys in the cowboy Western matinees I'd glimpsed. I could see the rounded, hollowed-out tips of the bullets already loaded into the chamber. And I could hear him stirring outside my room, downstairs, his voice bellowing throughout the house since his drinking bout had already begun. I backed up to the wall where my own dried and faded bloodstains decorated the old gypsum board and faded paint, crouched low and steady, and I waited with that revolver of his in my hand pointed at the door. I knew full well what it looked like for that door to open wide and to see this face of a big man step out into the open of my little room. That door, it was shut because it was always shut because I wanted it shut for my own protection, and I wanted it shut to brace myself for the next beating (like it did any good), and I didn't want to leave that room or face that same man, my father, the devil incarnate. I could hear his footsteps trapsing up the stairs, staggering down the hallway. I could picture him slumping from side to side, off balance, leveraging his weight against the bannisters then to the wall on the other side and back, and somehow, some way, everything and anything made matters worse and fueled the fury inside that drunken stupor of his until he got to me. It was my warning call, the *tip-off. Get ready, kid! Your wholesale beating's on the way!* is what it said to me that little, unprotected boy all huddled in the corner of my own lonely room. But now for the first time I was protected, the gun was in my hand. I was ready.

So, when the door opened wide, and he and his reddened and bulbous face appeared with that drunken scowl sickeningly painted all over it, I leveled the barrel across my knee, took a nervous and cursory aim at first, drew a more deliberately deadly bead next, and then, with my teeth gritted, pulled slowly, resolutely in a glorious instant that curled, cold trigger until his gun in my hand went off in a blast.

The sound of the gunshot, that blast, it was loud and startling then magically stupendous, clairvoyant, and heaven-sent. A cacophonous, climactic cymbal clash inside a strident symphonic finale. But there again, J, it was just me, that little boy. Relief, liberation, empowerment, and atonement folded into one. In a pause, in an exaggerated exhale, I saw the world as never before, and that world was good, promising, and whole. The weight was lifted from my shackled spirit, and I could breathe for the first time in my short life.

That same drunken sot of an old man, my father, dropped like a villain at the end of a hangman's noose.

I, that same little small tiny boy, sat up straight, placed the gun on the floor, stood up with my back against the stained wall, took a long deep breath without a sniffle or a tear, looked at the dead man on the floor (no relation), stepped over his dead body, walked down the hallway down the flight of stairs, and left by the front door to go outside into the fresh, crisp, clean air and play. Just play. Life began anew. The pain, the scars, the reminiscent bludgeoning, it all remained in ways, but it had now been sorted in a split second of that hair trigger and put away for good in some unknowable attic for someone else to ponder."

(Eddie mopped another bead of sweat from his brow a second time. Maybe it was a third. In the reliving, he'd miraculously and laboriously risen again off the hardwood floor of that small, bloodstained room, his childhood cell, and stepped across that same dead body to make his way into the outdoors and the fresh air and the sunshine and the blue sky and the sounds of other children playing and calling out those same games that all those other children had been playing all along for all those years.)

"So, go ahead, mark it down, J. For the first time in my life, I had killed a man. And, yes, the man I killed was my father. And, yes, that very same man, my father was the devil himself, Lucifer and Beelzebub and Satan, a patchwork perhaps but all three rolled into one.

Caught the devil in the crosshairs, Jenkins. Caught the devil in his own crosshairs, and I shot him, and what's more, I killed him. Best thing I ever did, my man, best thing I ever did.

Most of the time, it's the devil catching *his* prey, the rest of us, in *his crosshairs*. Casting *his* net, and low and behold, there you are. The devil's toy, the devil's bidding, the devil's bait, the devil's bargaining chip in *his* next deal for *his* fun and *his* sport. But that day, this little boy (Eddie demonstrably and insistently poked his chest with his own index finger) I reversed the table on the devil himself. And that's all that mattered to me then, and it's all that matters to me now, J. Amen, I say. So be it, Edek Jablonski. That's right. You did good, little boy. You did really good indeed. A job well done.

Shot and killed my own father. I did. And what's more, lived to tell the tale. Maybe hard for some people to admit it, harder for some people to say it out loud, or maybe even hardest for others to hear it, but, again, it was a great day.

Should've received a medal for valor or a letter of commendation from the pope or a citation from the city mayor or the governor of the state because looking back I was ridding the world of one diehard, diabolical son of bitch, a miserable menace to all mankind but mainly me, and it was that same, despicable person who had created me in some offhanded way, which is too cruel and perverse and invasive for me to want to know the truth. That's what I got out of my childhood, J, and because of it, most of life. Crosshairs of the devil, Jenkins. Raised inside the crosshairs of the devil, and still, somehow, broke free. Chalk one up to the kid. (In a self-salute,

Eddie raised his hand with a godly pride, his head bowed, and tossed out the other half of that ceremonial gesture as congratulations.) Save the reverence and veneration for yourself when you come up the way I did."

Eddie sat in the recliner and looked outside into the courtyard beside his room through the clear pane. A chickadee sat in the cradle of the bird bath drenching itself and joyously flapping its wings. Two bright colored cardinals swooped in to displace the other smaller bird. Eddie grunted. Then, he grunted again. A contemplative grunt, a nudge from within you might say, before the contemplative, relinquishing sigh. Ideas piled on top of other ideas on top of other ideas as the past fomented and rose in his mind's eye as something that must have happened only because he could remember it just like he did every day just like it was all right there in the playbook of his mind exactly the way it had happened.

There was no talk or thought or replay of a 'tomorrow'. Might not be here, he'd say. It wasn't day to day any longer, more hour to hour. Eddie knew by the grunts and the recollection and the recollective grunts and sighs that you knew that Eddie knew. He was a man possessed of his yesterday and the past and the telling of that time or what he could remember and how he remembered it.

Getting things off his chest. No, not in a religious way, but just things to set the record straight for his own peace of mind … or as straight as they could be set. Like he said, *just to get it off my chest …* an autobiographical ornament of sorts atop his own Yuletide tree of fostered recollection.

He looked back inside his Garden dormitory room because the space was all that he had left. It was his world. A change of everyday clothes. A wrist watch. Two sport jackets. His dress trousers and matching dress socks and shoes and the small drawer full of handkerchiefs and lapel buttons. In the corner … a flickering tv. No sound. The way Eddie watched the world and the television.

"I can lip read," he said. "Besides, what they have to say is of no interest because they have nothing to say. Heard it all before. And it was nothing way back then. When you've heard it all before, that's when you know your time is just about up. Bull shit's bull shit. You can quote me. Feel free. So much of life is a nuisance. Full-fledged interference on the way to the next step and the step after that until you get to the end result, the end product, the end of the day, or sadly *The End*, the finish line, and the grave itself, and the hole you've dug for yourself. You can quote me on that one, too, if you like … and afterwards, they, that entire world, can all kiss off. The devil as well and first in line. Satan, he makes a mockery of the entire process. Without him wouldn't be so bad … tolerable even."

(He always laughed loudest in the dark after he said that.)

He was by now talking to the empty space of an empty room in the sterile facility and its complimentary furnishings. It was just Eddie and Eddie in his borrowed room, and Eddie just waiting his turn to die. The fraternal order of things, all things present, past, and future for an old man with no dreams, no pretense, no longer impressed or needy, simply going through the motions with what he had left.

His coincidental misdeeds carried him through the night into midday. Remembrance or dream? It was all the same. *Living the dream* is what Eddie said. That's what he told himself. Living the dream and remembering it the way he wanted it remembered.

A misty-eyed Jenkins had reappeared in the room wiping a bead of sweat from his own brow.

Eddie looked over and shot Jenkins a thumbs up.

Jenkins looked back and returned the same thumbs up and smiled.

"Simpatico, Jenkins," said Eddie. "Simpatico sons a bitches, you and me."

In a robust and complimentary stir, the two men readied themselves for the noonday lunch downstairs in The Garden cafeteria.

"Feeling healthy today for a change with a bit of an appetite," said Eddie. "Plus, it's already paid for. Soon, I'll lose my place in line for good. Might as well make the most of it while I can," said Eddie purposelessly sad, bootless, and straightforward. "Time to go. Let's do it."

Eddie's voice trailed off as the two men walked slowly at Eddie's pace down the hallway. You could just make it out as they rounded the corner … "The old women here love me, J, just love me. What can I say? Play the hand you're dealt. Some men got it, some men don't."

The two were then out of earshot.

A Prayer Session with Cousin Rich

From the Cold Case Files & Confessions of Richard 'The Ice Man' Kuklinski Entry #17. For over three decades, Richard Kuklinski served as a notorious contract killer for the East Coast Mafia. The real number of Kuklinski's victims is said to be somewhere between one and two hundred. Selected events herein are recorded, recreated, and transcribed by Edek Jablonski, a successful, retired author-crime writer as well as purported kinsman to 'The Ice Man' himself. Room 315. Voices from within. Bringing the dead to life one last time in a murder victim tell-all.

From the desk of Eddie 'The Icicle' Jablonski. The next chapter as interpolative exposé. The victim's narrative as it might have been told.

Sitting at his desk, Eddie wrote:

It turned out to be a hapless endeavor… Waking up that is. What a day. Getting out of bed in such a nonchalant and unmotivated fashion. Unsuspectingly, I … Paolo Polyachenko, the Big Bad Apple, that's me … sat quietly drinking my second cup of coffee and talking shit with Aldo and Grease about the upcoming deal we had going down. Factitious by all counts. The usual. A group effort no matter how coincidental, but mostly my idea. I was on a roll. Taking in good money. Turning it. Taking in more good money. Then turning it again until it had spiraled full circle and back into our grasp but mostly mine. Just bought a new car and paid cash.

I was *too smart for my own good*. That's the way I described it. *Too smart for my own good.* Saying it made me feel good, like a big shot. It was exhilarating. Aldo and Grease, they both agreed. Grease, he would snap his fingers, a double snap, click, click, and laugh quoting me. They thought they were too smart for their own good as well. Just like that and he (Grease) would snap his fingers again. A heartier click. Aldo and Grease, they quoted me like I was an ancient philosopher or Shakespeare or a famous general. *Too smart for my own good.* It was a smug and smart-ass salvo for the three of us as well as a confidence builder among us undisciplined reprobates. Sometimes you say something, have some success, and you really do think you're too smart for your own good. In fact, I was certain. I really *was* the cat's meow.

Until that morning on that day, and that day was today.

He hadn't knocked. In an instant, all of sudden, more like a blink or a burst or a cough to clear your throat, he was standing there. No introduction. No pleasantries. No salutation or pretense of a greeting. Just this one man, reaching almost motionlessly into his coat pocket and drawing out a large hand gun and pointing the barrel confrontationally, unambiguously, unequivocally with purpose and premeditation at the bridge of my nose. Crosshairs fixed at the front of my face. What could I say? So, I said nothing. I backed up two short steps and took a very long and deep breath. I could feel the beads of sweat forming on my brow, and I stopped thinking clearly at that very moment in time. Life was on hold. I was spellbound and inexplicably surrounded from all sides… even if by only this one individual.

He was a shadowy figure of a man. Oversized, bulky, even a bit frowsty from over here where I stood, and with the pistol cupped in this hand, he looked even bigger, mightier, and certainly more menacing than at first. Somehow, he appeared unraveled or just about to be unraveled and unwound and unglued all at my expense. He muttered in a sleepy voice, "You owe Captain D (DeMeo) some money. I've come to collect." He stared and stopped talking and walking forward.

That was it. The entrance, forced … the stare, detached but resolute … the stature, demonstrative and sizeable at the same time, and the announcement, the demand with no strings attached. That was it. With me standing there, suspended, limp, helpless, destiny's knave, a kitten in the palm of a lion.

I stammered. My breathing had picked up quite quickly, skipping about and unrhythmically. "I don't have the money right now. But I promised I would get it to him. I just need a little more time." That's what I said. The words were more drawn out, elongated, and taffy-like. Maybe I knew that somehow in the moment I was trying to buy myself more time, when in fact I spoke about something so grave and incomprehensible and dread, that my words jumped to conclusions, the right conclusions even before the stranger, the big man, this stranger had time to tell me what was going to happen to me if he didn't collect then and there.

"Please." I was stammering again, harder this time. "Please, I'm pleading with you, mister, praying you don't kill me. Really, I will get your boss his money. I said that I would, so I will. Please God, don't let this man kill me."

"I don't make excuses," he said, "so you stop making excuses. Expect the worst. Hope for the best. What my mother always used to say before she beat the shit out of me," he said just before he paused as if lost for a brief moment in thought.

"Well," the big man continued deliberately, "you, my friend, have thirty minutes to get the money." He looked down at his watch. The gun was still pointed at my face. I could see the hollow points in the chamber of the revolver, its cylinder, captioned in broad daylight like small missiles cradled in their silos awaiting launch. "Thirty minutes after six months, so that's six months and thirty minutes by my timepiece. Suit yourself. Clock's ticking, my friend." He smiled … vacantly. Doom has a dismissiveness all its own.

"Tell you what I'll do," said the stranger in my house. He positioned himself then sat in the lounge chair that was my favorite. He motioned me with his free hand to sit on the stool beside the fireplace. "I'll give you thirty minutes. Stay calm. Like a good little boy. No need to bristle or pitch a tizzy. Won't do you any good. Lessens your odds of survival from whatever they are now to zero. You can just pray to God, then maybe God can come down and save you. If God comes down, I'll leave. No harm. No foul. If God doesn't come down, you're a dead man. So. You get busy and pray. Tell God you need some help. Pronto. Tell him to make it snappy. Put a rush on it just for you. Overnight express in thirty minutes. I'll wait. Tell him I'm here. Pops, Captain D, needs his money. All of it. Not part of it. It was a short-term loan. You knew that at the outset. Don't pretend you didn't know that it was a short-term loan, because I know, and Pops knows, and God knows, too, because as you know God knows everything. Right? … God knows … (the pause said *God knows* so it didn't need to be repeated) … He knows fucking everything. Right, right? So, God knows that you're late on your payments, and you would welch on the entire loan in a heartbeat if I weren't here. But here I am. We'll both just sit here in the meantime and wait. I've clocked about three minutes and thirty-nine seconds off my watch, (Kuklinski, Cousin Richie, taps on the face of his watch three times with the tip of the gun barrel. *Time's a' wasting.* It's what he's intimating.) so you've got about another twenty-six to twenty-seven minutes to talk to God and get the money, so go ahead. Pray yourself silly. Get busy. If God's on your side, he shows up, and you're off the hook. I for one don't believe in miracles. I believe in good luck. I believe in bad luck, too. I believe the cookie crumbles more often than you get the cookie. Hope God appears and brings the dough. Saves me a bullet. You get left in one piece. Bottom line … Captain D, Pops, needs to be made whole. You're in arrears. That's not good."

"Oh," I stammered. "Please dear Jesus, don't kill me, mister, whoever you are."

"Keep going," said Big Rich (Kuklinski). "That's fine. I like this. But don't pray to me. I ain't God. I'm just here to collect Captain D's money. That's it. Nineteen minutes and fourteen seconds to go. It's in God's hands, my friend. You know … *What a friend we have in Jesus.* Right? *How great Thou art.* Isn't that what they tell us? *Jesus loves the little children of the world.* Green and yellow, black and white … they are precious in his sight … something like that."

Big Rich Kuklinski holds up and out his wrist. He cocks the trigger and points again to his gold watch with the tip of his .357 Magnum and taps three times on the face of his watch with the tip of the barrel of his .357 Magnum handgun. Metal to glass, metal to glass, metal to glass. Tap, tap, tap. He points the handgun toward the man's face, then lowers it. He then blows off the barrel tip as if to sardonically whisper away the gun smoke from a spent round. He then lowers the trigger to neutral, un-cocked.

"Here's another one," said Big Rich, Cousin K. "*Now I lay me down to sleep. I pray the Lord my soul to keep. If I should die before I wake* … that's some morbid shit, huh, pal? That could be you, my friend … unless that is you come up with Captain D's money … but then again, maybe the Lord will come to the rescue … just like the nursery rhyme says." Kuklinski smiled. "Christians and nursery rhymes, they go together. Don't you think?"

Kuklinski looks again at his watch. He is cool. He is composed.

"Fourteen minutes and thirteen seconds until the half hour is up," Kuklinski said. "Better get busy and call on your God." Once again, he taps on the face of his watch with the barrel of the gun and smiles. He is the devil's own. He knows it.

"Personally, I don't believe in God. But I do believe in the slippery, cynical hand of fate," said Big Rich. "I said once … said it out loud … Hey God, I ain't playing games, so you quit playing games. I'm right here. If you've got something to say to me, speak up. I'm all ears." Big Rich, Cousin Richie smiled, another slippery, cynical, grin inside another sinister smile, just like fate's, he mused and continued. "But guess what? I never heard a peep from the big man in the sky. I got nothing. No feedback whatsoever. Just like you're getting nothing. But you keep praying. Maybe something good will come of it. I guess you never know. But we'll know or we won't know in just a little while. Seems so unfair sometimes, doesn't it? But we make our own bed so we get to lie in it. That's what my old man used to say to me just before he beat the shit out of me. And so it goes. Oh, and by the way, you've got nine minutes and twenty-six seconds before the money's due … Captain D's money … the money you borrowed and never paid back. Just a friendly reminder, my good pal."

Big Rich looked at his wrist watch, looked back at the other man kneeling and praying and whimpering and crying and sniffling, and Cousin Richie grinned.

"Scared shitless … it's not a good feeling, is it? I've been there a few times myself. I know, my friend, I know. Boy oh boy how I know," Big Rich said unaffectedly, with a grisly and unearthly and morbid and macabre nonchalance. "You should've thought of that before you borrowed the money from Captain D with no intention of paying it back. In case you haven't heard, Captain D takes offense to those that try to fuck him over. Captain D doesn't fuck around. Retribution's never far behind." Big Rich grinned, sucking air from the backside of his teeth, then continued. "Here's an oldie but a goodie for you … try this one … maybe it'll do better than whatever you're whispering over there … *'Our Father, who art in heaven, hallowed be thy name'*… You probably know the rest of it so you can take it from there. Never worked for me, and I've been in some hellacious pickles in my day. But you can try it if you like. I'm showing seven minutes and thirteen seconds left before the money's due."

"I guess you could say that if I was a gentleman, I could or would apologize for your discomfiture. But I'm not a gentleman, and I'm not in the *gentlemen* business. You've gotten yourself into this mess, and it's one hell of a fix.

Choices, we all make choices. Some good ones, some bad ones. I've made some good choices. I've made my share of bad choices, but I've never made as bad a choice as the one you've made, buddy boy. Horrible choice. Really horrible. Now you've been caught in the act. At present, seems your bravado's turned to mush. Your chutzpah to pablum. All of a sudden, you're a namby-pamby wuss. Maybe worse. Funny how that works when the tables are turned, ain't it?" Richie nods and grins even wider.

"Your crotch recedes, your brain freezes, your body cramps, your kidneys dilate and contract and dilate again and again, your bowels lose their purpose and composure, their memory (Rich grins wider still), your eyes blur, your senses stop sensing, all this because you're scared shitless. Some kind of scared, huh, pal?

But you had choices. You could've returned Captain D's money and none of this would be happening. I wouldn't be here. You wouldn't be here … kneeling like a little fucking helpless fawn at a babbling brook deep between the foliage of the protected forest … praying to some god out there for something that ain't going to happen. But, oh no. You, Robin Hood and Al Capone rolled into one, took Captain D's money, stuck it in your pocket, skipped down the yellow brick road, and hid out here until I came knocking. And to think … I didn't knock. Quite the surprise … huh? Pitiful. Wouldn't you say? Pathetic. That's what I'd call it. The door was wide open. And, by the way, for your information, *I am* why you lock your doors.

Four minutes and seven seconds to go. Maybe give a bigger, heartier, more vocal shout-out to God, the man upstairs. Maybe you've just got a bad connection and he can't hear you. Tell him you're up shit creek without a paddle. Tell him your yacht or your dingy or your canoe has sprung a leak. Mayday! Mayday! … you know … maybe he only answers distress calls… Three minutes and counting, buckaroo … wait … make that two minutes and fifty-five seconds and counting to be exact. Don't want to prolong the agony."

Cousin Richie grins. He is a happy and a diabolical Lucifer in the flesh. He rests comfortably in the leather lounge chair, his feet propped up on the ottoman, the barrel of the oversized handgun pointed directly at the man's head, the man kneeling, praying hard, his eyes in a squint, hands folded and sweaty, head bowed.

"Take no prisoners … Captain D's motto, amigo," said Cousin Rich. "I leave with the money, and you're still alive. Or, I leave without the money, and you're no longer among the living. You're dead. A flatline in the book of trivial tragedies. Capisce?" Big Rich smiled. "Sad but true. But think about it for a second. It cuts both ways. I came for the money. That's all I want. Captain D's money … in exchange … for *your* rest of today into tomorrow and next week and next month, and so forth and so on … capisce? It's that simple. Just doing my job, old buddy old pal. Just doing my job."

Big Rich looked away for a brief moment into the open space of the unfamiliar surroundings, then back.

"Whoops," he said in a sarcastic startle. "Looky here. Ain't it funny how time slips away. My watch says the jib's up."

The sound of the killing went unnoticed. One shot, two shots, three. In a muffle and a blur, a dubious, innocuous echo, no louder than the distant, far-off slamming of a door, slamming of a door, slamming of a door … until finally a third time, there was nothing. It's the luck of the devil always some would surely suggest (and forever).

Looking down at the body on the floor, Cousin Rich said, "My experience with prayer as well, buckaroo. Sky-guy never shows up."

On a quick search, Big Rich found most of the owed, uncollected money in an unlocked lockbox in the cluttered bottom drawer beneath the dead man's socks. He took the cash, stuffed some of it in his side jacket pocket left and the rest into side jacket pocket right, locked the box for posterity, placed it back under the dead man's socks as he'd found it, and then flushed the key with a wad of gum and a shell casing down the toilet. That, too, for posterity.

On his way out, the big man placed his hand gun away back in the concealed holster and wiped the door knob with the tail of his jacket. Out in the open air, walking down the sidewalk, the big man, Cousin Rich, he muttered to himself, "Once again, the devil gets the last laugh." Quittance obtained. Issue resolved. He dropped the other two brass shell casings, two and three, into the clear, small opening of a cluttered storm drain just before reaching his car. Number three bounced off the rusted, exposed grate twice before finding its way out of sight on a split roll and spiral. Both disappeared. It is the luck of the devil. But the devil makes his own. Always. Seemingly forever.

He left by the street-parked Cadillac rental to catch the next flight out.

If that's not the devil, I don't know who is.

CHAPTER 3

Creative Writing for Garden Seniors

Every Wednesday was creative writing for seniors, eleven until noon in Room 178 at The Garden of Eden. Instructed by Miss Erlene. Effortless Erlene. *Let your imagination take hold and soar!* That same Miss Erlene.

Today, Dombrowski, one of the senior participants in the day's class, looked up spontaneously (thought infused) and amazedly from his notepad over in the front left corner of Room 178. He was beside himself and almost giddy with delight. Dombrowski was a Creative Writing for Garden Seniors regular, devoted in fact. With his pencil in hand, he caught his breath, drew another deeper one more involved, and from that same faraway corner, then hollered out excitedly across to the back to the furthest far corner of that same room where Eddie sat. He was certain it was an epiphany and too good not to share with the entire class. Dombrowski said loudly, joyously:

"Hey Eddie, you're a writer. Why don't you write a nice, heartwarming story for all of us here at The Garden about Jesus Christ, our Lord and Savior, and the twelve apostles? Maybe something about Mary and Joseph as well?"

Dombrowski, with pencil in hand held as straight and vertical as the mast on a staysail schooner, looking out charitably and admiringly from behind his One Power Readers toward the other far corner in the rear, waited for Eddie's response hoping perhaps for a spontaneous high-five moment, maybe a fist bump as confirm, or even an old-fashioned hug and a handshake for old time's sake say after class, you know, between a couple of veteran, good ol' boy Garden old-timers.

Eddie was already hard at work on his own new story, his next project from his preferred position in the room over by the only window and source of natural light. Now irked and visibly irritated, he instantly looked up back over in Dombrowski's direction and yelled out:

"Hey, Dumbo, (*dead wood in the Garden forest,* muttered Eddie) why don't you do yourself a favor and stick a six pack of Roman candles up your sanctimonious wazoo … you know, where the sun don't shine … and set them off. I'll lend you my lighter. At least the rest of us can watch as they all ignite at once? Two things … we get a good-riddance chuckle … you get to heaven sooner rather than later. Lighter's in my pocket. Capisce?"

"Now, now," said Miss Erlene interrupting the disruptive classroom banter. "Let's let our imaginations take hold and soar, shall we?"

The other creative writing participants looked around and about and at one another seemingly more perplexed and confused than usual.

"Seeing Dumbo in a liftoff … it'd be the most excitement around here since toe-tag Paulson fell out in a dive at Arts'n'Crafts last Thursday," said Eddie.

"Now, now," said Miss Erlene. "Let's let our imaginations take hold and soar, shall we, Mister Jablonski."

"Tell that to Rocket Man," grumbled Eddie in a muffle. He was then back to work.

On this Wednesday, Eddie wrote his first semi-biographical essay opinion piece for next week's *The Garden Times* entitled:

The Ten Greatest (Hit) Men Who Ever Lived
By
Eddie 'The Icicle' Jablonski.

It was loaded and peppered with full-throated opinion and infused with red-blooded moxie in the wake of a front-line, morphemic cavalry charge. *Think habaneros!* Eddie wrote in a sidebar.

If you can rank quarterbacks and pulling guards, pitchers and catchers and centerfielders, big men in the paint, perimeter shooters from the outside, and small forwards as best off the bench, then I can rank Hit Men and the Greatest Mobsters who ever lived. So there. So be it. Great men one and all. My contention: Don't get enough respect or fanfare or credit for keeping things on the up and up, orderly, neat and tidy, and getting their hands dirty to get things done. A day when accomplishments and proficiency meant something. Rubbing out some slob in a quick-draw, quick shot was and is just an expedient way to get what's needed in a bulging society, refuse discarded, incinerated, buried, or destroyed. Ask me and I'll tell you the same today, tomorrow, next week, and next year. So there. Let's get right to it.

#1) Richard *'The Ice Man'* Kuklinski. Greatest Hit Man Ever. Take no prisoners. Bar none. Ice water in the man's veins. Cousin Richie. Rest in peace, bro. A man amongst boys. Made murder great again and revitalized the profession. Emblazoned the term forever into today's lexicon. New meaning to *still life*. Picture should be alongside the definition in Webster's. What's a hit man. It's Cousin

Rich. Big Rich. *The Ice Man.* Thanks, Rich, for the memories! You Da Man.

2) Carlo Gambino. A Palermo immigrant. Head of the Mangano-Gambino Crime Family. He then took control of The Commission. Anybody that lives life on the edge the way he lived life on the edge and dies of heart attack as an old man watching a frigging baseball game is top notch in my book. Hail, all hail to Carlo Gambino, mastermind of the modern day La Cosa Nostra, The Sicilian Mafia, aka Men of Honor. The crime boss of all crime bosses. Lived under the radar. Cool as a cucumber on ice. A billionaire with bucks to spare living in a prefab, double wide want-to-be. What a guy! The Don of all Dons. Don't make 'em like that anymore. It's a shame.

3) Vito Genovese. Joe Valachi. It's a tie. Penitentiary pals. Boss and underling. Genovese's murder plot against Valachi failed. Valachi suspected the worst and killed the Genovese hit man in prison. Genovese died in prison. Valachi wrote the Valachi Papers and became famous. Little man bad guy outsmarts big man the big cheese bad guy. Crime doesn't pay. Who says? Doesn't get any better than that.

4) Vincent 'The Chin' Gigante. Looney Tunes. Make believe. The Pantomime King. Puts Marcel Marceau to shame. Feigning madness and insanity in his pajamas, bathrobe and slippers while carrying on as the world renown lead gangster and mafia boss of the Genovese crime family. Brilliant! A doff of the newsboy Gatsby to you, Vincent. Twenty-one wins in the ring. Died in old age at 77.

5) Number five. This is a tie. I say Sammy 'The Bull' Gravano tied with Scar Face Tony Montana. Chip on his little Puerto Rican-Fidel Castro Cuban shoulder and a big ass scar across his cheek. Doesn't get any better than this except for his hot, blonde wife that he stole from his former boss. Got to love it. Yeah, I know it was movie, but irregardless (a spot of humor here in the telling… and I know it's *regardless,* so chill.), *Tony Scar* was The Man.

Sammy The Bull was the snitch of all snitches and rightfully so. Found out he was toast or going to be, so he fried the executive chef, the sous chef, the chef de partie, the pastry chef, the maître de, the wine steward, the busboys, the dishwashers, one and all, and then burned the place to the ground. Hit man's first rule, first inclination … self-preservation. Sammy personified the concept. Secondly … survival of the fittest. Sammy's still around being Sammy. The rest of the bunch, they're all history … **toast**. What else do you need to know. '*Witness Protection*' Gravano coming to a neighborhood near you.

6) Sam Giancana. So, sure, it's an obvious choice at number six. Master Don takes out the playboy president of the United States of America for tapping his mistress-girlfriend Judy Blue Eyes. Stones. Brass stones. Gives new meaning to payback. Profile that under courage, Camelot Jack, the rancid bootlegger's son. You, too, Jackie O.

7) Myer Lansky. A little, badass Jew and slick as an eel doused in whale shit. The definition of slick. His photo's beside the word in every dictionary. The ever-avuncular Uncle Myer.

6) John Gotti, The Dapper Don. The fuckup of all fuckups. He makes the ten top list just because he was so vain, so arrogant, so clueless, so destructive of the business that Carlo had taken seven decades to build, and yet he died in prison of natural causes which was too good for the mangy gumba. The definition of *threadbare* and with new meaning. An egoistic jerk of the first order. A blabber mouth big shot who beat the courts with hung juries so crooked it made porn stars look modest.

7) Lucky Luciano. Luck struck. Mister Lucky. They should issue a postage stamp with this guy's mugshot as the cover. When you lick it, the backside tastes like gun powder and oozes bloody red stains all over your tongue and teeth. Ah, how I long for the good old days.

8) Whitey Bulger. Not bad for an Irishman. On the lamb for sixteen years. Quite a feat. Died in prison at 89 years of age. Tough

guy's tough guy. If you dared refer to him as a *mick*, you only did it that one time. No nonsense Whitey. Brother to a top Massachusetts politician. All in the family. At least nineteen murders which included Balloonhead, big mouth bookmaker turned tough guy want to be, Louis the lip Litif. Armed robbery, truck hijacking, loansharking, cocaine trafficking, extortion, gambling, racketeering. All a part of Whitey's resume. There's got to be a special place in gangster heaven for James Joseph 'Whitey' Bulger Junior. Enough said.

9 & 10) Number 9 and 10 is a tie, as well. Just so you know.

Let me add here. *Honorable Mentions* to a couple of other celebrity types. I say, Pope John Paul the second, number two. He was a polack. What'd ya think, I was picking popes for the sake of picking popes. Not a gangster per se, but he was running maybe the biggest business organization in the world, right there from the Vatican, like it was a well-oiled machine. An inner circle any organization, straight or crooked, would envy.

And ... Sister Teresa, tied with Pope John in my book. Sister was a sister before she became a mother just like all the girls in my home town. I know, I know, this is about the ten greatest men and then I add a girl to list. Said she was a girl, but to me, she was a he. Looked like a he. Probably a cross-dresser at the very least. Just a little, do-gooder guy dressed in drag. Promoted (church-like) sister to mother. I know a lot of chicks that went from sister to mother. I, also, know a lot of little Italian guys, Polish guys, too, that look just like that (her) less the cap and gown. Forgive me if you're all politically contemporary, but that's what I think, so that's what I say. Not enough people speak up.

Eddie on Mother Teresa: Hey, I know what you're thinking. You're saying 'Hey, Eddie, how can a she be one of the greatest men al all time. She's a she, not a he. Well, give me a second and let me explain myself, me, Eddie *The Icicle* Jablonski.

She (Mother Teresa or Sister Teresa, whichever you prefer makes no difference to me. I'm just explaining myself here.) She, Mother T, was really a he. It wasn't like you've been told or had it explained to you beforehand. I'm here to explain it to you like it was. She (Mother T or Sister T, your call) was a *he* in drag. So, hear me out.

CHAPTER 4

Testament to the Times

Another day.

Eddie-ism #226. It came up early morning. Pre-breakfast. Post dawn. Eddie was an early riser, Monday through Friday. Laid back on the weekends both Saturday and Sunday. Skipped breakfast both days. Saved up for the big brunch at noon on Sunday after the teleprompter mass in small convention room #165 two doors down from the director's office and admissions. Complete with crumbly communion sippet and a snippet of wine. Never enough, said Eddie.

"Don't kid yourself, Jenkins," began Eddie. "I was a tough guy. And being a tough guy comes with a price tag. You probably already know that. A tough guy has to pay his dues. And, believe me, I paid my dues. In spades, mind you."

Eddie to Jenkins. Jenkins was finishing up. He was between the final swipe of his morning shave cream, straight razor, and the hot towel across the old man's face. These two, they'd been together going on four years. Convalescent and caregiver. Advisor and paid-to-listen advisee.

"Jenkins, just so you know… now get this straight; There might be a pop quiz on this next week … I want to make sure you get something out of knowing me, this old man." Eddie points to his chest with his forefinger. "Most of them, the palookas in here, will come and go. You'll have nothing to show for the wear, not even a kind word much less a thank you. Too demented. Too self-absorbed besides. But not with me. Not Eddie *The Icicle* Jablonski … Truths and tidbits of wisdom galore. A fountain of knowledge less the *youth.*" Eddie paused then continued. "Jenkins, you got grandkids?

Jenkins said, "No sir, Mister J. No grandkids. Not yet."

Eddie said to Jenkins, "Well, when you have a few and they get a little age on them, tell them this from me … just like I'm telling it to you." Eddie paused, braced himself next to his walker, one hand on a handle, the other perched and hanging on his shirt's lapel, the folding eatery-chair-table ensemble, he looked Jenkins in the eye, and said:

"Life is less a cavalry charge … more an accidental, unorthodox trudge on a broken switchback."

Eddie pulled back, stood up straight, taller, as tall as he could, erect, erect as an arrow, even for an old man, prideful say. He could feel a sudden adrenaline and new found virility and youthfulness reclaim his weathered body. It showed. Like he'd really just accomplished something, something very special, say something of military worthiness inside another even worthier cause.

"Tell them that. Give them that little nugget. It might help them get over the rough spots particularly when they feel most abandoned by God. As they'll come to find out, there are a lot of those little moments … some big ones, too … A curve ball, a sinker and a slider low and away … the pull, the draft, the intrusion of that a hulking, lurking, gasping horror figure positioned in the offstage (wings) and just about to make its grand entrance … Then, suddenly, God, that benevolent old caretaker, firecracker, and benefactor, is more the impudent court jester and suspiciously sardonic harlequin than the almighty grand master we've all come to expect, know, and somehow love (sort of) … or fear … with your own personal best interests in mind and a blueprint as plan to match your every need. But low and behold, you're actually standing open and broadside in the crosshairs of the devil."

In the moment, Eddie was Churchill, Gandhi, Sartre, Confucius, Langhorne Clemens, and Caesar rolled into one. At this stage of his life, *The Icicle*, Eddie, had a lot of these leveraged inner exchanges. Imposingly, he continued.

"And don't explain it to them, the grandchildren that is. Leave it open-ended. Let them soak it up, let them mull it (the expression, the witticism) over; you might get them to repeat it a few times so they get the rhythm and syntax along with the jive. The meaning and the significance and the intent will hit them later once they've overcome a little adversity or tried to or lived through turmoil and strife and come out the other side. I gave that to my kids to give to their kids so they can give it to their next generation of youngsters. You know… (Eddie begins the song, strikes up the tune, and waves his arms to and fro like a bandleader in free for all.) … Ninety-nine bottles of beer on the wall, ninety-nine bottles of beer, take one down, pass it around, ninety-eight bottles of beer on the wall. You get the idea. Life really is less a cavalry charge, Jenkins. Take it from me, an old man. For sure. You tell that to your grandkids when the time is right and they'll thank you for it later. Tell them …. Best regards, Uncle Eddie, Eddie *The Icicle* Jablonski. And not just another tough guy … tell them that, too … he was *The Icicle*."

Eddie winked at Jenkins. The two men headed off to breakfast.

"And for what it's worth … I mean what have I got left? … five maybe ten years if I stop eating potato chips and ice cream? Big deal. For all intents and purposes, it's over. Some of it was a good ride … a really good ride. No complaints worth airing."

Chapter 5

Eddie Flying Solo

A Soliloquy & Flashback

The back and forth return conversation went like this. A one-man soliloquy and flashback. Eddie to Eddie style. A Jablonski soliloquy and flashback. Eddie, the solo performance. It was Eddie to Eddie, one on one, self to self and back again. Sometimes he spoke intimately to Jenkins in his tell-alls and old man ramblings but only if Jenkins was listening. Today Jenkins wasn't listening. He'd fallen asleep in the chair opposite Eddie, but Eddie hadn't noticed. Eddie had feigned the nap bit. Jenkins saw it as an opportunity to catch a catnap, so Eddie proceeded without him as Jenkins quietly respired and snored, respired and snored, Jenkins' usual pattern. No doubt, all of it was subject matter for an old man and the informal yet dutiful subtext of his inner demons. His quiet, retirement-home histrionics were a bit Shakespearean in nature, elocution, range, and trajectory but effective nonetheless. Lear. Gielgud. Old Vic in timbre with a profoundness and clarity at the expense of cause, Eddie gallantly raised one index finger into the air and spoke.

"God is Providence. Providence God. No matter what anyone tells you, this is true.

God plays dice with all of us, all of our lives.

God does not play dice, said Eddie's other voice. It was his counter point to *self*.

Who are you, Eddie Jablonski, to tell God what he needs to do? said Eddie in return fire.

Okay then, God shuffles the deck, cuts the cards, then fixates over your destiny and mine in a game of twenty-one.

Come on now. Don't be ridiculous. God does not shuffle then cut the cards to play twenty-one. Blackjack is hardly God's game. So, again, who are you to tell God what he needs to do? He may shuffle, he may deal the cards, he may deal the cards from the bottom of the deck and to you useless cards of no significance or meaning, cards that will win nothing except frustration and gambling debt ... But so what. This is God. God, the Grand Croupier!"

God's plan? God's trickery? God's gamesmanship? Frightening questions all. But again, it was Eddie thanklessly, provocatively intimating to Eddie. The challenge ... matching wits, win, lose, or draw.

In the moment, Eddie Jablonki stood in front of the mirror and continued his ramble, Eddie Jablonski talking to Eddie Jablonski, the same man asking that same man's reflection questions of fate, fortune, and forgiveness. Eddie Jablonski said to Eddie Jablonski the same reflection and man in the mirror, that image of himself:

"God does not play dice." It was a mighty statement filled with reverent verve and philosophical force. He'd taken a stance.

Eddie stepped back, stood up taller while wagging his index finger and responded to that same person mirror-image.

"So, wait a minute. Who are you, Eddie Jablonski, to tell God what he needs to do? It's hardly your position or place."

Eddie from the other side of the mirror shifted his weight again right to left and said:

"I'm Eddie Jablonski, that's who."

Eddie said it with a balanced and impenetrable conviction. After all, he was Eddie Jablonski. He straightened his back to make himself and his own reflection taller with the appearance of being more the man from either side of the reflection than was left of him.

*"To be clear and to make my voice known, I am Eddie The Icicle Jablonski for your information. God knows me. We've spoken on occasion. Not often, but a time or two. An abbreviated discourse, perhaps, but we've talked. Just ask him. Bring up my name. See if He doesn't remember me. He'll reply. Sure, **The Icicle**, sure I know him. That would be God's reply. Of this I'm certain. God does not shuffle the deck then cut the cards to play twenty-one. He knows blackjack better than you. But again … Who are you and who am I to tell God what he needs to do?"*

Eddie backed away from the full-length mirror and sat down again in the hefty lounger to his right. Here, he was most comfortable, *a chair I could die in*, he confessed.

"Boss man, you don't need to talk that way," said Jenkins waking from his snooze. *"You can do better than that. You'll die on a grand throne somewhere as a great man. You'll see."*

Eddie smiled and each time repeated himself. *"Jenkins, you are the man. The man, J, for sure."*

Jenkins came back into the room carrying a hot towel, shaving cream, straight razor, talc and comb. He positioned himself near Eddie and listened.

"Old time Sicilian adage," Eddie said stoically to Jenkins. "Never shoot a man in the back." Eddie then paused, he looked out the window, held onto the arm rest, looked back in Jenkins' direction, and continued. "Not when you can get him to turn around. Just call him by name. Vanity'll get the better of him. Always does. He's a man. He'll turn around. Then shoot him. It's your guarantee. You know you took out the right guy." Eddie grinned.

If nothing else, Eddie always had his smile, and a nice smile it was. Warm, comforting, invitingly benign, and pleasantly suggestive, even for a hit man of sorts. Since he was a little boy, *Edek*, said his mama, *you have such a beautiful and charismatic smile, my precious little baby boy. Fresh as the morning flower. It is the breath of romance and distinction. Always you must smile, even when you are doing things not so good. Even when you, Edek, are doing the naughty and mischievous things of the good boy being bad. It is just what boys do.* Eddie could still swell with a son's pride at the memory of his mother's voice and maternal praise. Just the simple and dignified clarity and honesty offsetting her voice made him smile. From her, Eddie had learned the semblance of love and truth and honor so he insisted on it as a matter of principle and as often times a show of pragmatic will. But, of course, it was mostly and particularly his version of the truth that he loved most.

In greatest confidence, Eddie said to Jenkins.

"Take this with you wherever you go. It's for those of us on the inside.

The mafia, the mob, began and remains a novelty act inside a house of mirrors. That same house backs up to an underground transit connection stoically railed and trundling over a loosely balanced, flimsy, shoddy, and soiled house of cards. Jokers top the deck. Jokers are wild. In both good times and bad, these same wild card jesters carry more than their own weight for the player in need. Legerdemain is at large and on the loose at all times. This much is certain. Now you see it, now you don't. Just like it was planned from the beginning. Never meant it to be as bankable and lucrative as it has grown to be maybe … you could certainly argue that point … but hardly your average, clumsy, tinhorn pickpocket on some average, run of the mill, windswept city street corner unless that same cutpurse comes with an insatiable appetite for excessively large wallets too bulky for anyone's back pocket or mountainous amounts of loose change crammed inside a chinchilla-lined crocodile Gucci tote embossed with diamond studded straps and mother of pearl closures. But where in the world are you going to find a guy much less a gal on the street walking around with that kind of dough in a backdrop and setting such as the one I just described? Ain't happening," answered Eddie to Eddie. Jenkins was folding Eddie's clothes off to the side.

Eddie sat in his easy chair recliner. He nodded to himself. He liked what he'd said. Speaking these whip-smart words, these frilly and fancy pearls of wisdom off the cuff like that ... age let you do that. Age and experience and hard knocks and the mix and sweep of second-hand time both good and bad, melancholy and sad, accurate, inaccurate, linear or warped, morose, contemplative, and joyful, it all breathes life into the language and language into life. Eddie knew this as well as anyone.

He flavored his coffee with a mix of powdered chocolate, brown sugar, and truncated soliloquy. In that order. He percolated shaded truth and embellishment for the whimsy and in the telling. There is life, and there is death, and there's everything in between. Here was some of the stuff in between.

He squinted for the better view of whatever was making its way back into the life-before Eddie's Garden of Eden days ... into that old mind's eye of his. The approaching memory playback was as real as pepper flakes, table salt, and bratwurst to the taste buds. He closed his eyes to capture the clarity as old-man refuse and bring it to life once again. He smiled inviting the nostalgia. That same playback and recollection was a crapshoot just like the original life events had been, but more often than not, they came across softer and more pliable in the tough and mealy spots, less disturbing in the flinch and properly more amenable throughout the re-live and recall. So, Eddie was adequately and acceptably at ease and reticent with a look back. He'd survived it and now lived to remember it once more in the deep, soft cushion of his fat, stuffed, load-bearing lounge chair. He squinted a third time as if the eye cast, the slit and sliver eyelid to eyelid, would help him to recall and remember it at its finest, its grandest, or even more mellifluent than even that or the way it really happened. It was a chunk of his life, so why not, he thought. It really is a small world after all. The devil's in the detail, and today at this minute, the devil and his splendid detail had re-arrived. After all this time, it still wasn't over.

Vietnam, said the voice. Somehow, it's Eddie's voice. From way back. The same voice of the young Second Lieutenant Eddie Jablonski.

The year is 1965.

Note that here, the voice said, to remove all doubt as to time and place. No shapeless or shadowy tricks, no subtle or unstated obfuscation, obvious or formless omission from one old man's loose knit memory. We'll have none of that. The voice continued.

We never made Da Nang as promised, but we are too far off the beaten path to turn back now. We coordinate our mission from here. Orders must be carried out come hell or high water is what they, the superiors, tell us. Those are our orders.

To me from up here, it looked like both … *hell* … a steamy, monsoon, tropical heat, and … *highwater* … a turgid slough straight ahead slumping into a short drop-off below where I'm seated at the back of a rattly, fire-breathing *Loach*, the Cayuse OH-6. Inside this contraption, life's a freaking windswept, noisy clamor. You can probably sense and smell my sarcasm just like I'm drafting dying-to-dead, offshore plankton, diesel fuel, motor and gun oil even from way up here.

The voice of Lieutenant Jablonski spoke more clearly now and carried on. Realism was at stake. Like time, it was not to be wasted.

Too precious and too little of it left. At every stage of life, said the voice. But Eddie knew this then just as he knew it now. He had learned it in war and what better teaching grounds could a young man have had.

Somewhat surprisingly, he remembered it all very well. The images are clear, the sounds, the cadence, the alternating speech patterns are on pitch and queue, the urgency is reenacted with precision. After all this time, Eddie is amazed at the pinpoint accuracy. His memory too often now is piecemeal, crusty, stumbling, and stale, but not now, not today. *And I thought everyone had forgotten*, he heard himself say. *Pariah*, he said aloud, even to some *like we'd pissed in their cornflakes, like we were lightminded and frivolous young men there only for glory and a chest full of gallantry ribbons and medals over this halfcocked caper dubbed a war, pissing away our lives to something mightier than ourselves as self-sacrifice. Stuff it!* Called out the youthful Second Lieutenant Jablonski now in the sanctity of his own room 315 at The Garden of Eden. *You nabobs of negativism. Natters one and all,* said Eddie in a spark, a spry and spunky moment of vindication from a personally onerous fifty-year payback. From a festering backseat craw to the front of his own magic bus … *Touché*, said Eddie. Touché, indeed. He'd been lugging this baggage around for far too long like a tiny, rolling, pesky pebble in the heel of his shoe.

Nam Du is now in the backdrop then just as quickly the island is in the foreground as the helicopter circles and turns over almost broadside in an awkward tilt after a sudden, startling, unrehearsed maneuver. Not by the flight manual for certain. (It was uncanny. His voice repeated the dreadfully dire and dangerous circumstance exactly like that day from fifty, sixty years ago.)

Coming in low, much lower than anything I had experienced or heard of, and unprecedented as an approach, as approaches go, not like planned, and suddenly we're just above the treetops, I can see their leaves up close, the veins within the green that feeds them, a trickle of gray smoke from our rotor above is drifting downward into the cabin area where I'm seated, then we're skimming the branches and sheering them to pieces and then slamming into the trees and treetops themselves, me all hunched down in the back, and I am certain that this is not good. I say this to myself word for word as the entire flying machine is getting buried inside the shrubs and foliage and limbs, thick and thin alike, with sounds of crack, snap, screech and buckle, crunch, sheer, thud, thud again, and just as quickly, I, along with this flying machine I was traveling and depending on … we are perched in a stranglehold of brush on top of some random tree's crest. All of it has ended in a violently sudden stop. Everything, even my normal sense of breathing and vision, has come to a halt! The crash itself, it's done. Then there is near silence. A plummet into hell … I'm conditioned to expect the worst so why not out with it. A jumble of wreckage and it's all just outside the bent, open door of helicopter J 23 (reporting for duty, sir, I thought with a broken laugh). There's the chant and chatter of a nearby pack of birds. Probably discussing what they've just witnessed and have never seen before. As shocked as I am, I would bet as much or more. The rattle of cicada chimed in about this time. I remember that for some unknown reason while staring at tail remnants, ailerons, rudder, a bent propeller, opposite props side by side, and nose gear held up forcibly as if we're at takeoff (not the nose-down crash-landing position you might suspect) by vines and small limbs and leafy undergrowth. A bent wheel and other shredded rubber down the path were laid out like pie crust. I can see random pieces of helicopter strewn everywhere below me, beside me at eye level, and above me there are metal parts and army supplies all of a sudden perched like shiny tropical birds between tree branches or aboriginal monkeys at rest and at ease on their haunches mocking the entire debacle. And all this without warning.

My helmet is missing from my armpit. My rifle is AWOL. My flak jacket is torn and shredded. I notice the bleeding from my forehead but only because it is oozing into my left eye blurring my sight. Just as quickly, I can taste the same trickle of my own blood at the corner of my mouth. Looking down, my pants leg is torn lengthways raggedly in several places and small branches with their sprigs of leaves are looking up at me as if to say I've officially been invaded from all fronts by the jungles of Southeast Asia.

What just happened?

The voice goes on to answer the question it alone has posed just as efficiently and translucently as it did in the asking.

Oops! (says the voice of the young Lieutenant Jablonski, a voice dripping in sardonic condescension as one budding, youthful smartass). And welcome to all things Vietnam, Eddie, you pummel-witted neophyte of Special Forces United States Armed Services, 1st Cavalry Regiment, Unit 352 Squadron 4C. Welcome indeed, soldier and welcome aboard to another fouled up, wartime cloak and dagger from the hell hole and fiery spit they all call **Nam**, the voice replied sarcastically. And, what's more, you bought in, Eddie! said the voice ever more cruelly. And, as a grunt, no less, a second lieutenant, the very same rank of the most-killed, most-wounded dumb asses of this entire frapping, collapsing war … the grunt's grunt, mind you, too young to know the difference, too dumb to answer to your gut or question the call you've made by enlisting into the ensuing mess that has resulted and now dumped you off here. *Let me know how this works out, junior grade warrior-dude,* said the voice in a one-up jab. *You're on your own, killer.*

Am I ever! I reminded myself.

I heard the voice laugh derisively offstage in some kind of distant reprimand then it disappeared.

Next, I wiped the blood from my face with my shirt sleeve and unbuckled my copter harness with a free hand, my good hand, the one that didn't hurt, then tried to stand up ... but for what? There was nowhere to go. I was staring at a drop-off of forty or fifty feet from the helicopter edge and me with a damaged hand, the one, that was badly bruised in places... but my fingers worked, I told myself, which I took as a positive sign ... no, not from God, but just a positive sign, something to go on.

Since joining the military and shipping out, I became enamored and fixated by signs ... signs of all kinds ... religious signs, road signs (traffic and nontraffic alike and unrelated), heavenly signs (stars and shit), metaphysical signs (say, the heptagonal-hexagonal type as in Satan and devil worship where the occult comes to mind), luminary signs sequentially and particularly sun and moon, Eastern signs (talking native gibberish fraternizing Buddhist or Shinto slogans of how to), Western signs (almost completely Catholic), quixotic signs (we all have our windmills to battle and engage!), and germane signs which I interpreted as ordinary things punctuating what was right before me, sort of staring at me say like a gargoyle perched on the ledge of some highfalutin, historical monument or on the rim and crest of a city-center, metropolitan library or at the base of a well-endowed, overly-stodgy museum say, that (the despised-looking gargoyle) would rank as a sign for sure ... any of those at the time would most definitely be considered some kind of sign by Special Forces Lieutenant Eddie Jablonski ... whatever helped coordinate or retain my equilibrium in the next daunted or flagging moment of crisis and indecision.

Cloud formations ... yes, those worked as signs sometimes as well since they were usually readily available and easily accessible. You could just look straight up or out a window, see a wisp or a white fluff of puff or a gray mass, and there was your sign for the moment. Voila! Signs and desperation, signs and angst and signs and turmoil and signs and strife ... quite useful as a road map or directional if you think about it long enough ... they all seemed the quaint mix of futuristic telltale and omen for the time being. Whether there was anything to my newly formulated hypothesis, who knows. I was a young man, remember, a grunt for sure nevertheless bent on blithe. But I was giving it a shot (nonmilitary) and a military gung-ho-go to boot. What the hell. And just for the record, the aforementioned boot is non-combat related. Call it anti-war and peaceful. A cowboy to-boot. So there.

In retrospect … After the crash, the helicopter crash, Viet Nam, the war there, my transition to the mob and crime for hire was a piece of cake. Cake, ice cream, with whipped cream and a cherry on top.

Now, in the remembrance … a furtive and salty remembrance of things past … a voice from within and the story it told unfolds and begins.

Four Days in … Maybe Five …

Me, Mister Espionage, agent of death, killer, the kill of kill-or-be-killed, the slash of slash your fucking throat, the hybrid Lone Ranger less Tonto as chopper mongrel, the killing machine, a not-so-special special forces envoy dressed up in tattered undress and left out in the jungle to rot of that very same thing. My, my, what a coincidence. Makes unconventional look fluffy, plush, posh, a massage from both a queen and her princess. And then there's me … out here running around like a wild boar in disbelieving heat foraging under mango leaves and mottled pythons for a root or a berry to salvage my own skinny ass from starvation and scurvy. God, whatever possessed me to choose espionage. My mother said it was the kookiest idea I'd ever come up with and for me, a reasonable sort throughout childhood and pubescent adolescence, neither of us for the life of either of us could ever figure out what made me go through with it. But I did. There was always a surreal quality to the whole thing from the get-go. I mean I went from addressing labels on letterhead to ramming shunts into virgin dirt half way round the world with little or no probable cause. Figure that one out? No, I don't guess you can. I sure as hell can't nor couldn't at the time. The mind is maze unto itself. A contradiction in its own unsolvable, unknowable equation thus without answer until death solves the riddle for us. That's as philosophical as I get. Enough. It was either continue or disgrace myself in the eyes of my own mother so I continued. And here I am. Eight thousand miles in the middle of who-knows-where, undressed to a loin cloth and tattered head band and a cannibal wife would look better every time I look at my island alternatives. Monkeys, goats, and tasseled iguanas. As I understood it, my orders were: *don't come back until you've found the goods and destroyed the enemy.* I took it literally along with the other crew mates now vanished. So, so far after all this time traipsing about, I've neither found the goods nor destroyed the enemy. Welcome to my world.

Day Twelve … or was it thirteen?

Collecting my thoughts, they appeared in an uninhibited, spectral form and superimposed fashion and in this order.

I was a byzantine pirate. I told myself that on multiple occasions just because it sounded cool and capricious, helped to keep my chin up, a morale booster of sorts, and gave meaning and made sense of something I didn't understand … not even a little bit. But once again, as if I needed reminding, there I was smack dab in the middle of whatever, wherever, and however and all of this had just happened to me. It was my cloak and cover in both darkness and daylight. It went with the territory and gave purpose to my dreadfully purposeless mission. So, there you have it, the reason and the rhyme noted. Horns and daggers and pistols with a rabbit's foot as my shield in the place of a crucifix and a Gideon Bible and a dirty sock as the preferred placebo for any future, bloodcurdling pain or bloodletting! It's the way I saw myself.

In seconds and a nosedive, I found myself surrounded by an avalanche of despair over a cliff of doubt. That was just after the helicopter crashed and split into three pieces. Fuselage, tail, and rotors. The fire was minimal. The smoke, too. As well, three crew members, pilot, copilot, and machine gunner bailed out over offshore water before the rest of the machine disappeared with me into the canopy of the island jungle. Three small splashes into the big, blue sea. Eddie Jablonski watched aloft, rudderless, in a soft, steep, and surreal decline. That's what he said to himself at the time … soft … he was puzzled by how soft it really was, steep … no matter how soft, he and the helicopter were on a direct hit-course for the grove of mangrove and palms left of his best visual, and surreal … by far the best description of how he and the helicopter came rushing down through leaves and foliage and stalks and limbs, there was even a monkey in the way on the way down until he and the chopper rested sideways to normal with his seat belt twisted on a gaggle of green vines and hemp. He was left on board and stranded and alone but alive. He was conscious, real time, and thought *I'll take my chances in the bush*. He'd assumed the foliage would break the fall and he could crawl out from there. He was only right by a thumb nail and a second sliver of luck.

It was the strangest thing. He kept hearing Dusty Springfield singing, that pleasantly smokey voice of hers … *wishin' and* ho*pin'* … the Bachrach-David refrain … all the way down into the tops of the bushy treetops, the broken branches, the twigs and limbs snapping under the weight of the fuselage until he had to admit it was a curious song selection for the backside of his brain to drag out in full auditory reenactment and display, horn section and all, wishing and hoping at a time like this. A pack in his left breast pocket, a band aid on his ring finger, a sucker vine twisted over the front of his face and his right elbow, a whir of engine last gasp, and that was it. Broadside and bivouac and swaying in the heat of a gentle breeze and a quiet jungle setting. Welcome to Viet Nam, Eddie said to himself. And a big Ho Ho Ho Chi Minh to you, too. The old, stale, hackneyed joke always made him laugh so he told it to himself in his broken, Huey cradle because at the time, he had nothing else to do and no one else to converse or talk to. Roger that.

Three weeks in, maybe four, and counting, sort of but not sure ...

I am here. (His voice in the telling and in the recall, it is much younger sounding. Youthful if not naïve, less knocked-about but getting there. More certain of its own vitality while at the same time more uncertain of certainty itself. Lieutenant Eddie Jablonski, he has resurfaced in a flashback some fifty years or more before.)

No, that same voice says watchfully. **Here. I am over here.** At the base of the tropical Ceiba tree beyond the mangroves and the steamy marsh. You can barely see me even if you know where to look. Me amid the most preternatural, innermost jungle penumbra imaginable. At least that's what you might say as I just did. Nevertheless, it is what it is and it is where I am.

Haven't spotted me yet? Over here, just a bit more to the other side. Past the two hanging vines clumped as thick as a fist, past the thorny palm leaves all dangly as if something hauntingly forbidden is about to unfold. Look again. Even if you need to strain your eyes in the search, do so. It's worth the price of admission (free) just to watch me at work. With little or no braggadocio, I've gotten quite good at this over the last few weeks even if I do say so myself. Maybe five or six now that I think back. Not sure. It's really difficult to say without a time piece, a calendar, so much as an hour glass or a sun dial. I've lost track. Stopped counting. Besides, time flies (this is what they say) when you're having a good time!

Now, again in the remembrance … a furtive yet sharply edged and prickly remembrance of things past … a voice from within and the story it told continued this way.

Anyway. Back to the spot where I am hiding like a leopard in wait.

Below the foliage and to the left is where I'm positioned. Almost, but more to the left still.

Yes, that's it. Yes. Here. (Index finger on top of my head pointing downward purely for effect and a bit of comic relief.) The heat's pretty insufferable at this hour probably inducing a touch of giddiness to boot as I stand here as still as any of the unwavering broad-leafed branches surrounding me.

Yes. That's me with the soiled (filthy actually), khaki discarded shirt sleeve shredded and tied in a knot around my forehead to keep the sweat and prickly jungle fronds out of my eyes. I like to envision myself a resolute Comanche warrior, fit and sharp with razor-keen senses focused on the frontier surroundings. Sure, it's flattering you might say, but what the heck and a game I play with myself in this desolate survival contest before me. And besides, who's out here anyway (in this dense jungle) to compliment me? No one … no one except for me. Hah! Here, I answer to no one not even the blue-rumped parrots and sewer-less sewer rats, the military macaw and horny, filthy-mouthed monkeys jumping all about daybreak to dusk to taunt me like I'm oversized prey waiting to be had. They wish. Nevertheless, I don't answer. Not a word.

Killed a ruddy faced pochard last week with a club I made from driftwood. Discovered both by the water's edge parallel to one another. Copped the encounter as a sign when neither moved. After the whirlybird crash, I see stillness as opportunity and a short festival of sorts to plan ahead, prepare, and maneuver. The unfeathered duck butchered, dressed, cooked, and skewered was a dark meat delight. Charred the leafy green trimmings and daydreamed of a back home, backyard fourth amidst the perforated shade of cirrus clouds and wind-mangled palms cradled by serpent vines so thick I felt somehow nestled and protected. No longer have any idea what day it is much less the month. I could take a wild guess, but I have enough **wild** around me as it is. If I am here and made it to this point, there is no telling what you must go through to get to the end of one man's individual vale. An old man's life, right now, looks enchantingly delightful and enticing to say the least. We'll see. Life is a fractured ideal, a structured ordeal, and from where I sit, minute to minute unconnected chaos. You choose. I am only as smart as I am smart, lucky as I am unlucky, and somehow stuck here mid-boonies.

I can see the bare-chested monkey and his genitals, a proud male, in the tree above me. I am very still. Motionless. Okay, nearly motionless. I do not move or move very, very, very slowly most like a slug, maybe slower so that I go unnoticed and undetected as predator. I can even feel, even notice my own blinks, but it's okay. It makes no noise whatsoever and in the belly of the forest, it could just as easily be taken for the sway of a twig or the flutter of a loose-leaf groundward.

As usual, time is on my side. Since the beginning of my unfathomable ordeal, this over simplistic notion __ that time is on my side __ has become a personal mainstay, nearly a mantra. Little doubt this has reshaped and altered my view of living, life, and all that remains in its passing. As always, I breath with meticulous care. Even strokes in. Even strokes out. More like a fish in a bowl with tiny gills slurping up oxygen gulps in neutral buoyancy. Anyway, that's what I tell myself as the respiring, intrepid hunter: *Think of yourself as a fish in a bowl with tiny gills and acclimate your breathing, Jablonski.* It's the quick lecture of instruction that I give to myself in the waiting in order to break the monotony and tedium and boredom of standing there (here) feeling the mosquitoes and gnats and leeches bury themselves into my skin and extract their nasty pound of flesh and sticky dried blood from my arms and legs and the fat of my upper neck. Even my crotch has suddenly become fair game. And wouldn't you know it, they've now found and invaded my droopy nut sack and curly, pigtailed pubic hairs ... like pesky hornets circling a dangling, gray paper hive in the upper reaches of a porch atrium. This it seems is merely part of the price to be paid for a scrumptious jungle meal just now as I begin to take position and ready myself for the supreme kill. And oh my, this would be prime kill indeed. A tasty treat for sure. Maybe the best to date. The male is very fat, particularly for a tree monkey of his height. The thigh and torso, even the other appendages, would provide a most succulent dinner. With steamed banana and smoked papaya, roasted palm root and raw dates, he could make for a feast I haven't experienced in weeks.

I have dipped the dart into the poison twice at lengthy intervals prior to my long, nearly silent walk into the heavy thicket, this in order to guarantee the furry little bastard's death. Trust me, he is mine as sure as I stand here motionless taking the worst of the insect dread without so much as a flinch, a swat, a faint primal scream, or squelch. I tilt my neck slowly toward the base of my skull until they meet like a door latch to insert, the whole time keeping his fat cheeks in my line of sight. He nibbles away at the tree leaves as appetizer and looks about as if he's secure and confident just as I would have it. Go ahead. Take your sweet time, I say to him. Keep fattening yourself for the slaughter, oh mighty treetop chieftain. Cocky-fied, arrogant, insouciant all at the same time, why he approaches the semblance of a clownish and yet mockingly aloof disposition you might say way up there in his forked perch. *Don't worry*, I tell myself ever so patiently. *Don't worry. You're mine.*

With a fixed, resolute vision, I watch some more, making sure he, Mister Monkey, the one and the same Mister Loudmouthed

Monkey, is feeling smug and secure, dapper even, on the broad limb straight above me. Quasimodo aloft in his jungle campanile, the clock and the countdown to death is ticking, ticking, ticking. I, on the other hand, am like a vulture previewing a dying-to-dead carcass in the offing. Oh, and guess what, my fine, furry little creature, our roles here are reversed and reversed in my favor I'll have you know. Down here on the ground, a most bosky enclosure, I am the vulture. You, up there, are the carcass-to-be. I count to myself as slowly, as deliberately as I move, maybe even slower than in all the other hunts combined. One, two, three, four ... no it is slower even than that ... spread out are the numbers like the second hand of a wrist watch in five counts or maybe ten counts until the numbers finally pass methodically like a slow water drip into a vacant bowl ... five ... six ... seven ... eight ... nine ... ten ... eleven until the blow gun is raised to my lips in perfect placement. I must look like a rusty crane lifting a heavy, cumbersome load of steel or leaded weights the movement to my mouth is so, so very slow. I lick my lips once, twice, then a third time before placing the open, hollowed-out bamboo chute to my mouth. Until, it is .... There. Near the measure and shape of a reed flute less the intended intonation. It is done snug and comfortably between the soft tissue of top to bottom lip. I exhale more slowly still to assure my balance in striker's stance. It is just as my eyes and ears and senses want things to align. I inhale once again, smoothly. I exhale as heavily yet gently and then inhale again. Mister monkey, he is still nibbling away at his verdantly waxen tree leaves. I, as quickly, exhale with an inconspicuous yet hearty thrust a blow dart in an ever-so-slight, upward lean which always goes unnoticed by my prey. Voila and touché in one! And so it goes.

The dart has struck the animal in the abdomen which from here has the look of an oversized excrescence to the power of ten and the true size of a ripened cantaloupe. He pauses from the force of the projectile, backs up three or four steps toward the trunk of the tree, looks at his belly (poison's engaged), sees the dart embedded, displays momentarily the forlorn mask'n'face of an empty, would-be tirade, then falls head first, lengthways, ass over tea kettle, through the broad leafy foliage and into the thick canopy and densely thatched brush until he lands in a thud onto a soft, mossy tuffet in a bed of jungle debris no more than an arm's length from my left foot. It happened as if scripted.

There, he lays motionless. Somehow, yet mysteriously and for no apparent reason, and as if he'd intended to defy logic in the face of his own death, he's wearing (of all things) his own smiley happy face. The grin of a fool, a knave, or some lunatic and truculent court jester you might say! Maxillary incisors saliently showing (like some kind of audition for a toothpaste commercial), ridiculously pristine and glimmering, white on white with a sheen front and center. Canine incisors showing too, almost supernaturally, more pointy or pointier and razor sharp than you would imagine as if ground on a machinist wheel they are so ferociously adept and thorn-like. Eyes open wide. Wider still. Even wider than that. Like he is surprised and ecstatically glad to see me at the same time you might say. But, alas, he is dead. Just to make sure, I use the long branch to my left that I've spotted a couple of paces away (broke off the dead sprouts) to prod and poke his midsection three times to a one to two-inch indentation for good measure. Nothing. A leg poke once. Nothing still. Both arms twice until I displace the right arm back over his midsection so that actually he looks like a pleasant-enough gentleman seated on a park bench waiting on the mid-morning bus.

Once I didn't do this. The half dead little monster (the mister monkey from a few weeks back ... *me* the novice monkey hunter) was merely wounded. His eyes were shut, then suddenly opened wide, unhinged more like the jaws of a mamba. He came after me all enraged as if rabid and I'd insulted his mother treble-fold. He bit a two-inch hole in my arm the size of silver dollar. It nearly killed me as his bite gave way to a most diabolical infection followed by an excruciatingly painful high fever. Were it not for the ocean water, boiled and primed, topically poured into the open and malodorous flesh, I would have died. Very lucky. Very lucky indeed I must admit. Probably, no surely, lost twenty pounds in the ordeal and certainly didn't have it to lose. However, this one, this mister monkey, he is deader than a door knob and his half-brother from yesterday's kill-and-mini-feast and most fit to be gutted, skinned, roasted over an open fire with dates and guava juice, and eaten to the bone, balls, cartilage, carapace, pecker, gray matter, and all. Three bird eggs stir fried and the meal's complete. A hearty hi ho Silver … away.

The matching skeletal island dogs, Pol Pot and Meathead, can growl and tear and froth and spit over the negligible, uncooked refuse, skin, skull, scrotum, and hide. It's what they do even if they don't do it very well. Such is their life here. Mine, too.

When you lose your mind, lover, please don't lose mine, too. If it's not a song title, it should be. For now, this is Lieutenant Eddie Jablonski signing off from right here under the wide leafed coconut tree on some island somewhere off Southeast Asia. The radio's busted or on the blink for the time being so it's difficult to say exactly where I am. I'll attempt to climb the tree tomorrow or the next day and see what happens. Signal or no signal, I'm stuck here. Have some flares but nothing and nobody on the horizon to start popping off boomers for help. Will save the few bad boys in the bag for a more opportune occasion. Over and out.

Eclipse at dawn. Eclipse at dusk. The shadows are the same. The difference is left to right, only, then right to left and short as if long, narrower to the interpretive eye but only to the touch of death and memory's distance.

That night, the dream went like this.

Notes in a bottle. They floated ashore it seemed almost weekly for a time. Closer to twilight than not. There was a lull in the activity and frequency for another time. A couple of weeks or a month went by. It may have been six or eight weeks. I wasn't keeping score. Sometimes the bottles were wine bottle green. Other times clear as mayonnaise jars but cylindrical and yet properly, hermetically sealed with candle wax or paraffin perhaps. No reason for the interim that I could think of; it just was. I was curious enough. For sure. It was odd at least to have someone, somewhere, an adversary of sorts for sure, writing to me or to the world with such disregard and dislike. I carefully uncorked each vessel, not to get the inscription wet mind you, and unfurled the paper. Each one read in poor penmanship: *Yank, you die! Soon! Hate your ass! Tiếng Bansai! Mother is a whore! For sure! Banzai! Mother fucker!*

It was all a bit startling then I awoke.

Flip the switch. Dawn is breaking. My eyes open, then blink and flutter to focus. I hear voices subtle and awake and intentional. I can see the outline of unfamiliar figures around me so my eyes open wider. Trouble is all mine. I can feel the rounded, hollow end of a gun barrel in the meat of my neck left side. These men, these intruders, they mean business. This much I get. Military training isn't necessary to understand what's happening. I am a prisoner in the dim light of morning under the palm tree beneath the open sky and sandy soil beneath me. Dứng dậy, đứng dậy. Get up, get up, says the voice nearest to me.

I move forward on all fours then I stand up as commanded. I am disheveled. My clothes are tattered and dirty. I am partially bearded with dirt and grim all over my body. The strangers who have come into my tiny camp and awakened me aren't dressed much better.

Collectively, their breath stinks. Their bodies smell of rancid fish and campfire ash and charred incense, a token of their uncleanness. As the new sunlight spreads all around us, I can see that their hair is matted and filled with thistle and brush sticks like mine yet somehow, they are smiling at me one and all with moonstruck delight like they have captured Johnson and Westmoreland and McNamara in one. Hate to disappoint my captors, but it's just me, one lone American soldier bailed out from a dying to dead helicopter. Nothing more, nothing less.

Dem vật gì ra. Move out. Move out. Dem vật gì ra, the one says to me. All rifles are pointed my way. So, I walk off as if I know where I'm headed. The group, the leader in particular, intervenes. Người Mỹ. American. Không. Không. No. No. This way, cách này, he says with the point of his barrel. He shoves me in the back with the butt of his rifle. So, I change direction and trudge off into the jungle behind the sunrise. I am following now two small men out front making their own path as we go with three machetes and a half dozen rifle butts for clearance.

Evening is worse than this morning. I am handed a pitiful bowl of rice. Soiled, stained, watery, with small chunks of debris as if they've been added to insult and hastened my intestinal breakdown. My hands are bound. My ankles as well. Obviously, I can sleep on the ground where I want since I cannot escape hobbled and handcuffed the way that I am.

When we entered the village area, there are bamboo stakes planted in a swollen semi-circle. Mounted atop each stalk is a human head, a villager's head with the wilted look of a watercolor left out in the rain. Their eyes search for vision. Their mouths reach for expression of any kind. Their cheeks are sunken and dreadfully emaciated in death, more so than you might think. It reminds me or suggests that I might be next. I picture my head, my face, my visionless eyes, and sallow cheeks on a bamboo stake, but the projection is a waste of time. If it happens, I tell myself helplessly, it happens. I have somehow survived the chopper crash, perhaps I can or will survive this. Who knows? I fall asleep because I am exhausted from walking all day, mosquito bites, listening to strange voices in an uncommon language, and little sustenance to keep me going. Good morning, America, where are you? Don't you know me, I'm your native son? Apparently not, the voice says. Maybe tomorrow.

Day 2. I am ordered to stand, untied, hands and feet, then led across the village to a small spot in the broad sunlight. There I am told to squat and enter a bamboo cage perhaps two or three times the size of an American dog house. Besides, what choice do I have? I comply. As I bend over, I am jabbed in the small of the back with a shovel head. Even as dull as the blade is, I can feel the blood flow from that part of me but can do nothing to protect the wound. Inside this hut or cage, I have little or no room to maneuver and not enough room to stretch out. Sleep will be improbable no matter how weary I become. It's intentional. The sun beats down on the enclosure. I am sweating and dreadfully uncomfortable. Capturing and catching monkeys and ducks to eat seems now like paradise. Death … it is certain. I am convinced. Why not get it over with? But that isn't the way of the enemy. They are in no hurry. My lifelessness is their pleasure, a Vietnamese ritual I assume.

Day 3, Day 4, Day 5. I have lost count. Uncomfortable monotony. I sleep. I doze. I wake only to eat the demi-bowl of putrid rice proffered sometime in the morning, sometime in the evening. I'm not sure. The small opening is lifted, the bowl is shoved into the tiny space, then the door is latched shut and tied off. The time of day is a guess and only by the sunlight outside from between the slits in the bamboo strung together. Not the best of views. My captors chat, come and go, point in my direction but only for amusement or seemingly for gossip. I'm not sure why I haven't been killed along with the villagers. There is an angle, but I'm not sure what that angle is.

Day seven or day eight, maybe more. To be honest, I have no idea. Time is unmeasured just like my malnourishment which makes it incredibly difficult to focus or concentrate or care. A scant, half cup of rice is the highlight of my day. But I said this already, I know, I remember, but maybe I am delusional inside the throes of my rotting existence. I have the one-track mind of a starved animal, beaten and limp in submission.

But, then again, from out of the dribs and drabs of this dull, wearisome routine and this same lackluster encasement of my own isolated nonexistence, there is gunfire at close range. I'm sure I can hear the same campfire voices in front of me that captured me. However, they are now all of a sudden desperate and frantic and panicked. I can hear machine guns firing into the camp here. Shredding thatch, tree branches, palm leaves, and jungle brush. I can hear bullets piercing objects all around me. Bodies drop in the backdrop of smoke-filled air and other more familiar voices come into play from a distance. I am looking out through the small bamboo slits from inside my cage, but my view and vision is limited and captures only a small portion of what is happening around me. Two of my mangy captors collapse in an instant just outside my cage. One is shot through the head; his eye has vanished inside a trickle of blood. His tongue has been left outside his mouth like a panting dog that is no longer panting but closed as still life. If I weren't here in this bamboo cell, I could reach out and touch the wound with my bare hand, put my finger in the eye socket, and jab his brain. Wonderful to think considering what he and the others have put me through. The other captor is below my feet. His hand is limp and lying sideways to his corpse. Severed. Blown off. He is trying to breathe but his trying, his effort belies him. New meaning to *dies trying*. A last gasp and he is done. Good riddance to you, too. I had thought my captors might be coming to free me in the mayhem, but they are dead on the ground just a few feet from where I am caged and imprisoned. So much for that kind thought. A grenade detonates nearby. Other explosives follow. Two others go off. I would duck for cover, but I am shackled and defenseless. I am unharmed so far but the targets seem random. I could be next whether intended or not. Somehow and at last, I hear a familiar sound. English. Americanized. A wonderfully uplifting sound. I call out as loud as I can. Here, I say from behind my blanched voice. Over here, I say. Inside the cage, I call out even louder. Hello. Over here! Footsteps trample my way. A voice says, "Give me a second to open the door to free you." When the door falls off into the dirt, I crawl out and break into the open and the smoke-filled, fresh air. I see American GIs moving into and surrounding the village from all sides. Hallelujah, I say to myself and out loud. *Hallelujah.* Thank you, Jesus and you, Corporal Hamlin. His rank is on his collar. His name tag is clearly spelled out in American English on his chest. What a grand sight for sore eyes.

For that brief moment, I forgot God was the devil.

I then fast forward through another blur.

Headquarters over to Main terminal up to the second floor and down the hall to the left. Room 227. Says so over the doorway in black, block numerals. Home to Operation Chicken Hawk, brain child of chief strategist Steiger, NACOM, REPHI, military enlistee, CIA. Five copiers, six fax machines, a teletype in the corner though obsolete, and a dozen or more Remington and IBM desktop typewriters in front of cubicle desk modules lined up like urinals in a boot camp latrine. I am straddling a cardboard box of hand soap and laundry detergent. Counted thirty-six showers and ninety-six meals since getting here safely and in one piece. The flight over was a bit hairy but judging from my recent history, I had every reason to be nervous. In the big, springy office chair, Gasper, code name Elmer Fudd for the lazy tongue, is typing up my orders out of the country. Terms of endearment you might say. Gaspar, short for Gaspar Cleveland, head runner and chief of staff. Korean veteran. CIA operative. Thai boxing champion, 3rd Battalion, 2nd regiment 1963 at one-forty-six. He's slightly over two-twenty-two at present. Can barely touch his toes from a seated position. So, it goes.

Three weeks later, I am stateside.

R & R included ... Two hippie girls befriended and bedded in week one by recanting and altering my commissioned officer soldier status to antiwar. War is hell. Bamboo shoots now lodged eternally and forever in my dejected soul. Poor me. Both bought it. Two-and-one-half weeks in ... a pair of hookers both named Sonia sexed separately in a post-traumatic, recidivistic slip-and-slide back to the relapsed, as-yet-canonized wartime POW GI. Liberty bonds and patriotism at work. War is still hell but now less painful and more personable in the arms of love.

Onward.

Next up then to a steak dinner at an all you can eat buffet with two old resident Army buddies who had recently hired on to something they called *the syndicate*. Clicked my heels together three times and said to myself, *There's no place like home, Lieutenant Jablonski. There's no place like home.*

When Eddie awoke, he dressed, and, with Jenkins by his side, made his way downstairs to the cafeteria. *Ain't life grand,* he said aloud in the first-floor hallway to a fellow Garden passerby.

It sure is, said the other. *And beats the heck out of the alternative.*

You know it, replied Eddie rounding the bend with a thumbs up.

CHAPTER 6

The Scenic Highway

From the Cold Case Files & Confessions of Richard 'The Ice Man' Kuklinski Entry #32. For over three decades, Richard Kuklinski served as a notorious contract killer for the East Coast Mafia. The real number of Kuklinski's victims is said to be somewhere between one and two hundred. Selected events herein are recorded, recreated, and transcribed by Edek Jablonski, a successful, retired author-crime writer as well as purported kinsman to 'The Ice Man' himself. Room 315. Voices from within. Bringing the dead to life one last time in a murder victim tell-all.

From the desk of Eddie 'The Icicle' Jablonski. The next chapter as interpolative exposé. The victim's narrative as it might have been told.

Sitting at his desk, Eddie wrote:

Inexplicably their paths crossed.

Inexplicably through chance, fate, the devil's summon, or happenstance, Cousin Rich had decided to take the mountain backroad, the switchback scenic route, to get to his next stopover and business rendezvous three hours away. He'd done this years before with the wife and kids before he worked for DeMeo, before DeMeo passed, before he was employed full time as an *enforcer*. He needed to relax, loosen up, get the kinks out, before his next *venture*, put his mind at ease before *the closing* as he called it. The mountains, the overview, the panoramic scenery, it could be just the ticket if it was all the way he remembered it. Quiet and serene, visual therapy (his thought), there was a comforting stillness all about wherever his eye turned, a pastoral tour de force, this from a man who hardly if ever thought in such tangential and harmonious terms. The bucolic splendor, the perfect and natural blend of foliage and beauteous undulation in a bosky cascading confluence of the distant rise and fall, peak to valley all spread before him from every viewpoint and overlook as he drove up and over and around this swath of an old, mountaintop byway.

But it wouldn't last. He knew that. Not in his line of work. It never did. He knew that, too. But enjoy it for this small, little stretch of blacktop in the Appalachian outback while it lasts was his one passing thought, his own words in his own even-keeled voice in a fair exchange with himself as he drove.

He saw the approaching car in the distance from a glance into his rearview mirror but thought little or nothing of it. An oncoming car. Rather rapid in its advance. He centered his vision forward and then looked out again to his left over the splendid setting and pleasantly motored ahead.

Inexplicably as well on that same mountain road …

My pals and me … we were driving on the backroad just like before. Seneca rocks highway but this road was less traveled. Switchbacks galore. Hairpin curves and zig zags against the face of sharp rocks and boulders jutting out from all angles and somehow at some time, someone had carved a road up here. Freaking spooky. Little or no traffic with no adults to speak of. Party time, party time, it was in the air. We were sixteen, most of us, or close enough. A beer or two or ten between each of us. Most of those were in the backseat cooler propped up under Joey's feet, not counting the ones we were holding or the ones we'd already pitched out the side window or chugged or spilled or crushed in the offing.

Pictures of naked women from nudey men's magazines spread all over the dash and on the floorboard. Junior Mike pinned one into the ceiling so when you looked up you almost got a woody. Yeeha! Miss May, she was something else. Joey and I liked Miss April best. Miss July would do in a pinch if you know what I mean. That's what Pluto said to Timmy over a puff of smoke from a half lite cigar inside one of the armrest ashtrays. Two, uncharred menthol cigarettes rested unspoiled under the sun visor and another half pack on the front seat vinyl pulldown.

Only five of us this time going down the road to make more party history just like so many times over the last year or two. Sometimes it's six of us or more … or however many we can fit into my old man's sedan. Once we crowded in nine counting the three, frothy nubiles that came along for the ride and a little extracurricular. (Joey came up with *nubiles*. It stuck. Thanks, Joey!) There was always hell to raise and girls to chase and the endless, stream-less talk-the-talk. So, hanging out the car windows, both left and right, front and back, hollering into the wind coming full blast into our faces fit the bill. Screaming obscenities and spewing beer foam at the roadside signs like we were prehistoric beasts with a bone to pick, it was the *way we roll*. And don't you forget it.

I was driving. Full throttle, the only way, hammer down, balls to the wall, teenage waste land all the way whatever that means. We were empowered, impudent, ruthless (that's what Pluto and Junior called us) and a lusty band of lascivious gypsies. *Lascivious gypsies,* that was my line. At least on this stretch of the road, top speed was way too slow and way too legal and way too adult and grownup for these curvy, mountainous conditions of a West Virginia blacktop, so I sped up again and went faster.

But guess what? I didn't give a fuck and Joey didn't give a fuck and Timmy, he didn't give a fuck and Pluto (Paul real name) he didn't give a fuck and Junior (Mike Junior son of Mike Senior) he really, really, really didn't give a fuck because he was the drunkest of the five of us and hanging out the rear right window puking his guts out because that was his thing just like blue is some people's color.

"Jesus, Junior. Get a grip," I said from the front seat, driver's side laughing like a twisted hyena in heat. *"Man up, dude."* That's what I told him so he brought his head back inside the car and chugged the rest of the tall boy he'd straddled between his legs for safekeeping to afford himself a quick recovery. *Hair of the dog …* between all of us serious, over the top party hounds cause we get it. Besides, the five of us, we knew it wouldn't last. Junior always got the drunkest, heaved his guts out the most, drank some more, heaved some more, then always passed out before we ever got to where we were going or finished doing whatever it was we were doing.

More specifically, it was just Junior Mike and *how we rolled.* It was Pluto Paul and *how we rolled.* It was Timmy and Joey and me and *how we rolled, too.*

"Roll on, Big Mama," I hollered out. *"I like the way you roll."*

Sounded cool. Had to be there, I guess.

When I goosed it and then stomped on the gas pedal some more and passed the big burgundy Cadillac even-steven with the don't pass-double yellow line staring at me and other guy driving alongside, I thought the guys were going to bust a gut they were laughing so hard with the five of us taunting the old man driving that big ass, red hearse knock-off. Pluto dropped trou, pushed his ass checks up against the back glass, and got a big round of applause and a whoop-whoop from all of us. "Good job, Pluto from Mars," said somebody in the backseat. "Way to go, Moon Man," said another. "The most ass that old fart's seen in thirty or forty years," said another.

"Slow down, Perv, my man, (Perv, that was me) and I'll give him another round of moon pie, ass cheek, and two balls to grow on," said Pluto the Psycho Mission from Outer Space.

So, I obliged, my man, my pal Pluto and tapped the brakes just long enough to get the Caddy flush with my rear bumper then stood on them for a second or so longer just to fuck with the old man in the Cadillac behind me … you know, scare the shit out of him, get his heart rate and pulse above nothing and off dead. And I could see him in the rearview mirror clearly now how visibly shaken and irritated he was. Him … Bald or balding. The scruffy beard. The beady eyes. A chubby face but he looked like an oversized guy at least from a car length away. "*Just fucking with you, old man,*" I yelled out into the hollow of my dad's car and beyond the rearview mirror. West Virginia, older than the hills, take me home, country roads. We were working on getting drunk so when you're working on getting drunk you sing along regardless … even when you only know a couple of the words here and there to the song like … Mountain mama!

Just as quickly, the Cadillac pulled ahead of me and sped up and then made an even quicker stop across the blacktop so I slowed down as well.

"What's he doing?" someone asked.

"I don't know," I replied.

"He just straddled the highway up ahead in front of us," someone said.

"He's blocking us from going around," another backseat someone said.

The Cadillac had swerved to a T in the narrow mountain road. Now there was the big Cadillac sedan straight ahead of us, a thousand-foot precipice and drop-off to the left and a steep, impenetrable-granite, five-hundred-foot cliff to the right with clear spring seepage raining down the chest of the rocky formation like a soft spring mist.

I came to a stop thirty or so feet away from the parked car ahead of us and watched, speechless and numb and dumb and quizzical and anxiously motionless and now frozen.

The old man got out of his car, and as I first thought, he was a big man, huge as a matter of fact. He was slightly bearded and balding like I said, but he wasn't as old as I thought. He was dressed properly for a business guy in a gray tweed sport coat, turtleneck, slacks, and dress shoes and looked harmless enough, I suppose, you know, business-man-like or something.

Figured he was pissed. Told that to the guys.

Figured he was going to give us an ass-chewing … like we hadn't had one of those before … so what's new, old man? Said that to the others, too.

Figured he wanted the parents phone numbers and addresses to set the record straight and tell them what bad boys we were. Everyone snickered at that one. Been there, done that.

Figured all of this is in the first split second.

In the next …

Figured he'd notify the highway patrol … like we hadn't been down that road before now. Good one, huh … down that road … highway patrol. *I crack me up.*

Figured he'd give them my dad's license plate number, get my driver's license, and my dad's car registration, the make and model of the car, all to turn over to the authorities as well. But he wasn't carrying a pen and paper that I could tell.

Figured he'd get us busted for a D.U.I. … like we hadn't been there before now either. At least Pluto had. That's why I was driving.

Figured he'd threaten us with some tough talk and a bundle of grownup bad ass jive … like we hadn't heard it all before. Five of us. One of him. Like five of us couldn't whip this old dude one-of-him in a contest of five man one-on-one … a big old fat man for sure … burly … and so, he's the size of a small grizzly. The bigger they are, the harder they fall … that's what they say … you know. Him, in his business suit and dress shores … bring it on old man. But then he got out, walked to the back of his Caddy, opened the trunk of his car, and pulled out a twelve gauge … just like my dad's and I said, "*Holy shit,*" just like that. It came out my mouth ad lib and louder than I intended. Now he had my attention. Guess he isn't fucking around, I thought, but I didn't blurt that out to the group just to keep things hell-raiser normal, dust off any rising tension and anxiety and fear among us five, young tough-guy-want-to-be-s.

"He's still in the back of the trunk of his car," someone said.

"What's he doing?" someone said.

"Hey, mister," I called out from inside my dad's car. I'm thirty feet away. "Sorry about that. Thought you were somebody else. Our mistake. Kids being kids. You know. We get it. My apologies, sir."

But he didn't say anything, he didn't get it, he just kept walking toward the car with this blank look on his face and these beady eyes glaring at the five of us from behind those double-tinted sunglasses he'd adjusted once in the walk over.

Counting down …

I hadn't figured on him lowering his shotgun to chest level and blasting Pluto in the face behind my dad's front seat, car windshield.

I hadn't figured on the second blast coming through the side door and killing Joey instantly as he attempted to escape over the guard rail and down the cliff into the scrub brush on the other side. The big man drew a bead, fired, and Joey was down and dead.

I hadn't figured on the old man, a sizeable dude for sure, raising the gun to his shoulder again and firing straight away into Timmy's back as he struggled to crawl through the broken back window of my Dad's sedan and over the hood of the trunk. That's where Timmy died, right there. He was dead before I could turn around good, draped lifelessly in a sprawl between the broken glass, the backseat and the hood of the trunk so I turned around slumped to the floorboard, thought for another split second, and decided to play dead … possum something I'd only heard about … with my eyes shut tight breathing but barely. Smeared some of Pluto's blood across my face to look like I'd been wounded, hurt, lying there dead.

On the floorboard with my eyes shut to a squint and barely inhaling, I could see in my mind's eye the same big, angry man, the oversized guy draw a rifle, his shotgun from a slip cover and clutch the lever, shuffle it back and forward to loaded as he then walked toward our car, my dad's, until he raised the gun and began to shoot. The blast hit the windshield first. I know. I was reliving it again in my mind's eye. I flinched in the crouch. I flashed back and saw myself as I ducked behind the steering wheel. Pluto, his face was bleeding badly as he moaned and whined and gathered the blood from his wounds into his hands like precious droplets of drinking water from an empty canteen on a parched desert death trek. I heard Pluto moan loudest as the man walked toward the car, firing round after round after round. Timmy never saw the shot that killed him. I did. But he was looking backwards trying to escape through the rear window. Joey made a run for it out the front door passenger side but he was cut down at the bar ditch landed face first in the early spring runoff piled up in a puddle now bloodied and vibrant red. I played dead and counted and counted with my eyes closed, but I could feel the man almost as if his breath and his eyes were looking inside and he knew I wasn't hurt or wounded, and then I felt both barrels of the gun poke me in the side of the head close to my temple and then heard the man mutter …

"As you were saying."

And that was the last thing I recall. Into those words, his words, the gun went off.

Almost heaven. West Virginia. Take me home. Country road.

The driver's head was severed almost completely off read the autopsy report.

"Lights out," said the man leveling the shotgun to his side.

Richard *The Ice Man* Kuklinski turned from his spot in the middle of the mountain blacktop and walked back to his Cadillac. He moved in behind the wheel, closed the driver's side door, put the car in reverse, turned it downwind from the scene of the crime, straightened the wheel to forward, slipped the gear notation to drive, and pulled away guiltlessly into the afternoon setting sun. No other persons around. Five dead bodies. An abandoned late model sedan now bloodstained, buck shot riddled, with shattered glass all about. No survivors. No witnesses. No villain. No crime. Another issue resolved Kuklinski style.

CHAPTER 7

Hit Men Don't Do Confessionals

First off …

Hit men … we don't do confessionals. Not going there. Censer sensitive for starters … allergic let's just say. Sitting in a little, ventilated leftover three-by-three-by-five, old-timey phone booth talking to a mysterious and complete stranger on the other side of a flimsy venetian blind and telling him how many assholes I shot and killed in the past week … No … I don't think so. Or, me yapping softly about how many bodies I've got to entomb in various, marshy and boggy estuaries around the city harbor in the upcoming days … No. Again … Ain't happening. Father Cachotterie, Monsignor Spiritato, he can find another lightweight to spill his guts (and give it up) and another sucker to fleece at tithing time. I don't beg nobody for forgiveness because it's a waste of my very, very valuable time. Life's like a parking meter. You keep putting good money in the slot until you run out of coins, then your time simply runs out on the back end. You could be out back or around the corner, still out shopping or loading the back of the car with stuff you just bought or having a beer across the street at Big Lou's Tavern but the meter ran out of time and just like that and it's over. You're salami along with the other cold cuts. Begging Father Cachotterie for forgiveness and a night off is bull shit. Not happening. And it doesn't happen like that.

A hit man … you do what you do … end of subject. Then, you go home, put your stuff away in the front hall closet, top coat, gun and holster, jacket over the two, the other smaller pistol from your ankle holster, loosen your tie, remove the jewelry and chains beneath that, have a nice, quiet dinner, talk about your day leaving out the gory details, kiss your wife and kids good night, shower off the day's slim and residue (scrub and brush those cuticles mind you), go to bed … then you get up in the morning have a big stiff cup of black coffee and do it all over again the next day just like before. So why would I want to confess to something as mundane and day to day as that? I don't get it. You feeling guilty and remorseful and anxious … well, you go confess. Put in a good word for me. Maybe I can use it. Don't know. But I don't buy into the confession game.

Killed a man one time and three days later his entire family thanked me. So there. The guy's family wasn't even sure it was me they should be thanking. It was, but I couldn't let on so I just smiled politely and nodded and shrugged like I had no frigging clue what they were talking about … the whole time knowing full well I'd put two bullets in the center of his forehead, one in the top of his skull where the toupee stopped, and three more directly into his heart for good measure. An open field, overcast, chilly with a stiff breeze, no pretense, no formality, no apologies. After I finished kicking his dead ass out of the back seat of my car and stuffing the pistol, the murder weapon, back inside my windbreaker, I dusted and brushed my hands off … brush, brush, dust, dust … like I'd been digging ditches in a salt mine. To be honest, it was a prideful moment … come to think of it … one of the most prideful moments in my entire life simply because I knew what a slimeball dirtbag the guy was. The only shameful or remorseful part of the ordeal was I ran out of bullets, otherwise I'd have emptied another clip into his slumped-over carcass just for posterity's sake and the fun of it. The creep's creep. Rest in peace … I don't think so and not if I can help it.

So, stuff that one in your collection plate, Father Cachotterie.

Hit man this, hit man that, hit man … yeah, yeah, yeah.

But it's not all fun and games and certainly not as glamorous as you might imagine. Not like some people would have you think. Not at all really. The hot babes, the wild parties, orgies here and there, first cut on the best drugs and premium booze, the Kosher killings where everything goes as planned, even perfectly, the affairs with other men's wives, the hot, voluptuous types with curves to die for. It ain't like that. Not twenty-four seven anyway.

In the life of a hit man, there's plenty of pain and suffering to go around as well. Bruised knuckles, a busted metacarpal here and there, misappropriated car jackings, carpel tunnel syndrome (gun range related), hearing loss (gun range related), a stitch or two or ten over the crest of one eyebrow or the other, condom misplacement, the miscalculated hijackings, loan sharking where the shark is left alone holding his pud with nothing to show for the loan … it's quite an embarrassment plus the time wasted, and then there's the one where the lackey embezzles the embezzlement (had that happen once), a drug shipment ends up at the wrong address one house over and the wrong side of the street, or the prepackaged cadaver, the deceased, somehow ends up at his own legal residence and the spouse scribbles her punctuation as proof of delivery on the return receipt. Talk about embarrassing. Jeez. Then there's legal expenses, lawyers on the gouge, other gangsters on the gouge, other gangster's lawyers on the gouge, middle men on the gouge, girlfriends on the gouge, would-be mistresses on the gouge … always gouging … gouge, gouge, gouge, etc., etc. … you get the picture. Note here, there are no family portraits of the family, the mob family … no honorees-at-the-honorariums amongst the same group of thieves either … none to speak of anyway. And for that, there's a reason.

So, if you think it's a Sunday stroll in the park, go ahead, be my guest, walk this way. Step right up. Boogaloo down Broadway. Waltz across Texas. Walk a mile in my shoes. Just make sure someone's got your back while you're strolling or waltzing or sashaying or moon walking wherever. Take it from me, Eddie *The Icicle* Jablonski and cousin to Big Rich, *The Ice Man* himself, the life of a hit man ain't all it's cracked up to be.

And just for the record since you brought it up, not everybody in the business is a blood lusting psychopath. Mostly, a lot of hardworking guys doing their thing to keep things in order and straightened out ... above board but under the table ... at the same time you might say. And that's not easy. That's what I mean ... It takes a lot of hard work.

And, just for the sake of all things elucidatively rhetorical, let's say that you think you're special, really, really special say ... you're convinced that you are really, really something else, a big shot, the cat, the meow, the fur ball as well as the entire ball of wax rolled into one ... (I get this a lot in my line of work and this business, more than I like to let on) ... and so if you think you're that important and that freaking special, then I say, go ahead, build yourself a great big, gargantuan mausoleum ... a giant edifice the size and shape of the Chrysler Building or something really, really large and garish, Washington-monument-like, a phallus no less, to and by and of and for yourself ... I, Eddie Jablonski, *The Icicle* himself, said you could. Be advised. There's no law that says you can't. You just need to come up with the dough. That's it. You don't even need to tell anyone you built it. Let them think it was constructed by your other admirers, prestigious ones, celebrities, big shots, movie stars, business moguls, full of shit politicians, for example. Have no clue who would do such a thing? But because you were such a big deal, such a mover and a shaker, the tide-turning bon vivant, the unprecedented, inimitable hot shit, Tootsie Roll romance king, the luster of lusters and moonglow of and unto itself, you as the Hi and the Ho of that same deceased, gold-toothed grinning Cab Calloway … with his toe-tapping, big band jazz wonderment and Broadway style … all that and much, much more … Then stop and see how many people actually show up to pay tribute or stop to tip their hats in a curtsey or pay their respects in any meaningful manner much less actually remember who you were or what you did or where you lived or anything else about you.

And just for the record, you won't be around to count the attendees or put a name to a face much less peruse the John Hancocks on the sign-in sheet afterwards. So, let that sink in. You're dead, Einstein. Entombed. Embalmed maybe but nevertheless dead … and as *dead* as one of those slime bags you packed headfirst into the remnant of an old empty fifty-gallon oil drum that you then rolled off the back side of some outdated, dilapidated trawler into the expansive ocean swell on that pitch-black evening in some unnamed horizonless harbor … Ahh! I can almost smell the deep, really deep dark salt water at an hour and a half past midnight … when not even the drone, the low, lone note that same old D minor seventh of an unseen tugboat way, way, way off in the distant night air can console your dead ass much less bring you back to life to reminisce about the *good life … for the good times (sing it Ray)* … not even for an instant.

The crackling, smoldering, ambient fire beneath a pig roast spit has more bearing on the planet than you did. So, maybe you shouldn't take yourself quite so seriously. Loosen your suspenders before the braces cut off the remaining blood flow to the few parts of your anatomy still working and the part-time, sporadic circulation to your old and crusty and useless balls … those gonads you've bragged so much about and so long about for all this time. More than likely, it's the only section of your brain that's even partially or remotely still working properly if even on libidinal standby via remote control, VHS.

Might have built my dead brother a mausoleum … one of an appropriate, commemorative size say, but no one could locate the body. Someone told me later over a game of Canasta and single malt that DeMeo turned him into a tar baby … painted, slathered, daubed, then smeared and brushed on the blackened goop from a fifty pound twenty gallon open pail of road patch and kerosene… a gooey mess for sure … filled his mouth with wheat straw (if I only had a brain), propped open both eyes wider than the devil would allow and wider than their widest, mockingly tailored his hair to a point, and then lit him on fire like a girl scout campfire at dusk in mid-July. Twenty minutes later, once the flames had died down and subsided, dusted off his charred remains, scooped him up with a flat billed snow shovel, tossed his gray ashes into a Smokey Bear, park service county campground trash bin, and then left casually and as thoughtlessly, cavalierly as a veteran exotic dancer dismounting from a stripper pole, in a trendy, oversized, late model European sedan. All this over a three-thousand-four-hundred-dollar gambling debt. And that included the triple digit interest.

I had warned him several times. It was always in the fall of the year. *Never bet on the Jets*, I said to him … *particularly the late-season Jets …* I said to him in those exact words in that exact same tone of voice. But I'm a *diehard*, he always replied … *a diehard*, he said and that very same echo (echo, echo) always and forever bounces off the backside of my skull like the broken soundtrack of a budgie's mock-and-squawk inside its wire cage somewhere in the nearby backdrop … that same ceaseless, pesky parakeet-recital that you can't see and you can't locate long enough to blanket the little bastard goodnight … But, alas, my brother, and a hearty oh-well, my kinsman … him, Mister Diehard, sporting his green and white number seven jersey … my wouldn't-listen, hardheaded brother with his matching, green and white cap turned around backwards, the standard *diehard* schtick. But then again, he just couldn't hear what I was saying. Would have none of it. Didn't get it. Never did. So, he went up in flames … literally … over a football game … winner take all.

So, for all you ego aficionados, if it's an edifice you want, then it's a freaking edifice you'll get, or make it a maudlin mausoleum, or the fancy, satin-lined executive casket of solid cherry with solid gold pall bearer handles, or, as your dead man's rite (right) of passage, a high-rise funeral pyre built on a stack of expensive, exotic hardwoods (you're the man!) … mahogany and teak and Brazilian koa and driftwood just because you can afford it … and for you, only the best … right there in the bowels of some deep, dark ill-begotten forest, say Sleeping Beauty's mise-en-scène or maybe Riding Hood's underwood. Take your pick … goes along nicely with your own personal, self-absorbed solipsistic veneer, your fairy tale … so have at it. Just don't ask me to come visit any time soon or pay my respects or buy a token for the toll or intercede, suggestively or otherwise, with the grand Supreme Being in closeted, sanctimonious confessionals or the likes. Once again, and to make myself crystal clear so we're all on the same page, *The Icicle* doesn't do confessionals. Capisce?

So, for now, this is me, Eddie, signing off … Au revoir, addio, and *cześć* … from Eddie *The Icicle* Jablonski, tough guy, the rough guy's ruffian, storyteller, bullshitter, imbiber, the best friend a mobster ever had, embellisher and fabricator to gangsters and high-stake rascals wherever they may be „, those loathsome rabble rousers one and all … and (last but certainly not least) the ladies' man … to all you beautiful and lovely gals out there in Eddie-land … Ready or not, girls … Here I come! From the heart … in no particular order … You choose. And while we're at it, ladies, how about a slow dance cheek to cheek?

CHAPTER 8

A Man of Color

From the Cold Case Files & Confessions of Richard 'The Ice Man' Kuklinski Entry #81. For over three decades, Richard Kuklinski served as a notorious contract killer for the East Coast Mafia. The real number of Kuklinski's victims is said to be somewhere between one and two hundred. Selected events herein are recorded, recreated, and transcribed by Edek Jablonski, a successful, retired author-crime writer as well as purported kinsman to 'The Ice Man' himself. Room 315. Voices from within. Bringing the dead to life one last time in a murder victim tell-all.

From the desk of Eddie 'The Icicle' Jablonski. The next chapter as interpolative exposé. The victim's narrative as it might have been told.

Sitting at his desk, Eddie wrote:

He was a man of color of African descent of Newark's southside of little use to anyone, but we decided to take a chance and welcome him into the fold and give him a shot at the business since proverbially he talked the talk. A raw recruit, una recluta grezza, so to speak. He was a Negro, haphazardly prideful and objectionably vain. Went by

Soul on Ice. The word was: he was a bad man. Exceptionally strident and verbose in odd venues, this according to more than one source. A penchant toward the violent with a macabre twist toward cruelty. Perversion in tow when deemed appropriate. Torture wasn't his forte but not out of the question when pressed. Not hard pressed, just pressed. Merciless in nearly all respects which complimented the widely circulated on-the-street employer-employee inquiry/profile. In some respects, he was just what we were looking for and possibly just what the doctor ordered. But …

Colored outside the lines you might say. Not sometimes … constantly. Teacher said to him you can't color outside the lines. Everyone else told him you can't color outside the lines. Everyone over here told him you can't color outside the lines. And even I told him three or four times, you can't color outside the lines. But it didn't stick. Still, *Soul* colored outside the lines. He wouldn't hear it. Which, by the way, is far worse than he wouldn't listen. *Soul* wouldn't pour piss out of a boot with directions on the heel. So, Mister Too-big-for-his-britches, (an insider's endearment), this same guy, the soul brother with the Dacron-polyester disco trousers flared at the end of the crease over string-tied platforms, this hot dog dandy, he was expelled from the school of hard knocks and the crosstown mob's school of know-how at the same time on the same day by the same group of people who had hired him. *A goner,* to quote one of our own. *Had to bring him back down to Earth,* said another. Kept calling the head capo *'homie'.* Homie this, homie that.

Takin' it to the house, homie.

Bet you making millions, homie?

How 'bout some more percentage of the take, homie?

Where's your bitch, homie?

How 'bout a little kickback on the really good shit, just for Soul, homie?

You gotta picture of your old lady, homie?

Bet she's fine, huh, homie?

Bet you got a good-looking daughter, huh, homie? Which was the final straw. Didn't sit well with capo *homie* or any of the rest of us. You don't go there. Even a dumb ass knows that. Disrespectful. Verboten in fact. Where's the employee-to-employer etiquette, bro'? *Homie* isn't *homie, Soul,* he's your boss. Caporegime. Capo dei capi. Unnecessary all the way around. Everyone agreed. Fuck rock, scissors, paper. He was done and had to go. Outta here. Hadn't been for us he'd have been back out on the street a long time ago selling dime bags for a nickel. Pimping white girls and las chicas for reefer hoping and praying for a blow job when he was coherent and straight enough to get it up. *Soul on Ice,* his preferential personal treatment and precinct moniker in one. *Five will get you ten.* If he used that line once (after another one of his multitudinous fuckups), he used it a thousand times. Yeah, right, *Soul on Ice?* Gotcha, pal.

Okay. So, just for the record … His soul maybe on ice but his dead ass is now in a deep freezer just around the corner in Kuklinski's basement. And as with all of Coach K's understudies missing in action (MIAs one and all), he'll reappear in a seasonal spring thaw inside a lined trash receptacle just a few feet away from a nearby, shaded park bench on the scheduled trash pickup day within the hour. Coach K knows his x's and o's.

Color barrier one oh one is what I say is what you get. An education can be hard to come by and even harder to learn. And never forget … always, always, and forever, there's a price tag no matter what. From the kitchen of Mama Linguine … *It's either too steep to peep or too cheap to keep so read it and weep before you lose any more sleep* … in her own words. And God bless you, Mama Linguine. It's in the Guinea handbook of How-To. On the same shelf next to the Guinea Book of World Records.

Look it up yourself if you don't believe me.

CHAPTER 9

Writings Within the Cloister

The caption read in its entirety … Day-Timer entry under Schedule of Events Calendar: Retiree Meeting with Chief Administrator.

9:53 AM on a staid and unremarkable Wednesday.

Hillenbrand Lauterbach held the papers firmly in her hand out in front of her half an arm's length. Quickly, she scanned her notes and margin notations as she paused waiting to speak to her constituent, her retiree-client and customer-patient, Mr. Jablonski. Her demeanor was serious if not stern, dutifully passive if not plausible, but politely forthright by all means and manner. She peeked over sparkly bifocals, cleared her throat behind her feather dressed scarf and addressed Eddie Jablonski of room 315 this way.

"Mister Jablonski, it's come to my attention that you've been circulating your creative writings to numerous members of our facility here at The Garden of Eden … some patients and customers in good standing as well as to patient visitors, staff and other administrators. First off, Mr. Jablonski, let me applaud your efforts for staying active in your free time … occupied, creative, and making the best use of your time and talents. Those of us here love to see our clientele excel and reach for the stars. It's our duty as professionals and caregivers. However, I must ask that you forgo distributing the pamphlets and papers to members and staff of The Garden of Eden without first checking with members of the nursing staff before doing so. Apparently, some of our patients, and that includes friends and acquaintances of yours, Mister Jablonski, have been deeply troubled receiving and then reading the things that you've written. Keep in mind many of these same people that you consider your readers are frail, less than lucid at times, and trailing off as their lives come to an end. According to some of the readers, you attempt to convince or you have convinced them that your writings, these obvious pieces of fiction, are actual happenings from your past. As you might imagine, Mr. Jablonski, murderous crime and contract killing and body disposition to garbage waste sites and offshore shark infested waters is not something we could or would tolerate here at the Garden either as reading material or actual, real-life experience. Needless to say, you and anyone participating in such heinous acts should be or would be in prison, Mister. Jablonski, and not here living amongst us at this lovely Christian facility."

Hillenbrand Lauterbach paused to didactically illustrate her own salvation's sign in an up, down, right, left crisscross, followed by a double Dutch of mumbo jumbo, personalized circuitry, then she continued.

"I have read excerpts from some your latest writings, Mister. Jablonski, and I must say you have a way with words. Less the cruel and often time vile subject matter, the verbiage and syntax alone can be or could be highly entertaining … say if the material was of a more palatable variety … say, nature scenes or loving relationships between family members, a faithful and devoted husband and wife, or their children … even a good, old fashioned Biblical discourse might work. New Testament over Old would be my preference. Here again, less violence, more forgiving, gentle, kind, and spiritual. And, for goodness sake, let's not leave out *merciful.* Maybe you could incorporate some of those concepts into your next work.

Let me add here that I take exception to your use of the word 'Gulag' when describing The Garden of Eden, Mister Jablonski. It seems a bit harsh and particularly unfair to put it mildly. As you should know from your own personal experience, we provide exemplary care for the elderly. We maintain the highest standards in the industry as noted by the state and federal health agencies. *Gulag the Garden* and *Gulag and Eden's Gulag Archipelago are* not an appropriate much less a reasonable description in any way, shape, or form. In the future, please, Mister Jablonski, restrain yourself. Please refrain from the use of the word in reference to all things Garden … facility personnel, customers, and patients alike. Such an obtuse and punitively derogatory hyperbole is little more than *going for the jugular,* wouldn't you say? As a crime writer, you should know this. You are much too intelligent to go there, Mr. Jablonski. Instead of the term *Gulag,* maybe you could substitute *Care Environment* or *Health Facility* or maybe *Christian Center for the Elderly* as we like to describe the Garden in our public brochures and sales literature.

So, as it stands, Mister Jablonski, I'm going to have to ask you to discontinue passing these writing of yours, these papers or stories out to members of our Garden of Eden community residents. To put it plainly, many members of the Garden community are offended by your work. Others say they feel threatened. Some members are confused by the stories, the dialogue, and events within your writings and think that you mean them harm, personal bodily harm. Or, worse than that, they think that you might actually kill them. Besides, they are defenseless creatures, God's creatures one and all, who for the most part are close enough to death as it is, Mr. Jablonski, so why rub their noses in it so to speak.

I'm sure you get my drift. You're a very smart and observant man, Mister Jablonski. I can tell by your self-published sketches. Maybe you could spruce some these up a bit, say brighten the content, and thereby lift the spirits of those here that are dejected and anxious over their future, however limited and short-term. Being here at The Garden can be quite overwhelming for many of those same readers who you've targeted. They have issues, too … their health, financial woes, their waning love interests, displaced as they are from their own other loved ones and the homes they've left behind during their aged lurch… and so forth and so on. To use one of your own analogies, Mister Jablonski, yes, all of us here at The Garden are in the batter's box of life for sure. It's no doubt their final at-bat. However, consolation … instead of a dark, grim reminder, Mister Jablonski … might go a long way to relieving and-or quieting some of the angst that all of our residents feel at this stage of their passing lives. I'm sure you can understand.

Oh, and by the way, one last thing, Mr. Jablonski, we here at The Garden of Eden, we do *not* have a *Writer in Residence* per say. The titular heading or title doesn't exist. At least not yet anyway. Please refrain from the letterhead designation in the future … in what will hopefully be more pleasant, uplifting, and Christian-like stories and missives while you reside here within the confines of our community.

So. In closing, let's shine a bright light on the positive things in life for a change, Mister Jablonski, as we praise God for our many blessings and the good in one another. After all, God is great. God is good. Let us thank Him for all that He has done for us His children. So … like I said … Less of the criminal, tough-guy tabloid stuff, Mister Jablonski, and more of a Gideon giddy-up let's just say in an Old Testament, clarion sound-off praising the Almighty for His bountiful way towards us all. Now doesn't that sound like a plan? What do you say?"

Unaligned, Eddie observed. He rose from his seat in a creak, he said nothing, and left the room in his own unsure but deliberate gait.

Later, (back in his room, Room 315) Eddie dusted off his journal, the top eight-by-twelve yellow legal pad stacked on top of the other fifteen or twenty legal pads (some yellow, some white, all with lines and margins embossed) at the back of his desk. Eddie grabbed the nearest ballpoint and wrote lengthways in a stab and jab by way of his daily-weekly journal …

From the gulag. This is me, Eddie, again. I've got to speak up. Someone has to. These brain-dead old farts just let themselves get pushed around like shopping carts in a deserted shopping mall. I can't take much more of this Stalinistic treatment and abuse. Here goes.

Stuff it, LaWanda! You puffed-up Amazonian reprieve. Golgotha's Mary Magdalene and Gethsemane's very own Delilah … in spades. I'll write what I want, when I want, mean what I say, distribute to whom I please (reader be damned) and relive the past the way it happened and the way it was whether you approve of it or not, you Elizabethan stuffed shirt. It's history, by God! History, the instant replay of what was and how it was that needs to be told for the sake of an ongoing civilization by the one living son of a bitch who lived it … **me** *… whether it was pleasant or not, palatable or unpalatable, and whether you like it or not … game on. Rubber stamp the truth or trash it, Field Marshall Hillenbrand* Lauterbach. *History is history, and not to be tampered with or tamped down. Facts, just give me the facts. I can decide for myself. You and these old disconnected and dying Methuselahs in here will never and can never imagine what it was like to be The Icicle, Eddie The Icicle Jablonski in his heyday. And not just your ordinary tough guy, Der Fuhrer Fraulein … but an extraordinary, old school tough guy. Oh, yeah, and while you're at it, do me a really, really big favor … Oh, please, please, please …*

pretty please with sugar on top ... Kick me out of this hell hole! A big heave ho over your shoulder I go, you big beefy Hilda-Matilda! You bug-eyed wildebeest and Bohemian Rhapsody personified! Toss me back into that thorny, thistly briar patch while you're at it ... back where I belong.

CHAPTER 10

The Prize Fighter

In the morning hours, Joey Tagalong met Romeo Nosferatu Mosconi (Lover Boy Nosferatu Mosconi) in a vacant back lot four blocks off the entrance-exit ramp to the eight-lane interstate. They'd each already had their morning coffee. There outside, the air was foul. The stench waffled about so indefinitely that the birds flew away. Even the terns. The sky was overcast. The wind was always leeward or windward … always in your face. You turn left, the wind is there. You turn right, the wind is there, no matter, The odor, too. Cars passed by but only at a distance in a constant stream but always at a high speed as if they were being chased by a spirit possessed. Drivers and passengers avoided eye contact with the outside world. Contagion was all about. You could smell it. You were certain you could see it. Those same passengers and passersby had separated themselves from the drab view and desolate milieu in front of them. The highway was the quickest getaway.

With his hands in his pockets, Joey looked Romeo Nosferatu (Nos) Mosconi straight in the eye and said simply: "Make it happen."

Romeo or Nos (Nosferatu Mosconi), with both hands cupped to his mouth for the warmth of his own breath, now breathing heavily into his palms, Romeo Nosferatu Mosconi said back to Joey Tagalong, "Tags, any special instructions? You know … particular flavors, assorted colors, ribbons, bows, maybe a corsage or say a big, fluffy chrysanthemum? Our motto: We aim to please. We make a difference. Kill or be killed. Kill 'em with kindness or otherwise. Killing me softly? Titanic to tulips. Anything but indifference." Romeo Nos (Nosferatu) Mosconi grinned. He chuckled.

Joey didn't (*inappropriate humor at a time like this …* Joey Tagalong's words mumbled verbatim) so Romeo Nosferatu Mosconi quickly knocked it off. Tags was the man.

Joey Tagalong replied, "No. Just make it happen. Make him pay."

Romeo Nosferatu Mosconi, but sometimes *Nos* to Joey Tagalong, sometimes Romeo to Joey Tagalong, sometimes Mosconi to Joey Tagalong, sometimes *you no good, nail-biting Diego so and so,* depending on the Tagalong's mood and gratuitous inflection and purposeful disclosure in the moment and sometimes not. *Willynilly,* Tags would say. Just like life, everything with me is *willy-nilly.* I say what fits. When it don't fit, I change things up, you know, in the moment. After that, I start all over … just like that … you know, *willy-nilly* all over again like before.

Romeo Nosferatu Mosconi said, "Sure, boss. But you can think about it. If you change your mind remember, we do gift wrapped to-go or *dismissively delivered.* Sloppy served. Disposed, decomposed, chicken of the sea, chum or chunky? Shredded, sliced, and diced. Don't worry, all of the pieces slip through the (fishing) net. We do gratuitously gift wrapped as well. So, boss, let's maybe be a little more specific. How do you want him served up?" Romeo Nosferatu Mosconi looked to Joey Tagalong. Joey Tagalong didn't respond. Romeo Nosferatu Mosconi continued, "We do *over easy? Sunny side up? Scrambled, hardboiled, fried? Medium rare* or *well done?* You know me, Mister End-Different & Company, we aim to please.

Anything but indifferent, boss, as you well know. *"Half shell* or *Rockefeller? Pigs in* a *blanket* or uncovered? Catering available. Take out, too."

Joey Tagalong nodded. He paused and thought for a moment. The idea hit him like a swift left hook in the middle of the ring … him with his guard down. "Sweet," he said, then, he grinned. "Let's make it *gift wrapped*. Gratuitously gift wrapped like you said. Drop it off at his mistress's place, on the back patio next to the grill beside his wife's the million-dollar wine bucket so his wife finds out."

The two men swap gestures.

Gestures … just so you know and quoting …

Tags … A thumbs up, a *fuckin'* guinea thumbs up, a *fuckin'* guinea semaphore, Sistine sign language, then another *fuckin'* guinea semaphore with a smile and a grin to back it up which means *very positive, happy times, good to go*, etc.; it's posturing, pure posturing, something akin to Sicilian supplication and similitude. In other circles … recompense, recoil, repeal, and restitution. All of the aforementioned in one single *thumb*, the *thumbs up*, a gesture so profound and discreet and deserving it hasn't been used this effectively since lions, tigers, and Colosseum days. or simply something out of the ordinary but then again maybe, maybe not … over to Romeo the Lover Boy (Romeo Nosferatu Mosconi) then a replicate thumbs up back over to Tags.

Take this as an aside … a bit of a break in the action:

The two men met first in an alleyway behind an address-less back door in front of the stack of dilapidated cardboard boxes behind the pile of broken glass chest high and in front of the scrap lumber, a tear-out-throw-away junk pile that had been abandoned in months prior (more evidence that it was secluded and off the beaten path) so it was for all practical purposes a safe place, listener-free with no observers, eyeballs, no people traffic persons short-fat-tall-skinny or average, no smells, no odors, no bodies alive or dead or decomposing. Again, it was a relatively and innocuously secret place to talk out in the open without interruption or intrusion. It was the first time the two had squared off. Sure, there were actual and implied confidential statements in the undertones off the cuff for no apparent or real reason when the two first met. It just *was* ... part of a feeling out process. In private, Romeo Nosferatu Mosconi said this to the guy who at the time and for a short while he considered a complete unknown, another friend's friend, a confidante's confidante maybe, but to someone else with a less than desirable reputation, say, or maybe you could say that he thought of him as someone he might like to get to know if only from a business standpoint, circumstances permitting. They were hardly best pals. (Sometimes his new girlfriend but not so much; she was still too new. Too unfamiliar with the other's history and timelines and what all of that meant. It would come with time or it wouldn't. Just not right now. No rush, as Romeo said to her. They were still too new, unfounded, and novel at being a pair.).

However, from the get-go, the mix and rapport between the two men was sufficient, familial. For all intents and purposes, it appeared genuine, a feeling shared by both men. As a matter of fact, and at the time, it felt quite apropos or savvy maybe business-wise and street smart at the same time. Familial was probably a stretch, but regardless, it was almost like they'd met somewhere in another similar venue, place and time ... serial if not tangential. The two looked off in an opposite direction. Note: it was a feeling out process.

Romeo would go first. He spoke up casually, politely, firmly. Someone had to. Looking directly at the man in front of him, Joey Tagalong, he began speaking ... slightly above a whisper ... in a conciliatory low tone of voice ... self-effacingly without the hint of expression ... pointedly ... as if he was the listener as well as the one doing the talking ... he felt this was most important at a time like this ... so he began this way ... with his own series of personal questions as answers saying ... sort of like *Romeo on Romeo* ... a quick take ... one on one ... A one-man interview with another man present.

Who me? Who am I did you ask? Okay. Me? Here goes. He shrugged as he ran his fingers through his windswept, un-parted hair, but it was little more than a nervous reflex and quick groom before the spiel.

So, who asked? So, what does he want to know? Both questions that came to mind. It really was like interviewing for a job; *I ain't but I am*, he thought. Anyway, here goes, he said to himself. So, it was as if someone said "Who are you? So, without holding back, almost without thinking, Romeo Nosferatu Mosconi said nervously out loud, "*For the record, so to speak.*" It's the way he began and then he continued ...

So, who am I? you ask. And how'd I get here? A little introduction, Italian style.

I am Romeo Nosferatu Mosconi. You know this. No pretense in the claim. Clearly, I am who I am. It's all me.

The bridge of my nose is left of center. There's a salient scar along the curve of my right brow. My brightly colored eyes cross when I make them but only for fun, you know, to be funny, cut-up, clown around. It makes a pretty girl smile, even giggle, so it's worth it.

There's a wad, a clump of scar tissue in my lower lip, and my hairline stops before it should. But so it goes. Again, no pretense in the claim. No real fear. No real disgrace or want for forgiveness. It's just me, stem to stern.

For starters ... Completed thirteen professional fights with seven knockouts and a draw. Time in the gym, hours in the ring; punching bags, speed bags, heavy bag, endless rounds with headgear and bob and weave and crouch, bob and weave and crouch, duck, always duck, duck, duck, pow, pow, pow on the return, pow, pow, pow on the return again. Sure ... it dictates my persona. You could say that.

Or so I've been told by people that claim to be a whole lot smarter than me. Anyway.

The last fight, my last fight, was a draw. It was pure bullshit. I was robbed. That's why I gave up prize fighting. The fight … sure, I ground it out. Two to one. Rounds five, seven, and nine … eleven, too … three to one or more in my favor. He never hurt me. Not a blemish. I worked up a heck of sweat but that was from throwing and landing so many connective punches that my hands, both my two fists (wrecking balls) were swollen for two straight days from dishing it out. Even with ice packs regularly on the hour… Looked like lobster claws … I swear to you on my mother's grave.

The other guy was a mess. Cut over his right eye the size of a seamstress' nightmare … like a fat man blew out his trousers in a squat and crouch. Bruised left eye socket, a shiner, contusion bigger than a saucer of dark, organic applesauce (think lunar eclipse). Cut on his chin … I'm being gracious …not just talking smack here … it was a nasty gash. You could have slipped a subway token into the opening. What a horrific wound. Another bloody dimple where he never had one. A brand spanking new cleft palate look-a-like twin top lip compliments of Romeo Nosferatu Mosconi, me, the challenger. Not to mention a bloody nose (broke in two places) and a busted left ear. Twelve rounds of one-way (my way) mayhem. Hit him with a left hook in the tenth that would have unseated a king from his throne. The lucky stiff bounced off the turnbuckle wobbly as vertigo on a broken unicycle, (he was specifically and wantonly extricated from his equilibrium and any other sensory perception he might have been carrying as memorabilia), backpedaled into the center of the ring only to be saved by the bell and his cagey corner man with a bucket of ice water and a half pint of smelling sauce. The son of a bitch was so beat up it looked like me and another fellow gym rat had had our way with him for a solid day and a half, but it was just little old me, the **Lover Boy** *himself.*

Romeo, Romeo, wherefore art thou, Romeo Nosferatu Mosconi?

Answer: I'm here in the center of the ring making minced meat out of Juliet, the bitch and the supposed champ! No way that was a fucking draw.

The prize ($$$) money, cha-ching, cha-ching, cha-ching, went to my manager, his manager, my promoter, his promoter, two bookies and the three leggy hookers and a tall, lanky, lavender and buxom sugar-mistress waiting in the lobby by the green-leafed banana palm next to the gold-plated phone booth. No ... each one was waiting for a different promoter, not me. I didn't make enough to pay my cab fare back to my dingy flat. My girlfriend was packed up and gone by the time I got home at two p.m.

That night I started drinking. (Scotch.) In a small glass; the only clean one nearby. (Loved it right off.) With a quick splash from the faucet. (Macallan.) Chilled inside a two-ice cube roundabout, swish and throwdown. (Was the ex-girlfriend's stash in the cupboard, top shelf, behind the paper plates, wooden matches, and pine-scented cleaning solution.) Free-poured a second go as well. A hardier delivery. Just like the first round, it, too, was on me. The ex, she left in a hurry, I guess. (Twelve-year-old single malt.) Smooth as satin lingerie. (Premium aged.) Triumphantly and resolutely I smacked my lips. It was delectably engrossing and as newly, miraculously discovered as my first French kiss. (Never drank before that night.) I haven't stopped since. Just hitting my stride with a bit of a paunch now as evidence. Proof is in the pudding or the tiramisu, the single malt, or the midriff. What the hey.

*Two and half months later, I get a call. Voice said, **Need a favor**. He lightly identified himself as a friend of a friend and an acquaintance of another person and a nebulous unknown that I couldn't recollect or didn't know. Called the **favor** the mercenary kind. Called me his **intermediate** ... twice. Cash on the barrelhead is what he said or at least intimated. **Fetch the dough**, he kept saying in* *a distant, cavernous voice over his accommodating speaker (phone) … **Fetch the dough**, like I was Fido, the Rottweiler.*

So, three days later with very, very little preparation, I showed up at the designated site and beat a man (matched the wallet-sized, black and white photo) half to death because he owed money. He was delinquent. Told him so. Fair is fair. No, not to me. Told him that, too. Okay? I said that (Okay?) twice, maybe three times, (between blows) just to let it sink in. Thinking back, I'm certain it was three times (that I said … Okay? Trying to give the stiff a break.). His quizzical, vague and uncompromising look as an improper alternative said he didn't have the money or he wasn't going to give it up. But for sure he was playing games. But, there again and for sure and for certain one more time, he was playing games with the wrong guy, me, Romeo Nosferatu Mosconi. Three strikes (okays) and you're out. And fuck fair. The dirty hand of fate I guess you could say.

So actually, I was little more than the strong-armed, pugilistic proxy to some other full-blown, whining vaunter … a rich-guy-gelid-nobody (an "ice-water-in-his-veins" nobody, he liked to boast) out for revenge, a guy that I barely knew who was looking for someone else to sully his hands while he, Richie Rich, stayed home talking pug and rough-and-tough and foretelling my predisposition as his, my preponderance as his, my proclivity once again as his, my fondness along with my penchant for adjudication and rectification as his own where in fact, I was simply collecting for his chicken-shit recreancy, his disingenuous bellicose bravado (shoveled out in spades), and caretaking (performing) his own little pile of dirty laundry (work) as mine.

The money? Sure, I got the money. My work was completed so I got my cut. Then I paid off some severely overdue bills and most of my outstanding debt including two loan shark infractions and a smaller sum to another questionable so-and-so that I will leave unnamed.

Free at last, free at last. (That's a quote from somebody, somewhere. You can look it up if you want. Love quotes that fit the occasion.)

Took myself and my new girlfriend out for a fancy dinner at an upscale restaurant where the foppish and loquacious owner (Caesar of Caesar's) recognized me as Romeo **The Lover Boy** *Mosconi, Nosferatu the Neapolitan Nightmare, (Romeo Nosferatu Mosconi) The Raucous & Ruffian Ringmaster, the fight-fan's fighter ... the one man free-for-all and wrecking ball, the pugilistic dynamo aka Evil's Upheaval. Comped the entire tab. So ... Thank you very much for the hospitality, Caesar of Caesar's!*

I used to love it when on fight nights the ring announcer would bellow lengthways in a preposterously drawn-out and longwinded phonetic, monosyllabic, verbal edifice all its own and all **me**, *the entire list of my most notable Queensberry monikers ... with me over in my corner dripping, nearly soaking wet in a pre-sweat warmup, bouncing up and down, bouncing up and down, just to bounce up and down, jabbing, jabbing, jabbing just to jab reflexively at nothing and midair, slapping myself once or twice or three times and more just to slap and paw myself to be ready as ready and pawing and slapping yourself can get you ... a couple to the chin, the brow, the broader face, both cheeks, and a glance off the forehead, with an open glove, then disrobing in short order.*

And what a robe it was! Soi-disant and Magnifico! Neapolitan verde and rosso with white sequins (bianco) all in a row! Beautiful to see and me inside wrapped up like a beauteous bespoke bellicose butterfly ready to emerge! It was showtime. And again, me spinning about center ring to a full house of my most ardent fans going ape-shit just waiting for me to pounce, punch, sock and perform, flail, whip some ass, and do my thing. What a feeling! Better than sex, murder, and Scotch whiskey all wrapped into one, all combined with whipped cream on top.

I was certain I was destined to have escaped into my own world of fame and fortune ... me ... Romeo Nosferatu Mosconi, the Knockout Knight ... Knight Knockout ... The Italian Sandman himself, in living color... at your service ... The WOP with a pop.

But it wasn't to be. Fate had other plans.

Instead and simultaneously, I found a new job with steady income plus the new, glamorous girlfriend with ample, side-by-side cleavage, deliciously bifurcated as focal point, and legs enough to wrap the backside return of a moonshot, and my new favorite, five-star restaurant. So, I guess you could say, it all worked out. I felt good. Human for a change. Manly as well. Not too bad. Feeling good's not a bad thing.

An appropriate and fitting footnote: Warily, it should be identified here as a pass and abeyance (culpability's companion and friend) ... My ex-girlfriend ... she died tragically in a coincidental automobile explosion giving head to the other boxing promoter turned snitch. What a shame. But not really. Rest in peace, and so sometimes what goes around, comes around.

Life after death ... I get this on occasion ... it just pops up ... and frankly, to have lived through all of this stuff, the day-to-day eventualities of what I have lived though, in and around, and then endured ... what is and has been shelled out to me whether I was looking for it or not, and even more than that, what I was not or never expecting ... and then, say, I die ... just like that... (I'm dead) ... and then after I die, I go straight to hell ... Well, that's what the pew-sniffing, ecclesiastical religious types try and tell me. But ... Whoa, whoa, whoa, I say in return. Hold on. Wait a minute. No, no, no. I think, Mister Religious Type, you've got it all wrong ... Backwards to be forthright, on the level, straightforward, and in all honesty... The way I see it ... God (the backstabber) owes me ... not the other way around. With what I've experienced and encountered and endured and weathered (me, the hardscrabble Jack!) and put up with ...

heaven, the pearly gates, the glistening, resonant harps, the piped-in, surround-sound Muzak twenty-four-seven, the puffy clouds and fine wine, Dom Perignon by the case on ice over in the corner, the peace of mind (not a care in the world) and free dinners (fine dining buffet style) should be assured, a gimmie, a layup, the surest of sure things, a guarantee on the back side of a gold seal with a triple A rating and a matching box of chocolates to boot ... with premium, blanched almonds not the disgusting cheap-ass fruit center.

So, Jesus, you say, is in my corner? He's the answer, you claim. Heavenly Father as cut man, cornerman, coach and trainer? That's what you want me to believe? Oh, really?

Don't buy it.

Not knocking the Almighty (if there is one?) ... He's doing his thing. Maybe in all actuality unlike what I'm told, He can't be in two places at once. No offense taken. Life is after all for the living. I'm doing my thing, too. Just sticking up for myself. If I don't, nobody will. Life boiled down and extracted ... Generally, it's an unfair game. A stacked deck where I never get to deal much less be the sure-thing, sure-handed dealer with the subtly marked cards turning pointlessly droll and hollow cards into winning hands time after time after time. Exempli gratia: Straight fours, clubs, spades, diamonds, hearts looking right up at me. Three tens and a pair of aces suddenly as a kickstart, surefire full house. Deftly dealt next ... two nines and three fives, another more subtle winner-take-all but a full house is still and forever a full house; chips stacked like model skyscrapers at a small, cramped table for six. And remember, were I the dealer? ... Oh, my! Then, four sevens on the seventh deal followed by another full house out of legerdemain's veiled curtain of misty, murky thin air. Shit like that. I was never afforded the pleasure. Christ! Maybe in the next life, but it hasn't happened in this one.

Before my last fight (The Shellacking I call it. Shortchanged and left out in the cold.), I was a regular guy. Nine to five sometimes six ...

gymnasium hours for lefties with a nice, stiff, straight right jab. Paid up, squared up, and always ready to square off. It was my job, my profession. This from a proud man, a working man, very good maybe even really, really exceptional at my craft. Ain't bragging if you can back it up. A standup guy just trying to make ends meet. Stayed out of trouble. Didn't look for any either. On my way to the top, I said with the comparative adulation and encouragement of others, gamesmen and gamblers alike.

Then ... Hey, what happened God? Where were you when I needed you, dude? Or, Mister Dude, the big shot? Could've used some help that night. Just saying. A fair decision is a fair decision, but instead I get jilted by a bunch of hooligans. Yo, God ... rationalize that one, Big Guy Upstairs. And, up yours, I say. Stuff it. Ruined my life. What's left is payback. And Romeo Nosferatu Mosconi is still here working his ass off in spite of the setback. And don't get the idea or the notion that criminal behavior and malfeasance is easy work, or, say, a cake walk, because it isn't. But at least now I'm getting a paycheck. Take it from me ... Things never end the way you think they will.

As for the metaphysical add-on ... the crusty taunt ... things never end the way you know they should.

This just in. Joey called. Said the old lady at the nursing home wants to talk. In private. Has money. We'll see.

CHAPTER 11

Exercise in Futility

First floor. Room 189. Eden's Exercise Emporium. Where youthfulness meets maturity and fitness counts.

Remember when?

So, challenge yourself. Power up! Be all you can be. Make a difference in your life so you can make difference in someone else's.

This just down the hall and around the corner from Admissions and Administration. Beware all those that enter here.

Today, it's just Eddie and Jenkins inside room number 189. As usual, the two had it all to themselves. Twelve shiny, silver-handled barbells sat on a pristine, standing metal weight rack. Matching pairs. One pound. Two pounds. Three pounds. Five pounds. Seven pounds. Ten pounds. A stray fifteen-pound weight sat off to the side on the floor by itself unused, ungripped like a stale piece of bread at an unattended but full-blown banquet. Five disconnected, unused recumbents lined the outer perimeter in a lurch like toothless tattletales in a school yard. Six yoga mats leaned against the same wall new, tied up in seamless bundles, never used, never approached, like awkward, unadjusted adolescents at their first soirée. The single, multi-functional streamline treadmill was unplugged, its electrical power cord draped over the computer readout like a blown out, post-hurricane, downed transmission line. A big screen TV unplugged, the remote in a sling, reflected the same images in dark black and green of whoever walked in through the front door, it's only use like a mirror to the macabre. A stack of eight clean, unused sweat towels in one corner were last changed out in the spring prior to the one before that. The clear, blue twenty-gallon water bottle fountain with side cup attachment and cups galore shone brightest, lite up like an evening, storefront display case in some Amsterdam, red light district. In the opposite corner, a clean-handled pulley bar weight ensemble-contraption entitled Power Master was idle as well. Tension set at neutral. It most resembled a tireless, engineless, decaled race car up on blocks.

On the far-righthand wall, large, five black and white photographs were silver-frame-mounted side by side. Each portrayed a beefy, behemoth, lifelike muscle-sculpted photograph of bodybuilders from their prime in their posing, fitness-freak heydays… a muscle sculpted and smiling Schwarzenegger, Conan, in a roundoff, thigh bulge, brawny bicep side pose clothed singly in his skimpy man-sling, alongside a muscle sculpted Haney, Total-Lee, in round off and a gut-popping grimace, alongside Columbo fit and flexed as repeat Mister Olympia grinning almost foolishly but pleased, alongside Ferrigno, the Hulk, the fleshy side of green, forward flexed, double-fisted, abdominals rippling, biceps brimming, he, too, is grinning, he as Mister Universe, alongside and lastly, in the corner was The Chemist, Insane Zane, serious, pensive, pleasantly puffed up and pectoral, a dashing g string-ed Michelangelo statue rock-hard and chiseled. Bygone days for each and every one commemoratively resurrected and depicted in a forgotten part of the facility.

At the far end standing erect and enchantingly chauvinistic, chest-proud and glowing was a larger-than-life, life-size portrait of the grandmaster of fitness gurus himself … Francois Henri Lalanne

… Jack Lalanne… The Godfather of Fitness … the nutrition Wunderkind … Juicer extraordinaire and inventor and grandmaster … the Power Juicer personified. Grinning. Power stance. Jut-jawed. Gut tucked, concave and taunt. Biceps bulging. Perfectly coiffed and chiseled and as always etched in perfect symmetry. Everything less the halo and a pair of bronzed, adorned angel wings from on high. The semi-sleeveless, one-piece, belted trainer jumpsuit with signature, matching ballet slippers, color coordinated in Jack's favorite azure to cerulean. This was the muscle sculpted and smiling Lalanne, so lifelike that this the friendlier Lalanne could almost talk to you from his full frontal shot on the wall in front of you, with double biceps boosted and lifted up like a brand, spanking new pair of prize twin baby boys resting above and between elbow and shoulder, something off a snapshot at a Fourth of July family picnic. Wow! Why do you think they call them Jumping Jacks?

The photo portrait caption … **Can't die, it'll ruin my image!**

Around the room above that were other Garden pep slogans and Eden sententia for all the fitness go-getters therein.

Your best isn't good enough; try harder.

Touch your toes then reach for the sky!

Today is your tomorrow, so tomorrow's within reach.

Take a deep breath and go for it! And while you're at it, Picture this: You on a jumbotron! So, get busy.

Here at The G of E, Perseverance takes Precedence, and our number one precedent is your preservation; and don't you forget it.

Our motto is *YOU!*

Think big. Atrophy's not an option! | Your cholesterol count is depending on you! So, get motoring! | One, two, one, two. Jump, two, three, four. We're ready to pump you up!

Today it was just Eddie. Eddie and Jenkins. Mentor and mentor-in-training.

A dim fluorescent light flickered overhead. Muzak played. Handel for those who knew. *Faramondo*. Who would? Eddie didn't. Nor Jenkins. *The Icicle* preferred Brubeck. In a moody, whimsical pinch, he fancied Marty Robbins over Elvis. On altering weekends and in between, Como over Sinatra, Bennett to Tormé. But Handel would have to do. As Eddie was always quick to note: It's always piped in from the *warden's* office. Like you couldn't tell, he'd add in disgust.

"J, how many sit-ups was that?" Eddie asked.

"That's two, maybe three," answered Jenkins. "Three and a quarter if I really fudge."

"Jesus, Mary, and Joseph," replied Eddie. "You sure? Felt like four hundred. Maybe a thousand. Are you sure?"

"Yeah, boss," replied Jenkins. "And I'm counting by twos."

"Damn it, J, don't mess with me," replied Eddie. "I'm out of breath. One more and I'm done for the day. You hear?"

Seated in his regular sideline, foldout chair, Jenkins held the hand towel folded over twice in a bite-and-clinch like Tarkanian, UNLV Tarkanian. Talked through and around the terrycloth like he was coaching an entire team and an elite one at that. It was just team Eddie.

"Got it, boss," replied Jenkins. Jenkins threw the hand towel back over his shoulder to help Eddie up off the floor.

"Jenkins," said Eddie trying to regain his balance. "How many pushups did I do?"

"Two," replied Jenkins.

"Two?" said Eddie, an incredulous Eddie. "It was four."

"No," replied Jenkins. "It was two. And you cheated on the second one so call it one and half." Jenkins grinned.

"Aw, bull shit," said Eddie. "You're screwing with me. Me an old man. Shame on you, Jenkins. It had to be four. I'm sore from the strain and just thinking about it."

"One and half," replied Jenkins again. "You went up and then down and then up in a bow with the help of your right knee and then down again. Actually, you fell out like you'd been shot out of a cannon just before hitting the net. One and a half. I'm spotting you the half because you collapsed back to the floor so hard on the downstroke it's hard not to credit you for the intensity in the dismount ... or the flop. Remember, your long-term goal is five. You said so yourself yesterday."

"Five?" said Eddie. He was even more incredulous, now disbelieving. "Five? Five, hell. I'll never get to five with you counting. I'll be lucky to get to two and a half, you bastard. Use the calculator on your phone for Christ's sake. This is hard work."

Eddie stooped ... then kneeled ... then bent over until he was on the floor again.

"Here, count these," said Eddie. "And pay attention. I'll rattle these off, and you'll be looking the wrong way. Here goes."

Eddie lay flat on the floor, stretched out like an alligator in full sun ... but more a bearskin rug just back from the taxidermist, his arms folded underneath his chest, palms flat. "I could take a nap from this position," he said. Then he shoved off naval-like in knee-deep, shallow water. Little happened. He then sucked in, expelled the same breath, and lifted himself like a floppy, loose-fitting hundred-pound sack of flour, only to crash back to the floor mat underneath him once again.

"How many?" asked Eddie.

"Two," said Jenkins. Jenkins chuckled.

"Two, my ass," replied Eddie muttering to Eddie. "Now, help me get up off the floor. I don't want to die down here on the floor particularly in this position. Fetal. Anal. Anal-fetal. Something. Whatever. It's embarrassing ... and while doing these stupid exercises. I could use a good belt about now. Barkeep! And you're no help. Can't count or give me credit for what I've accomplished, me an old, old, feeble son of a bitch. Shame on you again, Jenkins. You know I hate this.

And for your information, Lalanne contracted with Satan just before he died. Wasn't supposed to die. Not for another twenty or thirty years. Said so himself. So, just before his time was up, he signed off. It's been proven. These days, he's running the devil's sweatshop in hell. Hear it's brutal with that little, ragtag, fitness-freak guru S.O.B. barking instructions twenty-four seven. Up, down, up, down, up, down … let's pickup those knees, ladies. Flex those thighs, girls. Any fool can suck in his gut and poke out his chest while flexing his biceps. A minute and a half or less, then lets it all go. Big deal. Hated the slippery, little showoff. No telling what he really looked like on the exhale. Bet it was a big one. My wager … his biceps were implants."

From his kneeling position on the floor, Eddie paused. He was in a pant. He looked up and over at the Jack Lalanne figure.

"Maybe a skimpy leotard with a pair of ballet slippers would help?"

"Might be worth a try, boss," said Jenkins. "Particularly, if you're going to meet those goals of yours."

Eddie a bit frazzled, looking sallow and out of breath said:

"How many minutes on the recumbent?"

"By my watch, ninety-nine seconds. Just shy of two minutes."

"Oh, for the love of God," said Eddie. "I'm calling it three minutes just because you're being such a dick. And I thought you were pulling for me? I know bastards I knocked off that would give me more respect than this. Three minutes it is."

Jenkins grinned.

Eddie stood up. He reclaimed his balance, his stooped posture; his mouth was agape, his eyes widened while he caught another breath in a heave, and looked around at his tiny space in the oversized room. His dementia circled. Buzzards in the blue and on high. Inside that labyrinth, he continued like nothing had happened.

"Jenkins, there was this time, see. Coordinated the rendezvous with Satan himself," Eddie looked over at Jenkins. He smiled. "I know, I know, you don't buy it, but I'm telling you, it's the truth. Me and the devil face to face. Mano e mano. The little bastard looked at me and said, 'Eddie, let's arm wrestle. So, I said, 'Dude, you're on.' So, we did. Me and the devil. The little bastard and me, we step over to the bar, over in the corner, move the whiskey, shot glasses, ashtrays, and overflow off to the side, and place our elbows onto the oak top steady-like, firmly planted, and ready to go. He's sneaky. But, then again, He's the devil. What do you expect? I keep one eye on him the whole time expecting him to cheat or pull a fast one, but to my surprise he plays it straight, Jenkins. Straight as an arrow. Couldn't believe it. We settle in. Lock arms. Grab a thumb, a palm. Flesh to flesh. And, I wait. Somebody's got to say 'Go!', so I'm frozen in arm-wrestling anticipation like you do. Had never lost one time in my entire life, Jenkins. A strong son of a bitch, Jenkins, as you can see from these workouts. Kept fit my entire life. Job description. Be prepared. Boy scout motto and all. Take names. Kick ass. The fraternity of Hit Men, Jenkins. I can't tell you how important it was.

So, anyway, the devil, he's got his eye on my wrist and the lock I've got on his wrist and thumb and palm, and I'm sure he was thinking old Eddie's nothing like the pushover he was expecting. Been doing the devil's work all my life, J. Why would I or should I be afraid of the little man himself? Besides, he was a fucking dwarf. Nothing like I expected. The devil. Five something. Less than a hundred thirty pounds. Full blown male. Dark complexion. Sure, ruddy to reddish, just like you'd expect. Eyes set too far apart. Made eye contact and looking at him difficult. Hairline just so, not too thick, not too thin. A strange looking fellow, the devil, just the same."

Dementia circled, this time away. Eddie looked back over his shoulder like he was expecting someone else to be there in the room, but it was just Eddie, Eddie and Jenkins standing beside him waiting to complete their time together one more day. Eddie remembered now. He was finished here, finished here in Room 189 just down the hall and around the corner from Admissions and Administration. All of it effortless with Jenkins' patience and help.

"Back at it, J," said Eddie. "Onward. Charge of the light brigade, you and me." Eddie threw a triumphant, single fist into the air and looked around for the exit.

The two men kept walking until they'd turned the corner and were out of sight. Another workout completed Eddie-style and one for the books.

CHAPTER 12

Conversation with the Devil

In his dream, Eddie is partnered with the devil. Amigo to amigo. We talked on occasion, said Eddie's dream voice. It was casual-like. Nothing strained or convoluted. I never asked for anything, and he never offered. Some people tried to say it was me just having hallucinations or making up stuff to get attention or the likes. Dementia said the old man at the end of the hall, but what would he know. He was eaten up with jealousy when it came to me. I had all the women, had my health, all my teeth. Only needed glasses on occasion just to read the fine print or my own illegible signature. If required, could hit a sparrow (bull's eye!) at thirty yards. I said baloney even though euphemisms weren't my go-to much less a trademark. Anyway, it was nothing of the sort. It was as real as the ring on my pinky, the nose on my face, or the flick and curl of white at the crawl of my nape. And, just for your information, He, Lucifer, was there, and I was there with him. The devil, he is a cool cat. That's for sure.

In our own way, we agreed on most things. He, we, me and him, we weren't nearly as heady or judgmental or invasive or persuasive, tactical or hurried or prompt, lackadaisical or calculating or really anything as you might assume. He, this Beelzebub cat, was a lot more laid back than I would ever have imagined. Not unlike me, I guess, but quite a bit more confidant in the rhyme. Guess you could say that's why we hit it off. "*Hit it off*' … hell yeah, that's a pun, a wise guy pun, and a good one.

He sat on a pillow cushion in the middle of the room like an oversized Buddha. This time, he was big man. Bigger than me, bigger than Cousin Rich, and were big men, both of us. Eddie's voice spoke up. He sipped ginseng barehanded from a copper kettle. Added sugar by the spoonful and stroked a smile that would take the worry and a heavy frost off an entire, freshly mowed, October stand of alfalfa field-side. I have to admit I was somewhat in awe, but then again, we're talking the devil here. The devil … Satan, the man, the myth, the legend. He hitched his trousers twice in the rise and shook my hand with a firm grip just shy of oppressive. I got it. You would too.

Compressed regeneration, I thought. Compressed validation, I surmised. Compressed upheaval followed by a compressed nurturing into the devil's own compressed and jubilant celebration. At this point, I could hear the devil cackle like a magpie over a rabbit's carcass … him playing his games and toying with me like gusty wind over a ripe wheat field. *Another soul stolen and tossed below into the fiery bowels of hell,* a voice summoned.

And what would cousin Richie do in a situation like this?

I always said to him, *If I could be a hitman just a for an hour or a day or maybe even better a week, I could fix things or fix things the way I know they should be fixed for good.* At least that's what I told myself.

The devil read my mind and responded.

Resentment and revenge … right up my ally in fact; my forte; a specialty and field of expertise reservedly all mine. Let me explain. First …

In point of fact, there is no follow-through in resentment. Resentment is little more than an empty mood, humorless, debased, and bald-faced leaving everyone and everything involved landlocked and surrounded by its unnavigable circumstance. A constant, exacerbated reminder, if you will, and the other side of enough. Enough already. A full-blown annoyance to body and soul. A holdover from unmanifested choice and freedom lost. A closeted voice that says naggingly, "Alright, alright, already. Alright". But you don't listen, or you didn't listen, or worse, you won't or wouldn't hear it so like an impudent jackal who's just missed the swifter, more nimble prey in a final lunge and is now mired up to his neck in ungrounded quicksand, you, too, are stuck in some bootless and barren jungle of entanglement christened **resentment***. Pity the fool, a great man once said.*

Revenge, on the other hand, hellbent or otherwise, is multifaceted from the outset, endlessly pliable, poised and on call, a schizophrenic inversion, containment to conversion at a whim, angry or angerless, placid even, or, at first appearance, docile, warm and friendly (a friend in need … that kind of thing) in demeanor as often as not … or tempestuous if you so choose, as well as creative by design, with chronically indubitable rights and freedom of expression all its own and akin to no one and nobody and no one thing. No relatives or kinfolk to speak of. Sultry and seductive as well. Revenge … what's not to like? It begs the question with an even easier, more apparent answer. Revenge, sure, it's mayhem's partner in crime. No question about it. It's certain and smacks of a kind of justified arrogance. Mark it down, and at the same time get it off your chest, settle the score, put matters to rest and a good night's sleep. Auld lang syne. Again, what's not to like? Revenge can live without mayhem but not the other way around. It's far more discreet. No time restraints or restrictions to speak of. Go with the flow. At will, on your terms, at your pleasure, in a whim in a flick, twist, or the snap of your two fingers. Chance per se with incalculable returns in the cradle of risk with limitless possibilities and advantage to the server with untold, tremendous upside. Revenge is so full of possibilities it even reeks of a grandiloquent potential all its own. Performance oriented, grounded in its latent intent and purpose. Something to love, and something to make love to (assuming you, you sexual beast, you, play your cards right) … revenge … sweet, simple, curvaceous, and enchanting all in one and at the same time. As refined as you make it, as refined and dandy and irrepressibly resilient as you want it to be. It remains up for consideration at all times. So again (ad nauseum), what's not to like? That is … unless you get caught. Never forget … just as long as you don't get caught. Ah, there's the rub.

Stranger still, the devil looked down his nose at me decidedly and said: *"Somewhere inside a lost casket inside some dead-man-derelict's top inside breast pocket is an expired winning lottery ticket with a sarcastic goodbye note addressed to the finder that reads: To all the rest & to whom it may concern … million$ have gone to waste. But it's just the devil's way."* He then sighed and smiled spontaneously, cruelly, a smile so thoroughly crowded with his own admixture of irony and sarcasm and dread, it could have been doused in the sour, tart, bite, and bitterness of pepper flakes, garlic, thyme, and lemon juice, made ready to feast.

"Most will do anything to meet with the devil's approval," he said. *"Even though they won't admit it in private, much less public. They pray to God for all the goodies and glory, but in their tried and tested and tired subconscious … I'm the one they call on for favor in their regressive revenge and reprisal out of spite. It's the baneful echo of dismissiveness, the sting and sere of denigration and disparagement, the bite of derogation, that aligns all of us against one another in an everyday onslaught toward petty retribution. It's the mainstay of my work, my mission. Simply put, it's what keeps me in business. It's the way I make my living.*

Honesty is not always the best policy. It's what you can get away with. It's what flies. What sticks. How you cash in.

Another nugget … looking back this is such a priceless entry and observation from earlier today. God and the devil … one in the same. If not in total, for the most part. Prayer … the dialogue bandied about in private when you're alone with no one to talk to but yourself, and always when it's not going your way … or something worse than that … then you see the whole thing journaled, channeled, jockeyed about with mixed results at best. The outcomes … good, bad, indifferent, and disastrous. There you have it."

The devil smiled.

As if to fully embrace the narrative, an intraspecific voice trumpeted plainly and pragmatically from out of nowhere: *Let's go see what the devil has in store for us today.*

In the faint final analysis, He, the devil, is no doubt collecting souls. Mine, yours, the neighbors, the man and woman down the street as well. And for what purpose? They are like runs batted in, I say. Runs batted in at the end of an inning, but there is no end to the game. It sprawls to infinity beneath a dark curtain. I believe this with my whole mind, heart, and soul even as heartless as it may sound or seem.

Or, maybe like collectable coins, not so rare, but coins minted like some meaningless and concocted cyber currency.

For what purpose and why? I don't know. I have asked the question thousands of times and there is no response, no note tacked to the wall, no hidden clue beneath the secret space, no sign across the sky to reveal the true, indistinguishable meaning of life. It's all such a mystery. So, I move on. I leave that day and that hour behind and proceed to the next task before my time is up … my time of completing or tackling tasks at all.

The devil knows. In his own way, He knows. But, just maybe, he is a she and the match game that we play, we are little more than bobbleheads, little more than Santa Mierda puppets all in a row. Not the prize, but more the cheap, little, weightless plastic ducks all in a row bobbing about in a water turnstile at the carney's fairground. Step right up, step right up.

The dream ended just as abruptly as it had begun. It left Eddie disconcerted if not wistful and confused. Yet somehow in a stretch and yawn, he felt resuscitated and revived, refreshed and ready to fight on. At least in the moment that was how Eddie translated and interpreted his dream's message. He moved to his desk to write the next chapter in his new novel.

Chapter 13

7 AM Breakfast with Cousin Rich

Eggs over easy, kielbasa links with a couple of slices of babka and a splash of orange marmalade out of something no bigger than a petri dish. It was just the two of us that morning, me and cousin Rich. By my watch, it was seven o one.

Location: LaGuardia's, the 24/7 diner, cross town. No airplanes, just good-as-it-gets food off the end of a spatula, a blackened griddle alongside the smell of fried onions, a worn, bent deep fryer, a sticky squirter bottle full of cooking oil, two double boilers and a Dutch oven behind a long and tawdry Formica countertop in front of a dozen or so floor fixed-swivel, hardback seats with a dozen or so hearty, heavier patrons as inserts chatting it up and preparing to face the day. A bunch of us no names … each and every one trying to find our way into the remainder of the rest of our work week on a full stomach.

So, there we were. The booth midway at the end of a short, fat, cozy corridor. Number eleven. A four top, but just me and cousin Rich. As previously stated, Rich was a big man and in need of his space. We'd been there long enough to chow down and enjoy the usual, and begin a third round and refill of black coffee. Rich did most of the talking. I listened, nodded some, responded when appropriate. We'd finished up the second cup of coffee and highlights from the last time, our last breakfast meeting … or maybe it was an early lunch … can't remember … we did this say once every eight to ten months or so. A catchup or a check-in call it, and always great material for my next book. It went something like this.

"Bury the hatchet," said Big Rich. "So, I did." He smiled that smile of his, the devil's own, and continued. "Right in the back of his thick skull. Never knew what hit him. Lights out. Clean as whistle except for the pool of red blood on the floor where he lay and bled out. The hatchet wasn't mine so I left it where I left it. At a glance-over and last sight, it was like a crank handle on an old-timey well pump … less the water of course. Like I said, blood was everywhere and all about. From my perspective, served him right."

Rich took another sip of coffee, added some cream, another packet of sugar, and continued as he stirred.

"Another time, same as before almost. Bury the hatchet they said. Make amends. Get over it. You'll be better off in the long run. Make peace with your inner sanctum, whatever that meant. Resolution … it's such a small price to pay for such a huge reward.

Might as well have been reciting or regurgitating nursery rhymes or fairy tales was my take on it, but that's some more of what they told me. Settle your differences, that was the last piece of advice I got. So, I did. Left the two-pound, hickory-handled, fireman's axe right of center in the back of his thick skull. By his own admission, he was hardheaded. Said so himself to a mutual buddy of ours the week before all this came down. Didn't cost me a penny. Borrowed the bright red hatchet from one of the guys, a neighbor sort of, down at Station 13 on Elm and 33rd. Brought it back spit-shined and in mint condition without a trace of daredevil or duplicity. Waved so-long with a smile to the rest of guys in the back of the shop by the shiny, red firemen's truck … engine, engine number nine … then

I was away. Just like the other gumba, Joey Two Shoes was dead as an eviscerated rat. Killed him indiscriminately and by the manual. No more carbon footprint. At least not in his size eleven D. The environmentalists and eco-nutjobs should thank me.

There are so many men that want to be like me, but they can't. Not enough testosterone in the makeup. Not balls enough or ego enough to chill and congeal the wrong into right. Murder's not an easy calling. Not a vocation for the weak-kneed or the unsure. I came to it with lust and gratuitous foreplay like a champion cliff diver off the gangplank of the Queen Anne's Revenge over a deep, blue Caribbean Sea. A cakewalk. Anxiety-less, unrepentant, and guiltless. Me, with a free and undisciplined conscience at all times. My unaccountable rules were my own, free of next-door and neighborly religion and homespun morality. To me, that was all bull shit. Coming up, my buddies wanted to be firemen, farmers, policemen, something like that. But not me. I just wanted to whack people and, in the process, get paid to settle scores. What's more, I was good at it, so it made perfect sense."

Rich added another packet of sugar to his coffee. The waitress stopped over and added coffee to his cup. Rich added cream. He picked up his cheap, diner spoon in his big, right hand, and circled the cup three times, then stirred and stirred in a back-to-back motion bisecting the middle in a gentle stroke as ritual, a cousin Rich ritual.

"The last time," he continued. "Same as the other two. Bury the hatchet, they told me. This time it was Federico. You would think the word would get out, particularly with someone like Speak Easy, Never-pay-up Freddie. You know … one ear close to the ground … cover your butt … but I guess not.

Federico rounded the corner in full stride. Happy, whistling, humming an up-tempo, perky tune, *I will survive* maybe, left hand in the left pocket of his disco trousers when I buried the hatchet at the back of his thick skull for the money he owed me and half the rest of the world. Bald as he was, lying there limp as a dish rag, his noggin was suddenly and aptly displayed like a decorative chess piece on a side table in a fancy parlor. The money was all there, buried deep in his pants' pocket and clasped tightly inside his dead paw. New meaning to *death grip* guess you could say. I stepped over the body. It meant little. Nothing actually. Another body. Another dead man. Little more than ho hum. Same cash that's buying this morning's breakfast. The technique, the bury the hatchet thing, it got old, traceable according to some close associates. So, I actually buried the hatchet in a city dumpster on pickup day and moved on to other, more stealth and elaborate ways of killing. It served its purpose. Besides, it's better not to look back ... at least not too far. I've forgotten the past pretty much by the next speck of sunlight at dawn the next morning. It's more convenient that way."

Big Rich added some cream to his coffee, another packet of sugar, stirred it in with a once-around with the cheap, diner spoon, and continued.

"It was meant to be," he said frankly. In an offhanded comment, a conversational sidebar, he said, "I've never known *content*, never been *content*. It's a strange and foreign word to me. Meaningless. Driven by the fact that everyday someone somewhere for some very good reason needs to die. Put down like an old horse past his working prime, winless at the track, useless on the farm. Maybe even cagey and feral and too difficult to tame. For whatever reason, *content* for me means nothing. Murder, on the other hand ... I get it." Big Rich smiled the devil's grin again, suggestive, gibelike, wily, and pleasantly foreboding, so I smiled back.

"There's a huge difference between forgiveness and keeping score," he said. "I don't forgive. Forgive all you want. Forgiveness ... it's for suckers, fall guys, and dipsticks. However, I do keep score."

Big Rich smiled and continued.

"I was always out of step with reality. I knew it, but it never mattered. So, I made up my own. I'm not sure that it matters now. I simply put one foot in front of the other, one step at a time, and move on. It's too difficult to change after all this time and all the *improper success* (shall we call it) I've had doing what I do. You could easily say that all along I had one fist in the tar from the get-go, of course targeted at the tar baby's head near the jugular, then another swipe with the free hand. Pretty soon I was goop and glued and blackened in sync for the rest of time and the remainder of my life up until right now. Okay. I get that, too. In America and the world, men have become little more than wet nurses and unflavored, uncompensated harlots useless to the overall masculinity of yesteryear."

Big Rich relayed it like an aside from a practical philosopher or a professional sociologist or maybe a noted, out-of-step psychiatrist watching the historical meltdown, failure, and passing of his own species.

"Besides," he said, "the mystery was in being me. And until recently, I actually believed that. Said that very same line out loud so many times I convinced myself of how interesting I was, how fascinating and casually mysterious I had grown to be, how invincible and invisible I had become as well. Laughable now ... sure. Easy looking back. Self-consumed by a mile, but not the only vanity-ridden, contemptible chiseler and unhinged mercenary to inherent and repeat the notion to himself. There've been others. I wasn't the only one, not by a long shot."

Seated comfortably in booth eleven, Big Rich reached into his back pocket and drew out his billfold. Inside was a piece of paper that he unfolded in front of me.

"Read this once in a book. Caught my eye. Thought it was interesting. My line of work, so I tore it out carefully by hand and saved it just like it was written ... as if it was written for me. Famous author or somebody. Don't recall. Says here ...

Some people want to sell death as an iridescent inevitability or comfortably claustrophobic salvation. Others lean in and strong arm the darker side, intrinsic iniquity, the horror-horrific side of the inevitable, the menacing dimension of blackness inside a seamless strand of lightless, soundless forever. And after all, that's a long time. So, murder is not something most people are drawn to."

Cousin Rich paused. He folded the small piece of paper back into his billfold, then looked up and across at me.

"Just so happens I *was*," he said with that same wry and seamless Luciferian grin of his. "Bully for me … maybe … maybe not. A sort of détente with the Devil I like to call it.

The straight razor was a favorite for a while. I toyed with big men, tough men, men full of bravado, full of sausage, sauerkraut, mustard, piss and vinegar. They were all the same. They led charmed lives. At least until they met me … little more than a slobbering, spit-shined hyena from the Serengeti.

I took the one man by his lashed and sockless toes and carved pumpkins into the soles of his feet, asked him to tango, then drug him down a flight of stairs into a basement and around the cinder block stairway head first into the bucket of a mason's wheel barrow. Oddly, when I'd finished, all of him fit into the belly of the thing like they were meant for one another. Wheeled him out and dumped into a vat (more a low-slung caldron) of hydrochloric acid for the sake of safekeeping. Didn't know I had it in me until I'd finished. Felt good actually. Mission accomplished so to speak.

But nothing's really that interesting anymore. When my time comes, I'm out. Seen it all. Done most of it.

And did I get to all of them … the people I wanted to kill? Oh, hell no. Not by a mile. There were at least a dozen or more just as a dust off or cleanup in a casual rethink from off the top of my head. Me, a private guillotine for hire no less. Others that should've been killed just on principle alone or just for the sake of it, they got away or escaped or faded into the massive, undefined backdrop and black hole of namelessness. Not enough hours in the day to get to them all, but I certainly got to more than my share.

Religious trinkets and gadgets and spotted good luck charms all to get into heaven where in fact you don't deserve less than twenty lifetimes in hell, nonetheless, I carried them throughout the day like I was a holy man or a devout servant of God almighty. Nothing further from the truth, but I did.

For the record and what it's worth, I was always at odds with the big man upstairs. Jesus, too. The holy spirit never factored into any of it. Never understood that part of religion in the slightest. Just me and Beelzebub on our own private, little mission working for the mob and doing our thing week in, week out."

Cousin Rich took another sip of his coffee, exhaled relievedly, and started again.

"All the religion, the straight talk, the abstinence, chanting, sobriety of language and gut, none of it will save you. You know that, Eddie.

You die.

The number kills you. The aged number. Say, fifty-two. Or, maybe sixty-three. Sixty-nine, seventy, seventy-five or even eighty. Seriously, it's the number. But, the number, it kills you. It's your number. It's over. Your time is up.

Death, it's the mystic in our midst. It's the clock on the wall. With no alarm. Not a gong or a chime of caution. Then, you and me, we are over. Done. It makes no sense, but here we are. Here it is. No one calls out as if to warn you even though you've suspected it the whole time. So, you've been told your entire life, and you knew it from birth. But, then, sure enough, the door closes. The curtain slowly and deliberately and passively falls without incident or suspense, noiselessly, perfunctorily you're abandoned like a willow branch in a gentle stream, and you're left in a heap an un-staged, unsung pitiful actor without an audience, you, to your own dimly lit, tracked and dirty stage floor. The end. But there is no signoff. No finale. No exit, either. Death has no impostor, no twin, or clone. There is no deus ex machina, no escape, no catapult to freedom and youth, no god machine, no saving grace, no trick wire harness pulling you up and over the next trouble spot, or white knight riding up to the rescue as we have been told or has been written in. No fault. No blame. No excuses. Death belies the lie, our lie, just as much as the life we have led, good or bad. It betrays the traitor and subsequently wrests deceit from the hands of the most gracious and gifted grifter. I've peered into the abyss many times. Just as many times, through the eyes of another man dying or getting ready to die, … and by my hand, me the grim reaper of sorts. So long, I would say.

Sell whatever brand of life you want. Sell it to whoever you want and to whoever will buy it. And sell it for whatever you can get for it. It's yours to sell. I chose a life of crime and malefaction and misdeed. Most won't go that route. My view … the fewer in my line of work the more money left on the table for me, more for the take. Not bad in my opinion at least from where I sit.

Besides, we're forever winning the argument in our own head no matter the subject. Who isn't?

And just for the record, most people spend their entire lives tripping over rainbows then stumbling headlong into misfortune and never making enough to pay off the mortgage. Disproportionately out of touch and dreadfully out of tune is what I call it. They die broke, destitute, and loyal to something they can't define much less put a finger on … kidding themselves the whole time. That's not for me. Never was.

The preacher's platitudes never make it past the back pew much less out the front door. Feel free to quote me. And keep in mind, there's no real hate in what I do. It's a job. Some say I'm a deranged mercenary, a cad, and a deliriously twisted soldier of fortune. Okay.

So be it. But it's not about hate. Hate has nothing to do with what I do. Capisce?

Here you go …

The far side of hate described … Once knew a guy so consumed with hate that he lusted for revenge. Plotted revenge. Mapped it out night and day. Transcribed all the where's and wherefores into a notebook, the dos and don'ts and the how's and why's, as well. He'd planned each and every bit of his revenge down to the letter, the date, the time of day, the season, the alibi, and the evidence to cover his tracks. You could even go so far as to say this guy stalked revenge just like a twisted, wanton voyeur peering through a peephole at some shapely and naked beauty on the inside of her sequestered boudoir.

When he heard the other man, the fixation of his revenge, had died and saw the date of the funeral in the newspaper, he was thunder-struck and aghast. At first, he groused and grumbled. He then fumed and ranted incoherently. In the moment, he realized that he wouldn't be able to exact revenge and taste and savor the succulent, tart sweetness he'd already imagined. It was gone. Up in smoke. Flown the coup. He'd been abandoned shoeless, on foot, and left by the side of the road. He said this exact same thing to himself repeatedly for hours on end. *I've been abandoned shoeless, on foot, and left by the side of the road.* He said the words in such a self-pitying reach it made the whole thing even more plausible, creditable, and real. He became despondent. This was not the way it should have played out, he muttered in indecipherable language all to himself in off hours and away from the madding crowd. I'll be damned if this is the way it ends.

So, he waited three days. The *ascension* or some such nonsense came into play. He then journeyed to the cemetery, dug up the body from the loose soil, opened the casket, pulled his pistol, and shot the dead man seven times in the face at point blank range just because.

Why? someone asked him. *Why would you do that?*

Just because, he replied.

Hate is a strange emotion. More an engulfment than an obsession. Like unneeded kindling to a bonfire or lighter fluid to a burning house already afire and mostly razed. Hate, it burns deep. It never falters or wavers. It never leaves the surface or the underbelly, and yet it seems to feed on itself repeatedly.

The guy, the venomous man, he emptied the shell casings into the lined coffin, slammed shut the pearl-inlay lid on the deceased's mahogany coffin, and then walked away, Formaldehyde and cartilage splattered everywhere in a mess.

Eddie, for the record, I don't do hate. No money in it. Plus, it's not part of my job description. I just take care of business no matter how ticklish, disquieting, or disagreeable to the doubters on the other side."

Cousin Rich grinned most artfully in the moment and finished his coffee.

CHAPTER 14

Police Headquarters

The Opening Scene was The Metro Police Station downtown, Rigby and 5th.

The Place, the setting, was the Police Chief's office. Chief Friday. After thirty-one years on the job, this was where he had settled.

Props: The main prop was the police chief's desk. There were the twin chairs positioned in front of Chief Friday's desk. The twin chairs did not match the desk. The bastard twin chairs didn't match one another. They were from police storage, confiscated belongings, unclaimed, matchless and mate-less to the oversized, bastard desk also from the same police storage.

Persons today: There was a threesome, a trifecta, gathered in the center of the room inside the small office tucked into the center of the hallway of the same cinder block municipal building approximately the size of three or four convenience store-service stations or two Quonset huts squared off with a flat roof. Inside, there was one small, similar-to-identical window left and right, chest height for a short adult, each with no decorative flair in the least. Institutionally drab, stale, and innately or naturally dystopian in fact in every way.

Chief Friday was seated professionally. He looked on considerately at the two elderly visitors, a man to his left, a woman to his right. He was wearing his best, most attentive face and the best one he could feign. Remember, as he might quickly remind you, he did this for a living, twenty-four seven. *Tedious is tedious no matter.* His words. *I am the chief of police* was his countenance, in the business of being the police chief for better or worse.

Both visitors were dressed in terry cloth house coats over pajamas and bedroom slippers over fuzzy woolen socks. Cold feet comes with age. The older gentleman was wearing a paisley ascot beneath the stubble of expressive gray and white beard. A retiree thing. The older gentlewoman, she was symmetrically coiffed yet looked confluently perturbed while shuffling a deck of tarot cards in a preoccupied fidget with her Coptic-style rosary on a crucifix kneaded thumb to forefinger in the opposite hand as guidance, security, and portent. She was unwilfully patient, and it showed.

Chief Friday looked on quietly waiting for their next move.

Eddie led off. He mumbled audibly to Eve into the small, open office space, "As I told you earlier before you drug me over here, this isn't a good idea."

Straightaway, Eve replied softly to Eddie, "Eddie, this is the right thing to do. This is long overdue." She looked back to Eddie, stopped, and stared.

"This is dumb," said Eddie. "No hit man ever walks into a police station and turns himself in. Never. Ever. Not in the history of hit men. It never happens."

"Maybe not, Mister Eddie *The Icicle* Jablonski, but you can be the first. You'll set a precedent," said Eve.

"A precedent? For what, stupidity?" replied Eddie.

"We'll discuss that later after you've turned yourself in," said Eve. "Now, go ahead and tell Captain Friday why we're here."

Eve turned to the police captain and said aloud firmly with subtle conviction, "Chief Friday, this is difficult for me to say, but Eddie won't say it so I will. This is not just idle twaddle as you at first may think. Eddie, he would like to turn himself in. This is about his criminal past you see."

Eve looked down and turned over a tarot card. The high priestess … the very sign that she can and must continue. Eve crossed herself with an extra up and down. She paused almost reverently, cleared her throat, and continued, "For murders that he committed years ago, mind you, but there were the past murders of multiple men in his old line of work. He'll have to give you the particulars on these crimes. I wasn't there. (Thank, Jesus.) He knows the time and place of each one of these foul deeds which he has confided to me in our most intimate moments (Dear Jesus deliver me.). As a former law enforcement officer and police woman, I simply cannot keep it all straight much less keep this to myself any longer. I'm sure you understand."

Eddie held up his hand as semaphore. Enough. He then began on his own.

"First off, I'm going to give it to you straight, chief. And just so you understand where I'm coming from, the last three times I prayed, I got no response. Nothing. Not so much as a slap on the wrist or a Dear John or a Dear Eddie. Nothing. So, guess what, I quit praying. At my age, I guess you could say that's a bit of a concern. It might be or it could be a premonition as hinderance or deterrent to the afterlife thing. I get it, but what the hey. If I want to talk to myself in private, it doesn't cost anything. Not one red cent. No tithing to some loudmouth yakety yak know-it-all at the front of a holy lectern.

As it is, I don't expect an answer of any kind. Plus, I save time, energy, and money. That's all we've got. I leave off the *Dear Lord* and the *Amen* and just like that, the conversation's over. It's just me conversing with me on a foregone conclusion. Quick as a wink. In part, that's why I'm here. Came to see you to get this off my chest before it's too late. Eve insisted. She's made it a priority for both of us. Me … in all honesty … I don't really give a flip. Water under the bridge and over the turnstile, I say."

Eddie took a deep breath. He looked across the desk at the police chief and continued.

"Fellow asked me once not long ago did I know Roy DeMeo? Said it like this … Hey, Jablonski, you old mafia goat, did you know Roy DeMeo?

So, here you go, Chief. This is the way it all went down. Now, buckle up. You've got a front row seat. Your ticket's paid for. In story form just for you with all the gory details to back up my experience. It's an admission to culpability as well so you might want to take notes. I doubt very seriously you get a lot of guys stopping by to offer up their own personal criminal reminiscences, statute of limitations or not."

Eddie straightened his ascot then sat up as erect as his time would allow.

"DeMeo. Roy DeMeo. The Gambino crime family mobster. Follow along.

It was poker night. Three fours beats two pair. He didn't see it that way. Typical DeMeo. Had to convince him. Roy, we all said, three fours beats two pair … all of us in unison … all day long. Subtle like. Persuasive but demure sort of, if that's what you want to call it. Okay, we were being demure, duplicitously demure just so we didn't piss off Raucous Roy, and he then pulls out the hardware and goes to war on all of us, his poker gambling and drinking buddies. Jeez la weez and then some. Namby-pamby gangster-like just for the sake of appeasement (insincere, coddling, like to an infant, fake … nauseous actually).

Told him once … *Three fours beats two pair, your queens and jacks.* Had to explain it again … *Roy, three fours beats two pair, queens and jacks.* Then a third time … *Roy, honestly, the three fours, those three cards that Richie's holding, they beat what you've got in your hand, Roy, the queens and jacks. Believe us,* we all said again. That's what we said when we all chipped in, all of us once. Jeez, said the looks all round. Grudgingly he gave in. Still don't think he got it. Said he got it, but I don't think he did. It was DeMeo. DeMeo's way or the highway. There's no way, he was famous for saying. But as it turned out, it didn't.

Ten minutes later. Outside to smoke a cigar. Breathing in the fresh, cool air along with teeming, centrifugal, aromatic exhale all round. Cigar smoke, the Cubans are so sublime. Quite the momentary enchantment, so it seemed. There was the breeze, a light, lift and stir as well. The starlight, too. Pacific quiet in the backdrop to cap an evening with the boys only to be interrupted by a faint and blunt … bang, bang … bang, bang … four silencer type blips more than bangs and in that order. The cadence of a soft, kid's cap pistol, or an oversized stapler hitting its mark. DeMeo, he hit the pavement, his eyes wide open, but he didn't see *nothing* as they say. *Nothing* then or on his way out because he was dead before he could finish the next drag off his Cohiba Robustos Supremos Edicion Limitada. He'd already hit the turf.

It was classic Kuklinski. A genuine Kuklinski moment if ever there was one. Snap, crackle, pop. One for all the *serial* lovers out there … wherever you may be. Cousin Richie at his finest, at his best.

Hail, hail, the *King of Kill* was no more.

Gone, someone said.

No one said *what a shame* … or *God rest his soul* … or *too bad, so sad* … nothing. Not one person. Not one tear shed. Not one. Dry eyes all the way around. To the contrary, a pat on the back from a couple of guys. *Job well done,* another mumbled like he hadn't said it. A couple of high fives exchanged as I recall. Nobody commiserated. Nobody boohooed. None of that stuff. DeMeo was dead. So long. And on your way out, don't let the door hit you in the ass.

Me and Richie and the guys, we went to work on the disposal of the body right then and there. *No body, no crime.* Instruction from the master himself. *No body, no crime.* Got it."

Eddie sat up taller.

"Did I know Roy DeMeo?" Eddie asked surrealistically and sarcastically aloud. "Hah!" said Eddie louder. "Did I know Roy DeMeo? The name alone sullies my saliva and hogties my tonsils. DeMeo. Roy DeMeo? The sawed-off little prick? That Roy DeMeo? And, did I know him? That's what the guy asked me, chief?" Eddie repeated incredulously, "Did I! I'm the son of gun that permanently transplanted the so and so into the trunk of his own car. The big, wide, purple-to-pink pimp mobile, the Caddy. Flat chested … his hair was a bloody mess, tucked his knees to his chin, shoved his ass forward against the spare tire, lifted the limp arm over the fold of his corpse into his other armpit, flipped both feet into place like he was walking backward … you can do that with a corpse … bet you didn't know that … it gave me great pleasure ... and then slammed the lid on the trunk of the car. That smile of his wiped permanently off his face. Buried neatly in the trunk of his own Caddy next to all of that razor-sharp German cutlery shrouded in Egyptian cotton, the original and authentic DeMeo gourmet Westhof set, from the nine inch paring knife to the eight inch chef's knife to the twelve inch honing steel, the same set he packed around from murder site to crime scene all to dismember his prey … the poor bastards ... popped their heads off in a single twist-and-snap like red tomatoes off a green vine … let the blood drain down the bath tub … washed that away with Clorox bleach … wrapped the remains in the victim's bath towels and bedsheets and then feed the disguised mess into the sidewalk trash bin for the city's next day weekly pickup … gone forever under a millions of pounds of refuse, dirty diapers, discarded leftover fettuccini, and crumpled beer cans. No one's going looking for those relatives of someone there. Not in a trillion years. What a sick fuck. All that and for the last time. How's that for knowing Roy DeMeo, says me, fast Eddie, Eddie *The Icicle* Jablonski? Huh?"

Eddie grinned sheepishly.

"That's the last time I saw him. That's how we met … if that's what you want to call it. And that's that."

"He was a murdering prima donna. Gave hit men a bad name. A visceral skunk. Platitudinous vermin, DeMeo and his entire crew. DeMeo … the textbook pseudonym for psycho. A virtual viral infection with legs and arms. Made murder meaningless. Too lowlife to be above ground."

Eddie looked away into the short distance, tugged again on his pajama shirt lapel front and center, straightened his ascot, and looked back again.

"Okay, chief. Go ahead. Ask me about Galante. Go ahead. I dare you. I double dare you. I know you want to know what happened to Galante," said Eddie. "Everybody wants to know what happened that day. You want stories, chief, I got stories coming out the wazoo."

CHAPTER 15

If Looks Could Kill

From the Cold Case Files & Confessions of Richard 'The Ice Man' Kuklinski Entry #39. For over three decades, Richard Kuklinski served as a notorious contract killer for the East Coast Mafia. The real number of Kuklinski's victims is said to be somewhere between one and two hundred. Selected events herein are recorded, recreated, and transcribed by Edek Jablonski, a successful, retired author-crime writer as well as purported kinsman to 'The Ice Man' himself. Room 315. Voices from within. Bringing the dead to life one last time in a murder victim tell-all.

From the desk of Eddie 'The Icicle' Jablonski. The next chapter as interpolative exposé. The victim's narrative as it might have been told.

Sitting at his desk, Eddie wrote:

Within his own existential web in an unpunctuated and understated plainness, Merchant Mike said to himself, *I came here in the wrong skin. It should have been different. Better by some measure for sure. Something more, maybe something less. I'm not sure. Bigger or stronger. More compact or grander in some fashion just so things would have turned out differently for me. Better as in a bit more glorious, particularly more lucrative somehow in my favor.*

I never mapped it out the way things should have gone or could have gone just because I didn't. It never occurred to me at the time. But it should have been different. Different as in **I made out** *... you know ... like a bandit, as they say ... and that's all I'm saying. You understand. The don's life, le vita del don, the fat-cat, easy life, the life of Riley, that stroke of light and darkness shading all the right corners and crevices like a fine painting or the perfect, shadowy, unrecognizable stickup ... it just wasn't in the cards, not for me anyway. Should've been me I always thought. Said it a million times. I worked hard. Did the heavy lifting. Carried out more than my share of the dirty laundry for sure. (I know, puns galore.) But it wasn't to be. It never happened.*

And then, there I am ... standing all alone ...looking down at all those dead bodies laid out in a row and at the end of that same row (picture it from an overhead through a wide-angle lens) ... that's me, the only upright guy in the photo. The smoking gun, the hangman's noose, the pills, the pipe, the pistol, the perpetrated perturbance and mayhem, all at my behest and my bidding no less. Everything laid out simple like ... the butler, the candlestick from off the Steinway, in the library. And me, the gangster, murderer, syndicate strong man? Apparently, I didn't have a clue. Nobody to blame but myself. No excuses.

Merchant Mike had two pair of shoes in the back of the car. Not in the trunk but in the back. Not on the backseat but on the floorboard between the crumpled, discarded shopping bag and the identically crumpled, discarded sandwich wrapper. Merchant Mike didn't give two shits. That's what he said. *I don't give two shits.* Out loud. To himself. He was in a hurry. He was trying to get away from a man named Richard or Rich. And he was trying to get away from the constant, bloodcurdling thoughts haranguing him about this man named Richard or Rich. He had been forewarned. If Richard or Rich comes looking for you, he will find you. And, when he finds you, because he will, you (Merchant Mike) are a dead man. Rich, he had been told was a hit man, a *can't-miss* hit man, so Merchant Mike, he knew that. He feared for his life because he had been an angry man and a bad man all of his adult life. No two ways about it. That catches up with you. Merchant Mike had always said that. Out loud as well. To himself and anyone listening *that sooner or later it, the lifestyle, catches up with you.* So, he stepped on it … the gas pedal that is … *like it was going to do any good.* He merely listened as he heard himself say that over and over and over … like it's going to do any good, like it's going to do any good, like it's going to do any good.

Every car he passed with a lone, large, dark figure of an adult male at the wheel, Merchant Mike said to himself, "*That's Rich.*" It wasn't, but that's what Merchant Mike thought each time. Just as often, he said it out loud. "*That's the guy who's coming to kill me.*" And there was never anyone in the car but Merchant Mike when he said "*That's him,*" but that's how he knew it was getting to him, that the paranoia was settling in and driving him crazy and close to insane. But he had no idea what to do about it, or what to do next, or what overall course of action he should take. So, Merchant Mike just crossed his fingers and hoped for the best because prayer wasn't an option … certainly not in his line of work.

It wasn't the neatest burial job in the world. You could argue that. There were loose ends. Not good, I know now. Things could have been tidier, more fastidious for sure. No one really said I should do what I did or should do it how I did it. Point well made, well taken. But I had a hunch. And the hunch was this would put me in line for a promotion, cause a stir within the rank and file, and I'd be seen in a different more favorable light by the decision-making muckety-mucks, the higher ups in the know making the real money, and I would come out on the other side as some kind of hero, a man of prominence, even a savior of sorts to the guys in the business at my own level. 'Hey, Merch, you should be a capo!' … I could hear them say this about me afterwards before I found out I'd fucked up and fucked myself for real, big time. So, this once, I went with my gut feel. So, guess it didn't go over as well as I'd hoped. (You think?) Guess my hunch wasn't such a great one after all … now that Rich or Richard, the mystery man, is somewhere out there and hot on my trail.

So, Merchant Mike drove on … *moving right along* as he liked to say to pacify his worry.

A day passed.

Then the man, the dreaded man, he finally showed up just as predicted. Unexpectedly. Problematically. Horrifyingly. Dreadfully. Drearily. In a baleful, solitary twist that cast the bleakest shadow imaginable, one even broader and more ominous than he at first feared. And, to be quite frank, it was actually worse than all that.

This badass bugbear, Richard the riddle, the punitive-puzzle of a hit man Rich, he appeared in the doorway … malevolently impromptu … if there is such a thing… and if so, it's the way it happened in spades.

Cousin Rich, it turns out, came by foot. Over the back wall. Down the alley. Through the opening in the chain link fence. (Almost snagged his sweater.) Until he, Richie-the-hit-man, Richard *The Ice Man* was standing in front of Merchant Mike like they were old, long lost pals in the opening seconds of a fortieth-year reunion … Richie with a slight smile and a sparkle in his eye and his signature … his notorious, ceremonious, "*Hi ya.*" Sometimes Richie, he would say "*Howdy*" (a borrowed or plagiarized or embellished Owen Wister-ism) but today he stood flatfooted in front of Merchant Mike and just said "*Hi ya.*"

Just like that. It was the way it happened.

How can you be astonished (yes, *astonished*, that's the word) when you know you know the outcome? The telegraphs are sent and received, messages are forwarded and read, gossip is confirmed and legitimatized, plot and summary have already been unveiled, intent and motive have long since been established yet you sit there somehow *astonished* and frozen in your own fright and disbelief like it was all just going to go away on its own. Heal itself. Out, out damn spot. Be gone foul demon ... in some kind of half-baked exorcism from some hands-on, hard up, flimflam televangelist. But instead, this is it. And it's your own voice speaking to you in a distinctiveness and no-nonsense inflection like never before, and like a vapid jack, you didn't listen to yourself and hear what you were telling yourself, knowing full well the entire time that it was all truer than the day is long sitting right there in and alongside your own person, your own actuality however existential.

But just like that, Merchant Mike knew that he was a dead man. His words. *Dead motherfucker.* His thought, *I'm a dead motherfucker.* The notion flushed his innards, sparks beneath a covered short circuit. It bandied about in his head loosely like black birds on a taunt, high wire scoffing at one another in earnest.

Sad thing to know (much less think it) that right then and right there you are a dead man just the other side of a short conversation. But it happens to the best of them ... as well as to the worst. That's what Merchant Mike said to himself looking at Cousin Richie ... Richie *The Ice Man* himself. Come to find out, a pre-obituary *come to find out*, this guy Rich was like a big brother, mentor, *a particular* and *for instance* to heavies in the trade, guys like Gigante, cousin Eddie, even *DeMeo-Murder Inc.,* and *The Chin.* It was the word on the street. Learning from the best. Nothing wrong with that. You didn't encroach on the *Ice Man's* turf. But a tad late to do Merchant Mike much good.

"Can we do this bloodlessly?" asked Merchant Mike. "You know … for whoever finds me? The cleanup. The emotion. The shock. The open casket. Family minutia. The little kids, the teenagers, some are just little girls and such and won't get it. Last respects … like I deserve any. But you understand."

"Suit yourself," said the stranger who had come for me. "Turn around."

So, I slowly turned around glancing over my shoulder as I did since I had no other choice, but I was pretty sure in my own head it would soften the blow. In the slow turn, the voice in my head, some other mystical, psychedelic voice other than my own said:

Should I come back in another life, I won't know the people I've known in this one. Death is so disruptive. Such a distraction as well. Washes in like a sleepy tide in the middle of a calm, then subsides leaving nothing. Quite a shame, I say. All this time wasted on getting things just so … then death, the shameless, purposeless intruder shows up unannounced. Death really is such a disruption. And rude what's more. How am I thinking this as I turn to face the fireplace? The craziest set of thoughts to be thinking in my last breath now staring down at the gray ash under the andirons and the two charred logs.

And never knew what hit me.

But *bloodless* was in fact his last request. Request granted. Compliments of *the Ice Man*. What more can a man ask?

Death beside the stone, cold hearth in his own home. Multiple blows. Swipes both hard and fast and thorough and deep and in that same order. Blunt force. In the bludgeoning, a man's skull's traumatized and crushed, indentations a tire iron in depth, nothing more, nothing less, so Merchant Mike's anxiety had come to an end, and his end was assured. According to Merchant Mike, he'd died just as he'd figured everything out … in his last thoughts … his last at bat … like a last rite, everything that he should have figured out beforehand. It was his legacy, a peculiar final gift as the curtain closed.

Rich stepped back from the dead man Merchant Mike lying crumpled on the floor. He nudged the body with his left foot twice, surmised the situation a minute longer taking a breather, and with a right foot heave-ho nudged the body into a rollover face up. He took a small, pocket instamatic from inside his sweater pocket and snapped four images of the man lying dead on floor. The dead man Mike, his tongue, the tip of it, was exposed at the corner of his mouth like a school boy's prank imitating his own death. Work order confirmed. Proof of purchase authenticated. One picture each for the decision-making muckety-mucks and the higher ups in the know making all the real money. Case closed.

Big Rich then left by way of the front door. He closed it quietly and snugly behind him, wiped his fingerprints off the door knob, and walked away down the neighborhood sidewalk as noiselessly as freshly falling snowflakes.

CHAPTER 16

Styx and Stones

A New Crime-Buster
From
Eddie *The Icicle* Jablonski

Foreword by the author.

So, here's another great story I've written for all of my readers and fans wherever you may be. I'm currently being held captive in a nihilistically mangy retirement home (or Orwellian bungalow but more properly a dystopian dormitory for the demented) against my will and better judgment. I have registered numerous protests with the city mayor, the chief of police, several city council members, the governor of my home state, as well as with the United States Supreme Court through my worthless, take-the-money-&-run attorney, Claptrap Valentino. As of today, nothing back. But don't worry about me. All hope's not lost. I'm okay, making the best of a horrific situation by writing every day, getting in shape through rigorous exercise, and mastering the gaggle and savoir faire of Scarlett O'Hara and Rhett Butler by channeling from within. The usual.

I hope you enjoy the new novella. It's a real sidewinder. Here's an excerpt. If you like it, pass it on. Recommend it to your other erudite reader-pals and crypto, pseudo-intellectual, bibliophile buddies … one big, perplexedly quasi happy-to-unhappy family … little more than a bunch of misfits and misanthropes fooling ourselves into believing we belong and fit in. Ha! Maybe someday the rest of mankind can catch up with the likes of us. Until then, soak up the enchantment, *The Icicle's* magic, the syndicate folklore and criminal abstract wherewithal of yours truly, Eddie *The Icicle* Jablonski, crime writer extraordinaire and pulp fiction mahatma. I may be one old man by today's count, but still, everybody's favorite contemporary tough guy.

All the best, EJ.

Postscript & Synopsis: This is one heck of a story about one not so lucky, young fellow made Destiny's fool at the hands of his own capricious and impetuous choice. Great sex with a hot babe, worse as damsel in distress, will do it to you every time. Take it from me, Eddie, the ladies' man, Jablonski. Read away. Be my guest. Never a better story to captivate any feisty, unwavering, and perspicacious reader.

Styx and Stones

It was a Tuesday, but maybe it was Wednesday. I should remember since I was the one being incarcerated, wearing leg irons, handcuffs, and an orange jumpsuit. You would think I would remember which day it was, but honestly, it was all a big, open-faced blur. A deputy either side of me, another behind me, and two uniformed guys out front leading the way down the long corridor through a set of double doors and then a free elevator ride upstairs. Sure, it was all about me, celebrity-like, sort of, in procession as if at the outset of my own Christmas parade? But hardly. I was inmate 439867. Second floor. Fourth cell on the left, top bunk.

I had never been in prison. At least not up until now. Pointedly …me … from my own vantage … I was … how do I say this simply enough without implicating myself in such a way as to come off as haughty and cocksure, supercilious and vain without any appreciable measure of reproach or guilt in this minuscule and introductory narrative? … but in all honesty, I was too aloof. Too crafty. Too smart. Invisible for the most part and as much as possible. No footprints. No timeline. No tracks. No loose ends. No ties that bind. Untrodden. Untraceable. Things that bedraggle lesser men. At least that's what I liked to think. That's what I told myself as well. In addition, that's what I purported in private for those gullible, loyal, fastidious, or disinterested enough to buy in. I should have been a professional smart ass, not a wise guy, or maybe a wise-ass wise guy. And believe me, there's a difference. Trouble is, it doesn't pay well or well enough or at all. Prison … serving time … is truly a needless exercise in futility in my opinion. Quite the misstep to put it mildly. They, those very same incarcerated jailbirds, dullards one and all, simply hadn't thought it through. Again … seemly and unnecessary I said to myself at the time. But now look who's talking… here I am. For starters …

From the beginning, we were an *item*. She said so herself. I simply repeated her claim. We really were an *item,* at least that's what I heard myself say above my own voice from over in my corner of the bed. I'd said it out loud so vainly and promiscuously it was like a lone wolf's cry in some deep, cavernous hollow or a bugler's call to arms from a mountaintop awaiting the indented echo, note for note, note for note, note for note in a Swiss fade. She was at the foot of the bed naked and smiling, voluptuous and Rubenesque enough. Me, I was one sexy devil because she said so, and I believed her every word.

Not to sound silly and jejune, naïve or compliant, but for me, it still spills over into servile frothiness just to hear myself quoting her. She was smitten, she said. I was smitten and agreed with her wholeheartedly. Together we were smitten while lasciviously sweltering in the company of one another morning, noon, and night. Obsessively brash, passionately bold, lifegiving exchanges between the two of us, punctuated by silly bits of folderol here, and codswallop there, bordering on twofold, twin mollycoddling. *Folderol,* that was hers; *codswallop* was mine. We both agreed on *mollycoddling* because we both agreed on everything. Foremost, we were unfledged intellectuals. Furthermore, unfledged intellectual sex fiends pretending to be unfledged intellectuals, too smart for the rest of the world, too engrossed in one another to know the difference, and too big for our own britches. That little aside ... *too big for our own britches* ... was *our* little private joke, a buck-naked knee slapper for the ages. Puerile banter (both of us just loved the phrase), seamless swearing (wily and as often alliterative just for sport), name-calling (infantile I admit), spitting (melon seeds mostly from the breakfast table at midnight), cursing (again familial and rambunctious), choking on one frenzied onomatopoeia after another just to satisfy the urge, and our endless practical jokes of any and all description, dirty jokes, both randy and raunchy, rough housing, everything except pillow and food fights, but don't think we hadn't sported the notion, at least suggestively if even just for fun and our own entertainment. We had it all, she exclaimed lovingly. The two of us, we had it all. I agreed again out loud and recited those very same words to myself like lyrics to an old, familiar childhood ditty throughout the day. How wonderful it was to be so clever and so in love.

Happiness is enchantment, the carrot, the stick, the string from which it dangles, devoured and swallowed whole with but a brief belch and a touch of stunted, wholesome flatulence in the next exhale on the way to nowhere in particular at the end of another busy day.

Look at me … here I go again. Just another one of her marvelously refreshing and brilliantly shimmering quotes to kick off another one of our days together. She was so easy to love, so easy indeed inside a sigh and respite, respire, respite, and sigh. Love is breath, love is air, love is a steamy breath of salty sexual fresh air for certain. We were one. Happenstance had proven itself best friend and fateful fulfillment in a mated pair. Who's to say it wasn't heaven sent. I still pine in remembrance of that time together. The winsome look of Cleopatra, the tenacious guile and savagery of Caesar and Antony combined, she prevailed. Her *ex's* … she noted in a tiny, seductive confession while licking longways my cheek stubble, nibbling away at the plump curvature of my lower lip, suckling my adjacent earlobe in a distinct if not suggestively faint, ever so soft whisper with my face now buried and cradled in her cleavage … *Left them one and all,* she said, *each and every one,* she continued, *in a lurch like loose hay in a manger's corner loft.*

But, craftily, I told myself, *I'm different.*

So, raise the curtain. Let the players play, the actors act, and a broader excitement ensue. Next up, it was: How we met! As played out in Act one. Scene 1 of *Partners in Crime.* By none other than yours truly, Mister Masters of Fine Arts.

Gale force winds and snowing ducks. Later that week … when the temperature spiked, the rains hit … raining sideways into September, someone said. But it was only May by a day and a half.

Bad weather, you asked?

I'll say, said I.

I drove straight where the road forked only to slow to a crawl to avoid the figure of a pedestrian in front of me on the righthand side of the street.

She looked at me and said, "Going my way?"

I took one second look at her and said, "For you, I'll change direction." So, I did.

She folded her umbrella and hopped into the front seat of my collector's '67 Volvo convertible. And, yes, of course, the top was up, and we were quickly off to our first stop along the way.

She had strudel, tea with honey and lemon, a glass of chardonnay back. I ordered spaghetti, the Bolognese with meatballs, red wine to look sophisticated and vino-literate … and cover the wantonly, wistfully venereal side of myself. *Double-sided, three-dimensional seduction*, she called *our encounter* out of nowhere. It seemed a most feminine to manly advance at the time, and somehow a show, a cast, and display of my own virility I thought while twirling the pasta around my fork like I was a culinary master and part Italian perhaps as well, but in all actuality was neither. Little did she know, less didn't seem to care. We were still strangers of fortuity and foul weather and a suggestion of horny in the midst of overlying steamy, sweltering, titillation and mutual attraction.

A few days later and my, my, my how things had changed. I had transformed myself from an electrified sexual participant to an insinuated, willing fiancée to the full-fledged, snookered holdup bandit all at once and in the name of love at her insistence. Never once did I ever think to myself that this was so unlike me because apparently it wasn't. I nodded and smiled with gleeful willfulness as she contrived our (my) next move while mangling my future.

As luck would have it and for the love of God, not to mention money and one scintillatingly hot, hot woman, I couldn't rob a Seven Eleven in a one-horse town on the outskirts of nowhere and make a clean getaway. It simply wasn't in the cards. It's what the little voice inside my head said to me later on. But, of course, this after it was much too late, and now I'm practicing my bedside manner fettered with another con in a soulless and distant correctional facility on the outskirts of forever.

Details of the heist were as follows.

I arrive. Case the joint. The convenience store is all lit up. A landscape view and side to side survey and back tells me ... There's not one car in the parking lot, not one car at the eight, discounted-priced (ten cents less a gallon! I almost filled up) fuel pumps, not one car parked in front of the plate glass front door or the broad, clear, plate glass windows left to right. Add to that, nobody is parked in either of the blue tinted, clearly marked wheelchair logoed, handicapped spots right and left of the front entrance. Plus, that same front entrance, it's a wide, swinging single door (for an extra-easy getaway) with a **"hello"**- customer's-in-the-house chime or a bell or a buzzer, whatever, take your pick. Once again, ripe for the picking. Neon signs hawking a variety of beers and snack treats, posters of burgers and the house specialty chile slaw dogs to-order-to-go and an assortment of lottery tickets and confectionary tryouts and try on-s. Cash is written all over this place, right here, where cash is king, credit cards secondary and frowned upon, so it's just me and the cashier as an open ticket to *theft* strikes it rich. *Theft*, that's me. *Theft's* delight ... that's this place. Prime for the picking.

I walk in, move to the back (villain's go-to first maneuver always), pull on the restroom door handle (empty), then move back around to the counter like I'm getting ready to order Slim Jim's or cigarettes or a quick-pick, trifecta double-down, double-or-nothing lotto Powerball printout winner, but instead I lower my wraparound sunglasses (broad banded, thick, in an indecipherable garish tint) and tell the cashier ... the pipe-cleaner-skinny cashier woman fast approaching sixty ... I tell her coolly, "Now, you be a good girl, and you won't get hurt. Open the cash drawer and place all the bills on the counter ... right here so I can see them. In a nice, neat stack. The ones with the unbroken seal are best, but I want the loose bills and rolled coins, as well. Like I said, you be a good girl, and you won't get hurt."

I disported my freshly drawn semi-automatic, nine-millimeter pistol from my vest pocket insert and held it next to my cheek as I grinned. Gangster-like.

Oddly, the woman behind the counter looked at me straightaway somehow like I was *a sight for sore eyes*. And I thought in that same flash, *a sight for sore eyes? What? A sight for sore eyes?* The thought repeated itself. Yes. That's right, that's what her look said … it spoke volumes, said my criminal detective alert-meter monitor, but somehow it didn't fully register … that's the look the pipe-cleaner-skinny little woman cashier fast approaching sixty gave me.

I thought … How odd? This is a stickup and she's looking at me like what? … like she knows me? … or like she's happy to see me? … or she can't believe it's me? … once again, like I (me, a complete and total stranger-robber-bandit with a loaded gun in my hand that's pointed at her) I'm *a sight for her sore eyes?* … like she's been waiting all this time for me to come around and stop by so she could pass along a big, old howdy doody from the good old days now duly and dearly departed? It just simply didn't add up … I thought this repeatedly in a hovering nano split with a perplexed-to-discomposed-to-fidgety smile changing as it morphed across my face like colors in time lapse. Until and when …

The trap door beneath me opened up so fast and furiously that I was swallowed whole in the superimposed wing-beat of a ruby-throated hummingbird. The hole, it seemed, wasn't that big or that deep, but I was flat on my back and now looking up at the pipe-cleaner-skinny, little cashier woman, the same one fast approaching sixty but who was now showing not only her age but her own true, old-school cashier craftiness and ring-it-up toughness, looking back down at me … the holdup king … empty-handed because I'd landed on my pistol with the small of my back. And while looking down at me, the cashier, she was smiling and chuckling and grinning

… grinning some more and smiling and chuckling ever wider and wider every second.

"Well, it works," she said satisfactorily of the trap door. "Works really good," she said approvingly aloud. "You're our first catch as well as *Catch of the Day*." Then she (just her face) disappeared as she closed and sealed the trap door cover with a thud.

In an attenuated muffle I was sure I heard her say, "Shoot your way out of there, Baby Face Nelson. And for your information, them bullets of yours will ricochet off half inch plate steel. Best of luck, Sundance. And thanks for stopping by to shop with us."

I was alone and in the dark.

The sheriff's face was the next thing I remember seeing. That and the end of the barrel of his Remington twelve-gauge, pump-action shotgun pointed indiscriminately into the trap door hole at the front of my face. For your information, thirty to forty minutes of pure, dark-side of the moon black and lightlessness … it takes a minute for your eyes to adjust again to daylight, or more specifically the overhead store-fluorescents burning down upon the back of my retinal cavity both left and right eye socket alike. More like the flagellant crack of a whip in a full-frontal assault across one's visual acuity and by any measure, cacophonously blinding. Disconcerting, too, to say the least.

Sheriff *Come and get it!* To townsfolk … *Waring thin as in his patience is* … Sheriff Waring McCain. Fourth cousin to Senator Hanoi Hilton John, and don't you forget it because he wouldn't let you. Sheriff McCain started out by saying …

"Once I drop this step ladder into the hole, I'm going to count to three, and you drop that peashooter you were carrying in here earlier right where you're laying now, then get your ass off the floor of that dungeon, put your hands on top of your head, and put one foot onto the first step of the ladder, then the next foot on the second step and so forth until you've cleared the opening.

And here's the most important part of your instruction." Sherriff Waring looks back over his shoulder holding the shotgun firmly on the target (my face). He calls out back over that same shoulder from his crouch, the unsupported shooting position, saying, "You say his name's Baby Face, Juanita?"

Juanita (or J Girl), she yells back to the sheriff, "That's just what I named him. Don't know who he is or what his real name is and don't care. Just want him out of here and down the road and into your jailhouse." Juanita adds, "Answers to Sundance as well. You're welcome to try that. Whatever gets best results. He ain't going nowhere. 's down there in the hole with the leftover rutabaga, two sacks of dry beans, some parsnip, and a crate of eggplant, all cool and dark."

"Got it, J girl," said Sheriff McCain. "So, Baby Face Nelson … Sundance, I'm only going to say this once, so listen up. You with me? (Sheriff verifies the nod, my affirmative from down inside the trap) … When you come up out of that hole, you simply slide belly down, snake-like, and slither onto the floor in front of the counter and stay there. So, next, you'll put your hands behind your back cause I'm going to cuff you. That or I blow your head clean off for resisting arrest, armed robbery, attempted first degree murder … the list goes on and on and on. It's just my word versus yours because remember you'll be dead without any kind of big, happy, gloating family of well-wishers or commiserators cause you blew the heist. Do you read me, Baby Face … Sundance?"

I nodded from inside the hole, my eyesight a flagitious blur.

"I read you," I muttered softly, villain-less, the suddenly impossible recidivist, crime-cured, captured, cooperative, demi-reformed, and hapless troubadour of trouble. Never in my short life had I answered to either *Baby Face* or *Baby Face Nelson* much less *Sundance*. Humiliating as it was, I had no choice. *Humiliation steams both the wrinkle and the starch right out of choice. It's in the* manual I've yet but soon to write: **Crime Doesn't Pay, Volume 1**. You can look it up real soon. Hark, alas … prison calls. I am stuck and up to my neck in a vat of void. Hark and alas once more … With emotional issues as well.

Right off, Sheriff wanted to know if I was alone? … who put me up to this? Said specifically, "Boy, who put you up to this?" Just like that.

Then, Sheriff Waring, he said, "You flying solo?" and continued without a breath or a break saying, "Are there more of you out there hiding in the bushes or waiting down the road a piece?"

Told him I was alone. Said, "This time." But it was a slip up, a thoughtless slip and slip of the tongue, the … *this time*. As if I hadn't already opened enough of Pandora's box … whoever she is or was … and like I know her, too? And for God's sake, don't bring up the name to Sheriff Waring. He'll be off on another tear is all I thought after saying it to myself.

"*This time*?" he said incredulously. "So, what other times have there been, Baby Boy?" He stared at me with a pair of cold, cold eyes with two steely double, buckshot barrels to back it up. "Huh," he said. "Talk," was all he said next as he waggled (and a perverse, intrusive, and intimidating waggle it was) the shotgun barrel in the open light down and into the area where I now lay.

"Oh, nothing much," I said repentantly, handcuffed face to the floor. I could feel my breath ricocheting off the dirty linoleum back into my face. The whole thing was putrid. I, somehow, with all those countless hours and hours in ivy-wrapped academia and stone-monuments-their-libraries, thought of myself as much too smart, elite, and refined for such a petty and perverse predicament, the one at hand, but here I was.

Feeling more and more uncomfortable by the second, Sheriff finally rolled me over on my back on top of my two hands and the brand-new pair of handcuffs attached.

"Painful," is what I said.

"Painful?" Sheriff repeated. "What are you getting at, Boy?"

"The handcuffs … they're painful underneath my butt," I said.

"Is Baby Boy a *widdle* uncomfortable?" whined Sheriff sarcastically. "Poor, poor Baby Face. So sad, Mister nine-millimeter. Hear that J Girl? His ass hurts because of the handcuffs. Why don't you call the humane society, Juanita?"

"Sounds like a plan, Sheriff," said Juanita in a more elaborately sarcastic shout out. "I'll get right on it." She stood pat with her smirk, arms crossed and never flinched.

Sheriff rolled me back over on my belly like he was carving the other side of a holiday turkey. A flop and a tuck with a second wrenching flip-over as punitive good measure. It wasn't great but better, less painful, not comfortable but less annoying and cramping down my right-side sternum to clavicle toward my left and right hamstrings.

"Explain yourself, Sunny Shades," he said. Now, all of a sudden, I'm *Sunny Shades*. What gives?

It all came back to me as sheriff finished his question. I readjusted my crouch or squat and would have gently lifted the wraparound dark glasses from my face (like a cool guy) making the view from the hole a bit more seeable but I couldn't, not with the handcuffs on and my hands behind my back. Having opened just about enough and as much of the proverbial can of worms as I could handle in one day, I fell silent and politely added in a fixed and premeditated voice, "I'd like to speak with my attorney."

From Baby Face to Sundance and now Boy and Baby Boy to finally Sunny Shades. But somehow, I liked it. It was a pitiful improvement from where I had started but an improvement nonetheless. For some reason, it seemed more personable and gender friendly or gender appropriate … a prep, perhaps, I thought rapidly … for jail time. Oh, sweet Jesus … I rethought my previous thought. Perhaps and all this for some other more appropriately defined role that I, at this inopportune moment, refused to give credence.

"Attorney?" said Sheriff. "Attorney?" said Sheriff just like he'd said it the first time, this as if after hearing the punch line of an incredibly funny joke, just before the belly laugh and the engendered snort. "You hear that, Juanita? Says he wants his attorney. Golly gee, and what's next? Your preacher?" Sheriff Waring laughed. What a punch line! Sheriff, J Girl, and yours truly … All three of us thought in different ways. "You ain't got no attorney, Boy. You ain't got two nickels to rub together much less an attorney." Sheriff laughed again louder than the first time out loud. A big belly laugh with a guffaw on the end of it like the puff of steam at the end of a train whistle. "We'll let you talk to Sleepy Joe Treadwell down at the People's Court once we get you printed, plain-clothed in orange, and assigned your new roommate. Hasn't won a case in over two decades. Right up your alley, Sundance."

J Girl, too. I could hear her in the backdrop, J Girl aka Juanita, laughing in sniffles and snorts. Hers with a devilish hiss on the tail end and all its own. She seemed the one most amused at this point … and of course at me, Baby Face, the holdup bandit … or, me, Sundance, pistolero … or Me, Baby-Boy, Sheriff's boy-toy … all three. I started it. J Girl aka Juanita, she finished it. So, here we were, all three of us together like two's company, three's a crowd. It was funny all right I guess … if I hadn't been the handcuffed and hobbled brunt and butt of all the jokes.

Appendage: I wasn't taught this (or they didn't teach this) in graduate school. I had no training for or in felonious predicament management. Felony do-overs were not in the Masters of Fine Art curriculum U of P. What would Picasso do? (Never discussed.) Rembrandt's masterpiece 911? (Never came up.) Nor was there a course entitled lamebrain mis-encounters of the wrong kind … nowhere that I could recall. I was on my own, and armed only to some extent with a vibrant and determined and creative lexicon that I was fairly sure was enough to baffle the pope and senior foreign peace treaty negotiators at the tail end of a bloody and protracted war or intended and forced genocide … I would have to see my way through this mess.

Had drawn a picture once … a painting … second semester of grad school … a complete mural … 4 x 6 … Warhol-esque … a standup … a single, lone Slim Jim in the wrapper … (no, not the Campbell's Soup can, but a borrowed likeness in kind or genre) … subliminal, serendipitous you might say, inspiration (sort of I guess) for the stickup, the robbery-gone-South or awry, you might say. Oh, my. Oh, well. Better days to come, I hope. Not looking too promising from here at present.

She said she would marry me, but only if I came back and asked proper-like and proposed to her with a ring, a big, shiny new one, a catalog diamond, Tiffany's, already picked out like every newly engaged girl should have and had the right to have. That's the way she described it. Last Friday, I didn't have the money or a job or even the pretense of a formal application landing me a job, the one I told her I was going to land or was about to land is the way I put it. She bought in. But I had nothing except student loans (a payment coming due) and next month's rent past due four days from next Saturday so call it Monday morning when the bank opened. If you have no money and you have no job and your girlfriend, my fiancée she called herself, is luffing in my wind-lessness over my unplanned, overwrought anxiety and fervent sex drive which leads to even greater and more meaninglessness than before, you become desperate, delusional, guilt-ridden, depressed, and then deranged. So, I was all of those things when I pulled into the country-stop-shop all lit up with Christmas type lights in late July thinking I could solve most of my short-term problems with a quick, flagrantly harmless bluff of a burglary out here in the middle of nowhere.

Wrong.

Such was my own open personal can of worms. Self-inflicted, tiresome, counterproductive, and self-defeating. Bull shit is bull shit and always easily identifiable before too much time has passed, I always say, travelling and abiding on an incalculable vector all its own no matter how easily tracked, traced, or spotted, burning up like would-be meteorites on its own fumes. It's bull shit.

A can of worms … open, distracting, dreadful, and smelly.

As in love, as in lust, the incalculable libido, it could only, would only allow me or let me fall into the frothy side of my own homemade irrationality. The singular sense that confiscates morality and high-mindedness and decency, some sort of social identity as querulous as it may be. Horney, the proletariat catchall, to boot, the cherubic nomenclature, permissive and vulgar simultaneously yet universally accepted, saying it's okay. Now … so that's what made me do it and started my oblivious spiral into J Girl's stop and shop homemade dungeon, the hole, her stickup trap.

My new love, the new, short term fiancée, she'd made herself available with malice aforethought. No question about it now. But how was I to know? I should have known better you'd think, but then again, I (this same person) am handcuffed face down on the floor of a country-shop convenience store facing attempted robbery charges in a failed attempt at gathering proceeds for a wedding ring. Obviously, I am a slow learner.

Once… it was early on … very much in the beginning … in the mix of sex and sleep and coffee and more sex and post-sex laughter, taunt and tease … I had described her as *colorful*. In the following week in a dire, secretive moment in a muffle understated like I wasn't supposed to hear or shouldn't be listening, I heard another someone say she was *clever*, adding *anything but dull*. I was certain they were talking about her, my new lover, but it's hard to be positively sure I was standing so far away at the time. I can only assume. It sounded flattering, on her behalf, her square of the court, so I let it go or scored the point in her favor. Fifteen love. An ex-roommate called her something between an *angel in distress* and a *complete whack job*. My preservation antenna rose but retracted almost as quickly. We were too busy having sex, performing, testing stuff on one another, having sex, performing some more untried positions and laughing at the plight of others who weren't nearly as smitten with themselves as the two of us were with each other. *Boring* is what came to mind for both of us, and we said so with particular delight fondling all the way.

For the love of a good woman, I told myself. The later image, her image, *whack job*, that image surfaced often enough and still comes back to haunt me on a regular basis. Her sister, who had only spoken to over the phone that one time, said she was *dangerously* possessive to a fault, she said *love hurts*, whatever that meant and a cheeky line, said she was the only person she ever knew who, one minute, could stand inside the target-palette-turnstile wearing the skimpy siren's costume for the knife thrower's toss, spinning, turning, spinning, spinning and turning, then switch places and throw the *fucking* (her sister's word) knives herself without drawing a breath or missing a beat. All of it her sister's words precisely. I didn't understand at the time what her sister meant even though I nodded and smiled and pretended I did. As it were, I was about to find out.

A streetwalker less *the street*, said another previous acquaintance … it may have been an ex, can't recall … but I got that one after the fact and it was too late to back out or move away or turn back time. *Less the street* … with most people their alarm bell (more like a freaking siren) would engage and go off, sighting … Warning! Warning! Danger on the horizon and close at hand. But not with me.

Coitus entwines with the pretense of intimacy and good inten-tion all the while framing the self-possessed moment, a powerfully numbing and playful elixir yet flammable as fleshy kindling, gaseous as a cool, fresh breeze, and unstable and addictive as the bend of nitroglycerin to an explosive psyche. The orgasm is truly the devil's delight, his creation, his playful taunt and tease, taunt and tease over the frailty of both man and woman but more man, the thoughtless, mindless, testosterone-driven of the pair. Things will get better, the voice says. Things are getting better, the voice repeats. There is little or no proof, but this is what you think and are led to believe. Coitus, its numbing effect, is the painless and pleasurable conundrum unto itself and all its own and frightfully and entirely at the devil's whim. Mark it down. You heard it here first. Like gravity, a misleading contrivance for sure … it's only there to keep you grounded … no, no, not at all, it's there to draw you ever closer to your grave, the devil's palace.

Swearing. Spitting. Name-calling. More spitting, cursing, jokes, then practical jokes, followed by dirty jokes (randy and raunchy) combined with rough housing, everything except pillow and food fights. There were even drinking contest, imbibe till you thrive, (imbibe till you can't drive more like it) into the wee-wee hours one man, one woman may the best imbiber win. She was more often the one lone soul standing at pre-dawn than not. An amazing woman no matter or whatever the knock. She prevailed. Left them one and all in a lurch like loose hay in a corner loft.

You can do it, she said.

I can do what? I asked.

"A stickup, a holdup, a robbery … how about (call it) a lite-heist. Or, a negligible nip," she said. "Just for us, you and me," she finished. Somehow, I felt flattered to be included in the would-be crime.

At the time, at that very moment, I had my hand on her left breast, she salivated into my ear, cooing, while her hand went down my open trousers and into my crotch, my phallus, massaging and cooing, massaging and cooing, the entire time some more and calculating the short-term effect. I melted on her further pleasure.

"So?" she asked.

"So what?" I answered.

"Then you'll do it," she finished.

A week later. Maybe it was two.

So, here I am … on the floor, face down at the stop and shop convenience store with the honorable Sheriff Waring and his double aught professionally pointed at my bowed and pointy head. You've picked a fine time to leave me, Camille? … to leave me and squeal. Now my ordeal.

From out of nowhere, she'd said, "Martyrdom isn't your forte." She said it with such conviction and philosophical authenticity that I accepted it as unquestionable truth, Socratic thunder, and spark of light, never realizing or recognizing it as hyperbole standing elbow to elbow, arm in arm, with his best pal premonition. I didn't think of it as the future, my future either.

Okay, okay, oaky … so there were three other times. Not to mislead the listener-reader, okay, maybe four. On two of those occasions (the robberies), she went with me. Wait … wait, wait one more time. I'm doubling down and doubling back and rethinking the retracement. So, there were three other occasions. Each time … there were in fact a grand total of four; she was there for three of them; I remember now counting on four fingers of my five, one, two, three, four … she waited outside in the car, car running, kissed me with a flagellant and demonstrably long and wet tongue (like a farewell) for good measure, before I vanished into the abode, the small business enclave. *No worries* … there was that kiss and that moist, supple, curvy-curly tongue, that forget-me-not tease as inspiration toward the task at hand plus she was a fast driver, a lead foot, a switchback-two-lane-country-road Andretti. I'd ridden with her before in my own car seatbelt drawn and tightly fastened.

I went in unphased, like a pro, a veteran, the Clyde of Bonnie and yesteryear, nine millimeter in tow, walked to the back by the soda casements … standard … checked out the restrooms … everything cleared … check and check … and from there, things went as smoothly as planned … cashier one, two, and three laid the money … loose bills, bound bills, and rolled coins … on the counter, complied, lay on the floor as I had instructed, said nothing, demanded nothing though two asked for mercy, not a problem, and I left by the front door and the peel-and-squeal of my getaway gal laid down exiting the parking lot.

Easier than an ATM withdrawal.

She said that steering and grinning and showing her splendid cleavage like hood-mounted dual exhaust in the getaway, and away we'd go … we were off … back to the house for more freestyle sexual intercourse in fits and starts and full tilt, unabashed writhing with hollowed out emotion. It was levity … or had I meant levitation and said levity? Blue collar crime … intellectual sex. Whatever, we both agreed. Each time of the three times … or make it four just because, but who's counting … the money lay uncounted at the foot of the bed like a misplaced fuzzy teddy from her unexplained youth.

"*Passion* has no bounds," she said selectively. That same afternoon, her tits were in my face while she straddled and rode me like Roy's palomino in full gallop. "It's the highest and purest form of love and has no boundaries, my love," she continued. *The riding* I assumed she meant. Didn't ask. Seemed inappropriate and pointless at the time.

If *passion* has no bounds, then neither does stupidity … I could attest as I lay there on the linoleum face down bound and gagged.

"*Passion* no less," she continued (there was that word again) perplexedly, "is a visceral treatise with the devil, Beelzebub himself to stoke the limp spirit and everlasting confinement."

Whatever that meant, I bought in.

"*Passion* leads to untold riches," she said.

"*Passion* leads to fame," she said.

"*Passion* leads the way. Complacency follows and lags," she said.

"The future, our future, is so perforated with dazzlingly tranquil possibilities," she claimed in an unchallenged aside.

I think that's what she said? It was in a mix of her first phrase the second time in the third sentence of her or our conversation though she did most of the talking and which, looking back, were as much tutorials as shared feeling or logic. I think back … but not altogether how she said it … a convincing yet tour de force with the curves (shoulders to hips to waist) and determined destiny to back it up. Okay, so I was pusillanimously pussy whipped, and gutlessly sidetracked by inguinal delight and issues of the … Okay, okay, you get the drift and I admit it and am now paying the price.

Picture this. It was very early morning. Dawn but barely. We touched at first under the covers, a hand, a foot to the other's, then one of us kissed ever so slightly by chance or mistake, until then excitedly we went all the way. Fornicative frolic. Fornicative folly. Take your pick. One and the same. A smattering of both. Basking in one another while entwined. We'd invented sex. We'd discovered love. Her words precisely. I went along. Her speech was morning blur so I think that's what she said but only if my groggy memory serves me correctly.

I was no doubt smitten with her sensual and most often salacious savoir faire however small time it may have appeared to an outsider. Her vision and pale yet intoxicating voice delighted me. I was a follower, her follower, though her unconnected and leaderless path went nowhere. We were little more than a celestial entanglement. Indelicate, tantalizing, and risqué bedroom capers. A cartwheel of pleasure that could be known only to the two of us.

Chapter 2
Styx & Stones

**Love was, as it turned out, a lie. Love is in the air, she said …
well, it wasn't.**

A fortnight later, the real story of the real person surfaced from a short stack of love letters tied up in a bow that I discovered by error and happenstance looking for a crescent wrench under dim light in the sidebar of leftover tools inside her garage. *I shouldn't have* you might say, but I did. I untied the bow, opened the letters one by one and read them each one in order to conclusion.

Dear Camille, the letter began. *You were remiss in not disclosing the money you'd stolen. Pilfered is a nice way of putting it. You're quite partial to euphemisms so there you go. Chew on that one, skanky bitch. And to think I trusted you. Obviously, sexual positions position you for life; one in the same. You are a thief. Sexy, for sure, but a thief. Shame on you. The money was all I had. You knew that, and still you took it without a word, without asking, and left (like a thief) in the night. Should I find you, you'll pay. Pun intended. Get it? Get it? You'll pay dearly. I promise. Hope I locate you before the cuckold, your husband. Hugs and kisses and coitus betrayed. Your ex-lover, your former paramour, your **cuddly**, again your word I believe and quite the scam, signing off, Rowdy-Rowdy Rough & Ready Mix, ex-bondage boy, one sex-trader to another sex-traitor, your garden hose, lawn and pool boy.*

Postscript: So … Heard you've caught another sucker. Who's the new stiff? He'll learn the hard way. Double-triple entendre, whatever. Too clever for my own good. Case in point: I met you. But wait. What a disaster. Now haunted. So long. Penniless in Pawtucket. Pete.

In the short stack was another letter, a second missive, in a different, less legible handwriting which said:

Camille, you f'ing windbag. Obviously, sex and fidelity for you are unmatched, unflavored yin and yang, oil and water, and mezcal con gusano psychedelia. But we won't go there. I thought you said we were bonding, growing together, experienced now as one … something like that. I didn't record the quiet, private moments like you recorded my phone conversations from the other side of the bedroom door which allowed you to lift the stash before it made landfall. Wow. I underestimated you by a mile. Sleep tight, baby cakes (your love moniker I believe for me). One day soon, you could wind up dead. Does your husband know where you are? Just a thought. Hope he gets to you before I do. Divorce ain't pretty, but that's the least of your worries. Noxiously yours, Psycho Johnny Underworld.

The third letter unfolded effortlessly, neatly, like a Christmas decoration, and told another story, another grim and fantastical tale all its own.

The reservoir of life and lies, by our little vixen and enchantress of disrepute, Camille Longfellow, poet laureate of the paranormal. Always thought of yourself as a poet. I remember that. Well, here goes. Here's one just for you. Made it up all by myself seated on a trash heap taking misplaced inventory. Love singed. You're the reason.

If witches were lookers with a great set of tits and an ass to match, you'd be the smoking hot photo-picture insert in every fairy tale storybook on the shelf.

If bullshit was butter and butter bullshit, you'd be a barnyard full and a hundred-head herd and a half of Holsteins and a dairy rolled into one. Sorry to say and sadly so, I was burned, boiled, churned, flip-fried, and am now charred the other side of well done.

Here's another one just to let off a little more steam. There's a cauldron's kettle full ((worth)) of this kind of hot, steamy, misty shit built up inside after dealing with your redacted BS.

Dogs dig up bones, cut from skeletons and carry 'em around like stones. If witches commandeered trolley cars, you'd be one but cut a meaner, wider swath and prepare a stronger brew. Cats in a gunny sack have nothing on you, all whiny and antsy they scratch and they claw. Snakes eat field mice in a nibble and a gnaw. Too bad they all can't converge and scratch your eyes out, bitch.

Chickens 'll come home to roost, Cammy. You'll get yours someday. Unlike you, it won't be pretty. Bobby Big Stones Bulger ... Lover Extraordinaire to Hot Babes Everywhere!

The fourth missive was a brief note, barely a note at all it was so short, half of a scratch pad tear-off, from her husband. It was signed T squared. The *two* was properly placed above and alongside the capital T, just like that with a personal flair. The message read ...

When I find you ... and I will ... you're dead ... in addition to whoever you're screwing at the time. Still your husband however unfortunate for me.

Each piece of mail was properly stamped, dated, with return addresses, and forwarded to her old address at her previous address, then to the P.O. box she'd rented under an assumed alias, then back over to the street and zip code here after she'd clandestinely and capriciously moved in with me. The roommate thing seemed a bit quick, but the sex was really good. Great in fact. *How could I be so lucky* I asked myself face down staring at the convenience store linoleum skid marks and heel travel and all? *That's how,* my own inner voice echoed and echoed again and then repeated itself in mocking chatter.

From the front door of the country convenience shop came a voice. That same suddenly familiar voice said, "Okay, Sheriff, put down the shotgun and place your hands on top of your head." In the same movement, the person, masked and ballcapped, had pulled a pistol from her pouch and again, more frenetically yelled, "Now!" She danced up and down moving from side to side in criminal angst, a kind of foreboding if not West African tribal dance. (That's what she later called it. A *foreboding dance.* No mention of West Africa.

Just something I read into the lean and sway, to and fro. Who would have known?)

Sheriff slowly slipped his double barrel to his side and onto the floor and then placed both his hands above his shoulders.

"On top your head, I said," said the mystery person robber rescuer, female ... five eight, five nine ... one hundred twenty-five pounds, no more ... blue eyes behind the mauve Ray Bans ... hair color indistinguishable under the New York Yankees ball cap ... busty on sight and obvious even in the loose fitting sweat.

A month before ... Said she hated guns. The same chick, looked the other way at on-screen violence, blushed, grimaced nervously at the thought, liked to think of herself as a Quaker pacifist, an Anabaptist type, an early-on hippie, a hippie before her time with peace and free love sprinkled on her open mind like giddy lyrics from the same decade's happy songs. Again ... Hated violence ... it begets violence she quoted herself quoting someone else but it sounded more profound and dramatic and benevolently more feminine, heartfelt, and absolute when leaving out the other someone.

Just as suddenly, standing flatfooted at the front of the convenience store opening, she opened the chamber of the Smith and Wesson revolver, spun it three time to check her ammunition, twirled it back again to neutral and snap-slapped the gun to ready, all with the professionalism of the head marksmen at a wartime shooting gallery.

From the shop floor I stammered, "Where'd that come from?

"A previous life," she replied. "Channeling my *Tania*. Survival of the fittest. Long before the beads and patchouli. Now, get up and let's get out of here. And don't forget the money."

Sheriff went first. J girl next. Down the ladder into the trick pit. Camille and I took turns latching the security clamps in prep for our getaway. We were out the front door in nothing flat and a second's mote.

"Just in the nick of time," I said.

"I sensed distress. Backup has arrived. Downtown shopping. Meter'd run out. Needed quarters. You were nowhere to be found. Figured I'd look here to see how it was going." So, she claimed.

An hour earlier, her text had been sent to three different individual men, all former lovers, one her estranged husband who she'd been cheating on (in more ways than one) for years. It read:

Meet me to settle up. And no funny business. Stop and shop country convenience on Highway 23. Giant Slim Jim decal in the window; another out by the pump aisle. Can't miss it, and two and a half miles past Gruber's Feed and Seed on the right. Again, no tricky maneuvers, double-dealing, attempted payback, retribution, or mix of the aforementioned. Have cover. Lethal. Will employ if need be. Think before you do something incredibly stupid. This is business. Final deal made good.

Fifty-two minutes later out front of stop and shop country convenience on Highway 23. There they were. All three. (Bobby Big Stones Bulger got the text but couldn't make it in time. He was on the west coast, robbing a string of jewelry stores in different malls along with random ATMs. No RSVP either. Word was he'd have showed had he been close by. Forgiveness for his Cammy was always and forever in his heart, a poem he'd written but hadn't yet sent.)

Out front on self serv Pump Number One stood estranged husband T Squared.

Out front on Self serv Pump Number Three stood Psycho Johnny Underworld.

Out front. Self serv Pump Number Five stood Terence Flashpoint O'Shenanigan, the Irish Meltdown, the Irish Melting Point & Misgivings, the Irish Melting Pot. All filling up at the same time. *What were the chances?* I asked her standing there in disbelief. She didn't answer or hesitate. Motioned me to the left, said "Draw your weapon and cover me," just like that. I drew my weapon hesitantly and watched as she moved to the fueling station and pump number one.

"Hands up, Square Bear," she said looking at the man with a cold and protected stare.

"Camille?" is all he could muster.

"Hands up, Square, or you can die standing in that puddle of Big Gulp."

"Geez-a-reez," said the estranged husband. "Fancy meeting you here. Looking all over for you. Styx misses you. I miss you, too, Cammy Bear."

"Cut the crap, Square," she said. "You'd cut my throat given half the chance and a dull pocket knife. I've got a little spot picked out just for you. Now, move along inside."

Inside, Camille moved T Squared to the counter, tapped on the trap door, and shouted out, "One more coming down to join you. Two's company, three's a blast." She pointed for me to open the hatch, dropped the ladder, and her estranged climbed into the hole with Sheriff and J Girl looking up wistfully for a breath of fresh air. After I'd removed the ladder, Camille slammed the trap door shut and we were back outside.

Out front in the parking lot beside self serv pump number one was a golden Cadillac. Next to it was a tall, broad shouldered man wearing a visor and reading glasses holding the gasoline pump handle and watching the meter. He looked up a second time when he saw us emerge from the shop. The man stared hard from across the way like he was looking for something he'd lost or found something he was looking for. Camille's ex-husband (T Squared) was on self-serv pump number one when we hit the parking lot. Parked behind the golden Cadillac on pump number five was a silver-back Mercedes. A man stood alongside measuring the fuel and staring out vacantly into mid-air. That was Psycho Johnny Underworld on pump five. You can't make this shit up, but there we all were. Camille turned her ball cap around backwards, put the sun glasses back over her eyes (yes, the mauve pair by Ray Ban), but she heard the voice before I did because I'd never heard the dude's voice.

"Camille?" said her estranged husband T squared loudly. "Camille," he said it this time like he was calling his Doberman *Styx*. And, yes, the two had a Doberman. And, yes, his name was Styx. From the back seat, Styx barked. Arf, arf, arf. And, yes, Camille had given up Styx in the unannounced separation that I was just learning about here in the convenience store parking lot.

Psycho Johnny Underworld called out at about that time, "Camille? Is that you? What the hell, girl? You stalking me?" said Psycho Johnny.

Another caller from pump number three, "Camille, hot dish, baby mama, is that you?" It was Terrence Flashpoint O'Shenanigan, lovingly T Flash, his nestle-name, the nuzzle, my one and only, My-heart-My-king, a previous lover driving the rocked-out Lincoln town car with oversized tires and the subwoofer portfolio tweeting in the backdrop.

"My previous life … it's all here. Here and now," said Camille. "How could this be? From one rabbit hole to another."

"Let me make it up to you, Cammy sugar," T Squared coddled.

"There's not enough life left, you sidewinder," she replied.

Camille motioned with her pistol … in the hole … in the hole, you, too … in the hole ... hurry up, hurry up. One by one by one. T Squared, *T Flash*, and Psycho Johnny Underworld. They all climbed down the ladder as she motioned. "Now," she said. When each one had descended into the pit, they all looked up at her like monkeys suddenly prehensile tailless, contrite, deprived, impish, and pale.

Camille, the self-anointed inscrutable spellbinding and tantalizing vamp, then turned brazenly to me, gun in hand, and motioned to me … *in the hole.*

"Me?" I said.

You, she motioned. "And drop the gun on the floor, Mister Master of Fine Arts," she said audibly, plainly, hurtfully with apparent subterfuge and malice aforethought. So, I did.

"Of all the audacity," I protested.

"Spunk," she countered.

"Fiendishly in love is what you said," I said.

"Love, fiendishly or otherwise, is little more than a meaningless proper noun on its best day," she replied. "Nothing more. Sexual desire its clone and makeshift entendre. Get over it, Master of Fine Arts, and for my sake, get over yourself."

"Execrable and odious," I responded.

"Unorthodox and check," she replied.

"Malevolent, impudent, and spiteful," I retorted.

"Demur, tactless and checkmate," she countered.

"I expected more of you than this," I said. "Waking up to me was your aphrodisiac, your morning elixir, dawn's delight and early light … an ante meridiem anthem, your tonic, you said."

"I said a lot of stuff," she replied tossing her hair away from her face and smiling. "From my vantage point, it was much too cavalier, provocative, and completely uncalled for." She continued in a heartless voice saying, "Making up shit is half the fun. It's life. Van Gogh was a bipolar pissant and a cad. A latent homosexual. He destroyed himself for no apparent reason. Consider your options, Vincent Junior and junior varsity at best." She looked away, her gun held steady and sighed mercilessly with exasperation and disgust. She continued …

"But to finalize this country convenience store treatise right here amidst Slim Jim's and Nehi colas, corn chips and stale popcorn, here you go, Ronny Rembrandt, just for you," she paused to catch her breath and then said, "Love … It's the flip side of seduction … seduction's the A-side … the mercurial feministic counterclaim to sexuality and sex itself … the physio-mystical element of gender as it is little more than witchcraft, voodoo, fantasy, and enchantment entangled and intertwined ... The very thing that binds us all, dearie. Pussy is the three-dimensional supplement ... sacrosanct, paramount, as well as precious to the psyche, and it feels good. You should know that by now ... You're well past the age of consent. For those of us in the *know*, we call it bondage ... the fourth and fifth dimension ... Zen on afterburners in its purest form some claim ... psychological, physiological, and spiritual enslavement ... a paradigm to live by. And horny clowns like you (she did the head count with the length of her pistol-barrel, one, two, three, four), you fall for it every time."

She smiled, licked her luscious lips, licked those same luscious lips again, flicked her tongue, flicked lasciviously that same, bewitching tongue exactly the same way again and winked twice to top it all off ... to all four of the men standing there stranded inside the hole. (Sheriff Waring just watched, baffled.) Ah, those big, brown eyes suggestively flaunted her true flair as the siren she was and knew herself to be. Somehow the situation, it was tantalizingly delightful, and I was all in as I backed down the final step into the darkening trap.

"But this isn't the time or place to discuss what's past ... yesterday's headlines ... nor what might have been ... or *the where to-s* or the *what ifs* ... much less our perceived problems by one party or the other." She paused, looked into the den, and said, "Right gentlemen?" She motioned to me, *Mister Fine Arts* all of a sudden, and said, "Now, you ... get in the hole."

But, what? ... *Me?* ... *Wait* ... *Why me?* I thought on the next to the last rung of the ladder (her gangplank or mine?) descending into the hole. My left hand was all that remained above board. *How could she?* Looking back, looking up, I stammered, "But what about us?"

"You can discuss that with the rest of Tag Team Camille," she replied. "And while you're at it down there in the dark, you can all compare sizes. Let me know the winner, and maybe I'll reconsider, but I doubt it," she said in closing as she slammed shut the floor-door. So caustic and determined … and I was so certain we were so in love.

She was a sensual wisp, a foible personified, immensely and grotesquely entertained by the misfortune of others. Humankind the stage as her comedic laugh-along. The more vulnerable and sadder, pathetic and dystopian, the more pronounced the suffering and pain, the more she was at one with her superiority, an invincible superiority built on emaciated and quotable fantasy as well as razed and feeble daydreams and even grander illusions. A *moon sparrow*, she claimed in self-analysis, with its psychic vibe, she said once describing herself. Knowing the difference between right and wrong and having the wherewithal, the *chutzpa* (her word carefully selected) to look the other way makes all the difference. Ouch, I thought, when I first heard this the first time. But it was, like it or not, *her*. Flitting about here and there by day by night, lighting only long enough to snag her next catch, then fly off again.

"This fire breathing alchemist is out of here," were her final words as the six of us from inside the hole heard the door slam behind her. The overhead exit-entry bell at the front of the store was a dead giveaway and she was gone. "Exacerbated desire," she said walking out the front door. Freudian promiscuity, and a world all its own … best described.

Just then, it hit me like a ton of bricks. I was fiendishly in love with a fast talker ... very fast. Oh, my.

Moments later. Quiet. Dark. Dank. Six separate strangers sunk and subdued into their clumsy confines.

The pit was now crowded, standing room only, cramped and uncomfortable as she slid the trap door shut. Darkness ensued.

"Like a stone across the door of a tomb," said Terrence Flashpoint O'Shenanigan, the Irish Madman, Mad Dog. For what it was worth, Psycho had his lighter.

Stones of a man, said T Squared, her estranged husband.

Stones of two dudes, said Psycho Johnny Underworld. *Maybe three.*

We've been had, said Terrence Flashpoint, the Irish Madman, Mad Dog, whimpering a bit. *Had … a second time or more. Me, I'd given it my all, my best, and it still wasn't enough.*

Whimpering in the dark is so unbecoming, said J Girl like a voice from beyond. *Grow a pair, you three.*

And somehow wasn't it all worth it? said I. But not out loud. I was pressed up against J Girl who was elbowing me back to get out of the way and give her more room. It was cramped. Sheriff Waring stood alongside, none too happy to say the least. I was still in hot water.

Look in the back, she said. "No, the trunk. That's where he keeps his stash. It should be there." That was the word from her beguiled insider, another would-be seductress's prey, another Cammy sucker. In the narrative, her source was quite free flowing. Pertinent information all round. Diamonds. Where he kept them. How many. Street value, etc. "Cleavage works wonders. Libertine, I am," said Camille. "Nothing more and nothing less. Take it or leave it. A birthright and positively proud of it. Don't forget *moon sparrow.*"

The uncut stones, the diamonds were in the backseat of T Squared's Caddy with Styx the Doberman. Camille opened the door, snuzzled with Styx, grabbed the bag of diamonds along with the dog, and hopped into the front seat of Matchstick's 300L. Matchstick McCaw, her latest, newest accomplice, her latest, newest paramour, explosives expert, car thief, jewel thief, mob wannabe, but little more with a rap sheet a mile long. The two kissed with grandiloquent and familiar and ulterior intimacy, held the other's face with both hands as further proof, clasped in wanton, sexual simulation, brushed back the hair of the other, smiled indulgently into the face of the other, turned away, and sped off at top speed.

This could be a scene from a great Hollywood movie, he said.

Or, a not-so-great scene from a not-so-great Hollywood movie, she added. Matchstick only grinned. She was always right, he told himself in hypnotic agreement. The gold star filling in his front tooth sparkled beneath the sunlight overhead.

The slow blow fuze detonated sixty seconds after her getaway car left the stop and shop convenience store parking lot just as planned. Five cars, a motorcycle, eight gas pumps and the front facade of the store blown away inside emblematic, expressive, and mind-scorching flames and billowing black smoke. Slim Jim banners were heat-shredded and incinerated at the same time, blowup ads and posterboards one and all.

Years later.

Other men are fooled by attractive women ... sultry women ... attractive, sultry, and intelligent women, passionately disingenuous, artful and alive ... but not me.

And to think I, Mister Master of Fine Arts, actually told myself that time after time, night after night in that same recurring dream here from the same tiny, cramped top bunk of this, my same tiny, cold, cramped prison cell. The voice was so earnest and forthright and lucid, I still almost want to believe it to this very day.

But what the hey. Gotta go. The early morning wake up-mess hall bell just rang. Steamy, hot chow, a tin cup of black coffee, then off to stamping plates for eight hours on the dayshift prison factory assembly line ... it's been so long, so many years now that the three almost seem to go together … that along with team Cammy. That's what we call ourselves. Me, T Squared, Psycho Johnny Underworld, and Flashpoint the Irish Madman, Mad Dog, all of us seated and taking up space at table J and talking trash for a half hour or so before work detail … us with our plastic utensils and unbreakable serving trays … us, little Cammy-ites in *throwaway* … each and every one.

One day out of the blue, Matchstick showed up … this was some months later … looking all the worse for wear. Sitting down with team Cammy at table J, he explained. Said he'd have been better off if Sherriff Waring had picked him up that day back at the convenience store, the day of the explosion (his creation) … said she drove him like a plow mule for the next year and a half … fraud, theft, forgery, stealing, drugs, more theft, more fraud, contraband, more drugs, three other on-the-job explosion-detonations, even lifted a kid's bike in a quick getaway once in Fresno … left him (him, Matchstick, not the kid) stranded south of Albuquerque this side of Gallop along (Route) 66 the final time … then ratted him out to the cops and blamed the entire thing on him.

"*Cleavage*," said an expressionless Matchstick. "*Cleavage,*" he said it again, this time tonelessly. "Two life sentences and an add-on for me," Match explained spiritlessly, shamelessly yet seemingly on the verge of tears. "She flashes a little cleavage, that concupiscent smile of hers as tease, those wraparound, curvaceous legs fully exposed beneath that hot pink, silken mini-skirt she loved to sport just before the shit really hits the fan … you guys get it … the full body exposé … and the high heels … let's not forget those f'ing high heels, the foxy red, hooker pumps … then runs off scot-free with the arresting officer who she ditched for the judge, who she ditched for the two jurors before landing the old guy, the Kiwi, a septuagenarian and packaging tycoon … still prima donna enough although a shadow of his former self … but his wallet still packed a wallop. Libido'd ground to a halt, but his bank account more than made up the difference … then she goes straight. By all accounts is now the model citizen if you can believe that. I, on the other hand, will never see the light of day. So, tell me something I don't know. How about a good word from one of you for your new inmate buddy and old pal, the Match-made-in-heaven here," said a doleful and forlorn Matchstick McCaw.

Not a one of us at table J said a thing.

The End

Styx & Stones, A Novella, by Edek Jablonski

*From my new collection of short stories
entitled, 'A Little Short on Time'.
To all my reader fans. That's all for now. Hope you enjoyed it!*

CHAPTER 17

A Family Affair

From the Cold Case Files & Confessions of Richard 'The Ice Man' Kuklinski Entry #84. For over three decades, Richard Kuklinski served as a notorious contract killer for the East Coast Mafia. The real number of Kuklinski's victims is said to be somewhere between one and two hundred. Selected events herein are recorded, recreated, and transcribed by Edek Jablonski, a successful, retired author-crime writer as well as purported kinsman to 'The Ice Man' himself. Room 315. Voices from within. Bringing the dead to life one last time in a murder victim tell-all.

From the desk of Eddie 'The Icicle' Jablonski. The next chapter as interpolative exposé. The victim's narrative as it might have been told.

Sitting at his desk, Eddie wrote:

I knew he would come for me. Eddie said he would. If only in passing, I got the message loud and clear, and he said nothing. At the traffic light, he smiled. I didn't. I looked back at him quizzically and feigned disgust and disgruntlement … *what's your fucking problem?* Actually, I didn't say that because I didn't say anything, but if I had that's what I would've said. I didn't say *chump* either, but it was written all over my face, the word in capital letters and bold italics … **Chump**. Additionally, my look was supposed to incredulously convey … *How dare you?* … but I don't think it did. His smile, that fucking smirk on his face, said simply *you've pissed off everyone in the family including me, but mostly me.* Then Eddie just drove off into the light-change-to-green. He, or him, *this man,* let's call him, *this man* for the sake of narration and getting straight to the point would be coming for me … whatever that meant … so I could only assume *HE* was some kind of professional bad ass or something worse and would be gunning for me somewhere, somehow, sometime into the not-too-distant future, at some unknown, unannounced date and time. But that's all I was left with as I pressed down on the accelerator and followed the flow of traffic at that same crosswalk.

I wasn't particularly alarmed. And really not frightened in the least. I was over it fifty yards passed the intersection. My perplexed passenger girlfriend in tow, she didn't even ask for an explanation or the identity of the man talking (or insinuating) smack in the car one over to my left, and for her, that was a first.

A week later, I received this mysterious note, a ragtag, handwritten missive, inside the letter drop box at my front door. It read:

Respect is different than fear yet akin. Cousins, no doubt. Brothers, as often times for certain. However, there is no fear in respect. Whereas there is always a mountain of respect in fear. It goes with the territory. That territory is pure, unquantified danger in and of itself. Before this is over, you'll come to know the two (and the difference) firsthand. Unlike you, I solemnly believe in the slippery slope and hand of fate. Pip-pip.

So, I knew something might happen, or let's just say something could happen. I just didn't know when or what or who or that it would be Eddie's cousin. Before now, *The Ice Man* didn't ring a bell. None of it had any significance to me whatsoever. Why would I care? Why would I be scared? Had I known the answer at the end of the riddle, I would have left the country, certainly the county or the state just to sleep better and go about my daily routine without the anxiety, fear, and dread.

Jesus, Mary, & Joseph. As I learned later, Eddie's cousin, Richie, *The Ice Man*, it doesn't get any worse than that.

He, this guy cousin Richie, he pulled back the curtain and there he was. Voila. Olivier, but a much larger and darker version …Act 3, Scene 1 … what's more I'd never seen the play, let alone the smirk on this guy's face.

It was around nine thirty. He arrived at exactly nine thirty-one. The oversized clock over by the fireplace was aligned with his entry. Time stamped. You could say that. The back door was unlocked. (I always lock the back door.) But it was unlocked. The breeze playing with the drapes, like an unmanned sail between a luff and a light wind, there stood big Rich, Eddie's cousin Richie. He was even larger than I had imagined or thought that the person coming for me would be. He smiled, almost nodded. And that's what I'd heard in my private thoughts away from the whole thing. It was rumor but as of right now a substantiated rumor. Story had it in my head … When he arrived and he saw you and you saw him, he always smiled. Oh, yeah, said a clearer voice, he smiled alright just before he killed you. I suppose it was a friendlier vision and version of the devil himself entering pitch fork in hand, but, come on, that's not saying much. You somehow know you're done for, your goose is cooked, the timer's gone off, and your time is up, but there you are in your house, and there he is in your house with you grinning like he belongs there and you don't. You're in your own house … to repeat … he belongs and you don't … again, I'm repeating myself, but I'm sure you got it the second time. That's how off balanced and out of focus the whole thing was. Wow! What an unprotected and impotent and powerless feeling. Blanket-less, shirtless, shoeless, and bareboned in the coldest and wintriest of outdoor conditions … I'm freezing to death, but I've been told that's what fear, real fear, the death grip type of fear, feels like.

Again. I'm in my house.

Needlessly, I kept repeating that to myself in protest as an inclusion and a God given right like it was going to make a difference or make things better or solve my problem and make this whole thing go away, the man, the intruder disappears, the certainty of my own death vanishes into thin air. And like I said, you're standing there (you in this case is Me!) and there's Richie, cousin Rich, Eddie's cousin *The Ice Man just* standing there, too. For God's sake, it's my house. But I was silent and stupefied and catatonic. I *mean in my house* … and he's grinning … with that glint of gold three spaces off the front left tooth. This day he had his pistol raised ever so slightly, already drawn so of course I didn't have to ask why he was there standing in the doorway of my living room.

What, do you think I would have hung around if I thought *The Ice Man* was stopping by? This Grim Reaper in the flesh, real name Kuklinski, Richard Kuklinski, yeah, yeah, Eddie's cousin and all that, *The Ice Man*, okay, so I get it now, but nobody told me that earlier… that and that he does this for a living. Someone just kept saying Grim Reaper … Kuklinski... Ice Man this, and Grim Reaper that. Words or names printed on tiny slips of paper indiscriminately handpicked from a fish bowl. I didn't take it seriously. I had no idea. Sure, we're all going to die. I know that. I knew that then. No big deal. For me at my age in my current health, I had plenty of time on the calendar and plenty of money in the bank. The insurance company settlement had cleared and made me whole just like I'd planned. But now, it had all gone up in smoke. I'm staring lights out.

He'd stopped by in the fifth week, the fifth day after my wife mysteriously died. She drowned. Over by the rock quarry. In the mirky water just below the steep drop. It was too late at night to see everything that had happened. I left and came back the next morning and found her floating upside down, lifeless and bloated. Her feet and hands atop the water. Her face and head were indistinguishable, almost indecipherable even void like they were no longer attached. It was a bizarre sight and not at all what I thought I might find.

Paddled out in the family (my wife's) kayak, the one she'd bought for herself the time she'd decided to take up whitewater rafting or something nonsensical in the spur of the moment. I had no interest. She'd taken up a dozen or more of these pastimes, hobbies, a scrolled bucket list so long you needed a cash register printout roll to keep up. Homemade papyrus was on that same list as well. Save me. Retrieving her body was only the second time I'd been in the thing. *Wobbly* … someone hell bent on drowning … it's all I could think. Who in the world would want to do this for fun? I tossed the lifeline and snagged the back of her dress. Pulled her body closer to the small craft, and paddled back to the clearance on the bank over by our parked car. I couldn't help but breathe a sigh of relief in that no one saw me. I felt free at least for a guiltless to guilt-plagued moment. For the average murderer, your once in blue moon killer, guilt is such a nuisance.

Okay. Okay. So, I pushed her off the ledge, and she fell to her death. I hadn't said that until now. I know, it changes the dynamic of the story. Okay. I get it. I didn't think anyone would notice. Much less anyone would come for me.

A big man with a sizeable gun standing inside your home unannounced … the guilty man's truth serum, on the spot confessional 101, a quick trip down memory lane into due process rolled into a tailormade, home course cram session right before your very own eyes. Reality front and center, at attention.

Some of her family had died off. Her father. A half-brother. A cousin or two. Three distant cousins and one of her best girlfriends as well. I thought enough of them were now gone so her death wouldn't play out with such vengeful and premeditative force with revenge as the dominant and pressing narrative. I never saw it coming. The reaction, that is. Not to this point. I never thought her death would cause much of a stir. I should have made greater haste collecting the insurance money for sure, then, left town. A suspect … possibly. Who's to say? No harm, no foul. Truant perhaps, but out of sight out of mind for all intents and purposes. Let things cool down. Stretch out on a Caribbean beach. Bananas, palms, reticent surf, and sweet, tangy cocktails with pineapple slices and tiny bright colored, paper umbrellas. Chill.

But then out of nowhere, what's his name, Richie or *The Ice Man* or the Ice Machine or Tasty Freeze Rich, he arrived. No name tag. *The Ice Man* is all he said, or all I heard. Gruff. Gravelly voiced with a quiet demeanor it seemed. Got my attention even though at first, I wasn't intimidated or frightened. Puzzled more than anything. Thought he'd come to the wrong house, wrong address, got his message mixed up with one of the neighbors' stuff. They were always battling problems I never had and never wanted. Steered clear of them and the likes for the same reasons. Waved from a distance. Hello. Goodbye. Until next time. Later. But then again, here was this guy standing inside the doorway, now inside my living room, looking accomplished, professional, as if directed. No handshake, no greeting, no warning, no explanation for his presence much less his intrusion, just because and, regrettably, I knew the other side of *because* without asking.

There's always that split second when you say to yourself *the devil's in charge here. He's intervened.* And so it goes. Standing right where I was, I knew the devil was in charge. In the interim, all I could do is sit back and wait it out … then see if I survive the fireworks and come out on the other side.

The Ice Man. Said that's what people called him. Didn't say which people. Just people. I learned the hard way why.

My wife had had enough of me. I'd had enough of her. The feeling was mutual, more mutual than anything since our engagement. A shame to let all that money go to seed. That's what I thought and told my secret gal, my clandestine lover. Every good, wholesome, red blooded American guy deserves a mistress. It was my line, a private, quiet fact and statement of faith. I'd told myself this for a decade. I fed it to myself as a retort and simple truth like sugar water to bumble bees. Cockamamie or not, I thought it up, I sold it to myself, so I owned it because I thought it was witty and the younger woman proved it.

Some suspected as much. Others said they knew. Fingered the lovely young woman from a distance in a parking lot here and there and a shopping mall or two, the same woman I'd trailed, stalked, solicited, stalked and wooed some more, and courted, then bedded. She had no chance even from the beginning they all claimed. It was my own worst kept secret because she was a source of pride, a come-hither victory, and seductive, sprightly triumph. Look at me, I said. I've still got it. Even at my age. I am the man, her man, a man for all seasons, and a Bolt out of the blue for certain … wife excluded.

Frankly, I got rid of my wife before she got rid of me.

Sloughed … was my a one-word exposé to the younger woman mistress in my life.

Very dispassionate, she'd replied. Playing it close to the vest as usual, her specialty.

No, merciless, I'd responded to her. The displeasure cut deep.

Of course (not to mention the untempered untold) … this from a young woman, my soft, sensual, and sassy mistress, my seemingly better half, who didn't want the details to the missing person report … only the arrival date of the life insurance claim and her share in her bank account. The numbers were spelled out (*discompassionately* or otherwise) routing number, date, amount followed by the recipient's name, address, social, and other personal information. *Dispassionate* ... oh, please, spare me.

The wife was paying the bills, owned the house, both cars outright, two sets of car keys, I got one set for the older model Suburban, another property that she wouldn't list in both our names, so what the hey? At any time, for any reason, she could have left me and moved away to her other zip code, the majestic lakefront abode with the double bay boat house and handyman tractor-backhoe out in the garden shed. Never even hinted much less suggested I take over the other house ... excuse me ... *her* other house. No questions asked. No regrets. I would have been out of the way and out of her hair. But by my own calculation, one of us needed to cash in for a getaway. By my own additional calculation, she remained in the house and *in the marriage* exclusively just to *torment and torture me* and display her disdain on an hourly, daily basis for years on end. I said this to the man while he stood there in my living room while the curtains banked off the curl of their own tailored drape. I said it so maybe *he'd hear my side of the story* and then *maybe he'd understand* ... I said that, too ... *there're two sides to every story* ... I said it just like that in a raspy plea aimed at his common sense, a throw of decency, *man to man* (I mentioned that somewhere along in here) ... so then maybe he'd leave ... *you can go, you can leave, no questions asked, really* ... that's what I said to him like he was listening or paying attention... *no hard feelings, all's fair in love and war* ... I said that ... it came out spontaneously out of nowhere, cheesy-like, somehow from somewhere like I was quoting the one famous person he'd recognize, impress him just long enough so he'd change his mind ... and most importantly I'd be spared.

Ah, there's the rub. For certain. Turned out everyone paid the ultimate price when Eddie's cousin showed up.

I wasn't thinking very clearly in the first place. The dead, drowned wife. I'm faking sorrow, sorry, grief, and clandestinely mostly self-pity. Waiting on the next meeting with the police. Answering dumb questions from myself as practice in a living vortex of full-scale psychological pandemonium all the way around.

Then, here we are, all three of us, all three of us in the same room together, and all of us at the same time. And then there's this guy, this stranger standing there in the back foyer of my wife's lake cabin, her *fantaisie Chateau,* la grande maison ... she never let me forget *I am French fluent*, Je parle couramment en français. La carrière, the quarry, my dear, une carrière de calcaire, ma chère femme morte. Me in my boxer briefs, arms amorphously akimbo, and my lackadaisical, leftover midriff standing there like a gimpy bullfrog on morning blacktop. The girlfriend in her bra and panties had stalled and remained motionless with an indolent look of bewilderment and disbelief on her young face. Her puzzled visage was nearly the size of the luxury sports sedan I'd just bought her out of my wife's passbook savings account.

"Can I help you?" I said to the mystery man.

Yes. That is what I said. And, yes, it's the stupidest thing I've ever said in my entire adult life. *("Can I help you?")* I backed up two paces in my mind's eye and asked myself, *Self to yourself dude, did you just ask this complete stranger if you can help him? Have you lost your ever-loving mind?* The fucking guy, the stranger is standing in your lake house (my dead wife's lake house) in the back foyer beside the second freezer and the mounted deer hides and trophy antlers, and I ask a dumb-shit question like that like I'm locked in behind the customer service counter at Sears & Roebuck.

Mother Mary, Joseph, and baby Christ Jesus.

Get a grip. I thought it, but I didn't say anything. Instead, I waited on Rich, Ice Man Richie. The Ice Man finally spoke up. (Sort of.) In his free hand, he held up a photo of my dead wife then started slapping the inside of his palm with a jagged pipe. Hard at first, then harder.

It got my attention.

The girlfriend, the young gal with me standing there in her bra and panties with her hair a disheveled mess from too much dramatic sex in the lake cabin master bedroom on the California sized king bed, she sort of whimpered and caught herself and the blurt that she restrained since she, too, picked up on the gravity, the seriousness, the potential of death's come a-calling, which sounded like fear but neither of us (like idiots) wanted to let on that we were scared. I held out my hand in front of her, man-style, as if it would prevent what was coming or about to happen. It didn't.

Our sex, it was always dramatic if not romantic, for me at least. She claimed it was for her, too. More frothy and histrionic on her part than not. I don't know. Left well enough alone. She could replace me. Told me when I got out of hand and didn't comply, didn't get what she wanted, what she demanded ... the gifts, the cards, the bonbons, the negligees, the designer this and that, and access to my cash money machine, and the accounts which used to be the wife's.

If it ain't broke, don't try and fix it, my young girlfriend always said.

There is such a thing as predestination. I'm sure of it. It's always cast in such a negative light. I wanted so much to believe it wasn't so, but herein lies the proof.

This man, the ice man, he shot me in the groin first. The sex groin, my dick and one testicle felt it first, then he hit me twice with the jagged pipe across the head. I'd forgotten about the jagged pipe because my groin was still burning and now bleeding from the gunshot wound as I clutched the raw pain.

The man, then, shot the girl, the younger women, my mistress straight through the head the same as if you'd placed the slapstick phony arrow comedy bit side to side, then a second time right between the eyes. Literally.

She had such pretty eyes. He knew this. He knew what he was doing. He was a professional. It showed. Heartless. Cruel. Strike where it hurts the most. The accomplished mercenary. I noticed it even as I lay on the ground groveling and squirming for my own safety (fuck hers, she was dead laying there all lifeless and such, a nude breast, her tit had spilled from her see-through brassier on the way down) and one last chance. So far, so good. The marksmanship didn't fit or match at all, but it didn't matter. Not in the least. She crumpled in front of me and died before she hit the hardwood floor. Funny what you think of just before dying. I figured it would be just like this, just not in this way, not by this man, this big of a man, a big man this steely cold and unfeeling and uncaring and seemingly diabolical. But really … who am I to talk. I pushed my wife off a cliff, stepped back into the darkness, and walked away. Payback is payback, like it or not. I should've known better. Apparently, I didn't and didn't believe her brother. I didn't believe her mean old mother and her deceased father before his death and her sister when they all looked at me and the one said, we'll exact revenge for your wife's murder. We promise. They never said we promise, didn't have to, it was simply written in their collective visage from one set of eyes to the next to the next and across. I saw them all clearly now as I stared at his man glowering at me … with me on the floor writhing in pain and holding what was left of my crouch.

Death moves in shamelessly, mercilessly, sometimes silently as often with no commotion, no racket, not a peep or a squeak more the soft, deliberate closing of a solid door shutting away the interference, the elements and stark drafts. The seamless shift of a wanton breeze (wind) against a candle's flicker, till it's out, extinguished, and gone forever. How callous. How true. Just like death itself. Unfinished business, finally finished at last.

Cousin Rich stepped back over the young woman's body as if lost in thought to exact the rest of the plan.

Carrying a jagged pipe and snub-nosed pistol, derringer-like, derringer in size. Maybe it was. Didn't get to ask. Never came up. Didn't say, "Hey, Eddie, old buddy, old pal, what heat you packing, dude?" Didn't happen that way. Not at all. Maybe the pistol was, maybe it wasn't. We'll never know.

Just as the horse and jockey are one, the fiddle and fiddler, the killer is similarly and just as at one with the tools of his trade, killing. The missing, unfound weapon, the death in question, the mystic knell, the pretense and appearance of a mournful burial, it's superfluous, unimportant, little more than the rattle of a peppermill at the noon day meal or backyard barbeque. Murder, assassination, asphyxiation, stabbings, shootings, strangulation, detonation, all one in the same to the craftsman and his craft. I was content with my role, even fortified by my bit part in death's stage play.

Just my contention. There is a toll booth at death. The tokens free. Toll booth token to death. The devil sits inside the toll booth brutishly grinning, cackling, collecting the money. And he doesn't give change for fives, tens, twenties, or the like. You have no choice. You can't turn around. So, you pay up.

Chapter 18

The Garden's Eve

Evangelista La Dea Mosconi Morelli Spilotro. Or, Eve. The Garden's Eve. A relatively new admittee to the community, but by all accounts, an indomitable, take-charge type from day one. To most, just Eddie's girl. Third Floor. End of the hall on the right at The Garden of Eden, Retirement Village and Nursing Facility. Senior Living and Memory Care at its Finest.

An open, unfolded promissory note lay next to a small jar of assorted, sugar free jelly beans, all this beside her decoratively, multi-colored nation sack, a personal, sentimental article and pride-and-joy possession that rarely if ever left her side. The Snake Slayer derringer lay discreetly inside.

To the left on the same desk, two hardboiled, half-baked, exigent letters from her less than reputable attorney rested beside a bright red and gold notary's medallion stamp & guarantee. All this sat collectively next to a purple ink pad, a full-length yellow legal pad, and three unsigned Last Will & Testament documents stretched out for completion. All of the aforementioned stuff was inside Room 318, that and the craziest, most whimsical Senior scheme ever devised just four doors down the hall from syndicate author, resident-inpatient Edek Jablonski. Room 318 belonged to Eve. The Garden of Eden's Eve and the only Eve of import for all intents and purposes. Some like to think there's one in every town or say one in every facility, but this was the unabridged Eve, the real Eve, the real deal, the larger than life, fire-breathing, fire-eating, sword-swallowing, five-will-get-you-ten Eve. Evangelista La Dea Mosconi Morelli Spilotro at your service.

Now ... Have I made myself perfectly clear? That always came next. It was her go-to line. *Give credit where credit is due.* She would say that as well. Along with ... *never get the credit, always the blame.* Eve was quick to respond and even quicker with a quip. Far from shy and to the contrary, a shade or two the other side of bold and brazen. Subtle on occasion but why? *Life was not just for the living but in the living, so live it up.* Feel free to quote her. Be my guest. Still working it. A weathered but broad smile less the feathered boa, bouffant do, and no longer the sleek figure from back in the day. A West to Monroe to Mansfield cross with all her own, original teeth satirized by the recent, customized whitening and brightening by Doctor Toothpaste, a facility token. Eyes less glimmering but steady and watchful. A softer hand that still rested on her hip when for emphasis and drama needed *emphasis and drama*, production and theatre, lights, curtain, action, as well.

"As a law enforcement officer, I was so hot I made Angie Dickinson wish she were me!"

This was the Garden of Eden's Eve, the same Eve who'd had her eye on Eddie from day one along with the paper trail of this treasure trove of each and every Garden senior resident. On admittance she was heard to have said, "This is a layup." Of course, at the time, no one knew just what she meant, and she knew that and reminded herself of that almost daily. So, the process began.

Looking into her full-length mirror sideways (pause), back to the other side (pause) back to the other side and further pause,

Eve said to herself inside her own reflection, "I was the fire in the fireplace, the kindling, the coals, the flame, the heat. Men loved me.

I had legs clear up to here. Legs of an all-night saloon hall, cancan dancer. A Rockette centerpiece no less. Juliette Prowse, girl, you wish; she never had it so good. Eat your heart out. Shapely to the nines. Draped sinuously and just as sinuously mesmerizing and hypnotic to any man worth his salt and his own bucket of testosterone. The two together, that pair and a couple of deuces in a matchless game of straight poker were God's grace on the face of machismo and all mankind. In a room full of gorgeous men, short, fat, tall, slender, sensuous to muscular just so long as they were male, a girl didn't need *liberation* or a *ballot* not when you had a pair of legs and a face like mine. March all you want. Burn every brassiere. Panties, too. Placard yourself into tomorrow and next week. I was a true and unmixed marvel in the midst of unabashed manfulness. An hour glass figure that made time blush. Turned heads inside the beat of a stop watch. This in the day when a beautiful woman was meant to be pursued, admired, praised, and seduced by virility and money and power and handsome creatures one and all. Sex was for the sexual, the worthy, the deserving souls that borrowed their beauty and good looks for a time and made the most of it never apologizing for their encapsulated luck or splendid good fortune or the marvelously crafty DNA drama kit that afforded them this higher sensibility of self … the dragon of *do*.

Remember? There was Adam. Then, along came Eve. Evangelista La Dea Mosconi Morelli Spilotro. Me. I didn't need a snake, suture boy. I'm the same Eve that invented the crack and recoil in pussy-whipped and tempted Adam into multiple positions alongside every other man to follow. When I didn't get my way, I just assumed you were blind. *Feast your eyes on this chunk of hard change and hard charge. Red Rover, Red Rover …* that was my motto. Or at least one of them. I made them up to fit the occasion.

My feet, too. They matched the décor (me). Succulent, dainty, perfectly pointed, and appointed, you might say. Fit for a slipper princess no less. Rounded not tubular, fitted and extended, cuticles to die for, length and girth properly pronounced. What can I say? I'm an old woman now. But it was the way it was. And I was Eve!

"Love oughta treat me better than this."

"How many times did I hear that?" said Eve looking back into her reflection again.

"Or … *Love oughta treat me better than you do.*

That was the other one, the other line. But I wasn't in love with you Johnny Handcuffs, I would reply. Just diddling you until the curtain dropped, you were ensnared, I got off work, you were processed and sentenced, then I was away and back at work the next day to the next villain-suspect to capture and incarcerate. Men … hah … they're all so tenuous, pliable, and predictably overwhelmed. Never underestimate the power of pussy.

Unless you've had sex with three or four dozen capable (key word here) men, you can't call yourself a woman, a real woman, a woman by today's standards on today's terms. And for Pete's sake, when you're liberated, panties are so passé. And just for the record, Peter was something else … all three of them. I was a walking, talking Champs-Elysees … as well as a histrionically sexually-charged Arc De Triomphe! And voyeur on my own terms in my own time."

In her Garden mirror, Eve stood full frontal, puckered her lips, smoothed her eyebrows and continued.

"Femme is for fairies and farcical old fuddy-duddies," she said to herself front and center. "Fatale for psychosomatic psychopaths or limp-wristed, blue-lipped cowards on stretchers rolled out of some backroom, deep freeze storage inside an intangible and merciless crosstown city morgue. I was all woman and the hardcore estrogen infusion that pumps red blood cells to and through the libido of broad-backed men and back again full circle. High heels in a tell-all.

Never forget it because I won't, and I won't let you forget it either. Time, time, time is still on my side, and I have the photographs to prove it. No one will back me into a corner or drive me from my place. Cleopatra's throne became mine. Move over. I was the good golly to Miss Molly long before she'd heard her mamma call. It ain't bragging if you can do it, and I could."

Eve next to a lectern with a Bible tucked into the corner, she said lucidly: "Introduction. Exhibition. Presentation. Titillation. Seduction. Erection. Copulation. Conviction to Incarceration. In that order. You can quote me.' Tantra was foolproof and failsafe. Preternaturally knew shit they don't teach, can't teach, and won't teach at the police academy. Take it to the bank. I was the police academy and a tactical force rolled into the sumptuous embodiment of succulent transverse symmetry. Hear me out."

Eve picked up her phone from the dressing table. She poked the numbers and placed it at earshot under her diamond earring. On the hello on the other end, she said:

"Romeo, Romeo, wherefore art thou, Romeo." She continued, "It's me, Eve."

"I get that a lot," replied Romeo Nosferatu Mosconi.

"Pick your poison. Let me know the next step before you move." She waited for a response and signed off. "Okay." Then she placed the phone back in the exact same spot, same position along the dressing table, emery board in hand.

An hour later. Room 318.

"So, Mister McCormick, just sign here on the dotted line, and everything will be taken care of from here on out," said Eve. "Not to mention if you don't sign, you have no chance with me. You wanted to *do me,* if memory serves me correctly those were your very words."

Mister McCormick smiled at Eve then nodded. Those were his very words.

"Or else," said Romeo.

"You've met Romeo, Mister McCormick. Remember? He breaks legs. Remember? Have you ever had your leg broken, Mister McCormick?" asked Eve.

"Well, let me tell you," said Romeo without a pause. "It hurts. And I know. I've broken a dozen or more of them for different, uncooperative so and so-s, persons just like yourself, and you don't want to be next on my list. And at your age, it might not heal. My best advice is … sign the paperwork, nod, and keep your mouth shut. It will all come out in the wash, Capisce?" Romeo smiled, sort of.

Mister McCormick, very much perplexed, nodded and smiled (sort of, too) as he picked up the ballpoint pen and signed on the dotted line which was solid. "No broken legs for me," said Mister McCormick. Again, he smiled (sort of).

"Correct," said Eve. "No broken legs for you, Mister McCormick," repeated Eve. "You've been a very cooperative part-ner and that serves you well."

Mister McCormick, his two homes were now Eve's, her less than reputable attorney's, forty-five, forty-five split, with ten percent going to the ex-prizefighter now fistic strong-arm Romeo Nosferatu Mosconi.

"Who's up next?" asked Eve.

Romeo waved in *who's up next* (Mrs. Johnson) in an as friendly as possible mafioso gesture.

Mrs. Johnson filed in from the side door behind her walker with the pink honker.

"What's up?" asked Mrs. Johnson from behind her usual veil of vague.

Eve brushed her hair the way she did every morning as she looked at herself in the mirror. Long ways. Soft strokes. Hardy at times, gentle almost lovingly at others. Anymore, she hardly ever recognized herself as the woman she remembered herself to have been. Gone was the youth, the glow in her face, the lilt in her complexion, and the loft of her hair. It had disappeared like stillness in a rain storm, like starch and levity in a spring flower or seasonal limerick. She remembered it. The woman she was, it was still aglow in her mind's eye, but it had vanished from her face, its features and appealing contour. She had become, she thought alone, a blanket of plain, a pork barrel of unmixed paradigm, an ungainly sack of flower, and an unwieldy meal cart. Little more. It wasn't as sad as it was noted in that same mind's eye. Too late to mourn, she as often thought. Why bother? The day moves into night just as I have. It's what Eve felt most comfortable feeling. She told herself she could cover the demise with her cleverness though she knew full well no one does. Fate, as the old man, gets the last laugh in a sneeze or a yawn or a cackle or at the clap of his hand. Gone! You're done! It's life's final act, a magic act all its own. Lastly, the curtain falls.

God would forgive her. She knew this. Deep down she was certain of it. God would understand why she had been who she was, why she had been cross and nervous at times and vindictive and impatient and nearly vicious at others, and why she had been with so many, many men and so many, many bad men what's more. Robbers and thieves and cutthroats and renegades and unlicensed dealers and card sharks and flimflam artists and deadbeat poets who weren't deadbeats or poets at all but pretended to be just to be with her for one night or one week or however long it took to ingratiate themselves into the good graces of the lovely, inimitable Eve, Evangelista, Evangelista La Dea Mosconi Morelli Spilotro.

God, she reminded herself in closest confidence, He understood her, her moods, her dalliance, her motivation, her whim, her sight-unseen connivance, her delivery and dominance because God understood law enforcement, peacekeepers, catching and capturing bad guys. It was all part of the earthbound dirty game, her employment. God, of all people, would understand. She was certain of the fact, and so therefore God would overlook her judicious promiscuity. To God and to Eve both, she said to herself alone, it was little more than a speck of a tiny speck as the fly in her own ointment. That's all it was … in God's eyes. That's what Eve said to herself in moments of feel-good confession, forgiveness, and flashback. She told herself this same story (we all make excuses) knowing or hoping or praying that the repetitive jive turned into belief and solace, conviction and truth as well as a very, very special place in a more pleasant afterlife she hoped someday some way to experience.

Eve, in a random, flashback, her voice said, *So, you made love to a vagrant gentleman once. Okay, so maybe it was three times or maybe four, said the same voice. Who's counting?* responded Eve where in fact it was to void a sixty in a thirty-speeding ticket and then arrest him for soliciting a prostitute, larceny, money laundering, and bootlegging.

The devil's own. It was always lurking somewhere inside the shadows of her soul. She was first mate working just outside the devil's workshop.

Eve, she had thought long and hard on it. So what if heaven, the grand afterlife was little more than observational window on a passenger train car from here to there with little more than changing scenery, noiseless and unchallenging and non-confrontational filled with greenery and foliage then steel structures and abutments and banks and hairpin turns that rounded mountain rails all the while going nowhere in particular but going just the same and none the less the whole time making the appearance of heading somewhere as vacantly pleasurable as one could hope for or expect. She saw herself there in the club car staring out through the clear pane of glass and felt at ease at least with the notion. There, a green pasture, its grazing cattle and other fences freshly painted and kempt beside barnyards and horse trailers.

This heaven … it was all in the view and the view not bad considering some of the alternatives mentioned in the previous life.

She was an ice sculpture, clear and sleek and tailored … now melting. She thought it in a daily reminder. Her eyes (My eyes!) … what had happened? Once, they were dazzling and so bright but now pale and sallow. Her hands were little more than semi-pliable crepe paper, blotter paper, too. She mourned her own existence. All this before it ends. Call it before it ends. Sell it before it'd finished.

"Two down, two hundred and twenty to go," said Eve.

"I'm in for the duration," said Romeo.

"Bring your best suit and tie for tomorrow," said Eve. "We meet with the big cheese, the wealthy guy and his wife over on fourth floor. He's out to lunch twenty-four seven. She's Judy of Punch and Judy. Suspicious of her own wrist watch and the creak in the hinge on her shower door. If we get past her, we've broken the code, their estate is ours. Capisce?"

"Got it," said Romeo.

Counterfeit, classy criminals, grimy axe murderers, salty dog jailbirds, dapper yet deplorable mutineers … remember … bad boys cleanup, too. It's not to say some of them weren't sexy or couldn't be sexy and sometimes even a heck of a lot of fun. That's the way I saw them because that's the way they were, and that's what I signed on for and the way I knew it was going to be. Paid to play. Paid to take out the trash as well. The trash heap of life … it's where I left them all each and every one. After a good romp in the hay (okay, maybe a couple of times), a nice hot shower or a warm bath to wash off the residue, all's forgiven if not forgotten … in love and war, isn't that what they say… and I was back out on the street and hot on the trail of the next faint-hearted, rebellious backslider ready for his inglorious and piquant comeuppance. Never said rubbing elbows (and a lot more) wouldn't rub off. Apparently, it did. Okay. So, so be it. Never claimed to be a choirgirl. I learned a lot in my time on the street. So, here I am. Bored stiff (pun intended before truly giving in completely). A girl needs something to occupy her time. So, this is it. Absorb, meld, and confiscate as many properties as I can, cash in, then head for the Caribbean for a beachfront hacienda, a nice cabana for visitor friends and ex-s, and I'm fixed for the rest of my life.

In '67 (or was it '71?), I'd just performed a clean, flyaway dismount from atop Gangster Number 6, Marciano *The Headless Horseman* Lanzini. Him … Lanzini … He loved horses. That's what he told me. Loved the green, green grass of home, the pastures … *the grass is always greener* … those very same pastures, the mint juleps on the front veranda on the half shell inside the bucolic, autocratic, aristocratic lifestyle as heirloom avec servile butlers, curtsying maids one and all or so he claimed. And, oh, how he loved the quaint, contoured, snuggly equine riding pads properly fitted beneath its custom leather saddles counterpart, hand in glove, the glistening silver stirrups, the sheen of a newly coupled snaffle, the natural long stroke of a curry comb through horse sweat and tangled mane and tail alongside the rasp, snip, and clip of the stooped and brawny farrier. Quilted, fitted wintertime blankets draping sumptuous brood mares and stallions alike hillside in the deep solstice snow topped backdrop. Oh, God, how he loved it all. An exponentially expensive sport for the wealthiest of the elite of which he considered himself, the Neapolitan Gatsby (his words), an integral part. This horse racing that he so loved was brilliantly orchestrated, year in and year out, and a monument to mankind in all its splendor and pageantry in its entirety. Rome rekindled. (Lanzini again.) Caesar, all hail Caesar. (Lanzini in another aside.) At least, that's what he professed in every sound-off and claim challenging his listener in the pitch, swell, and pause of his own voice. He painted the image … between the verdure and those same sculpted hedges … the simple, smooth furrows … the perfectly pastured in-rows etched into the backdrop

… the terrestrial aroma of freshly tilled turf … the romantic and resonantly stated bugle blurts and bawls, and finally, those proud, prancing stallions processionally promenading single file in a hop, skip, and a lunge loading themselves and their chequered rider into the platinum gates before the final, magnanimous starter's call. He even sighed as he finished … *his love* conversationally consummated.

But it was bull crap. More horse feathers. And every bit of both.

After the big layout, he came clean and admitted that when all was said and done, the bottom line was all that really mattered. The tally had to be tallied at the end of each day, and every day was a day of reckoning. Both, Lanzini quotes. Furthermore, he hated losing more than anything in the entire known world. He said it this way … and I quote … *I love winning. The money. The rush. Seeing my horse, the right horse, cross the finish line before the other bastard's horse crosses the finish line.* It was both the sensation and the color … together as one, he explained, but he hated losing more than he loved winning. What a bizarre, pathetic, surreal if not specious take on this game we all play called life, but it was *Headless* Lanzini, the curator of fix, race track predestination, and outcome.

At a closer glance, the solution was apparent. (His words.) It came to him not in a radiant vision like open sunlight after a summer storm, not in climax at the end of some titillating sexual dream fantasy with one or two or three or more beauteous nubiles, not in a salient, abbreviated currency tease from within converting dollars to cents to Euros and back, but from the backend of a bawdy, stripped down, truck stop, Reno roulette table rolling loaded dice and infectious smiles with a seductive, red-dressed, longhaired, comely blonde croupier on the take. His *transcendent ideal* became the moniker for something which was little more than fixing races at Aqueduct, Belmont, and Pimlico by paying off jockeys in sequence and series from the inside. A neatly packaged wad of hundred-dollar bills never tipped a scale (said *Headless.*) Haylofts to mangers to paddocks to holding stalls to changing rooms with the neatly hung, inside trouser pockets of colored silks … Marciano, he was a known taskmaster, a stickler for detail, and the same guy who wouldn't take no for an answer much less wooden nickels or personal accountability. *Hobble the horse's rider (with hundred-dollar bills woven inside either rein), you hobble his destiny no matter the bloodline. Ka-ching. Payoff. You win.* That's what he said. A surefire affidavit to success and the only way he knew to get ahead and stay ahead for good. So, that's what he did.

Behind closed doors with his broadcloth boxers, Sansabelt slacks, Pantherella dress socks, Italian loafers, Armani jacket, and cherry blossom, turquoise silk tie all lying on the floor in a heap, he admitted he didn't know a bridle from a bride, a bit from an eighth of a buck, a cinch from a sure thing, jodhpurs from a pair of Big Boy bibb overalls, and what's more he didn't care. Window dressing as forte, all of it, he said. Marciano did, however, own a stable of experienced if only slightly to benignly compromised jockeys whose payoffs rivaled the stud fees of Kentucky's best breeders. After lighting a second cigarette, with my head resting on his bare chest, he confessed the rest in toto. He knew the ropes. They knew the ropes. Everyone was onboard and as well-balanced as the Wallendas under a spacious, still and draft-less big top, full net. Five will get you ten.

That defining moment … when races are determined before the starting gate opens, he liked to add. *You know,* he continued, *the way life should be.* Straight from the horse's mouth, *the Headless Horseman,* the trifecta of all trifectas and a long story short.

But back to us.

He was an X-rated, wanton, if not peculiar and particular sort. Liked his women long, leggy, with extenuated yet ample to full cleavage and moxie (*raunchy* language and '*show-me*' his preference; submissive wouldn't do; too much like his wife), plenty and plenty of moxie to back it up, which of course was me, an exact replica of what he said he'd always been looking for … to the T … his quote, verbatim, like I hadn't heard that line before.

I was young. A rookie. Hardly a beginner. When you come here looking like I did, *experienced* is built in alongside instinct and survival, felicity's go-to, trusted sidekicks. It's all in a manner of speaking. So, I was experienced for all intents and purposes and knew how to work it. Quite a bit younger than he was, but, there again, that was his preference, and it got my foot (and everything else) in the door.

We met. He grinned as he rose from his chair. We shook hands. We dined alone at some dank, schmalzy joint on the lower East side. He picked up the tab. Helped me with my stole while complimenting my pearls, the same strand of cultured pearls calling attention to and accentuating the loop, the swoop, and drape of the decolletage of my black dress and what lay beneath. (You men are all alike. Admit it.) We went back to my place, sexed around for an hour or more after the normal hide and seek foreplay, and then he told me everything that I needed to know to have him jailed before the clock struck dawn. Cinderella before, Cinderella after, Fairy Godmother, Prince Charming (hardly), carriage to pumpkin, stallions to mice, full circle. *Headless* spoke clearly into the hidden mic, everything short of age, rank, and serial number. '67 was a really good year. I'm pretty sure it was '67. '71 was a really good year, too. Seven down, five to go. I was just getting started. Chuga-chuga choo-choo, Rmm, rmm, said the little engine. I thought I could, I thought I could, and, so, I did.

Sure, I was drawn to the bad boys. Always said they saved their softer side for the bedroom, for me, for the striped sensuality, the spiritual laissez-faire. The touch and feel, it was our mainstay. You can quote me, but, please, softly, respectfully. There was never any hiding this or that, the time shared, the feelings in the moment, or hiding what I did or had done at the time. All for a good cause I felt. Crime and punishment, truncated and postponed. Reward and favor. Vindication to reverence. Sober, tantalizingly so, but necessary and vital, too. I made hay while the sun didn't shine. You could say that. I just did. Not many could get away with it, but I could. Throw a hip here, a leg out front, a bust line, and a delectably pretty face in the mix, and it worked every time.

It was hard to believe some of them were so hardened, so callous, murderous, and cold. But not with me," said Eve.

She spoke the words and looked wistfully into her dressing mirror where each day she inked in her mascara and eyeliner and pasted her lips with seductive colors of lavender and scarlet and rose and tangerine as only she could imagine. She threw her chest forward, outward, pulled in her chin, and inhaled to give herself conformation and lift.

"I was something," she continued. "Something else, indeed. With me, in our time, our intimacy, a leg over, an arm under, pressed flesh, they surrendered. It was magical to watch them melt and then always come back for more. I was their siren, their quixotic femme fatale, the petal to their heart strings. I knew it, worked it, propagated their demise as I had intended all along.

This is as far as we go. I said that on more than one occasion. Told all of them the same thing. Without equivocation or remorse, without hesitation or second-guessing. Age catches up to the best of us. Leaves nothing in its wake. Fumes? you say. No, no fumes. The fumes have vanished in the same breath. No residue. No. There's nothing left. Not even the silhouette of yourself has disappeared. You are less than an apparition of yourself from a begone life. You couldn't recognize yourself in a lineup of six people of the same sex in five tries. It's that sad. But true."

Eve paused and said,

"Not to change the subject, but" … In less than a head gesture, in walked Mrs. Johnson behind her double barrel, two-fisted walker with the Clara Bell honker, Romeo assisted.

"Mrs. Johnson, you have three properties listed here on the tri-county records," said Eve. "Now, if you'll just sign here on the dotted line, we'll complete the paperwork and you can go right back to your knitting in Arts & Crafts at 2 o'clock."

"Well, where does that leave me?" asked Mrs. Johnson.

"Right here," said Eve. "Nothing's changed. I'm just tidying up claims and probate for residents here at the Garden through my nephew Romeo and my attorney. Kind of a community service if you will," said Eve.

"And land grab," muttered Romeo through a leftover punch-drunk smile. Eve kicked him in the shin.

"So, I sign, and I don't miss Arts & Crafts?" said Mrs. Johnson.

"Yes," said Eve. "That's right. Sign here, and you're on your way over to Arts & Crafts."

"Done," said Mrs. Johnson picking up the pen. She signed off in a slow-motion cursive and repositioned herself behind her walker and shuffled out of Room 318.

"Money talks," said Eve. "So they say. Money just as often doesn't," she replied to herself as Romeo Nosferatu Mosconi stood close by.

"Hush money up front as requested, so keep it quiet," she repeated holding out a roll of cash.

Romeo took the money and tucked it inside his sport jacket for keeps.

"Silence is golden," she said specifically to Romeo Nosferatu Mosconi over the top of her chic readers. *Mum's* the word. Capisce?

Romeo smiled and nodded. "Le mie labbra sono sigillate," he replied. So, his lips were sealed.

Later on … quella sera …

In the thick of a soberingly stark evening, inside a stale fragrance of tobacco smoke and dark, musty air, Romeo Nosferatu Mosconi sat next to Gravel Pit Galvano, the two straddling a pair of lattice-backed barstools directly in front of bartender Freddie 'The Sandman' Giuseppe and his spit-shined copper top bar left of center and twenty paces inside at Caesar's the restaurant. Romeo on the left; Gravel Pit was on the right. Gravel Pit Galvano was a Romeo go-to accomplice and mastermind of a new website *Mysterious Ways to Die for Hire*. The two hooligans sat comfortably. For the most part, they were unknowns and mysterious to everyone in the converted downtown, speakeasy-tavern. It was just as the two would have it.

If you looked at Gravel Pit Galvano straight ahead, say from the bartender's vantage point like you were professionally serving or pouring him a drink and professionally putting out the bar napkin and professionally taking his first drink order, say a vodka tonic, and professionally, carefully, delicately dropping the lime wedge into the shaved ice, and placing it neatly in front of him, just so, into its proper place on that same properly-positioned bar napkin squared up and looking up at the customer, you could see or you would certainly notice the stocky metallic handle of the Deutsche Waffen und Munitionsfabriken (DWM) nine-millimeter, six/seven shot hand gun hanging from Gravel's (or The Pit's) left shoulder holster insert inside his all-wool, checkered English tweed sport jacket. Gravel Pit fiddled about (he was a fidgety guy, that Gravel Pit Galvano was) inside his lined right inside pocket and pulled out a pack of Pall Mall Lights, smoothly displaced a single cigarette from the flip top box, slipped the cigarette in and under his top lip, and lit up. To a mobster, to murder for hire, to *Mysterious Ways to Die (Deaths) for Hire*, that first long, hearty, unflinching first drag off the evening's first cigarette was purely and simply a breath of fresh air ... of *fucking* (The Pit's words) *fresh spring air*. Piece of cake.

That and a charbroiled filet. Salad back. Another vodka tonic. And so … as Gravel Pit Galvano always loved to say at the end of another and each and every work day … *All's forgiven from what hasn't already been forgotten.*

"A toast," said Romeo. "A toast to the two of us, to the old broad, la vecchia, la vecchia bella donna, Evangelista, to the trifecta, and our mutual success and the reverification of identities and funds alike."

"A toast," said Gravel.

Their barware touched in one single malt to Zyr clink.

CHAPTER 19

Time and Space

From the Cold Case Files & Confessions of Richard 'The Ice Man' Kuklinski Entry #59. For over three decades, Richard Kuklinski served as a notorious contract killer for the East Coast Mafia. The real number of Kuklinski's victims is said to be somewhere between one and two hundred. Selected events herein are recorded, recreated, and transcribed by Edek Jablonski, a successful, retired author-crime writer as well as purported kinsman to 'The Ice Man' himself. Room 315. Voices from within. Bringing the dead to life one last time in a murder victim tell-all.

From the desk of Eddie 'The Icicle' Jablonski. The next chapter as interpolative exposé. The victim's narrative as it might have been told.

Sitting at his desk, Eddie wrote:

Whole again.

In another time and space, we will be made whole again.

That momentary spin ... *time, space, whole again, et al* ... it sounded like I was writing a first-draft, unmailed, desperate love letter to some nearly-forgotten, long-lost, old girlfriend-lover leading with the cheesy 'time and space' bit as preamble to our unconfirmed reunion and some half-baked, uncalculated reconciliation and rendezvous. When it went off in my head, I had to step back and admit that the "time and place" thing plus the "made whole again' tidbit smacked of atrociously sappy, syrupy romantic and colloquial jive and was errantly pukey what's more. A long-distance garbled message, intentional, unintentional or otherwise, it just didn't seem like it would work in the context of much of anything, but who knows? A bit too surreal to leave as an obsequious voicemail much less spoken out loud in an open forum or meeting between two individuals after such a long and extended period of time apart.

However, 'this eleven-word line' in play had nothing to do with romance or an ex-lover or a girlfriend and her boyfriend or old times or hooking up or soulful, lovey-dovey poetic gongs going off or travelling or romantic getaways or one last fling or anything else remotely germane to that topic in any way.

It was, however, specifically and metaphorically speaking to my own dull and dreadful predicament. It spoke specifically and explicitly to the godawful mess I'd gotten myself into at that moment … that moment in *time and space*. Long lost loves recoupling? Hardly. Nothing could be further from the truth. The line, this mushy existential bit about … *be made whole again* b.s., is what somehow kept popping up in my head and some way telling me this, my own, pitifully personable cliché while kneeling more or less flatfooted, if you can believe that, inside a debris-filled bar ditch in a pair of leaky waders beside the clogged culvert next to the steady, rancid runoff from the downpour off Highway 19. Yes, that very same Highway 19, which in fact, was little more than a crumpled, barely-blacktop back road filled with watermelon sized potholes and broken branches and leftover, thirty-year-old unreadable road signs leading to just the other side of nowhere. Or less maybe. Not to mention the perfect place for a murder and an even more perfect place to hide the victim's body. God Almighty, I said to myself ... and more than once.

I was frightened (and I don't frighten easily), I was wet, I was cold, I was tired, and I was lost. Without a plan or fence post to call my own, I stood up for the first time in an hour and a half, took in a deep draw of cold air as revitalized nourishment, but looking around, I didn't recognize anything. Not a tree, a road sign, a scrub, a bush, a tuft of grass, a scrub or a bush on the other side of the road, not a dimple in the dark foliage or a crack in the distressingly shabby asphalt blacktop laid out in the dark straightaway. Not one single, solidarity thing. Nothing.

Poncho-covered in camouflage and darkness (it was nighttime by now and pitch black), the voice inside my head said, *What now, Sherlock?* But I didn't respond because it was useless. I'd heard that same voice and that same question asked repeatedly so many times over these many, many years, jeering and jawing at me in that same tone and identical inflection, it was little more than a magpie popping off at the mouth over a mound of torn carcass, fleshly remains, marrow, and dead bones. But mostly, I didn't have an answer to the question. That wasn't unusual for me and certainly not unusual at a time like this ... mayhem's first mile. However, as usual, I knew I'd rummage around inside the vacant space of this brain of mine and I'd come up with something ... right, wrong, or indifferent, maybe something just straight down the middle low and away, a sinker, a curveball, a spitter or a splitter, something that I couldn't hit, a fast ball say, but something. Anything was better than where I was and what I was doing here in the here and now. *Wet and rudderless*, that came to mind next, but I was too busy plowing my way out of the bar ditch, belongings and all, in the dead of a miserably rainy, cold night to worry about what *wet and rudderless* really meant or what *wet and rudderless* could mean or might mean or what the silly, subconscious and psychosomatic gist just might really mean in this life or another life or outside of a pinch like this.

Dagger of death deliver me.

Okay. So, we met again, and it didn't go as expected. In fact, it didn't go well at all. She kept bring up things from the past, our past, her past, my past, unpleasant things, things that I'd done, things that she'd done to help, and wouldn't or couldn't let it go. We hadn't been together half a day, and she started in. I asked her to stop, but she wouldn't. I said as much numerous times in the span of an hour or maybe two tops, but she didn't or wouldn't or couldn't. It really didn't matter then, and certainly it doesn't matter now. It's over and done. I've moved on. I finally told her to shut up, just like that. An abrupt shut up in the face argument and dissension and disheveled conversation usually gets everyone's attention, drunk or sober. Everyone shuts up. Everyone in the room. But not her. She wouldn't stop rehashing rehash. The same old stuff drug up, laid out, poked and prodded and relived until there was nothing left to say, nothing left to examine much less talk about or obsess over. The meeting had crossed borderline insanity. In fact, it had hopped the fence with the No Trespassing sign posted underneath. Picture yourself at the laundromat in front of the giant clothes dryer watching your clothes tumble over and over and over through the giant tv-screen-sized glass port in a prepaid endlessness and expecting something metaphysical and recuperative and comprehensible to come of it. That was us.

So, one thing led to another. The drinking no doubt exacerbated good intention and washed away what both of us had (I guess) hoped for. Elusive turned to brusque turned to bitterness turned to hostility turned to shouting and looks of stark hatred … just like the days of old. The last time was one too many times. She blurted out again in another dirty, filthy reminder stuff I'd done, stuff we'd done, and other stuff I'd done in particular to her without consideration of her feelings and her future or our future together and her reputation going forward which were all things I'd said must be left unsaid. I wouldn't hear it. Any of it. Not one word. I'd warned her. Repeatedly. Don't piss me off. I said that between shots. (Cuervo Gold.) Don't bring it up again, is what I said a fifth or sixth time with other hardier pops (Cuervo Gold and cheap, unlabeled schnapps) down the hatch. But she did. Three more times within the half hour. *You want to see time and space?* That's what I said waving the whiskey bottle in the air over my head around and around and around. *Is **that** what you want to see?* I said it again the same way with the accent over '**that**', for drunken emphasis something we both, mutually understood like identical twins in cameo. *Like it'll make us whole again,* she replied sarcastically (pungent derision dripping from her voice) stumbling over the word '*us*' just to show me how '*over me*' (her words verbatim) she was and had been for all these many years. *Piss off,* she said as she tipped her shot glass back to empty, then poured another, downed that one, then poured another, and then downed that one to then turn in a drunken tantrum and smash the shot glass against the back door leaving a dent the size of a musket ball misfire off a Portuguese muzzleloader. She might as well have been chugging clear water from a midsummer, desert oasis at the end of a long day's trek. I'd had enough. By this time, my courage was complete, robust if not a bit portly, and probably overblown, fiery if not insoluble and a bit gritty. Nevertheless, game on.

So, I let her have it. A shovel over the front of her forehead, and then she got *real quiet.* Fell left to right into or over toward the fireplace. Looked sober if not puzzled and quizzical on the way down like … *what'd I do, or … what'd I say?* In death, her face lay sunny-side up, a pancake between and on the other side of the shovel-side pancake.

You know what you did, I said as she lay there in an unconscious pile on the cabin floor. *You cunt.* I said just to finalize my own personal victory symbolizing that *I showed her. Hah*! That's the way it ended. My parting shot. Two words. All of it reduced to name-calling in a strafe and a dead body (someone I'd known once under different, more favorable circumstances as I drunkenly recalled) made ready for disposal. Jeez. And ain't life grand.

Buried her remains in the back in the rain, the damp, the cold, the leafy debris, the hard, dark soil with the same shovel, a dull spade shovel, that I'd used to separate her from that mouth of hers. No wonder we'd spent so much time apart. Tamping down the last shovel full of soil, I wiped my brow with the back of my parka sleeve, went back inside, and tucked myself into bed and slept like a newborn baby on black-market tranquilizers and two more shots of gold. Best shuteye in thirty-five years.

It would be the last time she would refer to me or anyone else on this planet, living or dead, as a totalitarian, pro-crypto Nazi degenerate faggoty dick-less son of a bitch hermaphroditic pedophile. I can attest to that. (How in the world could I have forgotten that *mouth*?) The last time, too, she'd stick out that middle finger of hers way up in midair (at me mind you, her business partner and ex this and ex that, and so forth) screaming a juggernaut of vile, loathsome obscenities and vulgarities and dozens of really hurtful, perfectly-placed personal insults and then chase the gesture and all the rest with a backwash and hard swallow of bootleg bourbon out of an unmarked quart bottle wiping off the overrun and her pale, leftover lipstick with the back of her grimy paw. I can attest to that, too. Oh, yeah, sure, I can hear the protests over our little dustup gone sour from all the pansies in the audience … in her defense (like she had a defense) and in the backdrop, all the liberal-minded bleeding heart so-and-sos, the unhinged suffragettes, the whacko feminazis, the babbling bra burners, etc. etc., catcalls and crying and whining and propagating … (goes like this) she was someone's daughter, she was someone's child, she was someone's sister, she was someone's sibling, someone's wife, someone's true love … or maybe someone's *failed* fucking business partner as well. Did you ever stop long enough to consider that last one? Oh, please. Stop with the crybaby crap already. Hold a gun to your head the same way she held the gun to my head, right at my temple, with full and complete, heavy metal malice aforethought, in a drug induced, recidivistic rage and her, little miss booze-addled, foul mouth, just two months out of the can (Metro State), and then you tell me what kind of daughter, sister, sibling, mother, spouse, business partner she was. That and the one-ounce bag of toot she'd just crammed up her left nostril, then the remainder up her right nostril after lining her gums right before the shovel-side reveille I put upside that smug, acerbic and sarcastic, impudent, fuck-you-pal look on her face followed by a second blow (just for good measure because it felt fantastic) … right upside that know-it-all, brainiac head of hers. Touché and nighty night … sweet dreams, my loveless … sleep tight, princess poontang fairy godmother dope dealing Diana bitch from hell. A fiery crash on the Paris-side of the Chunnel would've been too good for you.

Two months and two weeks go by. I was lying there in the same bed still half asleep from a few good, stiff pops the night before. When I opened my eyes fully, still in a grog, there was a very, very large figure of a man standing beside the bed and me lying there in my bed. He looked down at me and said simply, "That was uncalled for." And that was all that he said. I didn't respond. I simply stared at the man, this stranger, and lifted myself to a comfortable and practical equally distributed propped up position on both elbows. It was recognition enough for what was happening. An answer or acknowledgement of sorts, you could say that. That and I didn't get it. That's what my expression clearly said. I stared back at the man as the man stared down at me. After that, he drew back in a short, chopping motion and hit me forcibly once in the face with the same shovel I'd hit her with. Tit for tat, but I still didn't get it because it hadn't registered at that point. It hurt like hell but didn't register. The tit and the tat were two months and two weeks old, even if maybe a little overdue. Who's to say? Bygones had already become bygones, I thought clumsily. Then, he hit me again in the face this time even harder. Tit for tat, again. Bygones were apparently still in play. As I held my bloody, bleeding face in my two open hands, I started to get it and rather rapidly began putting two and two together as fast as my little, jostled mind would or could race. Blunt forced trauma makes for a strange bedfellow.

Said to this guy standing over me, "Hold on. Wait a minute, for god's sake." I was trying to stop the bleeding from my nose when he hit me again over the back of the head which sent me to the floor. I stopped talking after that since saying something only made matters worse.

With a gun in one hand and the shovel in the other, this guy nudges me in the back. "*Get up,*" he mutters then sticks the shovel handle in my ribs and pushes me out the back door to the dirt mound where the woman friend (associate) (business partner) (fuck from the past or past lover, reader's choice) of mine was buried. Tosses the shovel at me … I'm still bleeding from the nose and mouth and now at the back of my head because I can feel the trickle at the top of my neck … and says, "*Dig,*" just like that. Then without pause or explanation adds, "*I'll tell you when to stop digging. Get busy. Dig.*" With his small howitzer in hand, he's watching my every move and before too much time passes, I'm knee deeper or deeper in a black hole dressed in bedroom slippers, long johns, and a blood-stained Henley. A real sight for sore eyes, blood and snot and mucous and bloody matted hair and now sweat mixed with my new romantic outdoor look. My entire face ached and was a bleeding mess, little more than a deep woods, modern day, Tecumseh operatic aftermath on the other side of Atlanta.

When I got to waist deep, I hit roots, tree roots, several, one of size, started chopping, and started talking to break the silence and the boredom and the monotony of digging. Why not? I thought. In my own defense, I said to the stranger in between the heavy breathing, "She was supposed to bring the money. She didn't." Heavy breath, heavy breath. "She was supposed to bring the drugs, the next much bigger shipment, the next supply. She didn't." Another heavier breath followed by a long sigh… digging on command at an assassin spectator's pace is tiresome and harrowing … the entire time I'm wiping bloody snot off my face and out of my mouth and eyes with the back of my Henley forearm now soaked with rain, mist, cloud cover, dew, sweat, blood, and saliva. "She was supposed to bring a new, different, more tolerant, more amenable attitude with her as well, but she didn't do that either. Three strikes and you're out. I mean anybody. No matter the circumstance. That's what I told her. Told her that before she arrived. Numerous times. At least half a dozen or more. Don't come if you can't get your attitude straightened out. Stay home. How many times do you need to repeat yourself? How many times do you need to give instructions to someone to consummate a perfectly simple business transaction? We're drug dealers, for god's sake. A simpleton's enterprise and a lazy one at that. How difficult can it be dropping off a package of lightweight, illicit shit from one place to the other completely without interference in the moonless dark with no one around? Don't fuck this up, I said to her. Not this job. This one's too fricking important. You're running out of chances, I told her. You didn't know her like I did … one puffed up mother fucker. Worse than any guy I ever knew. And that's really, really saying something.

Sure, we'd been drinking. Thought a toddy or two might ease the tension, maybe I'd get lucky (we'd been there before), or lay old demons to rest, not to mention the latest incident of a good thing, a one-time sure thing as a matter of fact, already gone bad … at least for the evening or old times sake. Drink up. Regrettably, I said that. But it just made matters worse, I guess. Well, hell yes … I'm sure it did. She's dead." I nodded, cast my eyes and head over toward the other shallow grave as evidence and proof and my own personal admission of guilt, like the stranger, the man with the huge handgun didn't get it. He got it. "*Shut up and dig,*" is all he came back with.

I'm chest deep by now. Water's leaked into the trough of a hole I'd dug and my feet were turning blue or purple from the cold and wet. The guy with the big handgun, he couldn't care less. Hurry up is written all over his face like moonglow, but there was none. So, I just kept chipping away at the resentfully unrelenting hard ground making process one shovel full at a time. The debris chucked over my shoulder was almost as much water as dirt. For the sake of the sake of conversation-less conversation, like I didn't already know, I asked, "Hey, how much deeper do you want me to go?" He actually replied. Not what I wanted to hear, but he replied and said, "Until you're up over your neck, then you can stop." That was quite an image … me … the hole … the dark … the dirt mound … me and my Henley … my bloody face wet and dripping with rainwater and sweat and blood mix … up to my chin. At that very moment, I, too, got it.

"Close enough," was the next thing he said twenty minutes later. "Now, turn around," he said. So, I did. "Put these on," he said as he threw a pair of handcuffs at me into the five-six-foot ditch. So, I did. "Now, put these around your ankles," he said as he threw another set of handcuffs into my chest as I stood there as compliant as a trained retriever. "Shake your hands," he said. So, I shook my hands. "Shake your feet," he said. So, I shook my feet, sort of in a lean and clumsy bounce. He simply nodded, put down his handgun, and began filling in the hole all around me.

"Hey," I said practically, just this side of mercifully. "Don't you want to reconsider? I mean while you still can? I mean, can't we, you and me, can't we talk this thing out, maybe come to a better conclusion than the one you're drawing up right now? You know, it doesn't need to come to this or go this far. Certainly not any further. I can change. I'll come clean. You know this wasn't all my fault. You know that? I can make this right. You just tell me what I need to do, and I'll do it. I've got some money tucked away there in the cabin. You can have it. It's yours. I can even tell you where to find it if you want. Seriously, it's all yours. Every nickel of it. Down to the pennies in the Campbell soup can on top of the refrigerator. I think there's some loose change in an empty, oversized Excedrin bottle, extra strength, on the second shelf over the stove. Take the two shotguns and the three revolvers next to the chest of drawers by the closet. Vintage models. A Purdey. A Savage, too. Worth some bucks in a tradeoff as well. All yours for the asking and to relieve and take some of the pressure off both of us. You gotta feel really stressed about now … (speaking of Excedrin)." Mumbled that last part.

I was chest deep when I said that. My feet, bound and locked in above my bedroom slippers, the same lamb's wool lined slippers my real girlfriend gave me off the last drug deal gone right, were immoveable, stuck like everything was planted in cement, growing colder and more numb by the minute. I was shivering, but I didn't care. The quiver and seismic shit meant nothing, or actually it meant that I was still alive, so that was a good thing. At least that's what I thought and told myself at the time.

"Hey, just so you know, I've already called for backup. Reno's bringing in the shipment the chick fucked up. You can take the entire thing with you. I'm sure it's worth two, three hundred thousand dollars if it not a half million or more on the street. Trust me. I know dope. I know drugs. It's all yours. Reno said he'd be here by evening or first thing in the morning. He found the stuff in her apartment in the bathtub inside the planter behind the shower curtain, a funky mauve color, where she always stashes the stuff. This isn't the first time, believe me. She'd have kept the entire fucking thing for herself just as I suspected. She was poison. Trouble in spades. A mix of snake venom and gloriously twisted, psychotic twat. Great in bed, but hardly anybody you want to do business with. So, hey, … maybe that explains some of the stuff you didn't know about so you get it now in a clearer, more erudite picture so maybe I don't look quite as bad in the final analysis, huh? Look, before you go any further and keep filling this hole up with all the dirt I dug out, why don't you just wait for Reno to get here and see what he brings with him. What's a couple of more hours of your time, and who knows, it might really payoff? Wait and see. For old times. One human being to another. Should old acquaintance be forgot. De hombre a hombre. A guy thing. You can take the entire stash, the complete haul, the whole kit and caboodle. It's yours. Free and clear. No questions asked. No answers either. We've never met. I don't know you; you don't know me. After this is all over, everybody goes their own merry little way. You take the high road; I'll take the low road. Again, no questions. Capisce? With a cherry on top. Whataya say? I know you don't like talking. I got that. But, really, a little negotiation could go a long way about right now. You, me, the money inside the cabin, a drug shipment mother lode here in twelve to twenty hours, a warm fire, a hot meal … I make a mean omelet with bell peppers, sausage, and onions … you'd like it … a nice hot cup of joe … cream and sugar … just the way you like it. Really. Me and my ex old lady, we sat down a few years back, talked about why she hated me and why I hated her, we talked for a bit more, we both completely agreed on why we hated one another, it was cool, copacetic, then we moved on. Walked away still hating each other, but what the hay. At least we knew why. Sometimes understanding the root and the meaning of your hate is really important. At least that's what my ex told me so I bought in fingers crossed. One less dipstick to deal with … one step closer to heaven is what I say. Now, we swap Christmas cards and birthday best wishes. Hers is in May. The tenth. Another one coming up soon. Imagine that. So. Whataya say?" I was spitting dirt granules the whole time talking. Fast talking. Really fast. But buying time seemed not to have worked much less was there any mention of a negotiable price tag … as in a de facto tag and release, say, for all intents and purposes.

My hands and arms were now covered, immobile as well. I was little more than a caricature of myself in mud patch and wet, black mountain soil with a sniffle of blood red mixed in. The next pitch of shoveled dirt hit me in the face, but mostly in the mouth and chin. A sign? I thought. For me to shut the fuck up? I thought that next. Maybe. Maybe not. I could only guess, but I was pretty sure I got it. He didn't say. Him … mum… Mister Mum with the oversized handgun … whatever … so mum was still the word. I spit dirt for the next two minutes or more and by that time, my shoulders and my entire Henley were completely covered, and I could feel that whole earthen hyperbaric bull shit and strain going on and mounting around my chest, choking off my ability to breath. The in and out you take for granted was now a chore and laborsome. A half dozen more shovel-fulls and I was buried alive up to and past my jawline with no way out. The big guy with the big handgun planted and grounded the shovel firmly handle-side upright with one, body-weight step and push of his big right foot into a patch of broken, loose, black, leftover debris and disappeared quietly back into the cabin. Both of us … me and him … I guess we felt pretty sure I wasn't going anywhere. So, for the first time that day, I was left unguarded in my new safe haven of sorts. Mayday, mayday said a voice deep from within.

Some time had passed. Don't how much because I was buried. Up to my ass in alligators as they say. In an abrupt reappearance, there was the big fellow again carrying a 16-ounce squeeze bottle of tupelo honey, a leftover roasted chicken from inside the refrigerator, and a 12-ounce jar of crunchy Crazy Richard's peanut butter (a personal favorite). What? Is about all I could think. I'd lost most of the feeling in my toes and feet and hands by this point, and my breathing had slowed to a whisper. The big guy bends over and pours the honey over my face, smears the peanut butter into my eyebrows and facial stubble, and said to me, "Open your mouth," which I did. He then stuffed cold leftover roasted chicken into my mouth, a fat side drumstick as lead, and said, "Bon appetite" as he dropped the rest of the chicken carcass around my ears and the back of my head. He turned away, walked a few paces, then turned back slightly to say, "The critters will be here before dark." Jesus, I thought. Please, somebody shoot me ... to sounds of the forest and a slow, steady, soft drizzle all about.

The first was a raccoon. Hands of a cat burglar, the sharp, prickly teeth of Satan. The second a fox. Colorful, just like in the storybooks, curious, seemingly interested but not interested enough. He wandered off. The third a bobcat, he sniffed and smiled with a mouth chock-full of canines the size and texture of barbed wire barbs, whiskers and all, only for a brief time, then with a swipe of his left paw swatted and clawed out my right eye after a short tussle with the ligaments that momentarily held firm to my eye socket. I blacked out then but woke to deafness in my left ear. The same bobcat was gnawing on that bloody leftover over by a small pile of leaves. He seemed quite content. Ear, a forest delicacy? Who'd have guessed? That was my last thought. That, and that I was checking out of this life as one real live, rootin'-tootin', first class, honest to goodness, bona fide, true blue, authentic, smart-alecky, wisecracking, smart ass wise guy the same way I'd come in ... that's when I blacked out for good.

Reno, the backup, the backup bringing the stash found inside the dead drug dealer chick's apartment inside the ceramic planter centered in the bathtub behind the mauve, checkerboard-patterned shower curtain, walked through the cabin door carrying that same stash from the dope deal gone awry. It was wrapped and bound in plain brown shipping paper and duct tape just like in a cinematic drug dealer, drug scene payoff. The big man was there waiting with his howitzer in hand standing beside the refrigerator with one forearm propped up on top next to a stale loaf of bread and two bottles of unopened cheap wine. That's how tall he was. Reno stopped. The big man smiled. Reno spoke up. "Is …?" "No, he's dead," said the big man. "Put the package on the table." So, Reno leaned over and put the package with the dope from the dope deal gone awry in the middle of the cluttered table and stepped back twice. The big man leveled his handgun, aimed, and shot Reno once in the chest and twice in the head on his way backwards and down to a sprawl on the cabin floor as thank you and in his spirit of cooperation.

The big guy picked up the package, tucked it under his arm, and left by the front cabin door. Reno, now dead, or dead Reno, was booked into the records as the murderer of the two bodies found buried in the back behind the mountain cabin. Drug deal gone bad is all it said. His death, along with the other two dead bodies retrieved, were never investigated. "Good riddance," DEA crime officer Snyder noted at the scene, "Would that we could send a *thank you* card and flowers to the guy that did this. Saved us a lot of work." Case closed.

Richard Kuklinski was by this time home watching the Steelers beat the Browns on four touchdown passes and five sacks with two interceptions compliments of the Steel Curtain defense. Cousin Rich adjusted the lever on his Barcalounger to recline, sat back, and tipped his pilsner to the victors.

CHAPTER 20

Police Station Episode 2

It's Eddie once again … Eddie speaking inside Chief Friday's office. They're one on one of sorts with Eve. All of it at Eve's insistence. Eddie's giving himself up a third time. Anything for sex, said funny Eddie.

Eddie began where he'd left off.

"His victims. You could hear them sniffle, whimper, gag on their self-pity and their momentary worn-out, antediluvian guilt. New found cowardice. Let your foot off their neck, and they'd be right back to who they were, who they'd always been, their old selves, putridly grandiose, magnanimous, rancorously indulgent, fire-struck, fantabulous or worse. The core, the center, and the nucleus of egoism all rolled into a ball of fiery bombast, braggadocio, and self-aggrandizement. The lot of them, I'd thought. Keep doing what you're doing, Eddie, said my inner voice. If not for you, they'd bury kindly, little old ladies and bedraggled widows up to their necks in someone else's backyard in their destructive wake searching for invented, buried booty and inferred contraband. Eddie, I said to myself, you're the only man of valor and integrity, vim and virtuousness in this mix of slippery, hardcore libertines. Stand fast, I told myself. So, I did.

Simultaneously in the moment, I could read their descension as well as the surreptitious resolve and cross tie into their impervious past … that is until that very moment. Then, it was just me Eddie, Eddie *The Icicle*, standing up to Lucifer himself, the undertaker, the demented one on high, as he made his crazy entry to save the brigands one and all," said Eddie finishing up.

He was out of breath so he paused ad lib to rethink ad lib and translate ab lib what he'd just said.

Now, it was Police Chief Friday's turn. He'd listened to the entire story. Each time, he noted, this guy's story gets wilder and wilder and more exaggerated. He interrupted Eddie with a loose index finger.

Chief Friday began.

"Okay. Says here, Mister Jablonski, that you and Ms. Evangelista Spilotro were here twice last month?" (Looks over his bifocals quizzically.) "Says here, too, Mister Jablonski that you and Ms. Spilotro were here in June. Three times, as a matter of fact." (Chief looking over his bifocals again quizzically.) "Then twice in May? Am I reading that right? Yes, twice in May."

Chief looked beyond his bifocals at the elderly couple sitting across from him. "And then, three times (holds up three fingers), three times, mind you, in April the year before? Does that sound accurate?" (Chief looking down then back up and over his bifocals a fourth and fifth time.) "Twice you talked to Lieutenant Faraday. I have his notes. Same stuff. Murders. You did it. Time to confess, you told him on a Tuesday afternoon just before I came in for my shift. Shot one *'fucker'* (your word, Mister J, your word) in the back of the head. That's what you said, Mister Jablonski. Your words exactly. I can read Lieutenant Faraday's handwriting. It's plain as day. He has a nice, very legible handwriting for a guy."

Eddie sat quietly. Eddie thought this through. Then without a wince or pause, Eddie stared back at the chief, he nodded and shrugged an '*I guess so*' shrug … quizzically as well. Takes one 'quizzically' to know one, from the book of *Old School*.

"Okay, you two," Police Chief Friday said. "I have taken notes and recorded in detail your account of the events that took place. I hope you understand that your time here and the conversation you've provided could act as a confession down the road. Am I clear?"

He looked at Eddie.

Eddie looked back at Chief. Eddie nodded knowingly.

Chief looked over at Eve.

Eve looked back across the desk at Chief, then to Eddie, then back to Chief and she nodded knowingly, too.

Chief Friday, his index finger was still pointed in midair, unemphatically but yet still pointed, something like a stale and weathered carrot.

"Now," continued Police Chief Friday. "Let me finish by saying that this is either the ninth or tenth time, you two have been down here to the station to give your account of the various murders that took place here in the city over thirty or forty years ago. Some of them go back forty-five years. That's a long time. And I get it. But, listen, you don't need to come back. I'm going to hand this over to the D.A., D.A. Robbinsville, and if he decides that he wants to piece your story together and then press charges, so be it. We know where to find you. Do you understand, Mister Jablonski?"

"Eddie, do you hear Chief Friday?" asked Eve. "Eddie?"

"Yeah, yeah, yeah," replied Eddie. "I hear you, Chief. Loud and clear. Icicle's hearing isn't great, but it's not that far gone," said Eddie looking to Chief back to Eve, and back to Chief. Eddie smiled. "You do the crime, you gotta be prepared to do the time. That's what they say, right Chief? Comes with the territory. Hit man's instruction manual. (Eddie grinned ever wider.) Chapter Four, second section, paragraph three. 'You do the crime, be prepared to do the time.' You like that one, huh, Chief?"

"Yeah, that's great, Mister Jablonski, just great," replied Chief Friday.

"I'm a big boy, Chief. All grown up and then some." Eddie smiled some more and leaned in for a peck on the check from Eve. "Chief, say you're a mechanic, a car mechanic, and you're a good one, a really, really good one, you're still going to get grease on your knuckles. Capisce?"

Eve lip-syncs, *Attaboy, Eddie.*

"Now," continued Chief Friday. "You two get back on the shuttle and go on back to The Garden. They're probably worried sick wondering where you two have sauntered off to this time. AWOL's for deserters, Mister Jablonski. You don't seem like the type, much less you, Ms. Spilotro … and an ex-police officer at that. Probably looking for you both as we speak."

Chief Friday stood from behind his desk and reached out with an open hand to shake Eddie's, then Eve's. Token appreciation between parties, say, but relief and good riddance moreover.

Eve then looked to Eddie, looked to Chief, looked to Eddie again and back to Chief. Everyone on the same page? It appeared so at least for the moment. At least, sort of.

The shuttle was parked out front. The shuttle engine was running. Jenkins sat behind the wheel. Jenkins said, "You done, boss?" To which, Eddie waved and sealed it with a thumbs up.

The two sat on the bench seat in the middle of the shuttle van, holding hands as they left the police station.

"You know," said Eddie reflectively, "I always wanted to be a hit man." He then let out a hearty grin.

"Yeah, I know," replied Eve to Eddie. She smiled just as wide, looked back at Eddie, and said, "And I always wanted to be a cop, a really, really hot, sexy cop."

The two smiled at one another and looked away.

"A guy told me this once," said Eddie. He paused, took the toothpick out of the corner of his mouth, then continued. "An old Italian guy and mobster ... Said ... *Eddie, wait until you're older, an old man, then you can exact revenge on whoever you want, whenever you want. If you're caught, cuts prison time incrementally in half or more. At my age, jailtime means little or nothing. Just another place to park my hat and coat. Capisce? ...* So," said Eddie, "Now I am that old man, and I can do what I want, when I want. I get it. I know what he meant. Capisce, I say."

Chapter 21

Police Station Episode 3

At the police station sitting next to one another and across from Chief Friday, Eve said to Eddie, "I didn't tell you earlier, but I love the ascot. The deep paisley, the florescent hue and subtle tones, the contrasting colors, they complement and almost match those ferocious eyes of yours, Eddie, you tiger."

"Yeah, yeah, yeah," said Eddie. "I know, I know." Eddie almost blushes. "My daughter gave it to me for Christmas a few Christmases ago. Came to The Garden with the two sons, my two grandsons, little Eddie, Eddie three and little brother Jimmy Gianni the second after his great granddad on his father's side, my little Guido the Polack and the hit-men-in-training I call them. My daughter hates it, but I lay it on thicker than provolone so the little sons a bitches don't grow trans-mixed, crisscrossed, cross-wired, or something worse. Boys … you want to show them rough and tough and gruff so they grow up rough and tough and gruff or even tougher than that living in the fucked-up world of today. Christ, what a world. But their dear old granddad's looking out for them even in spite of their pushover mother. It's not going unnoticed by Eddie The Icicle". Pansy asses. Most of the kids today. Pansy asses. No grandkid of Eddie Jablonski, the notorious hit man slash gangster slash tough guy slash mobster slash your worst nightmare, is growing up a pansy ass. Ain't happening."

"Ha!" said Eve out loud. She quickly lifted a hand and slapped her knee, her good knee. "Don't let it happen, Eddie. Whatever you gotta do, do it, and don't let it happen." Eve brushed her hair back, flicked out a thumbs up, sat up lady-like, crossed her legs, pajamas, slippers and all, and cleared her throat. "Men are men," she said. She looked straight into Eddie's eyes, Eddie's ferocious eyes and repeated herself. "Men are men are men and forever and always will be. That's what I say. Nothing can change that, Eddie. Nothing like 'em. Woodies and all. Woodies or no woodies, men are men are men. A man's still a man. All hail manhood!"

"Here, here," said Eddie seconding the motion.

In a personal aside, Eve said casually to Eddie: "I've had my eye on you since the beginning."

In a follow-up personal aside, Eddie replied back to Eve: "Ha, all the women at the Garden have had their eye on me since the beginning."

Eddie winked at Chief Friday. It's a man-to-man wink, blanketed machismo to blanketed machismo, not the other kind of wink.

Police Chief Friday starred over his bifocals once again. He lifted the coffee cup to his lips, backed off, blew into it, then pleasurably slurped a warm-hot sip. He looked at Eddie *The Icicle* and continued.

"You know what this means, Mister Jablonski?" asked Police Chief Friday.

Eddie stared back across the desk from his side. Pajamas, bathrobe, slippers, and ascot (paisley, hot paisley the color of his eyes). Eddie said nothing.

"Mister Jablonski, you know what this means?" repeated Police Chief Friday a second time, the same question precisely worded precisely the same way.

(*Police Chief Friday*: it said so on the official desk brass monitor at the midsection of his desk, part i.d., part decoration, part officialdom persona, part decorum and protocol, part self-respect and self-aggrandizement, part boss, part bravado and bull feathers, part Hugh Wilson honorarium, part Tarrytown aborigine-legend inclusive, part machismo, and triple parts ego and legacy. So, *What's in a sign?...* it said. *The makeup and measure of the man,* it answered. He had (he surmised and eclectically assumed) always been slated for greatness.)

"Eddie?" said Eve. "Can you hear the policeman, Eddie? Do you have your hearing aids in?"

There was a faint pause. Eddie didn't answer. He looked back across the police chief's desk, back over to Eve dismissively, and then out and away and into the distant far corner of the nearby cinder block wall.

"It means you could go to jail for the rest of your life, Mister Jablonski. That's what it means," continued Police Chief Friday. "Mister Jablonski, do I make myself perfectly clear?" *Can you hear me* was inferred?

Eddie gave a big sigh. He shrugged, then sighed again (a greater breath). He smiled sheepishly and then precisely, categorically replied.

"Hello! Earth to Police Chief Friday!" declared Eddie. "Am I not a hit man, Mister chief of police? Don't you think that as a *paid-his-dues and* **made** member of the grand fraternal order of the mob and an alumnus of distinction of Hitman U, us hit men, we know that we (if caught) as top flight and embellished to-the-nines alien-criminals could spend the rest of our lives in prison! It's in the manual, kind sir. Page one. Paragraph one. Single spaced! In bold italics! A big *Double duh,* to you, Mister Police Chief." Eddie looked back across the desk at Police Chief Friday then back to Eve for clearance, support, adoration, and backup. He continued inelegantly, brusque, it was in the pit of his unwavering voice, "Now for the love of Jesus Christ and all the saints that laid down their lives in their line of duty, come up with something I haven't thought of or heard before, will you? Please."

He caught his breath. He re-crossed his legs, His left slipper front-and-center dangled to an unheard beat, a doo wop number perhaps. He adjusted his ascot from front to back. He looked across the desk from his side of the desk back to Police Chief Friday's side of the desk, he looked over to Eve sitting alongside in the standard witness protection issue chair and continued, "Let me introduce myself once more just so we're on the same playing field in the same ball park and on the same frigging page, your honor. I'm Eddie. Remember me? (Eddie points to his temple, question mark inferred.) You know, Eddie Jablonski, Eddie *The Icicle* Jablonski. Hit man extraordinaire. All of this … this … this stuff that you're telling me … guess what? It comes with the territory, chief, the territory of a notorious hit man living in the bowels of infamy day in and day out three hundred and sixty-five days a year and one more on leap years. Forty-five years of committing crimes, murders mind you, documenting them no less, and I have to come down here to the freaking police station at the behest of my policewoman-cop girlfriend and turn myself in in order that my high crimes and misdemeanors can be rectified in the county ledger. Thirty-six times! Or, if you count the Smithereens murder and the Clausen murder, make it thirty-seven or thirty-eight. But who's counting? Something you two would know nothing about. I wasn't sure where you were going with that (lead question). Places unknown perhaps, then you circle back. Chief, (Eddie sighs again louder than before.), it's who I am. Get it?"

"A feather duster, three c clamps, a pair of battery cables, a pack of plastic zip ties, accompanied by a see-through satin drape. Your earth will move, Eddie Jablonski and then you're mine. I will have melted *The Icicle* forever," said Eve. "For life," she finished whetting her old lips. She pulled out a stick of discount L'Oréal super gloss Danish Dark from her bathrobe side pouch and reapplied liberally.

"Eve, you kinky conundrum," replied Eddie. "You come on hotter than a ten-gallon vessel of Cramergesic sunny skies midday Mazatlán south beach mid-July. Liberating the wild in my wildebeest. Livening the shake in my rattle and roll. Me, you nerf kitten ... your bathtub toy."

Eddie blew Eve a kiss which she caught and cuddled to her cheek. Love in the eighties, they both concurred.

"Eddie," said Eve. She was the complicit seductress. "Honey, erotica calls. A spank on the tush, it's a blank check into Eve's lover-abyss. I've strangled on erections the size of winning, county fair cucumbers, Eddie. Bigger than anything 'The Icicle' can resurrect. Point of fact into the future, our future, my love."

"Oh, come now, Eve," replied Eddie. "It's not possible. You're bragging. It's so unlike you," said Eddie.

They laughed and laughed and laughed and laughed and laughed like drunken fools near the fourth bottle's bottom as they loved to laugh at one and the other's ill-mannered jokes.

A G-string. Tassels, too. Fuzzy handcuffs. A ruffled boa. A feather duster. A corn cob and three martinis. Perpetuity. Purgatory on ice (pun intended). Collect your $200, you beast. Pass Go. Another Get out of jail card free. All of it the randy side of sultry senility, and just a few of Eve's favorite quips that Eddie adored.

Looking at his watch, with the faded face, the analog one from his Vietnam tour, Eddie asked waggishly, "Am I dead yet?"

CHAPTER 22

Hands on the Clock

From the Cold Case Files & Confessions of Richard 'The Ice Man' Kuklinski Entry #106. For over three decades, Richard Kuklinski served as a notorious contract killer for the East Coast Mafia. The real number of Kuklinski's victims is said to be somewhere between one and two hundred. Selected events herein are recorded, recreated, and transcribed by Edek Jablonski, a successful, retired author-crime writer as well as purported kinsman to 'The Ice Man' himself. Room 315. Voices from within. Bringing the dead to life one last time in a murder victim tell-all.

From the desk of Eddie 'The Icicle' Jablonski. The next chapter as interpolative exposé. The victim's narrative as it might have been told.

Sitting at his desk, Eddie wrote:

Since my divorce, I'd been seeing several women. Each one was different. Each one served a different need. Each one served a different desire, a drawn-out fantasy, some lucid to filthy to absurdly lurid addon to my incomplete, obsequious, and tone-deaf marriage of sixteen years. I'd had enough. Picking up the pieces in a most appreciable and self-serving way seemed only natural and spontaneous. *Now* was all about me. Round and round she goes and where it stops nobody knows. *Why not?* I always say. *What pain?* Chalk it up to experience and move on. I have.

I'm pretty sure none of them knows about the others. I've been discreet. Tracks covered. Just our little secret which is actually my little secret. The panties, the teddies, the sheer and enticing lingerie and sex toys, they go home with them every time. No trace. No harm. No foul. Ignorance is bliss, at least in this case and as often as not. Trip the light fandango.

To be honest, it was no different when I was married. There was this one and that one and a time or two in between those other innocuous, lady ledger entries, women and women and more women at my leisure and whim since I was married to the boss's daughter. Except not just any boss. I was married to the *Boss of Bosses'* daughter. I liked to kid myself on occasion that it was my dazzling good looks that attracted all the hot babes ... but come on. The old man, my dear, beloved pops-in-law was head of the largest and most powerful of the five crime families in the known universe, Mister Beau Brummel himself, the lead dog, capo of capos, *Big Paulie* the original dapper don in the flesh. Millions blowing in by the hour like a flock of Canadian geese on a Mach-fed westerly on touchdown in the broad expanse of some open corn field at harvest ... it didn't inhibit his lifestyle or mine.

Frankly, looking back, I never fit in.

When Connie, my ex, moved out and in with her dad, I was relieved. Fear not, I told myself. She's finally rid of me. And she left me the townhouse, I said astonishingly to myself. He's (her old man) finally rid of me, too. We were never close by a mile. Off the payroll and out his hair, I told myself. Of course, it wasn't long before I got my eviction notice (alongside my walking papers) from daddy Paul's lawyer and three, menacing toughs who guided me down the long hallway, into the stout, sleek whisper jet of an elevator, down another longer hallway, into the lobby, and out curbside into the open, not-so-fresh air. Car fumes everywhere. Traffic. Car horns honking. Hustle and bustle. Pedestrians by the dozens, with conversations all about, and me now standing there all alone an arm's length over from a meter maid writing up a time-expired violation ticket. Foreboding if not ominous for sure. Shortly afterwards, I found myself picking up a few marital furniture leftovers abandoned next to the street side trash, Tuesday-pickup bin. Within the week, I was back at the same tiny apartment I'd lived in before I got married. Second floor. Suite D. Down the hall from the staircase and around the bend from the fire escape. A bit worse for the wear to put it mildly. So, a downgrade for sure but, hey, all in all, it was a good run. I could almost hear and feel the giant sigh of relief in a Big Apple exhale from way over there to all the way over here on this, the other side of town where I now lived. Me, the blue collar, butcher's boy, him the mafia don supreme whose daughter was little more than a dreadfully spoiled and self-absorbed Italian princess if ever there was one. A billionaire father-in-law and his ne'er-do-well, womanizing son-in-law … the match made in hell.

But, guess what … in spite of it all, I still got the ladies. Lots and lots and lots of women. Mostly by association with the old man's dough mind you. It helped. Immensely. It wasn't my money, I know. And never pretended it was. But let the beauties think what they want, I told myself. I was covered up in pun tang. Sicilian snatch, Ukrainian twat, Russian minge, American muff, Neapolitan fanny, you name it. Pablum for the soul. Not bad for a happy-go-lucky, fat guy swinging a meat cleaver by day and single malt by night.

Having said that, Sundays were my designated day-off. I chill. Put my feet up on the ottoman and read the paper (mostly ads), but I still like the comic strips and the sports section. I'm a statistics goof. PATs, batting averages, ERAs, QB ratings, aerial yards, shots on goal, knockouts, timed events down to the hundredth of a second, all that. Even steeplechase and Daytona 500-time trials. Some of the guys tell me I'm nuts. Takes all the fun out of watching the games or enjoying the event, they say, but I say, what the heck. Whatever floats your boat. Made money off it because I paid attention. Infuriated the father-in-law not to mention my ex-old lady. Made more in a weekend than all week splitting briskets into T bones and beef jerky.

It was a Sunday when my wife left me. The next thing I know, she's moved out all of her stuff and moved in with Daddy Paul, Mister Castellano, the big cheese, the head banana and man in charge. I figured at that point she was really serious. So far as her old man … I wasn't fearful. We always seemed to be on decent terms, cordial, amenable son-in-law to father-in-law. I worked the jobs he provided. I was punctual, reliable, conscientious, and personable. Too personable, I guess, with some of the other female employees, but every man is an island I say, every man's a king, or so I've been told, each to his own and every man drives his own bus, sees things his own way, but inside is hidden the child that wants to play. That's what I'd heard, too. So, I was just taking care of business with a little playtime for myself on the side. Full circle. The women, they were there. I was there. We got along. Then, things progressed. Let's just say they took a shine to me. It was my pearly white smile against my olive complexion you could say. So, one thing led to another and then we were back at my place or their place shagging like monkeys on the crisscross of tree limbs in a treetop. Me Tarzan, you Jane.

Silvia screamed loudest. Mamma mia, mamma mia! Tatyana, with a tramp stamp just above her butt crack and left breast, she proved a proud, bilingual adulteress. Unless you spoke it … you'd have to guess what sordid, passionate innuendo and dirty doubletalk sounded like in her native tongue. I didn't. So, I could only imagine … so that's what I did … *imagined.* Fishing off the company pier, and me a butcher. Too funny for words. From the sound of things,

Mary, who cursed like a sailor, was no virgin that's for sure. Sophia claimed dyslexia so we did it mostly from behind. Roxanne rode the pony, giddy up, giddy up. Sally drove a Mustang and a hard bargain, but we always came to terms. And so forth and so on.

Then came the following Sunday after the Thursday showdown with my ex at municipal family court. In the hearing, me and my attorney, we made all kinds of demands of my soon-to-be ex old lady. Daddy's money. You get it. House paid for in full, car and car insurance premiums, stipend for living expenses and upkeep, clothing and medical allowance, etcetera, etcetera … you know, living in the custom I'd grown accustomed to living during our factious matrimonial disjointedness. I came in with nothing. Zero. Okay, so I had a soft, jelly belly, a silly if not endearing smile, and a part time erection to go along with my dimples. But that was it. She had the money. Daddy's money and lots of it. She had it all right off the get-go. It's not too difficult getting used to having everything on demand. So, I had gotten used to luxury and expensive shit and everything on demand. With the brass balls of Attila the Hun, my lawyer in closing says … "You and your filthy rich old man are loaded. You pay my client what he's owed and what he deserves or else." Just like that. Badda bing, badda boom. Verbatim. Jesus, Mary, and Joseph … me making demands of the head of the Mafia like I'm Julius Caesar and Napoleon rolled into one. Zacarro, the wise guy attorney, Zorro for short, and me, we high-fived in the parking lot pre-settlement like it was a sure thing. We were brash. We showed 'em. We had them right where we wanted them. *Saluto!* *Celebrare! La vittoria è nostra!* as well. Zorro would wait on their counter offer in the coming days. The sun, the moon, and the stars in the sky were ours! He assured me. *Per alcuni.*

But back to Sunday morning.

"What time is it?" she said.

"Four minutes before nine," I replied looking down at my hefty, diamond-studded, *Big Paulie* lookalike Rolex clone.

After a peck on the cheek, Svetlana left by the front door. Shopping. Sunday Sales. Department stores. More sales. Nails in a new, more impulsive and persuasive color. Shoes to match. And still more sales. The frothy coordinated bra, thong, and garter set was certain to subvert even my hedonistic imagination. *Sheer*, she said as she closed the door in a whiff. "Then skedaddle," I replied in a nod. I never ever argued.

At around nine, nine fifteen, I'm out the front door. Hop in the late model sedan (chick magnet) and head off to one of three or four places for a nice brunch, eggs over easy, fresh fruit, a side of pancakes, coffee black, and wheat toast with marmalade. As often as not, a side of hash browns, Polish sausage, and a waffle on a side tray drenched in gold Irish butter and pure Vermont maple syrup. Always found room for a nice, tall Bloody Mary with a pilsner backup just to wash it all down. Frankie boy's (that's me) motto to live by: It's why God made fat.

After brunch, I always moved from Cynthia's place in the late afternoon to Janet's apartment for a quiet evening alone. Seamlessly. It was afternoon delight in pairs. I'd tested the waters for over five months. Neither suspected a thing. Business to business. Travel back and forth. I was usually early, rarely late. The time in between left them needy and wet and ready. I bore gifts as a testament to my true feelings where in fact I had none. Truth be known, it was all about ego, sexual healing, diversity, more sex, more ego, more healing, plus it beat the socks off of three hours of Sunday afternoon Parcheesi over at Dominick's listening to him scream and yell at the television every time the Jets screwed up or did something right. If I had a wife like his, I'd stay home, too. Whew. A regular rack of lamb. And loyal what's more. I tried. Smooth talk. Lover boy lingo. Told her what I'd do. Told her how I'd do it, and how I'd behave.

Told her how I'd misbehave, too, and turn the bedroom inside out if just this once but just for her. She wouldn't hear of it … cheating on her old man that is. What a disappointment, but life goes on. Other mountains to conquer and fish to fry.

Sitting at the intersection, I'm daydreaming. Minding my own business. For once. Sure, my problems were too numerous to name. List from here to the mailbox and back.

"You got the time?" he said from over in the other lane. It was lip-synced for the most part.

"What's that?" I said in return. I wasn't sure. My driver side window was up. His passenger side window was up. He then lowered his passenger side window, so I then lowered my driver side window. It seemed okay, normal curtesy, even for the Bronx, and hospitable enough for an unusually quiet, Sunday morning with little or no traffic or pedestrians or jaywalkers or cyclist. We were just sitting idling at a meaningless red light waiting on green. Not a soul in sight. Nothing. Nobody. The guy just asked for the time of day. No big deal. Harmless enough.

"Do you have the time?" he said again. It seemed a friendlier version of the first inquiry so I looked down at my watch. It read nine nineteen. Rolex standard time. Nine nineteen A.M. That's what I thought to myself. The wristwatch was a present from the ex, exactly like *Big Paulie's*, that's what she said to me when she handed it to me all wrapped up in a fancy birthday box with the big bow and the knee-slapper birthday card. But I kept it because it made me feel like a big shot, and I told myself that because the thing was so fricking heavy for all intents and purposes it was my exercise for the day just putting the watch on, taking the watch off, and turning my wrist over to catch the time of day. It beat pushups or curls or going to the gym. You know … me, the chubby boy sex symbol of sorts.

I looked up and across at the other driver and said politely, "It's nine nineteen."

The pistol had already been leveled at my face. It as quickly went off. Boom.

The light changed to green. The crime, the killing completed. The job finished. The man in the other car, the shooter, drove away at a slow to abnormally slow speed, hardly a getaway, more a drive-away or saunter-away, a leisurely Sunday drive-by mob style, *Ice Man* effected, for some fresh air and a look with full and complete premeditation and malice aforethought. The man, the shooter in the big sedan, disappeared between the stack of tall buildings at the fourth intersection in a right turn. No witnesses. No crime report. Nothing. Nothing at all. Leaving the dead man, the ex-son-in-law, slumped over his own oversized belly and double chin with a bloody face and his foot still on the brake, his car idling in a purr like it had all been staged ... and immaculately so.

There was a special *Big Paulie* reward on the other side of the signature hit. All this according to Cousin Rich in a passing conversation a few months later. Bought himself a brand-new sedan, a Cadillac, in midnight blue trimmed out everywhere imaginable in chrome and leather with doodads and interior mirrors galore, a sonic boom stereophonic sound system and push button gadgets throughout. Plush. "Like it should be, Eddie," he said to me with that assassin's smirk.

CHAPTER 23

Art Class with Eddie

Every Tuesday was Art in the Afternoon. Room 186. Sponsored by Lillian's Florist and Catering. Art class was a real Eddie-favorite.

Eddie sketched. He sat up straight in his artist, *director's chair* (Eddie vernacular), and looked into the broad-board, the senior's easel in front of him. His vision was fixed, tried, and targeted. He sketched the way he did every Tuesday afternoon in this very same time slot. Today, in big, bold, block letters one quarter of the way down the page, he wrote:

Down at the Post Office.

Eddie drew a big circle. Inside the circle, he drew one straight line down the center of the page top to bottom. Then, again inside the circle midway down, he drew another straight line that bisected that line perpendicular left to right. A Scope. An Eddie-*scope*. Crosshairs. It was a la Eddie. Vintage Eddie. His Garden of Eden signature. Eddie was *fucking with them*. His words. *I love fucking with them*. After all, it was Eddie. Then, Eddie continued with his Tuesday drawing entitled, **Down at the Post Office**. My picture, he wrote. It was just below the title. There he'd sketched himself. In pencil. Gray, a silhouette, properly curved and contoured. His hair was fuller, not thinned like now. His face more supple, less aged, but still *Eddie*. Anyone could tell it was Eddie looking at the drawing then back at Eddie the artist then back at the drawing. It was Eddie alright. Not a bad likeness either, he thought. Then, beneath that, he'd chalked in bold …

AMERICA'S 10 MOST WANTED LIST.

Then he etched in a smaller lettering (it was neat, tidy, precise, like font to a computer type …

WANTED for MURDER. Multiple homicides. BE Forewarned. This man is assumed to be armed and very dangerous and an Alleged Murder for Hire Criminal!!

Then he printed in large capital letters …

DEAD OR ALIVE.

Then, he highlighted the above captions with …

Hit Man Eddie '*The Icicle*' Jablonski.

Then …

REWARD $100,000.

Then he scrawled the disclaimer in cursive … *If you have seen or know the whereabouts of this MOST WANTED FUGITIVE Notify your local police, your local sheriff's department, the FBI or other law enforcement agencies immediately. Help stamp out CRIME.*

Wednesdays was Be-An-Author at The Garden of Eden. Today in room 184, Eddie wrote his third short story, one called **A Miscreant's Missives**. Alliteration was Eddie, and Eddie was so alliterative.

If I could swing at God, I would. If I could connect and knock Him down, I would. Even a sucker punch, the way He's done me. That would be better. If I decked God, sure, he would get up and kick my ass, just like all the other times before, but it would feel good just to get in a stiff overhand right followed by a really nice, well-planted uppercut as payback to seal, secure, and redress some of the pent-up hostility, make up for at least a trace of the indecency and the flagrant disrespect I've been dealt and suffered through my entire life on His watch.

Destiny is a cruel task master. Plenty of lessons learned. Plenty of lessons forgotten. Plenty of lessons to come. Plenty of lessons in the foreshadowing. Plenty of lessons in the sunlight and the shade and after dark. Plenty of lessons. Plenty of lessons enough. Okay. Chalk it up. I got it. Lessons aplenty. Not nearly enough for some people but more than enough for me, an old man who won't be getting much older. Just the facts, ma'am, just the facts.

Once someone said to me, *Eddie, your plan is a pipedream. Wake up.* So, I did. I woke up. And I responded: *my whole life is a pipedream, so … what? … you're telling me something I don't already know? Change now? Why? What for? I'm at the end of the road and the end of my rope, a hangman's noose, all in one. I'm almost done. You're a little late, partner, if you ask, me. I'll just keep on going. Luck's bound to change sometime. If not, you can sound off. That is if you outlive me.* Eddie guffawed just to hear himself guffaw. While he could still guffaw … while he could still hear it. Few people guffaw anymore. Outdated I suppose.

Over in the far corner of the morning's workshop, someone hollered out: "Hey, Jablonski. Can't teach an old dog new tricks!"

Eddie shot back again mainly talking to himself, "Don't need any new tricks. The old ones work fine. Learned them all the hard way."

Eddie's poem was entitled:

A Luckless Loon with Noble Intent.

Why do the noble die? Why don't they live on and give lessons in nobility alongside the virtuous and noble minutiae and particulars?

My sentiment:

The ones that should die, don't. But I could fix that.

A sentimental sojourn. In sentimental soup. Sentimental claptrap? Sentimental soap? Sentimental slave? Doused in Sentimental sauce?

A Poem entitled Cover Me Before I Die by Eddie 'The Icicle' Jablonski from Thursday morning Poetry Class 10 AM to 11 AM in Activity Room 122 with Instructor Ms. Irene Hamill. Or Miss Irene. Or … Eddie's take … Boom-Boom Hamill, with knockers the size of overripe muskmelons … Irene (I REEN) the siren (Sigh REEN) … again, this was Eddie. Nothing sexist about it. Speaking the truth. If its sincere and heartfelt, honest and spot on, all's fair in lust and war. (Eddie-ism # 88). Lust can be discrete if not innocent and purposeful, but indiscrete and jaded as well as indecent. Why not? Just ask *The Icicle*. Where wisdom's uncovered, truth revealed, one layer at a time.

To Ms. Irene:

Covered up in heartache. Covered up in life. Covered up in dread. Covered up in loneliness. Covered up in you. Covered up in sadness and sorrow. Covered up in a stoically painful tomorrow. Covered up in yesterday that I can't but would just as soon forget. Covered up in one-sided love affairs too numerous to neglect. Covered up in displaced want. Covered up in disconnected kindness. Covered up in love, and make-believe and sweat. Covered up in sweetness. Covered up in shameful intent. Covered up in fear. Covered up in bed. Covered up in liveliness. Covered up in you. Dreading tomorrow, I am so lost without you. Covered up in loss. Covered up in destiny. Covered up in what will be, won't be, and never was. Covered up in fantasy. Covered up in hardship, pain, and suffering.

To be young again and fitful enough again to be anxiously lustful and yearn and burn and crave my nubile hard body counterpart and then be able to do something about it.

Old age is the pits, and an open, still, and flameless one at that, but maybe it's just the dress rehearsal for a next, much better life to come. Onward. Avanti. Dalej.

Ms. Irene blushed when she read the note, Eddie's poem, but Eddie simply grinned while standing there in front of her all-alone pad and pencil in hand.

"That's quite sweet," she said.

Then Eddie turned and left Activity Room 122 a prouder and more confidant old man.

CHAPTER 24

Hallway 7th Floor

*F*rom the Cold Case Files & Confessions of Richard 'The Ice Man' *Kuklinski Entry #27. For over three decades, Richard Kuklinski served as a notorious contract killer for the East Coast Mafia. The real number of Kuklinski's victims is said to be somewhere between one and two hundred. Selected events herein are recorded, recreated, and transcribed by Edek Jablonski, a successful, retired author-crime writer as well as purported kinsman to 'The Ice Man' himself. Room 315. Voices from within. Bringing the dead to life one last time in a murder victim tell-all.*

From the desk of Eddie 'The Icicle' Jablonski. The next chapter as interpolative exposé. The victim's narrative as it might have been told.

Sitting at his desk, Eddie wrote:

The drugs were to be delivered to Apartment G 7th floor. That's my place. Surprisingly, the package never arrived. I pled innocent. No one believed me, but that's what I told them. I stand by my claim even though I was lying through my teeth and the gold cap two over top left. Told them I didn't know *nothing*. Couldn't understand what could have happened. Maybe the delivery boy got into it, I told them. Saw the contents, knew it was worth more than hourly wages driving a box truck around Manhattan and Newark. As for me … Better a bit nettlesome than dead. In my line of work, that's always a very fine line.

I was there all day and through the night. Told my girlfriend to take the night off just in case the guy showed up with the box, he was late, or something else unexpected happened. *You never know,* that's what I told her. That's what I told the others, too. It was a big payday for everyone including me. I knew that. No fucking around, I told them. No excuses. I said that as well … convincingly. (*Convincingly* was always my forte.) Instructions were … take delivery… then meet downtown. Nothing complicated about it. Capisce. Understood. I said that three or four times the day before in the seven telephone calls between head capos and crew. Capisce, capisce, capisce. All around. Just like that. Got it. I got it. You got it? I got it. With bells on. *Wild horses couldn't drag me away …* playing in the backdrop when the doorbell rang, and I got up from the recliner and the second quarter interception (trade the fricking QB for god's sake! He's no Namath. We all know that.) to see who was at the door.

Always used the peep hole. Always. I lead a dangerous lifestyle. Illicit. Crime infested, promiscuous, and debauched. Make no bones about it. It's the reason God invented peep holes. Gangster peeps. And, no, not people … spyholes. Sleaze blanketed, checking out sleaze. You choose what you choose. '*Eeny menny miny moe*' is not for me. I weigh the risks. I weigh the rewards. I weigh my options. I make my own decisions based on the facts, the past, the present, as well as my gut. And then I live by those same decisions; I abide by them and don't dwell on the outcome. Life's too short. You can second guess yourself into the grave. Somehow things take care of themselves. That's what I always tell myself in the final analysis.

So far, so good. I'm still upright and paying my bills. Day to day and as often as not, I'm covering my butt through the magic mirror at eye level on the front door of my rented apartment.

That and checking out the young, slim-waisted, busty, blonde receptionist, my nearly-next-door neighbor, coming and going and flaunting her wares in tight skirts and tighter blouses with her thighs exposed even in the winter under the open heavy overcoat with the fur trim but more so in the spring and summer and fall when I would watch her fumble with her purse strings just to find the key ring and the mess of keys attached until she found the right one to open the front door to her apartment. So fine. My, my.

Her … with this guy and that guy and then two Fridays ago, St. Patty's, nearly midnight, some guy, burly, dark haired with a topcoat draped over his arm, he's groping her, fondling her, sucking her jugular, licking her neck just below the big, round, dangling gold earring, then her earlobe, then pulling her dress up and banging her up against the wall in the hallway. Turns her on a dime and throws it to her from behind full blast. A couple of highly accomplished pugilists against the ropes giving as good as they get. All this at a quarter past the hour before the two would even go inside. Two dogs in heat and perfectly matched. Did everything but bark. She moaned. He moaned. She moaned. He moaned and whispered sweet nothings in the do. Her tits fell out, her crouch next, legs up to here, his bare chest against hers, then her one leg straddling his, then both in the air like she was riding Secretariat bareback, ass and all. It was all there just a few feet from me like I was meant to gawk and stare. Did everything but ring the doorbell and ask, '*Wanta watch*?' Who wouldn't? God was she lovely.

On a separate weekday, I pressed one eye of my binoculars into the portal and stared at her nipples showing through her blouse, this for several minutes while she searched again for her apartment key. I was wise to the routine, time of day, when she leaves, when she comes back. I hoped she wouldn't find the key. Then she could knock on my door perhaps and seek shelter or comfort or help with her dilemma, but she uncovered it hiking up her skirt with her bare thigh and one knee propping up her purse so I got a longer look. It was mesmerizing and wantonly wonderful. Rather, *she* was mesmerizing and wantonly wonderful. Make no mistake. I washed my face with cold water and took a number of long and deep breaths afterwards. My God.

Voyeuristically speaking, I suspected she knew what was going on nearby. In fact, I know she did. Must be nice. Thought that every time I watched her ... voyeuristically ... time after time after time ... standing twenty feet away with her hands on her hips, her chest just so and out to here, her makeup kit in the one hand, fumbling for her keys with the other while tossing her hair back just to taunt and tease and titillate me, her out-of-sight, out-of-mind hall-mate. I'm certain of it. And it's another reason God invented peepholes. Wide angle, for the record, is by far the best.

I always stood to the side, left of center. Sometimes I would place a pair of shoes, my slippers say, in front of the doorway as a decoy, in case someone shot at me through the wood panel. It was reinforced. I bolted a half inch steel plate midway on the inside of the door for protection. I'd seen enough Cagney movies in my day, so I knew what could happen to bad guys like me, Donnie Does Drugs at 1-800-Donnie-Does-Drugs. (We deliver.) Just my line of work and the line of work I'd chosen. No problem. We've all got problems. Some bigger than others. Some more dangerous and life-threatening. Risks. Rewards. I could deal with it. The good, the bad ...plenty of ugly, but I could deal with that, too. Then stretch out in a lean and peek through the glass portal to see who was there and what was cooking. Nobody's fool, mind you. Nobody's. I took precautions because I am who I am and knew where I'd been and what I'd done. Some of it was grotesquely foul, vicious and *insensitive*. (I love that word, *insensitive*. Can't do justice to the *injustice*, the crimes I've committed and the other ones I'd witnessed. Euphemism is too soft even on the underbelly of the meaning of the word. *Insensitive* … the euphemism of euphemisms if you know me and my line of work. Ha! Heinous more like it, and that doesn't begin to do it justice or compliment the task as the devil's own.)

A man lives for only so long. Day to day he works and toils and labors. Or, on the other hand, he works at not working. Some men secure success by virtue of their hard work. Other men find success by avoiding work altogether, that same work, toil, and labor the other man devotedly and fastidiously pursues. It cuts both ways. Common, undignified chance or plain, homespun, simple, and indifferent fate make success viable and attainable by either routine, either route, whatever the pursuit. One man's hell is another man's heaven. *It's all the same* some would say, and I contend that no truer words have ever been spoken. What's more, at the completion of the game and the end of the day, *success* is *success*. It's that simple. You've acted out and attained life's goal since your success has been achieved. It's no more the crooked path that counts, or the virtuous, streamlined highway you've travelled that counts, or the willy-nilly bumps and tumbles encountered along the way of how and where and why you got there that counts, it's simply that you did your thing and you achieved success.

A cheat, a liar, a thief, a forger, even the most common and bumbling adulterer, the most unsophisticated swindler, or sniveling murdering thug, is just as likely and liable to stumble onto success as the righteous, dignified, and honest man. Crossing your t's and dotting your i's scores points, it counts for something but from either side of the ledger, rightfully or wrongfully.

A liar purveys nonsense as truth so in someone's else's eyes it becomes just that, *truth*, words forged to concept, in and out of context no matter the circumstance, and voila! That same liar, he has won over his audience in full. The tale is told no matter how short or tall, twisted or preposterous, and made believable and noteworthy and exceptionally plausible at the same time by some or all of his listeners. It's the liar's gift. The cheater's, too. Prevarication and mendacity are their aim, their guise, their lot in life, and as often their crooked craft through some sort of disfigured talent which bestows credibility to their schlocky, seamless schtick. Think Flagstaff for a fleeting moment with a loftier, lazier purpose with a sharper glint and brighter twinkle in his eyes. That's the backdrop, and these are my people.

Long live the cheat and the liar, the bootlegger, the fraud, the louse, and those even worse! say I. Because for all intents and purposes, I am one of those. Me. From a long line and lineage of these same cheats and liars, rogues and miscreants, mind you. A murderer here and there not to mention a great uncle convicted of forgery and jailed sufficiently, but, when examined more closely and when all's said and done, the sum of money in question was well worth the effort, his risk, had he succeeded. Hear ye, hear ye! Select company, I say, one and all, one for the ages, and for certain.

So … long live the lot! Bon mot, bon mot, I crow. And I can bellow, boast, boo, and brag in a ruse with the best of them. Mark it down. You've never heard of me, but you will. Not by design but simply put, it's that I didn't fly low enough under the radar. Low, but not low enough. Here goes.

Conscience is frail and pitiful and a nuisance to real freedom and the criminal mind and its way of life. It is mainly for the weak-minded engrossed in their trivial pursuit of some absurd noble glory and moral high ground … trite and spineless in my opinion … for the clueless souls and clowns that mingle among us. Little more than ground fodder to a hedgehog. Those that travel the back roads like snake handlers from a tent revival, they should step out into the open and be counted, but only at the appropriate time and only then into a dim light.

The preacher laments this life, on this earth, and makes way for the next one in the hereafter. A preposterous pretense at best. The politician laments this same life and this same earthbound condition and makes way for this life and the one just around the corner through his idle jabber (promises, promises) and nebulous confection. Neither is worth much more than the other. Same outline. Same story. With two useless conclusions that trail off and never arrive at fruition or their claim and promise of some happy ending ... Except, that is, for the con man (preacher, politician) himself.

I can see better from here. From behind the small glass eye in the door frame. Little do they know I'm there watching and listening and examining the movements of passersby in the hallway, up and down the staircase that empties only a few feet from right here at my front door. I wouldn't have it any other way. It was the main reason I took up residence here. The peephole is the moat around my castle. With such well-deserved, argus-eyed surveillance, I am protected ... as well I should be ... even if I do say so myself. Particularly with my seedy history in this degenerate backdrop. After all, it's my ass on the line.

The day the doorbell rang I was more than a little suspicious and certain it was one of the mob bosses stopping by to pay me a little visit ... along with a few henchmen as muscle. *Where's my money? Why haven't you delivered the dope? Pay up or else?* That kind of thing. So, when I got to the front door and peered into the magic mirror, my spyhole, I was very, very pleasantly surprised to see the next-door neighbor in short shorts and a revealing, white, tight wife beater standing barefoot outside with her one hand on her hip, the other holding a Pyrex measuring cup waiting patiently for me to open up.

"Well, hello," I said swinging open the door wider and more hurriedly than ever before.

"Hate to bother you," she said, "but I'm baking cookies. Ran out of sugar. The bag looked half full, but it wasn't, so it's either bother you, one of the other neighbors down the hall, or get dressed and trapse down to the grocery store for one measly little old cup of Dixie Crystals. So, here I am. Do you mind?"

"Oh, no, no," I said. "No bother whatsoever. Come on in, and let me go to the kitchen and grab some sugar for you. Hang tight," I said backing up and disappearing into the other room. "Is sugar all you need?" I called out.

"I believe that's it," she replied from the front entry. "Butter's on the melt. Milk aplenty in the frig. Chocolate chips galore. Just the sugar."

I returned with a brand-new bag unopened. "Here you go," I said most chivalrously. "That should get you through a few batches or more."

"Oh, that's more than enough," she replied. "Thank you so much. And I'll be sure and return a new bag to you later today or tomorrow. I promise. With fresh baked cookies as a thank-you."

When she turned and started back down the hall, I watched and stared and kept looking until she turned to go back into her apartment. She waved. I waved back. She was more beautiful than I thought or had imagined. Then she was gone.

Another shadowy figure of a large man stood alone and silent in a lone silhouette and half-turn profile much further down the hallway, but it was no interest. She had come and gone and would return again. She promised. I closed the door, slicked back my hair, and caught my breath. My place was a wreck, I thought, but she didn't seem to mind and by her own admission was indebted to me. Finally.

The lone man, the same large man at the end of the hallway, waited four minutes. He moved closer to Donnie-Does-Drugs' front door and looked into the peephole from outside in using the peephole view reverser. He saw nothing. He bent down on all fours and looked under the front doorway through the open threshold and could see that the man's slippers had been removed. Again, it was clear sailing.

Minutes before, he'd listened carefully as the hall-hottie, the blonde, knocked on Donnie-Does-Drugs' front door … per instruction … at his request … with the promise of a cash reward for obtaining a cup of sugar from Donnie-Does-Drugs, 1-800-Donnie-Does-Drugs. (We Deliver.) That was all that he'd said.

As quickly, she'd replied, "*So, I go knock on his door and ask for a cup of sugar, get the sugar, and return to my apartment … And that's it?*" She asked incredulously. *And you'll pay me $100 in cash. That's it?* She asked again with an expression of excitement. Before the large man could reply she said, "*Sure. Makes my day.*" So that is what she did.

Standing at the far end of the hallway, the large, ominous figure of a man had listened carefully to the rhythm of the young woman's knock, the cadence, the loudness or volume, the number of raps, all of that so that now, as he prepared himself, he could mimic the sound of the hallway-hottie to a T … as bait … sex sells … every time … always has, always will … he knew that … his exact thought.

Taking the large pistol and suppressor from the inside pocket of his jacket, this same man, this looming figure of a man looked on one last time into his reverse peephole viewer. He dropped his scarf and nudged it between both feet and the front door threshold. He placed the barrel of the gun over the peephole. It had been measured for other jobs prior to this one and this moment, and so it fit perfectly. He then reached down at the exact location and height where the women had knocked on the same door and rapped …

knock, knock, knock, knock, delay … knock … just as the hallway-hottie had done minutes before.

"Coming," said the voice inside. "Sugar, sugar. I'll be right there. Cookies so soon?"

The man holding the gun on the outside waited, he looked through the reverse viewer one last time, saw the occupant, his eye, now just as quickly in front of the magic mirror, then cupped the tip of the silencer over the portal, and pulled the trigger. Thud, thud, sounded the gun. The shooter moved away from the door, removed his scarf from off the floor, and bent down again to look under the doorway to see the man inside the apartment dead in a heap. His one bloody, displaced and missing eye stared blankly straight away into space. The man's other eye went unnoticed. It didn't matter.

The Ice Man, Kuklinski, he stood up and stepped away. He fished into his other inside coat pocket and pulled out an envelope. He then walked twenty paces back down the hallway and stooped over to shove that same envelope containing one one-hundred-dollar bill beneath the next-door neighbor hottie's doorway sill. His thank-you note said simply, *Cheers*. Printed in a scrawl. Semi-legible. No signature. No message. Nothing else. She'd done what he'd asked … retrieved a cup of sugar and went back into her apartment. No questions. No discussion. She'd been perfectly marvelous and marvelously perfect for the job, matching her comely appeal and voluptuous looks at the same time. He told her he'd leave the cash reward in her mail slot on the first floor. Instead, he slid the unmarked envelope under her door having wiped away any leftover or possible fingerprints from any and all of the paper exchanged, bills, pad, sealed or unsealed.

He moved silently down the emergency exit stairwell floor by floor by floor by floor then seamlessly through a clearly marked overhead egress which emptied outside into the gray, cold afternoon air in the street side alleyway. He walked two blocks at a comfortable and casual pace, unlocked his sedan, moved in behind the steering wheel, looked about for oncoming traffic, and drove off without a hitch. His job completed.

CHAPTER 25

Eddie back at the Police Station. Round Five.

E ddie is seated across from Police Chief Friday. The two are looking at each other with quiet complacency. They've talked before. Here they are again. It's not like *old times*. It's more like *here we go again*. Eddie waits. The chief begins.

"Mister Jablonski, you told this story to me several months ago. This is the Paul Castellano story. The one about his murder at the steak house, Sparks, several decades ago. I know. You were there." The chief looked across his desk at Eddie and exhaled politely, visibly, a tinge of exasperation but respectful as respectful as he could muster.

"Well," said Eddie. He was polite as well. Incredulous though he was, he took another breath and continued. "You didn't do anything, chief. So, I'm back and telling it to you again. Maybe this time you'll get the magnitude of the event, the seismic happening of that evening, and then you'll arrest me. I was a really, really bad guy back in the day … a bad guy … a Hall of Fame criminal and felon. Hell on wheels what's more. Are you with me? I still don't think you get it. It hasn't hit you full force, the impact and implications of Big

Paulie's death, his murder much less my involvement. It changed the course of history, chief. I was a part of that, an integral part. Just like Gotti and Gravano and cousin Rich and the rest of the gang. We were all there.

I should be arrested, here and now. Put away forever … a life sentence, two life sentences, or more. But that's for the judge to decide. You just keep taking notes. Maybe you'll have an epiphany and see how important this visit really is. This is a tell-all. Not like the other visits. They were important in their own way. Warmups, so the two of us get to know each other a little better. You, the cop … me, the gangster mastermind, been there, done that, old school when *crime-don't-pay* meant something and nobody paid any attention. The good old days, chief. But you're too young to remember so I'm doing my best to fill you in on what was, who was who, and who I was and still am. You with me?"

Eddie stopped. He took a deep breath. He stared back over the desk at Police Chief Friday, then stood up and put out both hands in front of his chest with his wrists together.

"Go ahead. Slap the cuffs on me," said Eddie. It was the dramatic *Icicle* talking, the histrionic pro from olden days and days gone by. "I've been freer longer than I should have been. I'm turning myself in. They'll never miss me at the Garden. Besides, they're all brain dead. In the meantime, you can make a name for yourself so it's a win-win for both of us. Maybe you'll get a raise. And for me? Leg irons if you feel the need. At my age, I'm probably not a high-risk, AWOL-cut-and-run escapee kind of a guy, just not the type … you could ask my mother, she'd tell you, but she's been dead, thirty-five years almost to the day … but that all may change once I'm incarcerated. Don't know. You never can tell what a person might do in a certain, unspecified situation. Once known for a spot of cabin fever in my youth. It might resurface. Human nature. Be forewarned, chief, be forewarned. I bust out … you can't say I didn't give you plenty of notification and a fair warning on the backstamp of Eddie's honor … so be it hereby declared."

Eddie sits down and begins the story of the night Big Paulie was killed. He was there.

"It was like this. And I know, I was there," Eddie said. He backs up to the visitor's chair and sits down again. With a heavy inhale, Eddie began again.

"Castellano … Paul Castellano to be exact, he couldn't decide … gangster-mob-boss or Wall Street tycoon? Gangster-mob-boss or Wall Street tycoon? Hmm? What'll it be? Big Paulie couldn't decide. But you can't be both. Doesn't work. Besides, he wasn't both. He was a trust fund baby of sorts. Inherited what Carmen had left him all neatly bundled into the slickest racketeering and gambling and drug running enterprise in the history of mankind. Spun like a top except smoother. All Big Paulie had to do was not fuck it up. And, by the way, just so you know, driving around in a stretch Lincoln doesn't make you a Wall Street tycoon. It just means you're driving around Manhattan in a stretch Lincoln, and that's it. And in this case, on somebody else's money. As with so many trust fund babies, Big Paulie, he found out the hard way.

I was sitting in the car with Cousin Richie just across the street from Sparks, the steak house the night Paulie was murdered. Gun downed in cold blood. Rich and me, we were backup, but we weren't needed. Gotti and Sammy the Bull were three cars away, same side of the street, laughing and yucking it up the whole time in the front seat of the Dapper's Caddy. Richie and me, we could see them from where we were parked. Richie even said to me twice, "Look at those two idiots laughing and yucking it up waiting on Big Paulie to be assassinated," just like that. Nonchalance parked three cars down from nonchalance. Speaking of … at the same time, Big Paulie pulls up in the stretch Lincoln in front of Mister Steak. He's all dolled up. Top coat, hair slicked back, his matching Gucci glasses and loafers, with the Lord & Taylor cashmere scarf draped around his neck, the Brooks Brothers topcoat, like he's an aspiring Captain Blood and Errol Flynn in one. I admit it was kind of exciting. I'm sitting there watching knowing full well that Big Paulie is about to be no more, the man who thought of himself as the *epitome* of the *epitome*. I believe that's a quote. A famous person from somewhere in the past. So, you'd can look it up if you want.

Carneglia. He was all business, Carneglia. Not a man you wanted on your bad side. Hit man, criminal entrepreneur, ladies' man I was told … made no difference. Job at hand was job one. Appeared out of nowhere. Pistol drawn, he fired six shots straight into Castellano. Bang, bang, bang … there was no pretense to the hit. Hell, you could hear the shots as far away Seventh and 42nd. Bang, bang, bang again for good measure. Big Paulie fell like a blue spruce in an open canyon of his own concert jungle. That quick and it was over. Chief, you had to see it to believe it. It was cold as Hades, dark as Central Park at midnight, and strangely no one was around. Nobody on the street, in the alleyways, no pedestrians in front of the restaurant, left, right, or down the middle. I saw two cars pass five minutes before the Lincoln pulled up at Sparks. After that, nothing. Not one taxi, not one car. Someone knew. People had been tipped off.

Eerie is all I can say. And I'm a tough guy, a hit man. Has to be really, really eerie for me to call something *eerie*."

Eddie then paused.

"We'll see, Mr. Jablonski," said Chief Friday. "We'll see. That's a very interesting story for sure. Thanks for sharing."

Eddie left the police station at half past the hour, walked through the sliding glass doors, crossed the parking half circle, and returned to his front row seat on the Garden of Eden transportation shuttle. Jenkins greeted him.

"How'd it go, Mister J?" asked Jenkins with a concerned smile.

"Not good, Jenkins. Live to fight another day. Not good at all," said Eddie. "He still doesn't get the full ramifications of the dalliance and imposition on criminal history. He's a youngster I know, not a punk mind you, but he needs to take the admissions of criminal guilt seriously regardless of the timeline. I fully realize that I'm not in my killer prime. Some of the swagger and intimidation has faded. The look … the *if looks could kill* look … it doesn't have that same radioactive feel and glaring disposition from my youth. Youth really is wasted on the young, Jenkins. It really is."

Chapter 26

Del Rio

From the Cold Case Files & Confessions of Richard 'The Ice Man' Kuklinski Entry #80. For over three decades, Richard Kuklinski served as a notorious contract killer for the East Coast Mafia. The real number of Kuklinski's victims is said to be somewhere between one and two hundred. Selected events herein are recorded, recreated, and transcribed by Edek Jablonski, a successful, retired author-crime writer as well as purported kinsman to 'The Ice Man' himself. Room 315. Voices from within. Bringing the dead to life one last time in a murder victim tell-all.

From the desk of Eddie 'The Icicle' Jablonski. The next chapter as interpolative exposé. The victim's narrative as it might have been told.

Sitting at his desk, Eddie wrote:

Waiting around in Del Rio. Another layover. I was assured I could catch the next flight out later that day, an evening flight, so I said okay. Actually, I just nodded. Like I had a choice. And, no, Greyhound wasn't an option. So anyway, I stopped off at the nearest bar. The Del Rio Bar & Grill. Quite the catchy appellation. But what it was lacking in creativity (a sobering sobriquet) it made up for in old school, honky tonk ambience, small town, main street, truck stop-diner décor, and understated if not altogether ambivalent hospitality. The neon sign, red and green with flossy, dayglow white trim, said *Open for Business,* so, I took them at their word and walked in.

First things first.

There was no one at the front entrance. Not a soul. Not at all what you might expect anyway from an establishment that looked like this one. Not the oversized bulky dude with bulbous biceps, shaved scalp, and a scowl on his face all tripped out in grisly, garishly sidewinding tattoos and migratory facial hair. Not the atypical buxom and brawny bar mama with stacked, tinted hair (post '60s beehive), a lip, brow, and nose ring, and cowgirl eyelashes out to here looking naughty and down her nose acerbically at unsuspecting clientele … the same chick that's always fond of flirtatious trouble from the right macho-branded patron-types in tight jeans and sleeveless cowboy shirts. Nope. None of that either. There was no one. Not a person of any description large or small. So, there I was standing on the inside of this seedy, uninviting threshold all by myself, tortoiseshell Dolce & Gabbana's in hand, vision adjusting.

Looked around, left, right, and straight ahead, saw an empty space and an opening on the other side of the fluorescent jukebox (howling and wailing) next to the waitress station and a stack of freshly washed and wet barware. I just as quickly moved onto the first, most comfortable bar stool imaginable via a side straddle mount then followed up with a shot … Don Julio Blanco down the hatch … a lime wedge … death grip between the incisors … then a beer back … frosty to the touch and as quickly at the back of my throat. Aye. For the love of Saint Patty. As quickly, I felt right at home.

Onboard to my right were two tawdry, too-hot-to-handle waitresses. Straight ahead was the bar maid (*whoa and somehow, I just noticed which was so unlike me*) sliding the frosty mug (handle first) my way. *Whoa* again. A babe. Delightful. A real doll. Delicious. A local seductress, no doubt, suffocatingly sultry with an hour glass figure to tempt the eye of any man worth his salt. A scrumptious smile and heirloom breasts the size of country Tuscan-Italian melons. Tuscan face and features as well, straight from a High Renaissance oil on canvas. Sweetness and clarity of form, serenity, harmony, perfection and visual brilliance. She smiled, and I smiled back because I'm no fool. At least not that big of one. Predilection told me that that smile of hers was special and pointed directly at me like double index fingers in a gangster lineup. It was a present, a gift if you will, straight from heaven no less and from God on high, and a present and a gift just for me and mine all mine, something to embrace in the interim and the wherewithal of my dingy, little day, my teentsy unsettled tomorrow, into forever and the next unholy week and whatever it might bring.

Sometimes fate doesn't lie. It just spills the beans right in your lap. And on rarer occasions, that '*sometimes*' brings about a very pleasant surprise. This time I was certain I was on to something. (Whoa.) This was my lucky day; at least that's what I told myself. At a second glance and a longer stare, I was sure of it. At least that's what I told myself a third time in the mix. I assured myself that this telepathic, extrasensory forte of mine of sorts (all mine) particularly when a pretty woman like this one looks my way and smiles, and I know, without question, that smile, her smile had to be just for me. And if it wasn't, then I'd just go on believing that it *was* because it had flat-out made my entire day a whole lot brighter in an empty instant. She was something else.

"Lost your way?" she said.

"Not so," I replied chivalrously, impunity in play. "Now that I've met you, I'm right where I belong." Juggled intemperance and mock cleverness ... sometimes it pays off.

"Boy, that's original," she replied. "Never heard that line. But I give points for effort so keep trying."

"So, what's a beautiful girl like you doing in a dump like this?" I asked.

"Pays the rent," she said. "Customers like me."

"Count me in," I said. If she was keeping score, I was throwing up threes from half court.

"So, passing through?" she asked.

"Flight cancelled. Leaves later. Time to kill. Saw the sign outside. Here I am."

"If you're headed to Devil's Cay, I'm game," she said. "Or Kamalame. Either will do."

"Wow," I replied. It was an exceptionally smooth *wow*. She smiled in return. So, I was certain she got it, so there.

At the end of the bar were three cosmic cowboys with custom crushed straw cowboy hats and crapped out boots and jeans arguing about who won the bet. Pool cues in hand. Apparently, an eight ball in dispute. The one dude held the nine ball in his hand as a show of semi-temperance I suppose. But hardly the first stripes and solids melee I'd witnessed. I didn't belong, but I played along because of the bar maid, the delightful babe, the real doll, who was even better after a second, third, fourth, and fifth peek over and under, beneath and between my custom, designer European shades … like I wasn't checking her out the entire time and as if she couldn't tell … that is until the fight broke out in the far corner by the pool table, and I knew I didn't have a dog in the hunt, a cross to bear, milk spilled, an axe to grind, or beef in the broth.

Let every man skin his own skunk, I say quoting my derelict father. So, I seconded the motion and left after leaving a one-hundred-dollar tip for Tuscany on a ten-dollar tab. (Drug money lets you do that.) Sidestepped in a slip and reverse dismount amid all the commotion, and escaped out the side door into the Texas heat and a blacktop parking lot to a whole new life, one with bigger problems of a different variety. Associate to soldier to capo to made man to don. The sky was the limit, I kept telling myself, and my goals were all laid out in a row in a straight line at the back of my mind's eye. I could see my tomorrow. I'm just not so sure tomorrow could see me. Ever.

Before I could start the car, out of nowhere, the bar maid, the babe, the real doll, had hopped into the passenger-side seat beside me. Unannounced and unrehearsed, with that same big, adoring smile painted all the way across the front of that beautiful face of hers, she said to me, "Where to?" Just like that. No kidding. Which was the look on my face as well. And, that's what she said in return. She wasn't. An incandescent moment in the annals of my insignificant life … me … the existential misfit … Sartre's lap dog … Beckett's Bowser … from the unexplored, unpublished treatise entitled … *Untuned, Unloved, & Untamed … So, What's Your Problem?* (You can look it up if you don't believe me.) She leaned in with her eyes closed, puckered up, and history, our history, erupted. The rest was about us. Ours. Say what you will … heaven on Earth has its moments, and this was one.

We kissed for ten minutes straight. I timed it. The face of my knock-off Bulgari was looking back at me throughout. Without interruption. Lips to lips, neck, both sides up and down, earlobes one to the other and back again. We groped some more, then checked into a nearby motel, wrestled over, under, above, and between the sheets, until both of us were exhausted and spent. We left the motel in a synchronized heartbeat, drove to the airport where I bought two, first class tickets on an upgrade (drug money lets you do that) to the east coast as a mister and mistress Alphonse Gabriel Capone.

Don't expect love, I told her. *Don't expect normal or what you've grown accustomed to expecting normal to look like. Don't expect sanity. Don't expect the expected. And love comes with a disclaimer so know that, too. You're with me now. So, be a good scout. Be prepared. Prepared for the worst, the unexpected, as well as the shuck and jive of unseemliness. It's all just a prelude to the next step,* I explained like I was Guido and Plato's older brother. *Oh,* I added, *if you hadn't figured it out by now, I'm a walking caveat. So there.*

She looked at me with love in her eyes, at least that was my interpretation. But it may have been sheer befuddlement. Or maybe just some kind of unimportant addon that I had misinterpreted altogether where in fact it was little more than west Texas boredom and maybe just a touch of stark lunacy brought on by too many dust storms, oversized habanero hot tamales smothered in green chili, and unmeasured shots of cheap, unstarched, unbranded mezcal.

"But what the hell and whatever," she replied in a perfectly matched response. Since she was giving points, I was too, and she'd just scored big.

We'd closed in on something comfortable so we were off and on our way.

That was eight days ago. Not bad for tentative … exceptional for me. On day nine, my new sidekick, she mentioned baby or maybe it was babies. So, I called a taxi, told her to visit her mom and dad and friends back in Del Rio, pushed a wad of hundreds into the palm of her delicate, little hand (drug money lets you do that), kissed her forehead, her cheek, her lips, and waved from the driveway as the yellow cab pulled away.

I missed her, I admit it, until on day eleven, when I stopped in at Cassavetes's Lounge on 39th and Elm for happy hour, bellied up to the bar, and came face to face with Alessandra. Whoa all over again. Fidelity was never my strong suit. We loved until dawn until I was back at my place until I was back at work making devices that would blow you the fuck up and sky high at the same time. Hugs and kisses, that's how I signed off with Tuscany when she called later … which was intended to be the last time.

Even the sound of it, fatherhood, frightened me. I was unfit and knew it and troubled by the remotest prospect. Better men than I had tried with all their might and failed. And miserably. My own father, my old man, he was one such. An unlucky stiff if ever there was one.

And now look at me. On the lam. Two mangled and bungled prison sentences, though brief, before the age of thirty-five. A murder for hire that I can't and won't talk about. Two guys in a ditch on another occasion where I wasn't sure if it was me or the other, oncoming car driving on the wrong side of the road at the same time just before impact. Sure, I'll take credit just so long as I don't go to jail and I still get paid. And sure, I was trying to kill the son of a bitch. But it happened so fast who knows? A desired outcome is a desired outcome. Mission accomplished. Cash on the barrelhead; I got my money. *Moving right along*, that's another motto to live by in my business.

Long time capo *Sonny Boy* Delecante said to me, Zoomie (my time in the Air Force), start a fake business, something wholesome, American as apple pie, something that people love to love, something close to religion but not religious, with clean-cut and healthy overtones, something nice and sweet with whip cream and a cherry on top. Make it frilly if not patriotic, or say, maybe genteel but not too fancy. Inconspicuous and as out of sight, out of mind, and innocuous as you can make it. It's for your own protection. It's your disguise. That's your storefront. You can lower the shades anytime you want. Turn down the lights, as well. Then you can do business anyway you like and just point back at the storefront, the one with your great, big sign on it … the one that spells out *you* … the personification of one law-abiding United States of fucking America Citizen Kane *you* … like … what? … who me?... what'd I do? … when the shit hits the fan. They'll never suspect a fucking thing. That's what long-time capo *Sonny Boy* Delecante said to me.

Almost his exact words with the curse words exquisitely, perfectly, and properly placed as *Sonny Boy* Delecante so exquisitely, perfectly, and properly placed them every time he spoke. Old timers, they're worth their weight in gold, and never to be taken lightly. I've always said that.

So, I did exactly what long-time capo *Sonny Boy* Delecante told me to do. Bought a banged-up, abandoned Mister Softie (ice cream) truck, beat out the dents, gave it a fresh coat of paint, rejuvenated the logo into brighter blues and rosier reds, located a couple of shiny retreads onto the back, restored the freezer and the sliding side window, then drove around the neighborhood selling soft-serve popsicles and shit to all the little tykes, twerps, and nerdy brats with their smoking hot mothers situated along the route in their short-shorts, perky halter tops, and smiling at stupid me from the sidewalk's edge of their sprinkled, verdant front lawns. Would've loved to serve up some you-know-what to a few of those lovely ladies … little Johnny's hottie Madonna types of the suburban junior league and lawn club. But I was Clara Bell the clown on wheels, tunes and all. Almost drove myself nuts as well after a week or two listening to *Pop Goes the Weasel* twenty-four seven. Changed out the ghetto blaster in week three … at the *Flick of a Switch* with a *Stiff Upper Lip,* until I was *Back in Black* and headed around the corner toward that *Highway to Hell.* So, *Give It Up* (for me). *Come and Get it* … cause *Money Talks.* You get the picture.

In week four or five, I parked the used Mister Softie ice cream truck in the driveway just for effect. I had cast my spell, set up the storefront, ratified my citizenship, radiated love of country and community while fostering all things neighborhood, kids, kids' moms, summertime and the living's easy. I was Jersey boy Gershwin and Captain America personified and rolled into one. Fish were jumping and the cotton candy was high. Apple pie switched out and substituted with ice cream. Botta bing. Botta boom.

My mother, Mama Zoom to my service pals, used to say to me, *Son, you've got the looks of a movie star … a matiness idol.* She was all aglow with a mother's love that day. *Oh, you're so handsome,* she'd say in her own way in a kitchen tizzy. *You keep this up and you'll be more handsome than all of those beautiful men on the movie marquees combined.* So, I kept it up, at least I guess I did. *Almost pretty,* she'd say later kissing my cheek and pressing my face between her hands. But from the get-go, I took it in stride. I mean, come on, it was my mother. But I have to admit, women loved me. I smiled, the women they always smiled back. I could tell. Goes with the package, I guess. And what's not to like. It was me. And me, a lady's man without really even trying. Life, sometimes it's a frigging peach and a really succulent, sweet one to boot.

I'd moved into the rental house on a Tuesday, and the next thing I know the big guy with the sullen expression and enormous frame said, "Howdy," he was my neighbor. "Check this out," he said next.

So, I did.

Demolition was almost the first word out of his mouth. *Explosives expert wanted* is what he said unvoiced or nefariously intimated and inferred. I was, but he already knew that. With my new neighbor, everything in conversation was cloaked and somehow, if only subliminally, fiendishly juxtaposed … a wisp of thin air or an inconspicuous breeze next to a nearby firestorm only a block and a half away. This guy, the big man, he was like reading a weather vane at the top of El Capitan.

"From here to kingdom come," he said. "Our Father, who art in heaven, you know the rest. Then … nothing left," he said intimating almost licking his lips and nearly salivating in the moment. "Obliterated particles to nothingness," he orated. "Cosmic dust. Forlorn pieces of patchwork of somebody else's yesterday and a forgotten, unlived tomorrow. Shrapnel to smithereens. Front yard septic shock on the half shell," he said in that hermetic smile of his, sly, stealthy, unpleasantly seductive, foreshadowing the macabre and charnel. "Little more than the faint whiff of a fairy fart when all is said and done," he said lastly.

I had no fucking clue where this was going, but I listened.

I, too, was looking to become an associate. I, too, was looking to become a *made man*. If I had a game plan, and I'm not sure that I did at that point and time, that was my game plan and that's all that I knew. The girlfriend, the barmaid-babe-the real doll, back in Del Rio at this point, wasn't pregnant. But what if she was? And what about the others I'd been with recently. I thought futuristically, and I had never thought that far ahead in my whole life ... ever ... there'd be bills to pay ... then bills to pay future tense. And me the retired USAF grunt coming off six plus years of a government black hole specializing in depth chargers, IEDs, un-improvised and improvised, handheld detection to mine sweepers. A licensed and professional saboteur at your service. My future was bright, I thought, underworld bright with unlimited possibilities, me, a professional in a semi-employable circle of hucksters, dilettantes, and diabolically-driven miscreants. I could only succeed. I was destined to do well, if even by my own covert tyro-gangster guesstimate.

When I pulled it out of the garage, the big guy was all smiles ... giddy by big guy standards. We drove to the wooded area just beyond the obscure boat landing where the abandoned car was parked. A land yacht from a bygone era of foolproof automotive opulence and souped-up delinquency. I unleashed the contraption in a hail Mary and watched as the wobbly machine stumbled and sputtered to its resting spot beneath the parked car. We waited. I counted to ten. At seven or eight the abandoned car went up in flames, debris shattered the quiet, and cleared an opening between the hedges. Exploded shit was everywhere and all around. So, we left. The big guy was again all smiles. I even got a high five.

"Here's some dough for your trouble," he said congratulatorily palm down with a roll of twenties, fifties, and a couple of hundreds mixed in. "Now, let's do this again, real soon," he continued. "Got a job next week. This will fix the problem. Not my problem, but another guy's problem. Tie it up in a bow with a big, bright pink corsage and all the trimmings," he said happily, or as happily as the big guy seemed to get. "He'll never know what hit him," then let loose a full-scale grin.

You meet all kinds in my line of work. Good, bad, malicious, vicious, stir-crazy, vindictive, happy, sad, smart, crafty, and wily, too. But this guy ... the big, enormous fellow with the errant and sneaky smile ... I was certain from the start *now here's a freaking guy that's not playing with a full deck.* I had this uneasy feeling but kept it to myself. It was my first lesson of sorts in mob-associate self-preservation and a fast read 101 on La Cosa Nostra *associate-*to-*made man* self-awareness all at the same time. Mob boss axiom à la Sonny Boy Delecante: A lot of information makes you just a little smarter. Don't let it go to your head. You just might wind up worse off than you were before you learned what you learned ... maybe even dead. Capisce?

Back in Del Rio for a few days to check on Tuscany and well worth the quick trip. Contraband, narcotics, weed, speed, psychedelics, uppers, downers, smack, crazy pills and more coming across the border at will. A pirate's treasure chest of a dealer's booty coming to a town near you, and I'm the pirate. Then it was back on another evening flight to the East coast. After that, it was just me and the big guy back in Jersey. And no, I didn't mention the extracurricular business venture to big Rich. No need to make a shady deal a Sherwin-Williams shade darker, more contorted, or any less comfortable for yours truly, me. Left well enough alone.

Pals? I don't have any pals. Friends either. Just customers and people that like me, put up with me, tolerate me (mostly work related), dismiss me. Others of little or no importance don't like me, maybe hate me, or don't know me and couldn't care less about me because I don't matter. I'm sure there are a few here and there out and about that loathe my existence because of the dozens of beautiful women I have made love to (and they haven't), but really now, come on, I'm not important enough to loathe … even if I stole your girl for a night or two or maybe even for the entire weekend. But really. It's just little old me. Maybe later … you know … once I've become a *made man* say … and then a *don* … after years and years of murder, mayhem and getting even and doing deals and settling up, screwing and getting screwed … maybe then I'll be worth loathing, but not now. Hey, but give me time. I'm working on it.

"Devil's Cay," I said to Alessandro in our third romantic rendezvous somehow signaling commitment and caring and some sort of us-together continuum. "I'll meet you there," I said in parting.

So, I lied; it's all part of my profession. Personal and professional life are interchangeable. Again, it's the life of a rogue. An ardent misanthrope. An ardent philanderer. An ardent criminal. An ardent sociopath. Pick a hat. I wore them all with a smile, a glad hand, and petty, ready-made pontification off the cuff like razzle dazzle and sparkly glitz at an open, nickel and dime funfair venue. Ah, hell, who am I trying to kid … I'm half carney. I headed to the airport to board the flight, not to Devil's Cay, but back to Del Rio and Tuscany. *This can't end well, but I'll give it shot,* said my inner voice, and myself an A plus for effort.

One day the big guy took me aside. We were in the garage. I was finishing up the next project masterpiece. It even had a bell on the engine for effect. I flipped it with my index finger to show the big man that the bell actually worked; ring, ring.

He smiled and added, "Kaboom." Then he looked down at me in his own nonchalant and merciless way and said,

"There are always those people hanging around, people looking for and starved for attention, a handout, or maybe even a crumb. You see them every day. People without relevance. People looking for some kind of cockeyed recognition, looking for that very same purpose and pertinence and germaneness and relevance that comes about from hard work, trial and error, and testing the waters, often treacherous, because someone has the precept and gumption to churn out and glean success. But these so-and-sos, the hangers-on are clueless and clueless even by mob standards. Seeking a temporary (ego) fix merely because they have nothing going for themselves. Starved for attention, they attach themselves to notoriety in hopes of notoriety … thereby becoming or achieving *notorious*. That gives them relevance or that's what they like to think. What else do they have to talk about? *Nobodies* running off at the mouth and beating on their chests about nothing they did or ever accomplished in hopes of relevance, recognition, or some semblance of the two. Paparazzi-target wannabes less the flashbulbs, tall shrubbery, eucalyptus trees, tall parking garages, and other secret hiding places. But really. Come on. That's preposterous as we all know. Vicarious thrill seekers one and all at the expense of someone else's experience, thrills-sought, failures and successes, pain, and know-how. But it doesn't work that way. It never has, never will. That's not the way it works at all. You know it, and I know it. So there.

Besides, it takes all the honor out of cheating … not to mention, lying, stealing, murdering, racketeering, running drugs, money laundering, and just about illicit everything else." Big Rich had finished. He smiled and sat back.

I said nothing. Nodded but didn't answer. Just taking notes. Always taking notes.

We met the next week. I handed over my latest creation (a nasty, little gerbil on wheels) to the big guy. He was all smiles. Drove to the downtown location. Parked the car. Got out. Opened the trunk.

Fired it up, then he pointed it in the general, implied, and intended direction, at the target. With the big guy now in charge of the controls, he guided it beyond the median, over the speed bump, and underneath the blue Cadillac convertible. The top was up. Seated inside were two passengers. It was apparent even from this distance, inside there were two men. One in a fedora. The other in a Gatsby. The two shooting the breeze and smoking cigarettes flicking ashes out the side, tinted windows which were cracked with gray smoke billowing out in an exhale at their own muted leisure. The big guy looked at me. I looked back at him. He nods. I nod. He pushed down on the lever, the red button, and all hell broke loose across the way. Kabul before Kabul. The two guys in the blue Cadillac convertible had been converted to a volcanic puff of blue smoke and three rolling, topless, bottomless hubcaps which lay capsized and sprawled in the middle of the street next to the gutter, one rolling around next to the other like wobbly sputniks searching for a place to land. No idea what happened to the fourth hubcap. The blast was that powerful ... problem solved. We disappeared in an instant back onto the busy interstate.

"Problem solved," said the big guy with a wider smile on our way home.

Me, I was little more than a gangster greenhorn and *made man* wannabe learning from the best, but a first-rate gizmo-grenade and explosives saboteur nonetheless.

We did a few more of these over the next couple of months until one day, out of the blue, I said: *cyanide.* Cyanide poisoning via vapor spray via a poof and a puff and you're dead cyanide poisoning. I continued. The big fellow listened.

Knew a guy in the service who knew a guy that had another guy screw him over. *A big-time triangulation,* the (screwed over) guy explained. *Triangulated* him out of his wife, his money, his house, the good car, then his marriage *"and basically made a fool* (his word) *of me*," he said. "*The cuckold.*" (His words again.) The *fool, the cuckold* part of it was bigger than the money part or the wife part even though the wife was one really, really hot babe. That by all accounts. He added: "*Didn't know what a cuckold meant. My buddy from the next block over told me what it was. Over a cold beer and set of socket wrenches finishing up a tune-up ... while I'm getting a tune-up. Ironic, I know,*" he added. "*And me a grown man, but I didn't know ... that nor the shame attached to it. When I found out, I said to myself, I will never be the cuckold, much less any woman's fool. But then it happened. I was that very thing that I said I would never be. And with only one way out,*" he said finishing up.

So, a month to the day after his wife had left him, the jilted guy made the *cuckold* and the *fool*, he dresses up like a postman. The blue uniform, name, rank, serial number, the postal patches, the black knee socks with the all-purpose postman sneakers, with the beefy leather carrying pouch strapped and slung over his left shoulder. He bops around the corner down the sidewalk looking all professional ... waving to the neighbors all friendly and postman-like ... moustache in place with the blonde wig (him with the balding pate) and thick-rimmed, clear paned glasses just so to hide his identity ... through the white picket fence ... past the pint-sized, barking (yapping) dog ... up to the front porch where he lifts the brass knob and knocks ... then knocks again on the door of Mister Triangle, the guy *triangulating* him from his money, his wife, his house, the better car, and his marriage, and when the guy finally opens the front door, the postman-jilted-husband-fool says, "Need you sign for this one, sir." So, Triangle takes the cuckolded, fake postman's ballpoint pen, presses down on the dotted line and signs his signature in a scrawl ... this as the jilted-husband-postman draws the cyanide vapor dispenser breath freshener lookalike, covers his own face, and unleashes in the slightest puff a faint blast of the perfect lethal dose into Triangle's open face. Triangle man's living space and life had been breached, violated, and compromised. Triangle staggered about, gasped twice, then fell back into his house. The postman-jilted-husband pushed the dead man's foot back into the foyer and closed the door. His ex-wife discovered her new lover boy dead on the floor three hours later. The cause of death … Triangle's … an apparent heart attack.

So, I said to the big guy, consider reducing the collateral damage, the apparent and obvious mayhem, the visual, sideshow side effects, the cop commotion, the spectators, the gawking, the blue lights, the newspaper reporter assemblage, the neighborhood rubbernecking, etc., etc. You get it. Switch from *crazy to stealth*, I told him. *Peep show carney style* to *backyard voyeur*. Death is death, from the front side or rolled over on its back. A mission accomplished is a mission accomplished, I said.

The big guy, Kuklinski, he got it right away and was so excited he was grinning like a kid at his own birthday party … pony ride, popcorn, wrapped gifts, ice cream, cake with lit candles, the works.

It was a Tuesday. The breath freshener cyanide dispenser was in the inside pocket of big Rich's jacket. It was cold that day. Overcast. Brisk but invigorating. A deep breath felt wonderfully vivacious and invigorating enough for a test run to murder. I stayed in the car parked behind a van and watched. Kuklinski set out on foot. Sidewalk, afoot, down the way a bit, across the street at the light, then down a small alleyway where another man, a complete stranger walked toward him. An elderly soul, harmless, defenseless, unsteady in his gait, hunched over and apparently lost in thought, demented or otherwise, this man wasn't a threat to anyone. Kuklinski fished the dispenser from inside his jacket, uncapped the container, covered his face with his handkerchief, walked by the elderly man casting a fine mist just out in front and before the unsuspecting soul's next step. Kuklinski kept walking without breaking stride as the elderly man, the complete stranger slumped to the ground unnoticed. He was dead. Kuklinski walked back to the car in an unassuming and forgetful stride, opened the door, sat down in the passenger's seat, and said, "It works." Just like that. And that was it. Aimlessly arbitrary and so capricious it was almost devoid of capriciousness itself in the telling, in the witnessing like he'd just pitched the leftovers in with the table scraps, took out the trash, and flushed the crapper at the same time. Insouciance in spades.

Later that evening, I took the next flight out back to Del Rio. I'd seen enough. Plans to become a *made man* were on hold because I figured I was next. The awkward vision of myself was either me as an unmarked nameless nobody in some city landfill, or me as the next plume of smoke at the end of a fuse-less, homemade improvised explosive device under Mister Nobody's storefront aka his refurbished ice cream truck, or me in mid stride minding my own business walking to work keeling over from a whiff of baneful Binaca on the sly ... no thanks.

Texas barren never looked so good. Tuscany either. Fidelity took on a whole new meaning. Maybe it has its place and a face after all? Sanctity and sanctuary came to mind in the rethink. Time will tell. It always does. Or, it doesn't. You can never be too careful or too sure, which is just another long-time capo Sonny Boy Delecante-ism. (For the record, what he actually said was, "You can never be too *fucking* careful or too *fucking* sure." I mean after all, it *was* long-time capo Sonny Boy Delecante ... him speaking *gangster*, and he was really good at it. Actually, the best.)

It was a few weeks later when I got word that Kuklinski, the big guy, my Jersey neighbor, had been captured and incarcerated. Handcuffed, a dozen cops or more led him across his front yard, saw his wife being led out the front door in handcuffs behind him, then he went crazy, threw a few arresting officers around in the front yard all handcuffed and shackled, headbutting and biting and thrashing, until thirty minutes later he was subdued and carted off for good. As I said, he was a big man.

I flinched as I grimaced as I perused, and then ducked into the shadows to finish reading the big Rich's arrest story for more detail. Simply put … I wasn't really that interested in the big guy; I just didn't want to be implicated in any of the big fellow's misdeeds. In jail, people chirp. The longer they're there in jail, the more they chirp. Then they begin to sing. Operatic like. When pressed for details on top of the details they've already provided, these same songbirds prattle on like an Amazon parrot after a triple line of pure, uncut coke. Names and places appear in midair. And so forth and so on.

That day, I packed up and moved to the other side of Del Rio into a smaller rental unit, changed my last name to Tuscany's, laid low, and as quickly abandoned what property I'd left in Jersey including the ice cream truck (my make-believe mafia storefront) parked in the driveway to whoever wanted it. *Free* read the sign, retreads, ghetto blaster, refurbished cooler, and all. For all intents and purposes, I'd vanished. Drug money lets you do that … that and a lot more.

"Zoomie?" You ask.

"Who?" I reply. "Never heard of him."

My mother still doesn't know where I am, but Tuscany and me, we just got back from Devil's Cay. Sure, drug money lets you do that, too.

CHAPTER 27

The Final Chapter

Poolside. Fountain side. A Bird Bath. A Subchapter.

A chickadee, two robins, and a cardinal were gathered outside around the bird bath. Fluttering their wings, scant dives, splashing, chirping … But these were not songs of love or sounds of frivolity and happiness in springtime. This was bully chatter, bluster bickering, and hate speech, intimidating rants and mocking disparagement. Hitchcock's birds. A nastiness all their own. Pipsqueak bird snarl, all of it frothy and fiendish.

Eddie watched through his window. *An omen*, he thought. *If not, why not? And maybe as close to one as I get considering my age*, he said to himself. No sooner had he thought this than he made the decision to take matters into his own hands. *It's that time*, he said to himself, *that time in life when everything down to the smallest detail needs to be put into its proper place, proper perspective. For the record. For posterity. But more so for my own peace of mind …* That voice within continued … so *that my life cannot be altered from what it was to what someone else says it must have been.*

Last Rites, The Final Chapter.

So, Eddie Jablonski spoke up. *Who needs a priest? Priest are for sissies.* (Eddie's words.) *I will administer my own last rites.* It went something like this.

The final chapter … everyone has one. I, Eddie Jablonski the writer, *The Icicle* to some … I said so in each one of my books. It's all there. You win some, you lose some, but once it's over, we all end up down in the endzone with team Hoffa. Sadly, God and the devil appear to be one in the same. I have wrestled with that overwrought and overly dramatic notion, that impractical premise my entire life, but that is still the best, most worthy description and conclusion that I can come up with even now in this late stage of living. It may seem a surly sentiment to some, nevertheless it's mine.

Usually toward the end or at graveside, the complete story of the deceased becomes quite the yarn in the retelling, spun into something so limp, so vague, that it's stretched beyond recognition, loose ended even fashionably haphazard with all the bruhaha and activity surrounding each shred of minutiae leading up to this point. Emotional commotion along with the baggage in full, everything is finalized, cinched into a black bow or maybe just an erstwhile slip knot that won't undo no matter how hard and how long you tug on it from whatever angle. So, that is what the deceased becomes forevermore. It's over. So, it's important the dead man gets his story documented or dictated before they do. *Finally* is a long time into the future and rubberstamped without room for later revision. Left in the handwriting of the wrong someone else or the penmanship of other uncaring souls, you, the deceased, could become a dreadfully piss-poor impersonation of yourself. Vanity forbid!

The final plot, it's usually a reverential cheap shot filled with mindlessly clever if not disingenuous double entendre, puns, pranks, gags, gimmicks, witticism, and linguistic homebrew, all of it from start to finish in a vague attempt to make the deceased look better than he or she actually ever appeared in real life. And, in this case, that would be me. No matter how silly or apparent or undistinguished, I'm still Eddie, the man in full and open disclosure. It's what made me, Eddie Jablonski or Edek to my mom (now long gone), or just *Eddie* to fans and friends alike.

On Following Your Gut?

If gut is the same thing as your *dream*, well then, okay. Have at it. But don't expect too much. It may or may not work out the way you want, but you're welcome to give it a whirl. Take a shot. Give it a stab. All's not lost until it is. What's more, it's on the house.

On Life As The Lonely Writer?

Lonesome? you ask. Sure, I was lonesome sometimes … the lonesome life of the writer-author as everyone assumes, but I never let it get to me. I had my words, my stories, their uninhibited characters and the brash and bold notation that followed alongside those same earthy characters' misadventures … misadventures of their adventures and tangled misappropriation stacked and piled high, end to end because they were bad men and rapscallions, skunks and monsters for the most part, the worst of the worst and then some, wrongdoers and evil-doers, some so evil they seemed to have lost their darkened luster just by the unsanctimonious company they kept in the interim … chapter in, chapter out, you could count on a gloriously wild ride.

Of course, all of them, men and women alike, were flawed in a way that made them blessedly interesting to the masses of my readers and casually real to even the most untrained eye and the worst, most inattentive non-bibliophile imaginable, that same inattentive reader(s) who finds comic books and children's fodder, even scribbled and captioned cartoons, difficult to follow or grasp … even they could follow along and get to the finish of each and every one of my works. No Shakespeare. Not by a long shot. Nor a Dickens or a Dickens knockoff and never, ever a mainstream wannabe. But still, not half bad.

Besides, those same characters (vivaciously vile each and every one indiscriminately) made us … you and me … they made us feel so much better in the moment about ourselves. For me, the writer, the feedback and reviews were a sensational high, a feeling of genuine and impenetrable accomplishment as well. I was invincible, or so it seemed at the time. A certification and verification between this human being, me the writer, and another somebody (or somebodies) out there in the great abyss and beyond, that reader or group of bookmen/bookwomen, in some other place and time, all of us together around campfire *Eddie*. Somebody I'd never met and will never meet, yet there we were, the two of us in that same place enjoying the same madness, the identically same silly Jablonski composition without a whisper of apology or permission asked or permission granted.

On the rocks? Coincidence? Fate? Maybe so, but I'll take it either way as the lucky or luckless son of a bitch that I am.

Looking back, that swath of nihilistic loneliness with its dull, drab, depressing, visionless absence of interaction, it was most certainly a gift of sorts like wartime to the gallant hero that makes it to the other side of armistice and a final peace.

My loneliness, that lonesome feeling and aloneness, it was a gratuity from on high because it lifted me to that other station and that other time and a place I couldn't go without my imagination being set afire and fueled and stoked again and again by that wonderfully empty space. That fitfully abject feeling of loneliness no doubt was motivation and spark and incentive adding to my personal devotion like a tailormade mantra. We were attached at the hip and indivisibly one. Inside the dome, I could leave this world, my reality, the here and now, for another, and I could get to that stark, uncensored opening, absent of anyone else, that opening and blankness that I called my own, that interval and emptiness I felt cradling and comforting me just to do what I felt I was called upon to do. Me. And I could look down on the world as a whole and objectify and pontificate and bloviate about what I'd seen and what I'd found and what it all meant.

A *writer's life* you say ... it must be grand somehow? Maybe, maybe not. The aloneness, the trusted solitary ambience is something all its own, and it's all mine with a majestic finale as climax on the other side. That much I knew then; that much I know now. There was no *perhaps*. There was no *question* or *doubt* about it; it just *was* and thankfully so. I can't say for sure how it all worked or why much less speak to anyone else on how to do it or how to get it done ... it's just what worked for me, Edek Jablonski. It's the way it turned out ... the way it came together.

On Advice. Eddie's take. & Eddie on Purpose.

Sure, I took the two pills prescribed by old doc what's his name the day of, but I was never one to call back the next morning for another dose or the next appointment. Never followed the doctor's advice or anyone else's for that matter, only in part and only when it suited me and my gut said it was okay. Just kept on. The words, the syntax, the rhythm and cadence, that was my compass. The drivetrain, the steam engine, and caboose as well. It helped me navigate and fill the hours with something people wanted to read and see things by way of a shared lamplight, bifocals and clear vision alike, like we were kin or at least kindred spirits of some kind and enough of something similar that they read my schtick until the end and put the book down when they at last felt their parched soul was quenched or at least partially replenished for a time until I brought out another bound book of stories or another round of my patented and copyrighted lunacy complete with baited and embellished jaundice, old school rigor mortis, catatonia still respiring … all of it a rhythmic and wordy fermentation saturated and splattered in blood and guts and brain matter making another mess of a whole host of other characters' lives and their happenstance until those same readers, intoxicated and sober together, could point, stutter and stammer, then fumble about inside their very own little pea-brains foraging for some upbeat interpretation and introspection about what it all meant where in fact it was little more than *murder* … plain and simple … and good, old fashioned murder just for the sake of it … that and having fun at the expense of some fictitious dead man-dead woman's dying.

Get over yourself, why don't you? Reading isn't calisthenics … at least not my stuff. Cradling, nursing, and coddling stereotypes is something of a passion of mine. Like it or not. *No harm, no foul if you've been forewarned* is my motto. Or, at least one of the hundreds of thousands that I've lived by on a daily basis.

Looking for entertainment is one thing … *hidden meaning* is quite another, something completely different and as unalike as crocodiles and pablum. So, turn the pages one by one. Lap it up, all of it. Enjoy yourself in the read and read into it whatever you'd like to read in … every quaint, quirky, and indecipherable phrase … have it your way … agendas, protests, deep meaning, hidden feelings, hurt, social commentary, trauma for the ages, mustard, ketchup, mayonnaise with pickle relish and a slice of cheese if you like … all of it just for you … full force … within every nook and cranny of my ink-stained mania. A bloodletting amongst leeches. We are one. Dastardly crime reader mischiefs and misfits one and all. I laugh at the image, the thought which is my own, because I am so darned clever that it simply amazes me in the telling.

In short, I nailed it. And that's when I became me, Eddie *The Icicle* Jablonski, crime writer extraordinaire. A man on a mission, mission accomplished. So dubbed.

On Burial.

My own personal final burial plot is in the back, further back than even that … still further … in the desolate, far corner, an unmanicured, unpretentious cemetery with the excavation … a hole in the soil with little or no shade from the midday sun, no protection or drainage from the rain or runoff, and completely exposed to the elements at all times. "Just the way it was my entire life." I told someone that very same thing the week before. A corpse and a casket … neither suffocate in a closed setting … neither breathes better in an open space … and little more than Eddie Jablonski's contention. Crammed next to twenty other look-a-likes, little small, flat stone markers with names and dates etched inexpensively, illegibly, chipped, and indecipherable on the face of the stone marble juxtaposed to the tall, elaborate structures up front by the wrought iron gate and the four mausoleums (four, count 'em, decayed and decomposing, egoistic tinkerers tapped for greatness in their own minds), money-bought facades, then corpse one through twenty at the very back row living paycheck-to-paycheck, and now all of us crammed together like frankfurters in cellophane in a mostly unkempt, weedy, and open field. Come to think of it, there used to be a rose bush on the property somewhere nearby. I saw it over there once. I'm quite certain. Before now … as my time is apparently up as well. But it, the rose bush, must have died, too. Only fitting. Don't know if it counts, but there are dandelions here in abundance and all about. The mower's blade is set too high to clip them, but broadleaf green and yellow go nicely together out here in the expanse.

On Death Itself.

In death, I am still Eddie. Nothing more, nothing less. I am calm. Cool. Collected. Ready. The dead man, me, I am matter of fact and succinctly cooperative and in the mood. Death's mood is unperturbed and inflexible if not staunch. But it is mostly uncaring. I am unmoved by death's style, the lack of formality inside the naturalness and flow of the natural order of things. *What the hell,* I said to Jenkins the day before, *we're gonna die* ... every last one of us. I made the best of it for the most part in the allotted time provided. I carved out what I could. Made it my niche for sure. As well, I've been listening to the voices in my head for over eight decades. It's high time the harps take over. Classical-lite on the ride over followed by a twist of Sibelius toward destination's dead end. Not so bad.

On My Epitaph.

My epitaph: *Paczkis and Chopin into infinity and forever. Vivaldi, too. So be it. Amen. Amen. A brief aside: I have three Segovia recordings I'd like to pack if there's room. Breathtakingly stunning. Amen a third and final time.*

On My Graveside Service.

At the graveside, twelve to twenty people will gather. No one will bother to count. Family members and close friends will stand beside the casket, alongside a priest as hired gun, and my fumbling, estranged daughter alongside Mister Ne'er-do-well, her pitiful excuse for a husband of twenty plus years. The Roman Catholic priest in full regalia will read from his list, his notes, and an open Bible full of loose-leaf, shredded paper markers for easy reference, all in an ecumenical cadence to fit the occasion. Birth, baptism, marriage, eucharist, Easter, Christmas, and now, death, graveyard. He will bless the mourners. He will bless the onlookers. He will bless the day. He will follow-up and finally bless the life of Edek Anton Augustyn Jablonski, me, husband, widower, father, grandfather, and recent great grandfather to another, and yet we have never met. We are utter strangers. Neither one of us would recognize the other in a crime lab lineup or exiting a subway station at the same hour in the same garb for twenty months straight.

"We are here today to commemorate the life of a loving husband, father, grandfather, and great grandfather. (That's what he will say and yet we've never met.) A man who worked his entire life to support his family, his faith, his country, and his fellow countrymen. Edek Anton Augustyn Jablonski, may God take you in His arms and carry you to his heavenly throne. May you rest in peace forever in the cradle of the Holy Spirit and the Christ child who was crucified, died, and was buried but then rose again from the dead to sit on the right hand of God the Father Almighty."

In short, religion is all about the show … a front for dishonesty, the illusion of self-righteousness piety, and crowd control. Flimflam dealt from the bottom of the deck one, two, three.

Graveside, The Day Of. Another Subchapter.

Ne'er-do-well son-in-law Runo, he will come for the money, his wife's inheritance (my estranged daughter Christina), her inheritance, the unread reading of the will, his cut, another first-of-the-month grubstake not to mention the house in the country, another all-expenses-paid sneak getaway with his mistress, the down payment on his gambling debt, the payoff on his nearly new, lease-to-own Mercedes, overdue country club dues, overdrawn checking account, the neurotoxic protein injections for his undisguised yet aging brow to look more age appropriate (Ha! him with this gut draped over his trousers' belt! Please, spare me.) standing next to his faint-hearted mistress, the two superimposed on other, adjacent tropical getaways while his wife, my estranged daughter Christina, is away, out of town on an extended girl's night out-weekend away. What she sees in him I'll never understand. She could do better. I've told her so. Even she agrees with me and has said as much.

What present money (his grownup child's allowance) can't or won't buy, Numb-Nuts Ne'er-do-well will simply wait until the next round of royalty checks comes floating ashore then he will spend his way into stardom with the locals. A cocktail cockatiel and showboat and nothing less, nothing more.

Sure, I know about his new love interest. As of yet to his displeasure, it's unconsummated. She's little more than a lascivious glint in his wayward eye. What's new? Lateral foreplay at this point, younger than his current mistress, young enough to be his daughter. More delectable by a mile and desirable on all counts, teasing him in their ever more frequent crossings. She, the little twat, can smell my money from way over there all the way from way over here, old man Eddie's money as down payment on future encounters. It would make it all worthwhile having known the old man.

On My Estranged Daughter & the Dynamics of Family.
My estranged daughter Christina looks evermore haggard each year. Botox never lifts sadness or forlornness much less desperation and life lost and unattained; it simply, if only momentarily, freezes the inertia of failed living, the subjugation of windless moments and a rudderless relationship as marriage, and the disappointment in general. Filler for her lips, filler for her brow, filler for her boobs and neckline and cleavage and cheekbone … even her dimples have disappeared in the whimsical, back and fill, regenerative excavation. The once artful, feminine, and womanly drape and contour of a female's outline is now just a maudlin imitation in lieu of grownup-pretend, a Harlequin's mask, etch a sketch, paint by numbers at the whim of her surgeon's scalpel as currency for his fancy-house mortgage and private clubs. What's a girl to do? A woman who's no longer a girl? Fudge has replaced sex. Checkout clerks have supplanted friends. Frustration has long since overwhelmed resentment. Insinuation is now preference to discourse. But, what

the hey. It's the normal pattern toward dissension, dismissiveness, demise, divorce into death.

Juxtaposed to Ne'er-do-well's mistress and his other nubile wants, my estranged daughter Christina will never win. The dress that she wanted for this day and the burial and all of its affected pomp and circumstance, the one in the window from the boutique is two sizes too small, almost three, so she's chosen another similar wrap in a more somber color, less splash, more doom-appropriate, but germane enough for the occasion at hand, all nursed in bleakness. But who would know? Much less, who would care?

Hankie in hand, Christina, she is all sniffles for show. Histrionics have always been her forte. Sadness aside, she pretends to evoke *'Ain't life grand'* over melancholy and woe is me. The sadness on the sepulchral half shell is deference to protocol amidst (her words), "A *few fucking attendees that don't amount to a beaver pond in a flashflood who showed up like they're going to get something.*" Quoting my precious estranged daughter Christina to her husband Ne'er-do-well Runo stepping out of the mortuary limo graveside, it's painful, shameful as well, but it's really Christina at her formal best (or worst). So, now you understand our family chemistry, the tension and disdain. Of course, the family bit, it's all hogwash. I know it. You know it. They know it. We all know it. So, who's kidding who for god's sake?

Noted on page one of the script entitled *Me*, the words read ... Throughout Edek Anton Augustyn Jablonski's forty-nine-year service as a professional writer he was never once a Rotarian, never a beneficent Elk, not a Y member, nor a school booster. Neither Unitarian, humanitarian, Sierra Club wannabe, political affiliate or political hack. He wasn't a party man or a party goer. Nor was he ever a parishioner of St. Mary's Catholic Church Belleview where the presiding priest drove over in a quick stop crosstown, hired on the spot, prepaid-compensated, and once hired spoke ad lib without knowing the deceased, the man Eddie Jablonski at all. There was no mention of *The Icicle* or the mob or the mafia or a gangster or bad guys, just Edek Jablonski. Pretty formal, pretty boring, pretty staid, and pretty offensive to me the dead man in memoriam.

The mystery of life stops here. And I for one was never a believer. As previously stated, God and the devil are one in the same or much too much alike (ay, there's the rub) for my taste. And yet, Fate, as every man's own personal Judas Iscariot, has stepped in, thrown the silver pieces to the floor, and you are done, a goner, finished, and guilty by association from the number drawn from inside the Mad Hatter's crown. The guilt, the angst, the anxiety, the second guessing, it's all gone, over, swept under the rug or out to sea. Like a deep, dense, dark gray fog, you are covered up and engulfed and blanketed in a shroud and veil of certainty, the certainty of darkness and death itself, for the first and only time in your existence. It is now passe. No future, no escape, no failsafe plan, no getting out of what you've started or jumpstarting something else just to weasel out of this one … you and another one of your hairbrained schemes you cooked up in the middle of the night just to make a buck or please your mate or put off the obvious headed your way like a breakneck locomotive spewing steam and cinders and aimed directly at you. The hand of fate, yours, is now the backhand of fate. You're done and done for as was pledged, promised, and guaranteed from the start. A voice from elsewhere says, *I hope it was a good run, Buckaroo, because it's over.*

Eddie On Writing.
Tribune feature article '82 entitled: **Eddie Does Crime**. Quoting Eddie. Eddie on writing, Eddie on art, Eddie on life, and Eddie on the art of life:

It really boils down to who you can fool. Pick and choose carefully, but most of all, get lucky.

Early on my wish list looked like this: #1) Become a famous author and make a bunch of money and get all the hot women I could stand. #2) If that didn't work out, join the mob as a hit man and whack or bamboozle all the people that deserved to be whacked or bamboozled, make a bunch of money and get all the hot women I could stand. That was it.

After a bit of fame, I started reading things about myself that even I didn't know about myself. For a short while, I became something of a vassal, subordinate, and prostitute to that very same gossip … gossip as pimp with me as a bit of the scrubber. Then I realized it was nothing more than a nuisance, a hindrance, so I dropped the entire notoriety farce as a pesky distraction. The sooner the better I say.

Remember too, dignity and arrogance are as unakin as kerosene and snake oil even though they both come from within. One lights and leads the way to greatness; the other poisons and putrefies the soul onto the wrongful slippery slope of self-treachery and a coarse and jaded demise.

Trade secrets (aka tricks of the trade) are as follows …

Work your ass off. Write, write, write. Anything. Anything and everything will do. Get it all down. Shake out the writer's cramp. Then, write, write, write some more. All day and into the night if need be. That way you show your devotion to your craft even if only to yourself. You're all you've got. Of course, you don't for a minute suffer fools gladly or otherwise. Better yet, don't be one.

All of my life, I'd felt I was simply preparing to die. "Get to the end," the negligent, uncaring voice inside my head would say. "Let it be. Give up. Drop what you're doing. Quit. It's useless. Stop the pain, the agony, the day-to day flirtation as torture. Soon you'll succumb," said that gnawing reminder. "Why bother?"

But then, out of nowhere, some other kinder, more empathetic voice, my own, would exclaim, "Oh, no you don't. Champion the day, Eddie Jablonski! Your work's not complete." So, I listened and followed the advice of my own voice and that same instruction to a T. It was a marvelous feeling with a magnanimous conclusion. I finished my books and lived my life knowing full well that I could settle up with the devil at a later date and time, knowing, too, that I owed the red-faced, bullying, diversionary son of a bitch nothing.

Whine all you want. If need be, complain as well. Make excuses, too. Opine in front of your full-length mirror if that helps. It doesn't serve any purpose so go ahead. Once you realize that little blunt, irredeemable point of fact as an everyday tutorial, you'll tone it down and get back to the real issue, the unfinished writing at hand.

Semicolons aren't meant to be pathological and don't tell a story. The fewer the better. In general, as well as specifically, punctuation's not sociopathic. A great story could be told without it, but don't try and sell that heretical notion to some, know-it-all editor-wisenheimer least they're left peeved, befuddled, or maybe even ineffectual and jobless. And just for the record ... in a world full of wisenheimers, malaperts, and smarty-pants, I seem to have known them all. In the interim, you already have enough worries as well as detractors just showing up with a manuscript in hand or under your arm.

Better yet, capture all your bitching and moaning on paper and turn it into a story, specifically someone else's story as opposed to yours. No one will know it was you doing all the squawking but you. And, who knows, the story might turn out better than you first imagined it could or would. By taking the spotlight off yourself and placing it on some other affable or despised so-and-so, you're free to boast, brag, chastise, coddle, foment, or ridicule without conscience. Conscienceless writing, ah, there's the rub! And a little-known and unexplored fact for the ages. Villainy to trust, trust to confinement, confinement to all-out subjugation then back to trust and villainy, full circle. So, call this conscienceless writing, this penmanship, call it love or replenishment or hate or servile resentment or anything you choose, you're in charge because you're the writer, and you're in charge ('light brigade' or otherwise) of the manuscript's destiny and the fate of those within … so move forward. And, for the record, it's only one of the many **rubs** *in this life that you and I will face.*

Be harder on yourself than you would be on your detractors or people you don't like. Why not? You'll quietly beat them to the punch at their own game. See their folly, resentment, dissatisfaction, and criticism as incentive to succeed and strive toward your own perfection. It might pay off in some unexpected way as well. On second thought, flip those same traducers and backbiters into a potpourri of miserable, cast-of-character sons-a-bitches inside your own jamboree of cooked-up fictional applesauce, ripe or rotten. It doesn't matter. They'll never know … too vain, overly foppish, and egotistical to see themselves in such a dim and unfavorable bright light. But you will. You'll laugh, the last laugh, at 'Larry' or 'Joe' or 'Moe' (clowns one, two, and three, stooges in their entirety) every time you read the passage knowing that you know its them but they don't. Scores are best left unsettled if you can't win them on your own terms so let them die on their own accord. Life is made whole through small victories inside even smaller skirmishes.

Furthermore, be sassy, bold, adventurous, noble, wry and subtle, too, all within the context of grade school grammar and syntax. Language has already been invented. Use it to your advantage. You're neither slave nor master. You're the train's locomotive engineer (à la Casey Jones), not the manufacturer-inventor. Stoke the boiler, power the beast for god's sake. Give that same language room to breathe. In addition, give that same language its due. The makeup, distinctiveness, markup, and continuum of diction as language is the writer's best friend if the writer's worth his or her salt. In short, try anything … or anything in the process short of cutting off your fingers or poking out both your eyeballs. Good writing, excellent writing, or, better yet, great writing in particular, isn't a mishap. It's diligence, study, trial-and-error hard work, and perseverance as the norm.

Lastly, from my own personal experience, booze, drugs, and unsettlingly crafty women are a deterrent and hindrance to quality in the finished product. I say steer clear.

Eddie Jablonski, I am the writer here. So, it's up to me to compose my own epitaph, not leave it some skill-less so and so. Not in this instance. It's my farewell so that it mustn't be misinterpreted or glamorized or sterilized or embellished one way or the other, but particularly so that I can't even recognize myself and my own likeness even beyond the pale. I've said as much to anyone around me, anyone that would listen, but usually that's only Jenkins, the two of us strolling in the lamplight after dark before Jenkins returns home to his real family.

Eddie can hear voices in the distance inside his own head. "Amen," said the small crowd of Eddie enthusiasts in unison without instruction. "God bless you, Eddie Jablonski!" a lone voice cried out.

An honest man in a dishonest business? Maybe. Or perhaps just a distinctively dishonest man in a dishonest business? Regardless, the fact remains … I was *The Bard of Bad.*

Fireside at Eddie's place.

Post funeral. Relatives had dispersed. Housekeeping packed the old man's belongings, one by one, into a single cardboard box. The old man's desk was the last item left in the room. The photographs had been stacked and arranged for shipping. The books had been removed and boxed. The front half of that same room was bare, a bit messy and dusty but bare. It was where Eddie wanted to die, die in his sleep, in his own bed or even sitting in thought at his own desk, but in his own house, not in a nursing home. There, there was no dignity in the lurch, no real, down-to-earth decency either. Instead, merely a stale and withered cocoon surrounding a dispassionate, displaced, and permanently rotting diapause.

Crosshairs of the Devil, a novel, by Eddie Jablonski. The manuscript lay inside the desk drawer, properly folded, neatly stacked, orderly by design, third drawer down on the left. Handwritten notes in Eddie Jablonski's writing style were apparent in the margins both left and right. Asterisks and footnotes as well.

CROSSHAIRS OF THE DEVIL
A Novel by Edek Anton Augustyn Jablonski
Eddie's back!

The letters were printed in bold italics the same way he left each of his other manuscripts, each of the other bestsellers. Bestseller number 1. Bestseller number 2. Bestseller number 3. The fourth book was a bit off the mark but outsold the others over time. His last book, **Mistress to the Mob**, a #1 bestseller, sold over 4 million copies and still flying off the shelf.

From the *Daily Times*: Jablonski, crowned king of the murder-for-hire mystery ten years in a row. Or, was that twenty? Anyway, who's counting? Long live the King, the King of Kill.

From his 1997 Interview on *Kill or Be Killed*. Over three million copies sold to date. "The work of mine that I like best," said Eddie. "Personal and substantive. Suffocating detail in a stranglehold. Cringe with zing."

From *The Herald*: Jablonski, a shadowy prince of darkness, a mobster's best friend. Never met a mobster he didn't like. ***Bossa Nova with La Cosa Nostra.*** The hard-hitting story about the Cuban Mob by Eddie Jablonski is obviously a collaborative with the devil himself. Or the devil herself. Who says *he* can't be a *she*? You decide. But be sure and give the devil *his* due. Read it and weep before they come for you, sucker. Five stars said **Chicago's Echo**. Better than Five Stars said the **New York News Daily**, so I'm giving it Six for good measure. This book is so good; it breaks any measuring stick and tape rule.

From *The Daily News Journal*: Jablonski, caretaker to the underworld. La Cosa Nostra's Shakespeare.

From *The Bibliophile Beat*: Jablonski, a writer to envy; better yet a writer to read. Without question, Jablonski is The Mafia's Chairman of the Bard.

From *Reader to Reader*: Jablonski strikes again, full force. This one is well worth the reader's time. Subject matter to die for.

From the *Global Times*: Jablonski never met a mobster he didn't make you like. Go, Eddie!

Those were just a few of the clippings, a smattering of Eddie's reviews. Sales and accolades and memorabilia stuffed inside an adjoining closet with a scarlet ribbon hanging, dangling alone, from the clothes rod beside his winter coat. He hadn't bothered to take it with him (to the nursing home … The Garden of Eden). The medal. A Pulitzer. Another medal. The National Book Award. The last one, his least favorite. He hated politicized pandering. The Nobel Award for Literature, nominee … is what it said.

The book as manuscript, unpublished, unread, undiscovered, it lay in the third drawer. The chapters inscribed in Eddie Jablonski's scribble and arthritic handwriting, complete with dedication and a notarized last will and testament that read:

To Harold Conway Twitty Jenkins, My trainer, caretaker, confidante-accomplice, associate, and friend. I, Edek Anton Augustyn Jablonski, being of sound mind, do hereby bequeath to Harold Conway Twitty Jenkins, my most simpatico sons-a-bitch buddy of all time, my entire earthly possessions, royalties, collectibles, homes, and properties. To the best damned caregiver a man could ever ask for. J, after I'm gone, let the good times roll. Your pal, Eddie.

Crosshairs of the Devil a novel by Edek Jablonski.

Chapter 1) *The Making of a Hit Man*
Chapter 2) *Prayer Session with Cousin Rich*
Chapter 3) *Man of Color*
Chapter 4 *Scenic Highway*
Chapter 5) *If Looks Could Kill*
Chapter 6) *Hands on the Clock*
Chapter 7) *Hallway 7ᵗʰ Floor*
Chapter 9) *If Looks Could Kill*
Chapter 10) *Time and Space*
Chapter 11) *A Family Affair*
Chapter 12) *Del Rio*
And finally:

Styx & Stones
A Novella
by
Edek Anton Augustyn Jablonski, America's
Greatest Crime writer.

From the Gazette: Jablonski (is) … "Agatha Christie and Arthur Conan Doyle only grittier, more humorous, more gripping with a keener eye for detail. Crime fiction on steroids. Read it and weep. It gives new meaning to the phrase."

It was all there.

Eddie Jablonski, crime writer, bestselling author, fact, fiction, delusion, imagination, truth and dare. Bits and pieces of the man, the author, bits and pieces of other men he'd known, met, wished to have known, helped to embellish. It's what the author does.

"It's my craft, my calling, my salty salvation, my calculative spirit come to life. Without fiction, without my writing, I'd have been

relegated to a petty pickpocket in an unattended, small-town park. And not a very good one at that." **From the Life and Times of Eddie Jablonski, circa 1999.**

The Great Escape __ The Next Subchapter.

Eddie never liked Quisenberry. They'd shared the same hallway for months, and often times, other Gardeners mistook Quisenberry for Eddie and Eddie for Quisenberry. Same height, same weight, comparative facial structure and facial features similar but not twin, hair a similar gray to white mix, thinning but holding on in a last gasp. In old age, old men often inherit this aged trait, said other Gardeners in idle chatter in the offing. They all look alike. Most agreed.

When Eddie heard Quisenberry had taken ill, he applauded. Jenkins scolded him, but Eddie applauded anyway.

"Never liked the son of a bitch," said Eddie. "Pretends he's me. Takes credit for the books I've written. What's more, laid claims to my best works, my favorite works. Said they were his, where in fact he's a nobody, a parasite, a leech, a scoundrel, and a piss poor plagiarist and pretend. One of us has to go, and it should be Quisenberry the suck up, a latent, no account feather duster. For once in my lifetime, let justice be served. Hear an old man's last prayer, Mother Nature. Take him out before me."

Liturgically … *ask and it shall be given.* Eddie, somehow it seems, was the first to hear of Quisenberry's passing, his shortened death, pulmonary edema, an inner wrecking ball all its own. "What, the old windbag's MIA?" said Eddie. "Carpe Diem," said Eddie resolutely to Eve.

So, Eddie hitched a ride to the mortuary (Jenkins drove the Garden shuttle) with Eve in tow. Changed out the toe tag, Quisenberry to Jablonski (Eve's handwriting). Rambled through the medical records and entered Jablonski instead of Quisenberry.

Height, weight, gender, hair, left as is. Eve helped. She was a policewoman forgery crackerjack, remember?

Then, she and Eddie returned to The Garden, kissed on the lips in the parking lot, returned to their individual dormitory rooms, packed their brief belongings into one suitcase (their only), kissed again on the lips on the return to the parking lot where Jenkins waited once more inside The Garden shuttle van. He then drove the two Garden lovers to International Airport ... Flight 828 to Fort Lauderdale ... connecting to Belize and then on to the house that Eddie'd purchased online sight unseen with Eve's instruction. Oceanfront, calm, reflective, cerulean waters and even bluer skies, broad and tall palms left, right, and in the rear with a quaint garden of tropical flowers and succulent everyday fruit. A scene, a portrait, a snapshot ... like something out of a Hoagie Carmichael lyric. They both agreed.

Eddie was particularly fond of oranges in season not to mention bananas year-round. Eve was a guava aficionado having cultivated a taste for the peculiar fruit from way back in her undercover days vacationing with mob bosses in Havana and other Caribbean elsewheres.

"You two have fun," called out Jenkins with a thumbs up. "Sympatico," he said to himself from behind the airport glass as they boarded the plane.

Sympatico said the double, return thumbs up from Eddie off the tarmac in the distance. Jenkins watched until the retractable gear tucked itself away in liftoff and the plane was fully airborne then out of sight.

A Meeting of the Minds __ Another Subchapter.
Meanwhile, across town, two men looked at one another quizzically. Bafflement a-brewing. Confoundment in all directions,

up and down, right and left. The two were professionally as well as personally mystified as if left in a lurch.

"But wait a minute," said the senior undertaker. "The toe tags have been misplaced. Who was the man in bin number four? The toe tag said Jablonski … Edek Jablonski. But the other toe tag has nothing written on it at all, like nothing happened … like the man never died or was swapped out in between here and there. It's as if it's been discarded in some kind of clandestine switch. Hmmm."

"Can't be," said mortician junior-grade. "The dead man was the same dead man I brought over myself from The Garden the night before last. Unless, that is, somebody's jerking our chain, and the dead man isn't or wasn't the dead man after all."

"Don't mess with it," said the senior undertaker. "Let it go. We're in enough trouble for the Botticelli screwup six months ago when he was a she and neither of us caught that one."

From the shadows of Martini's morgue and mortuary just inside dead room #3 appeared a broad-shouldered man, not too tall but tall enough. Even in the dim light, the man's nose looked misplaced, or mangled perhaps. At a longer stare, it was obviously and disturbingly mashed. It was keenly apparent in better lighting. As well, there was unmistakable scar tissue above both his eyes. Ironically, he'd just entered death's makeover dressing room at the same time with the two lead makeup artists in tow and on call. Quite the coincidence, but not really. The stranger in their midst had intentionally, purposefully tracked them here for his own reasons, so he then spoke up softly and said,

"Good day, gentleman." The stranger signaled with his left hand held higher, something of a limp hello as he stepped into the light. Offhandedly, he continued. "You two look like a couple of smart fellows. Above average intellect. Educated. Well trained. Valets and varlets to the deceased it appears and as I understand the circumstance. Well-rounded professional types no less. So, listen up because I don't like repeating myself. Time is money, and something you both certainly understand in your line of work. I'm passing along a little message for your safeguard and safekeeping. So, you are hereby advised.

The dead man in your possession *is* Edek Jablonski. No two ways about it. Capisce? I'm just checking in so that you don't get too nosey and try to solve a riddle that doesn't need to be solved. Capisce? I'm also here just guarding the fort so to speak, the fort that I'm getting paid to guard. Capisce? Oh, and by the way and for your information, this is what I do for a living ... I pass along little, tiny tidbits of information to people in hopes they'll understand fully the nature of our little meeting and get the message (inferred, wordless, unspoken, or otherwise) passed along in the interim, then comply as requested. Go with the flow, you might say. My flow. Conform to our little, tacit and unperturbed plan of action. Once again ... the dead man in your possession *is* Edek Jablonski. No two ways about it, one last time. So, you have been officially placed on notice, gentlemen. Capisce? Now. There you have it; that's it. And that about wraps it up from over here on my end. Oh, and for the record. There's never a Q & A at the end of one of my little sessions ... *get-togethers* I like to call them ... because there are no answers and even fewer questions. Again, time is money. You understand that. And we all end up back here at your shop or one just like it sooner or later. No nuts, bolts, or axel grease, but a lot of Bondo. You get it. I get it.

I hope you two gentlemen have a wonderful rest of your day. If anyone asks, tell them Nosferatu the distempered prince of darkness, the former discounted world champ came calling. If you care to ask around, anyone that matters can validate or verify my credentials, my reputation, my whereabouts and what happens if you don't flex with the bend or bend with the flex as requested. You fuck up, say you bob instead of weave, and I'll be even easier to find because you won't have to come looking for me. See me in your dreams. Capisce?

Arrivederci, miei amici," he muttered turning about and waving with flighty fingers from atop one bulbously battered, weathered, and scarred-up right hand. "Fino a nuovo avviso." (Until further notice.)

The broad-shouldered man walked away silently and exited footstep for footstep by way of his same shadowy entrance.

Surfside __ Still Another & the Next Subchapter.
Belize International Airport. Touchdown. Arrived.

Eddie grabbed his bag from the airline carousel. Eve waited; her arms folded. She sighed, but patience was never her strong suit. The taxi driver smiled. "All aboard, he said. "Todos a bordo." His name was Eduardo. It was printed on the cabbie card dangling from the rearview mirror. "And where to? … a donde?"

"The Royal Placencia Hotel," said Eddie. "I can smell the ocean from here. And so long Garden. Living the dream, Eve, living the dream."

"We showed 'em, Eddie," said Eve. "They'll never know what hit 'em."

An hour later.

The two sat silently. The surf lapping at their tired feet. Eve watched for terns and gulls and osprey and cormorant, sea life, too, in the clear water. Eddie snoozed, then opened his beach satchel. He laid out his portable-writing lapboard, his #2 pencil with eraser, a fresh, unblemished yellow legal pad, then his iPad. Once a nuisance, he'd grown accustomed to its unmannered discharge, pretentious idiosyncrasies, and techno-uppitiness in recent years. So, he opened the case with aplomb, flipped the switch to on, and hit enter. He then began to type. My next novel, **Mob Murders Caribbean Style**, a novel, by Edek Aton Augustyn Jablonski. Then, he wrote … *The Icicle is back.*

Fake death and funeral aside, Eddie'd never really left.

THE END